Narrow Escape

Cheyne rushed down the narrow, winding streets, trying to remember just how he had found the Arcanum to begin with. He began to feel the edges of panic. He was a stranger with no name and no standing, and now no money, caught in a city where those were the only things that could pry you out of trouble. And trouble, he had been told time and again, always came out of the dark in Sumifa. His concentration caught up in this whirl of angst, he did not notice the beggar he tripped over until it was too late.

It was a fortunate fall. Had Cheyne's head not dropped as he rolled over the vagrant, the well-aimed throwing disk that sailed over them both would have taken it from his shoulders. The discus bounced hard off a basalt wall, brass blade ringing sweetly as it spun into the sand . . .

Look for
MAGIC: The Gathering

From HarperPrism

MAGIC
The Gathering™

SONG

OF

TIME

Teri McLaren

HarperPrism
An Imprint of HarperPaperbacks

HarperPaperbacks   *A Division of* HarperCollins*Publishers*
10 East 53rd Street, New York, N.Y. 10022

Copyright © 1996 by Wizards of the Coast, Inc.
All rights reserved. No part of this book may be used or reproduced in any manner whatsoever without written permission of the publisher, except in the case of brief quotations embodied in critical articles and reviews. For information address HarperCollins*Publishers,*
10 East 53rd Street, New York, N.Y. 10022.

Cover illustration by Bob Eggleton

First printing: June 1996

Printed in the United States of America

HarperPrism is an imprint of HarperPaperbacks. HarperPaperbacks, HarperPrism, and colophon are trademarks of HarperCollins*Publishers.*

❖ 10 9 8 7 6 5 4 3 2 1

For Janna Silverstein, Kathy Ice, and Dave Howell:
Fair winds and waters, my friends.

ACKNOWLEDGMENTS

Many thanks to Jim DeLong and Terri Johns for their support in word and prayer, to Mike Kimble for sharing his sensory impressions of desert climes, to Pete Venters for help with Dominian geography and Jana Wright for a diligent linguistic search. Thanks also to Amy Weber for her wonderful painting of the Armageddon Clock and to Mark Reynolds for graciously providing me with a copy of the card. Randy Asplund-Faith spent valuable time with me explaining details concerning his painting of the Elven Fortress and Bob Eggleton gave the book a marvelous cover. David Kirchhoff provided sound musical advice and made noteworthy suggestions. H. C. Patterson, veteran saltwater fisherman, spun long lines about time and tide, and Carla Vaananen offered much appreciated first reader response. Thanks very much to Nancy C. Hanger for her excellent copyedit of this manuscript, to Marsha Waggoner for meticulous research, to Michael Ryan for handling the book in its final stages, and to Gloria Beckner for her expertise with domestic animals. And thanks to John Hale and Stephanie Maloney who, years ago, provided me with the opportunity to work as an artist on the University of Louisville's dig at Torre de Palma, Portugal.

One last thing: Deuce Sapp—Doulos is for you, my friend.

PART

1

CHAPTER

1

Ancient Sumifa, 3000 BCE

THE WHITE MARBLE FACE OF SUMIFA'S monumental sundial brightened by small degrees as the red sun rose above the crawling dunes of the distant high desert. A tall, thin, basalt head of Caelus Nin, Sumifan god of time and patron of the ancestors formed the sundial's double-faced gnomon and stood silent entry at the village's main gate. The eastern face's weathered expression looked fiercely into the burning light, a full hourglass in its knotted hands, while the equally severe western face remained cloaked in cold darkness.

Samor the Collector moved quietly to his study, locked the door, and opened the only copy of the *Holy Book of the Confessors*, forbidden by Mishra since the first day he had seized power in Almaaz. Since it was written in a language that he himself could not read, Mishra did not trust the Book, or its followers. He feared their teachings almost as much as he feared losing his power to his brother Urza.

Samor raised his head, sang the oath of the Circle aloud and waited, while all over the countryside, certain

mages, members of Mishra's court and highest coun-
selors every one, stopped their work, their breakfasts,
their conversations, and withdrew to quiet places, making ready to receive the words only they could hear.
When he sensed their expectancy, Samor sang from the
precious Book its message for the day. "Fear not," the
spirit of the Book had commanded, its voice insistently
echoing in Samor's mind, the urgency more personal
than usual. Puzzled, Samor released the Circle, closed
the book, and retired to the courtyard to ponder the
words.

But before he could meditate on the message, there
came an odd summons, a message from Mishra borne
by Porros, one of the younger mages, who came racing
in on a thundercloud through the early morning sky.
Porros dropped to earth inside the courtyard and
handed Samor a message written on a torn corner of a
campaign map in three faint, sand-scrubbed words—
"Trouble. Come *now*."—with Mishra's royal imprint as
signature. A small circle around the Borderlands
marked the location.

"We fly to Mount Sarrazan. I will guide you,"
shouted Porros, dusting the sand from his robes into
the high winds. Samor caught a mouthful of it and
turned his head as Porros went on obliviously. "Call all
of the others to attend us. Mishra has need of our
greatest strength. It is a cockatrice, Samor. It seems
you were right; they are, indeed, real."

"Mishra is there? Why would he lead troops to fight
over a ch'mina crop? Does he yet live? It is said that
all who meet the gaze of such a beast die. And who
summoned this creature?" the Collector cried in alarm.

"It is Urza's doing. A trap for his brother. Urza must
have a spy in our midst; our lord Mishra was tricked
into leading the troops himself," Porros replied, his eyes
strangely fixed on the Collector's several gold rings.
"But there is no time. You are the only one who knows
the song. And the only one who knows every member of
the Circle and can bring us all." The unnatural storm

raged around them, whipping the palm fronds in every direction, threatening to denude the carefully attended gardens.

His robes tangling around his legs, Samor looked hard at the young man, but Porros refused to meet his eyes. "Wait here." The Collector ran to his study to gather and warn the Circle about the cockatrice. But he called only a handful of them, those whose voices would blend toward the old spell he hurriedly copied from his bestiary. He rejoined Porros and, quickly lifted by the dark magic of the thundercloud, they flew over the desert toward Mount Sarraza.

As they glided to earth, the beast flew around the other side of the mountain. The Circle's mages appeared one by one in winds of their own, each marking with unbelieving eyes a twenty-foot-deep crater, with a wide ring of split rocks and melted earth at its perimeter, as they set down in the confusion and din of the battlefield. Samor silently noted the arrival of everyone he had called as they scattered into a loose network across the torn land and began tending the wounded. When they were all in place, Samor gathered their strength to his own, each second passing in expectancy of the beast's return.

He had not long to wait. The beast tore around the peak with a scream that sent a hard chill down Samor's spine. When he lifted his eyes to gauge the creature's distance and, he had to admit, to see what sort of creature had caused the damage smoldering before them, he expected a huge monster, at least as large as Mishra's tower. But the cockatrice, winging around the mountaintop with seemingly impossible speed, was only the size of a large horse. Samor nearly forgot his caution and continued to look at it, his curiosity was so instantly fired by how the red-and-green-scaled creature could have ravaged such a huge portion of the fertile mountainside in such a small amount of time. But then he broke his stare and looked again at the battlefield, suddenly sure that he had never seen such ruin, even

when the brothers had fought before, even after they
had stripped whole Almaazan forests of timber, or
mined great open wounds into the earth. The cockatrice had already laid waste to an entire village and a
mountainside; the precious ch'mina crop Urza and
Mishra had gathered to fight over lay in total ruin. Even
the elves' water source, the headwaters of the Sarrazan
River, ran foul and dark.

Samor covered his eyes as the creature circled again
high above them. "How did it do such harm, Porros?"
he shouted over the din on the field.

"Three hours before dawn it came," said Porros, "and
at first we thought it one of Urza's machines. At the turn
of every new glass, it changed subtly in shape, direction,
and tactics. We could not see clearly what threatened us
until dawn. Most of those who died from its stare must
have looked upon it before the light came. Apparently, it
mutated the acids in its breath and the fire in its eyes,
countering all spells the novice mages tried to work on it.
By dawn, its breath had slain hundreds and its gaze
turned to stone hundreds more. As you see, the brothers
continue to glare at each other over their failing armies
and their defeated magicians. They have no answers. We
had to let the women and men who fought the creature
drop in their tracks, their bravery unmarked, the battle
raging over their bodies," Porros cried bitterly. "Finally,
Mishra sent me to fetch you."

Samor blotted his brow, wondering now if the old
song he had taken from the bestiary's pages really
would work. Again, he had little time to question; high
above them, the beast circled the peak, gathering
speed, winding its path outward like a clockspring. If
he did not act now, soon all of Almaaz would look like
Mount Sarraza.

"Shield your eyes!" Samor reminded the mages as
they heard the beast shrieking back down the mountain. "Look not upon it!" Porros took the word on
down the lines. Samor finally saw Mishra and moved
to his side.

"I know of only one song for such a creature, and that unpracticed," pleaded the Collector blindly to his lord as the hot wind rushed upon them.

"Well, use it or be damned with the rest of us!" Mishra bellowed from under his gauntlet, its bronze arm guard held hard against his face. Just then, the cockatrice swooped low over them, its glance vaporizing an unprepared warrior in his armor, the empty, seared plates falling to the ground in a molten heap. The beast crowed its exultation, exhaling a great gasp, its hot, foul breath splitting several huge boulders in its path, circling its rounded furrow again and again. As he waited for it to come near enough, Samor felt a sudden, overwhelming temptation to view the beast up close, just one time, to collect information, to get a look at it for the sake of giving the sketch in his bestiary the proper scale. Realizing his foolishness, Samor shook his head, chasing the feeling away.

Upon the next turn, with the cockatrice's brilliant red eyes shining through his sleeve, beckoning to him, unable to remember all the words or follow the unfamiliar music, the Collector sang for the first time the most intricate protection spell he had ever attempted. His heart beat painfully out of time with the music as the song filled the air. Some of the Circle linked their silent magic in protection, while Samor's oldest friends, risking discovery, joined their voices with his and amplified the music until the beast's crowing was lost in the song.

At first, nothing much changed; the beast only swerved and rolled in the air, righting itself and lashing out madly with its beak and claws. Then abruptly the sky cleared of its dark confusion, the waters of the elves' small lake stirred and leapt as the bright notes charged across their waves as their cascading tones interrupted the beast's flight, tangling its wings. *A moment more,* Samor thought, *and we'll have him down and dead.*

Then a sharp, foul note peeled out over the true

ones. Samor's voice broke in surprise as the song was altered, its power diverted and fouled with dark energy. Struck to earth by the music, the beast lay thrashing, merely confused. And far from dead.

Can it be? he wondered in amazement. *Someone has sung untrue. We have only sent it to sleep!* His eyes still covered by his sleeve, Samor could only listen in horror as the cockatrice tried to rise again and again, its beak clacking together and its wings beating at the air.

Worse still, he knew he was too close. Samor felt its evil breath, and a renewed temptation to look at the creature pounded at his mind. Stunned at the thought of a traitor within the Circle, his confidence lost in the only spell he knew for the creature, the Collector bowed to the unbearable pressure, flung out his arm, and dared to look directly at the beast.

He had expected an awful, ugly thing. He had expected to be repulsed. But instead, Samor was instantly mesmerized. He had never seen such beautiful colors, as if an entire rainbow had been captured in the beast's tail feathers and scales. As the capricious mountain light fell upon the creature, its jewel-like pinions changed hue, matching the brilliance of the sun as it broke through the clouds, fading as the shadows passed quickly over. The cockatrice flailed about, terrible and majestic as it fought the magical sleep, its yellow spurs gouging up great clods of the scorched earth, its clawed wings scraping raggedly across the shattered rocks where it had made its furrow. Samor quickly found his voice again, but could not look away before the beast turned one cruel red eye upon him and caught his stare, holding the Collector's gaze by the power of pure fear.

Samor's heart quelled within him. "Fear not," the Book had said. He fought to obey. But Porros had come too early; Samor had not had time to make the words his own, put them in his heart, where they would afford him protection. Spellbound, all Samor could see was the intelligence and cunning in that molten ruby eye, how the creature had learned him, learned the song; how it hated him and any other living thing that would dare challenge its territory.

Samor's legs gave way beneath him and he dropped to his knees. The beast twisted its beak into the ground in rage, unable to bring his head around so that both eyes could bear down on the Collector and turn him into stone where he knelt. Shaking, his death mirrored in that sleep-dulled, crimson eye, Samor knew surely that his spell would never work again.

In the strange silence, the other mages had begun to stir. The novice nearest Samor crawled over to see to his unmoving master. Samor felt the boy's eyes upon him, but he could not respond, could not tear his eyes from the deadly stare. The novice thought fast. As quietly and deftly as he could, the boy removed his heavy cloak and whirled it before Samor's dazzled eyes, instantly breaking the power of the creature's fell glance. The beast hissed and wrenched itself up on its wings, its spurs snatching and tearing the boy to shreds as Samor fell backward, fighting the paralyzing fear, caught by the sound of the boy's screams, frantically searching his mind for another song.

There was nothing, nothing.

Seconds passed and the beast began to turn around, throwing off the sleep. In the panic, all Samor could remember was a little minor key ley, which he had just used to help Lesta dig her gardens. It wasn't deadly, it wasn't heroic, and it could easily fail to produce an opening large enough to contain the creature, leaving Samor completely without recourse. But it was all he had. The mage rose to his feet, clapped his hands over his eyes in a supreme act of will, and gave all of his heart to the little planting song.

In desperation, his voice rose to a strength he had never known. The stones in one of his rings became fired with the power they gathered from the land, and their facets glowed as brilliantly as the monster's plumage. Before he had finished, the mountainside, already laid bare by the beast, began to split and crack open, at last swallowing the shrieking, flapping cockatrice. The Circle's several mages joined the Collector again for the last three notes, their counterpoint raising crystal from the burned earth and sealing it over the cockatrice in a shining door. The mountain itself shuddered and compacted as the Collector held the final note, and this time truly, at last, the beast was heard no more.

A moment or two passed in profound silence. Samor looked around him, the waves of the last song's power and the shifting of the mountain reverberating in his sensitive ears, pounding in his bones, making him nearly deaf. But at least he could count that Almaaz, and Sumifa, and all the lands and their peoples beyond, seemed safe again.

His short battle had been expensive.

Along with most of the elven villagers and an entire legion of Urza's finest lancers, four members of the senior Circle lay dead, some hand in hand, their eyes open and their bodies sundered or turned to stone. Some could not be found at all.

His ears ringing and sore, his heart withered by the power of the beast's feargaze, the Collector climbed through smoldering, shattered maples and bone-white birches, up the ruined terraces of the elves' ch'mina crop for his last duties. He found and saluted Urza's chief mage, then walked back to what remained of his beloved Circle. After the last song, they had wisely scattered, losing themselves with the regular mages among the wounded and dying, caring for their last or future needs.

"Samor—" Aswi the Sender surreptitiously caught his sleeve as he passed by. "It's Praden . . . I think he was caught by a spur while the beast struggled on the ground."

In the center of the largest crater, Samor's best friend, Praden the Sower, lay clutching a large, smooth, ovoid stone, his hands clamped to the oddly veined rock as though he had been trying to crush it. All the blood had been drained from Praden's corpse; an ugly gash about the width of Samor's hand opened his neck.

The Collector wept as he lifted the pale body and laid it gently with the others, and again, the bitter tears came when Aswi brought the body of the young novice. Samor could not remember his name.

"Samor, the chrysalis spell . . . you must lead us." Aswi beckoned to him.

"I cannot . . ." said Samor.

"You must, Samor. You are still our master," Aswi quietly declared. "We will follow you. Just begin."

They entombed them, then, all of the mages of Mishra wearily cooperating to hollow the earth and gently place the broken bodies in the newly made chambers. In the quiet song, no longer able to hold his emotions back, Samor, who had never before known hesitation or compromise, began to shake violently as he was thoroughly consumed by clawing, all-consuming fear.

Throughout the peace rites, the warring brothers looked on, angry still, all the more so since neither could claim the day, Urza from his distant post at the top of the mountain, Mishra upon his charger on the smoking battlefield.

"Well, is it dead?" said Mishra, walking the snorting steed over to Samor, who was the last left at the new tomb.

"No. These . . . these are dead." He held out a hand to the mound before him. "The beast only sleeps. It is planted like a seed. Contained. Were the wall to shatter, the cockatrice would certainly rise and fly again, probably to nest. Look at the pattern of its ruin." Samor pointed to the rings of desolation cut into the mountainside and hung his head in shame, trying to find the words that would bring Mishra's forgiveness.

Before he could utter a one of them, Mishra began to laugh and clapped him hard on the back.

"Well done, Samor, well done. Very clever of you not

to kill such a fine and deadly creature outright. Good use of resources. Since you have been away from court, you seem to have grown much in power—as if you shared the strength of a hundred or more mages. I wonder why that is? Especially since all Almaazan magical orders have been banned under my rule. You wouldn't have any knowledge of such things, now would you?"

Samor looked away from Mishra's burning black eyes, certain that the Artificer would see every member of the Circle in his own.

"Of course you wouldn't," Mishra continued. "Samor, I have an idea. It won't take a mage of your capabilities much trouble to arrange. Compose for me a spell that will *free* this beast. An undoing, if you will. And add a song to declare my triumph. Something simple, memorable, almost humble," Mishra said, smiling evilly. "And I want my brother to know this— that I will learn to control what he could only summon. Samor, let us put a great image, a sort of clock is what I see, upon the mountainside to remind him that the Beast of the Hours sleeps only as long as I choose not to wake it." He reached down and picked up a handful of the blackened sand and let it drain slowly between his fingers. "I will be the incarnation of Caelus Nin. Urza's time is in my hand." Mishra smiled.

Horrified, the image of the beast's eye overwhelming in his mind, the Collector instantly thought of his daughter, Claria, laughing with her parrots, of his lovely, bright-eyed wife, of his unsuspecting neighbors in Sumifa, of the faces he had seen and voices he had heard on his journeys. And what of his collection, all that knowledge and art? Of the fallen men and women to whom he had just sung the sleep of transformation? Of Praden, who had died during the short moments Samor had wrestled with the cockatrice's deadly stare? The nameless novice? What desolation would they rise to find, come the time of the Great Awakening? He could no longer protect them. He shuddered as he looked long into the hard, iron-colored eyes of his determined king. One thing Samor knew: if he could not slay the beast now, he could never slay it. If it were loosed, it would overcome Almaaz with total desolation. He slowly shook his dark head, refusing Mishra for the first time in the twenty-odd years since he had been bought and brought to the Artificer's court.

"Lord Mishra, I would beg you to take my life before I could agree to place the world at such risk again. I respectfully ask you to consider that it is not only your enemy this horror will attack. I pray instead you let me correct my mistake now and find a way to contain the beast forever, or perhaps send it deeper into the earth. Keeping it would mean nothing but the one and only end of all things. For where a way is made to release it, a will follows. Please do not ask me to make the way."

"Do it, or by the Six Curses of Caelus Nin, and by my sacred scepter, I will take from you forever your most beloved possessions, Samor." It took no divination to know that he meant Claria and her mother, Lesta. "Do you actually dare behave as though you were a free man? I can always find another mage while you decorate my rack. And how many others would follow you there, hmm? You have the grace of two days," growled Mishra.

The Collector could only bow, his eyes pained with unspilled tears, and nod his head. What did twenty years of honorable service mean when he was so easily replaced in Mishra's opinion? What did family mean to Mishra, who had set about to destroy his own brother? The Grand Artificer would have his will, and someone, eventually, would discover the way to wake and free the beast.

Long after the brothers and their armies had marched down the mountainside, Samor lingered, deep in thought, the smoke of burning trees heavy in his nostrils, the keening voices of grief-stricken elves playing across his heart all night long. There seemed to be no satisfactory answer. If he did what Mishra wanted, the world would likely see such ruin as had never before been. If he refused, Mishra would destroy his family and his life, and the Circle would be exposed, the Book burned, the Artificer's wrath poured out upon them, and Almaaz left without protection from his wanton whims. As it was, the Circle were the only ones who kept the land, who healed it after Mishra and Urza trampled it. And the only way to open a crystal wall that had been locked together by the Circle was with a sound so overwhelming that it would likely deafen the user. No human voice could produce such a vibration.

The constellation of the three sisters had risen at twilight and still he wrestled with his fear, his conscience, and his imagination. At midnight, when the moons rose, he began to walk blindly down the mountain.

By dawn he had blundered into a strange valley. All around him stood towers of glittering ganzite, some rising hundreds of feet in the sky, thin fingers that played the air as he moved among them, producing sighs and whispers of bright music like the voices of the elves themselves.

Then the Collector looked up to see the sun strike the crystal wall, producing a blinding, painful glare in his swollen eyes. It seemed that he had come no further toward a solution than when he started.

But when the sun rose upon the ganzite towers, the wind suddenly swept down through them and Collector found himself amid a thunderous chorus of glorious music and a thousand bizarre distortions of his own image. Samor began to laugh hysterically despite himself, despite his trouble and crushing care, causing echo upon echo upon echo, each reflected sound growing louder and more powerful. He began to try bits of melody against the crystals, from the lightest airs to the most ponderous dirges. In a few more moments, he believed he had found a way to give Mishra what he wanted.

He fell to work, walking through the strange valley, testing each spire for its peculiar properties of resonance and light. By dark, he had found the right spire. It was the tallest in the valley, with a small slit through its base at about the height of Samor's eyes. If the slit were plugged, the wind's voice across the spire would make the towers around it echo and repeat their own strange music, so loudly that eventually the noise would sunder them. The Collector knew what such violent tones could further do. Their vibration would call a great wind storm to pull through the deep recesses of the natural gorge. And the unfettered voice of that storm would gather, and gather strength as it poured through the barren, empty valley; when it reached the mountainside, the deafening surge would create the sound that would cause the crystal door to break open.

At length, Samor found a small piece of ganzite that would fit into the notch of his chosen spire, like a key. He sang a dividing song over it, carving it into a precise fit for the slit in the spire, and then placed the crystal in his sleeve. All that was left was Mishra's victory song.

He looked up the mountainside again at the shining wall that blocked the beast. Rainbows danced off its surface, reminding him of the glory of the creature's plumage. Immediately, his heart began to race at the remembrance of the creature's stare, almost as if the beast could yet sense his presence. Samor took a deep breath and said, "By the spirit of the Holy Book, you have no power over me. I condemn your evil! I swear this: the song that frees you will destroy you!"

Samor stood shaking as sudden power filled his words, freeing him from the crushing fear. He could feel the beast thrashing in his sleep, trying to draw him back into that awful memory, make it new, make it real again. "No," he said simply, and in his mind, the image of the beast flickered out, as if it had never troubled him, as if it had never held his imagination captive. Relieved beyond measure, exhausted, Samor knew there was work yet to do. Idly fingering a pendant around his neck, he thought of his little chroniclave's whirring, chiming song, the same tune as Claria's namesong—that simple, perfect little melody that always made order of chaos. It rang in his mind over and over.

He checked his calculations. Checked them again. And then he smiled. When Mishra inserted the ganzite key and sung his "song of triumph," that song would be Claria's little song, with its ringing harmonic overtones, and it would collapse the crystal door forever, sending the beast back to its own rightful place.

Mishra would have his clock. And Almaaz would still have time.

His steps lighter now, Samor walked back up the mountainside to the ruin of the battlefield. Huge green-bottle flies hovered over the still-smoking ravines and gullies, open wounds on the land itself. The smell of death filled Samor's nostrils. In another day, Mishra's masons would come here to begin the huge hourglass of standing stones that the Artificer had deemed the proper marker for his new grand armament. It should have been a gravestone, thought Samor, for the thousands who died in this obscene conflict. But the forest was healing itself, with help from the elves, apparent in the greening of the scarred ground and the tiny new leaves on the bare trees. Very soon the evidence of the Day of the Beast would be hidden altogether in the tightly woven undergrowth of the Sarrazan forest.

"Yes, it will. We will see to it," said a silvery voice. Disconcerted, Samor turned sharply to find a tall, fair-haired elf standing only a few feet behind him.

"You can hear my thoughts?" Samor queried, his curiosity piqued as his irritation diminished.

"Not exactly. But I can read your heart. And watch your eyes, where they go, what they find. We have watched you all night long. We wondered whether we should make it easy for you and put an arrow through your heart. But the tyrant would send someone else, and that one might not care for life as you do. We decided to wait and see if you would win over your fear. You have fought well."

Samor shook his head. "No, friend. I am but a slave, and I have chosen between evils. I have only picked the lesser, and that out of selfishness. I pray that Mishra will forget this place, this thing he has demanded. May there come one who can destroy this creature forever. It is not I."

"As you say. The beast, like all things, will find its way home. There will be time," said the elf.

"Yes. For now, there will be time. I pray there will be enough. Tell me, companion, who are you and what do you call this valley? I would have the name for my books."

The elf considered, standing silently for a long time, then answered, "I am called Sh'Daran. This place we call the Chimes. Though you know the name, soon not even the warring brothers will be able to find it again. Our worlds seem to be drifting apart, though they will probably always somehow be joined. Obey the unjust tyrant for now; that is your duty and your honor, though he be honorless. You will have help. Only watch well for yourself. Another, who spoils the harmony, has also followed your path this night and day." The elf quirked his mouth into a peculiar, knowing smile.

Before Samor could ask the identity of the traitor, the elf stepped back and shouted a word in his own language. A curtain of light became visible between them, and immediately, the vines and shrubs at their feet rustled and grew up, hiding the elf completely. A breeze diverted suddenly and trickled down the valley, taking the elf's command, echoing it back to the mountainside. The Collector watched in awe as the battlefield greened over before his eyes, the mound where his friends lay springing up with flowering vines and a mature forest replacing in an instant what the beast had rent.

But the crystal wall remained, a bright scar upon the mountain that could not be healed with the greening, no matter the gentle song of the breeze.

CHAPTER

2

A GUST OF AIR RATTLED THE OPEN SHUTTERS, dissipating instantly. Inside the village wall, Samor's large house began to cool in the long shade of a grove of date palms, their slender shadows playing through the high windows and over the blue-tiled floor. Samor wiped the gleam from his brow as he absently pondered his impossible choice, looking up from his untouched curry to find himself alone at the table, the patient steward waiting to clear the dishes and clean the room. Slightly embarrassed, Samor abandoned the cold dish and climbed the stairs to his study, looking in on his small daughter before shutting himself behind the heavy teakwood door for the night.

The girl lay sleeping in her bed, her exhausted nurse sprawled across the threshold, snoring softly, while one black-clad juma guard, her golden eyes glowing, sat alert in a darkening corner near the window. Samor hummed the girl's namesong as he stepped over the nurse and adjusted the netting over Claria's bed. The guard never changed her position, but the Collector saw her eyes on him and her hands flexing in the dying light, repeating the endless motions of the exercises she and her company constantly practiced.

The juma could kill with the flick of a finger, or the small quick thrust of an elbow. Samor bowed to the guard a silent goodnight and left his daughter to her sleep. A moment later, in the confines of his cluttered study, he sank his solid build comfortably into a red silk pillowed chair, the little tune still upon his lips.

Samor's only wife, Lesta, had busied herself downstairs in the sheltered courtyard with her women, their bright music now competing with the jewel-eyed parrots' talk and the gurgle of the pink-and-turquoise tiled fountains. The noise and the music rose and fell pleasantly. But as always, in a little while, the only sound Samor would notice would be the constant machinery of his chroniclave, its brass pendulum swinging back and forth like a heartbeat. The chroniclave, an odd combination of timepiece and music box, was the only thing he had from his homeland and the only remembrance of his freedom.

Though he had not enjoyed it for a while now, this was the Collector's favorite time of the day. He loved this wondrous building; loved this odd country with its chill, dry evenings, the spicy fragrance of night-blooming jasmine floating on a gentle breeze, and in the hazy distance, the rocks of his desert homeland, Halquina, glowing redly. No movement troubled the dunes, no sound stirred the air other than a near-constant chorus of heat-loving cicadas. Eastward, darkness already mantled the Grand Artificer's glorious palace, its soaring white towers outlined by thousands of everburning torches. But here in the fortified city of Sumifa, where Mishra had positioned Samor, his historian and sometime ambassador to Almaaz, there was a little light remaining, despite the sifted hourglass in the time god's western hands.

Samor checked the chroniclave for the hour. He could delay no longer. His gaze returned to the window as he took in a last look westward before the long night ahead. His forehead creased a bit when he noticed a small puff of dust, outlined by the sunset, dancing at

the base of the red rocks. Maybe a chariot, or a sea-
sonal wind squall, but it was too early for them by
nearly a fortnight.

He chased a darker thought from his mind. The
Circle often traveled by whirlwind, and one other—
the betrayer—knew what Samor was doing about
Mishra's demand. Though Samor had no proof or witness, he knew it surely in his heart: Porros, his
favorite, known among them as the Raptor, the prince
and future king of Sumifa, and too impatient, too
proud, to wait for Samor to give him the leadership of
the secret magical brotherhood, had broken his vow.
The puff of dust disappeared from the horizon.

Ah, no. Samor rubbed his eyes. *I am tired and my
imaginings are perhaps groundless. You could not
know more than you saw on the Day of the Beast.
There will be a better moment for you to try to take
me, I am sure.* Samor made a warding sign and
rebuked the darkness from his thoughts.

The insistent ticking of the chroniclave brought him
back to his immediate purpose. Turning the delicate
machine sideways and inserting the amulet he wore
around his neck into its keyhole, he wound the music
box, waited a moment, and then listened carefully as
the bright tune chimed. He sang along, searching for
harmonies and variations on its theme, letting his mind
be calmed as the pendulum's smooth movements kept
time with his improvisations. The chroniclave's
machinery always gave him a feeling of steadiness—of
rightness.

He relaxed, beginning to believe that he would make
Mishra's impossible deadline and could, in just a few
hours, meet Mishra's messenger with the news that he
had found a way to give the Artificer what he had
asked. Then Samor could rest as easily as his daughter
slept. The small chroniclave ticked steadily in the
room's sudden stillness.

The mage pushed his thoughts away, rang for the
steward, who came immediately and poured him a cup

of tea laced with visionbright, then left as silently as a shadow. The Collector lifted the dagger's-length of absolutely clear stone from under the false panel of the chroniclave's base.

He had decided that the glittering obelisk, the first key to Mishra's "clock" would be Claria's naming totem. As Mishra had ridden away from the desolation, Samor had asked permission and the Artificer, distracted, had granted it, asking only if she was old enough, having escaped the Nine Horrific Infant Diseases, to have one. Mishra cared not how or where Samor hid the spell, only that he have it.

The stone block tapered gracefully from base to blunted tip, a perfect prism, now catching the very last of the sun's strong rays in its crystalline heart and separating their colors, bouncing a rainbow off the gold rings on his left hand, magnifying it under the chroniclave's dome, and finally losing the bright beam in the thick scroll of Jerubian carpet at his feet.

The Collector hummed his tune again, adding the magic of his four-stone ring. The gemstones glowed, and the rainbow danced in response, its colors dividing and springing up into tendrils and curls in the air, weaving themselves through his song like the ribbons Claria wore in her long black hair. The Collector gave the song full voice, singing Claria's name in the glyph language, and the colors wove themselves into a woman's graceful handprint, the distinct shape of his beloved Lesta's hand, the fingers long and beautiful, the first and second fingers slightly crooked at the first joints. In Lesta's family, once in each generation a woman displayed this peculiar trait—the archer's hand, her family called it; no one knew why anymore. From the way her small fingers already curled over, Samor knew Claria's hand would fit this print someday, too.

The Collector ended the song and smiled as the rainbow rejoined and settled into its tight beam once more. He polished the smooth, cold stone with a soft cloth, removing his own fingerprints from its surface, but carefully leaving the thumbprint Claria had pressed upon it near the base. He placed a jeweler's loupe over his eye, and from under his scarf brought forth the chroniclave's key again, comparing its engraved print with the fresh one. Exactly the same. He took a clamp, a delicate hammer, and a miniature diamond chisel from the top desk drawer and laid them on his desk.

The breeze gathered strength, making for a sudden chill in the study. The end of even the most scorching day could leave one cold here in upper Sumifa. Could make you shiver and make your hands shake. It had to be the cold. The Collector took a sip of the hot, fragrant tea to settle his nerves and focus his eyes, pulled his rich purple robes more tightly around him, and concentrated on the shape of the names of his ancestors before he began to cut them into the totem. Even if none of the old ones would, one day maybe Claria, or one of her children, could understand what he had done. Maybe by then, if he hadn't found it himself, they would know how to kill the beast. The Collector allowed himself a glimmer of hope.

He placed the diamond chisel to one side of the prism's perfect face and began to carve, sending the rainbow into a kaleidoscopic dance. At the window, the wind picked up the white linen curtains and puffed them rhythmically with its tide, rocking the cedar shutters on their hinges. The musical clock chimed its tune again.

A few minutes later, little by exact little, the six glyphs covered one side of the totem, taking the history of his family down through the known generations, their ancient nameshapes purling the tribe together with the signs of sunshadow, skyboat, lightning, sword's edge, river, adding his own chosen sign of the basket, until he reached Claria's fingerprint, the pattern for the last glyph. In the intricate whorls of her left ring finger's print lay the actual letters of her name, marked upon her hand with the namesong at her birth. The print was small to begin with, the intricacies tedious to carve, even with the visionbright.

Pushing aside the loupe, the Collector looked up and rested his eyes on the book by his hand. He stretched his arms above his head and rose to pull the shutters over the large window; the breeze had risen considerably and it felt as though the sand squalls were indeed coming. The thought nagged at him again that it was early for the scouring storms—and there was an odd, high-pitched note to the sound of the wind. The Collector shut the cedar slats over the window and lit an oil lamp. Deciding to give his carving a bit of a rest before attempting the last glyph, he picked up his quill, turned to the last two pages in the Holy Book. Here, for the Circle, he would hide the only written record of the keys and their true mechanism.

But the quill passed over the thick paper without leaving a mark. He dabbed a second time at the well, and all that came up was a clotted smear. He had forgotten to cap the bottle again. Sighing wearily, the Collector rubbed at the stiffness in his neck, his eyes alighting triumphantly upon the bean jar standing beside the desk, the roomy receptacle that seemed to gather everything that strayed from his immediate grasp. He poked his hand around blindly in the jar until he found a new bottle of ink and sat down again, his knees stiff from the chill. In a little while, he had set the story down between the unreadable lines of the book. His tea had passed from tepid to cold. The steward would be in bed by now—his day began well before dawn. The Collector would not wake him for such a trifle. He could light a fire, but he was nearly done, and he would need all his energy to carve. Just Claria's name to finish.

It struck him how very lonely it was in the study. The parrots must have roosted. Lesta also had likely gone on to bed; she knew by now to leave him to his work undisturbed. Her juma women would no doubt

have taken their places outside her chambers and upon
the roof. They were the best guards in Sumifa, educated and companionable, and far more agile and
deadly with their hands and their borrowed silver
combs than Mishra's cavaliers were with their own
swords. The Collector had found Charga and her company wandering, dazed and homeless, on the western
dunes on a gathering trip several years back. He had
never regretted taking the three women in—they were
loyal fighters, and Samor knew what it was to be
unhomed. Mishra had taken him from his own village
long ago, another impressment in the war.

Two of the juma kept watch while the other slept, as
had been their pattern since joining the Collector's
household. That left him unguarded in Charga's opinion, but he felt safe enough here, far away from the
court and the workshop. And he had a trick or two of
his own. He was, after all, the best mage in the kingdom
of Almaaz, almost as good as the brothers themselves.

But there is Porros, he thought. *I should have
known. Should have seen it.* The pale, handsome,
aquiline features of the Circle's youngest mage flickered into Samor's mind. Talented and brazen, Porros
was also deeply flawed with an intense craving for
power. Porros had come to the Circle from this very
city, where he had been a phenomenon of sorts—a
prince whose magic could light candles, bring the
sheep home in the middle of the day, make a flower
bloom out of season.

One day, the Collector, newly installed in Sumifa,
had found the young man tangled like a broken kite in
a treetop, where he had landed after another failed
attempt at flight. The Collector had extricated him
from his perch, dropping him neatly, if a bit roughly,
to the ground with a little impromptu aria. Porros,
keenly insulted and angry, but suddenly aware of his
benefactor's gift for magic, had followed the Collector
all the way back to his home, begging to be taught. So
the Circle enlarged to include the Raptor, as the

Collector had introduced him. Though Porros probably would not believe it, The Collector had never told the others why he had given the boy that name, preferring to keep the small joke of their first meeting to himself.

In the brotherhood of the Circle, Porros had learned more magic, fighting first his own limitations, and then, at one time or the other, many of the senior members of the Circle. Always full of strife, even after a decade among the finest mages in Almaaz, Porros still could not fly on his own. *I should have known he cannot yet,* Samor chided himself.

But come what may, there was the work to finish. Samor picked up the diamond chisel again, expecting to be finished with Claria's totem before the next strike of the chroniclave's hammer. But another sound, the sharp slapping of the shutters against the wall, nearly made him miss his stroke. The squalls truly must be upon them already. With the mightiest gust yet, the window blew wide open, and the pale, wind-borne sand of distant Halquina's wastelands danced across the floor in a whirlwind.

No. It is no natural storm. So you have come this quickly. Who, I wonder, has taught you new tricks? thought the Collector, refusing to look up or appear to be bothered by the dramatic entrance of the impetuous prince. The Collector just shook his head, adjusted his loupe, blew away the sand from the crystal's face, and resumed his carving.

"How is it you do not greet your guest, Collector?" The voice seemed to materialize out of the very air. Porros stepped from the whirlwind and moved to the desk in a graceful, sweeping motion, his sleeves blown wide by the last gasp of the wind squall in the small room, his red hood obscuring his chiseled features.

"How is it my guest does not knock at my door and await admission? Like the friend and brother he has pretended to be . . ." said the Collector evenly. *If I do not startle him, perhaps I can delay this fight long enough to finish,* he thought, composing his voice and his face to blandness.

"My business with you is private. I would rather not have to run the gauntlet of your courtesy," came the low, melodious voice from beneath the hood.

"You mean the gauntlet of my guards. They can be most hospitable, you know. When you come in peace." The Collector laughed softly, looking up at the young man, his left eye dark and enormous through the magnifying lens.

"Give me the spell for the beast, Samor, and I can let you live. Consider that the show of my friendship. Especially since I have been chosen and commanded to kill you."

"So we have come to your purpose this quickly. . . . Porros, I would have given anything had it not been you," said the Collector, with more than a hint of hurt at the edges of his words. He steadily etched the first and second letters of Claria's name into the totem with his chisel.

"Save your sentiments for someone who cares, Samor. Your family lies within these walls. Would you expose them to Mishra's new weapon? Perhaps I should wake your daughter right now."

"You know better than to ask such a question. And you know better than to even mention Claria. She—and your two small princes, I might add—are why I will never hand over to you the secret of Mishra's Clock. Urza should never have summoned the cockatrice. Wherever he came from, perhaps they know how to fight him or control him. But not here. He is a creature out of his element." Thinking of his own battle with the beast, Samor bent again to his carving, as if the Raptor had not spoken.

"You stubborn fool! Do you not know that I can destroy you in this very moment?" The Raptor's voice rose to a high-pitched scream, not unlike the cry of his namesake.

"Are you that strong now?" Samor asked, his hands

faltering as the missing truths slowly dawned on him. "Ah, I see. It was you who brought forth the beast. It was you. So Urza had you in his snare long ago. You are the spy in Mishra's midst." The Collector looked up from his work, raising bushy brows over his black eyes.

The Raptor snarled from beneath his dark hood and clamped a cold hand around the Collector's wrist. The chisel dropped to the floor, landing softly in the folds of the lush carpet. The Collector looked straight up into the face of the man who had stood and served with him in the Circle for twelve years. The Raptor's pale gray eyes, the peculiar mark of the Sumifan royal family, glowed redly as the lamplight caught their lenses. Samor winced, remembering the stare of the beast. Porros, sure of his own strength now, slowly released the Collector's hand.

"Yes. I brought the cockatrice. Found the spell in one of your own books. What does it matter with whom I conspire and for what price? How dare you ask me such a question! I can fly now, too, no thanks to the Circle. Samor, for years, I have watched you gather the wealth of my kingdom to yourself, with Mishra's blessing. The Artificer's slave has better than Almaaz's royal family. Since the brothers began this fight, my kingdom has been overrun with their skirmishes; its waters and mines are used up, and my people are taken from their beds to stand and be killed in front of the next, grand, horrible machination. I am the prince of Sumifa, crown city of all Almaaz. And mark this, Samor—before I leave you, I will have the key to your crystal door, and then I will be rich again. Sumifa will be restored to its greatness, and I will watch while Urza and Mishra clash their forces upon my plains—like the battle at the End of All Things. What is it your *Book of the Confessors* calls it? Armageddon? Well, Armageddon will come early, for with the cockatrice in my power, I will be able to watch in safety as the brothers break themselves each upon the other, and then take the spoils of their kingdoms for my own. With the beast in my hand, they will not dare defy me.

"I watched you devise this magic, Samor. I saw you with the amulet you wear around your neck. That's it, isn't it? But for your elven friend, I'd have taken you in the valley of the spires. No matter—I will have the key to the Mishra's Clock, after all." He tugged gently at the chain on the Collector's neck where the chroniclave's key dangled under his robes. The Collector sighed.

"This is about wealth for you? Take whatever you see and go in peace. Of course it is yours. The Circle only protects it until the war is over. Surely you know that you, alone, will never rout the brothers from this land. Forgive me, my young friend, but such a thought is almost laughable." *And certainly insane,* thought Samor. "The best we can do is work within the Circle to hold the brothers off, deflect them, counsel them into diversions, try to bring an understanding that every war has no winners before they launch into such a conflict as this land, and no one in it, would survive. Look around my house. What is here? For Mishra, nothing of any value. He wants powerful machines and magical weapons. What does he need with art? With beauty? To him, I am nothing more than a fancy puppet. In the Circle lies my dignity and my freedom, and the greatest wealth I have: the chance to protect my family and my country from the worst of the brothers' furies.

"Porros—you would have been my successor. The Circle would have followed you without question. You were the rightful monarch of this land. A disciplined force of fighters, scholars, and magicians would have moved upon your command. Porros, one day the Circle will grow strong enough, will find the knowledge and the right words to stop this awful war. Why will you not wait for us to do it by peace? Our only chance is together."

The Collector stopped for a moment, then added, more softly, "Why, Porros, did you bring such evil? And why did you sing the foul note that caused my song to fail?"

His eyes never leaving the Raptor's, he concentrated and hummed Claria's namesong under his breath, the magic tracing the next two letters of her name deeply into the hard crystal, the effort taking all of his energy, all of his strength.

"Why? Because I could. Because I could not bear for you to destroy such a wondrous thing. Samor, I joined the Circle to learn magic—never to offer myself as servant to your idealism. Your quiet ways of peace will never change the Artificers. My family members are warriors! The only thing the brothers will ever understand is power and might. You waste my gifts. And there are those, Collector, there are those who think as I think. They stand with me now. We will take back the kingdom of Almaaz by strength. How else does the eagle feed?"

The Raptor began to scan the room, taking in every detail of the Collector's acquisitions. On the top shelf of a heavy mahogany case, the only copy of the *Book of Khem*, the greatest known compendium of cures in all of Almaaz. On the other side of the room, one of the Faces of the Night—the other part of the sculpture had never been found—its eerie dark stone seeming to engulf the light around it. And everywhere, stuffing every crevice of the study, music boxes of the finest and rarest make, of the richest materials, turned and tuned by the finest craftsmen in the known world. The Raptor shook his head and narrowed his eyes.

"I see now that you play games with me. You have expected me. Where have you hidden the real treasure? Where is my gold? Ah, of course. Where but under the mountain of the Clock?" Porros's eyes, alight with his madness, glowed like the beast's.

Done! The Collector breathed sharply as his low song engraved the last letter of the name upon the totem. The Raptor, startled by the sound, whirled upon the older man, throwing himself over the desk in unbalanced impatience. The Collector had no time to brace himself, no time to summon the magic to shield his body. He instinctively met the attack with the object in his hand, bringing the heavy stone totem toward Porros's head. But the Raptor dodged the blow fluidly, bringing his long, thin hands around the Collector's neck in a death grip.

The Collector gently dropped the totem, his thoughts flying over the time he would never have to see his daughter grow up, of what would become of the Clock, its fail-safe incompletely recorded. The Raptor mercilessly pressed upon the older man's throat, venting years of revenge and jealousy. With a ragged gasp, the Collector managed to summon a spark of fire between them, repelling the younger man backward, pitching him into a seven-hundred-year-old mirror, rending its delicate frame and breaking the glass. Three music boxes jangled down from their places and the room erupted into a glorious cacophony. The Collector felt movement on the floor below him, though he could not hear it. *Maybe the juma . . . Charga . . .* But then he remembered that the study door stood firmly bolted. He could hear Charga battering at it, ferociously attacking the hard, thick wood. But it would take her too long; Samor knew he was alone in this.

The stunned Raptor wasted no motion in rising from the wicked splinters, shook them angrily from his robes, and rejoined his attack, armed now with a crescent of the broken mirror. He swooped over the gasping mage, raking the sickle-shaped edge just under the Collector's jawline, three bright ribbons of red erupting in its wake. The Raptor seized the severed cord and its amulet triumphantly as the Collector clutched his neck with one hand, the other flailing at his desk, his fingertips finding the blood-spattered book and somehow managing to push it over into the bean jar. "You are deceived . . . may you find the truth before you find your death. However long that may take," he whispered, his breath failing.

"I need not your truth, Collector. You named me well, despite your little joke. Like the eagle, I shall seize with my own hand what I want. My shadow shall fall over all I possess and all I rule. No blade, no poison, no water or fire shall harm me. No mage shall overcome me! I have all the Circle's magic now."

"You have broken the Circle, and there is one thing you never learned about its magic, Porros. It works best when the many voices agree. You will never have what you could have had. You have broken your country and you have broken your own family with it. Think of your sons! But none of the Circle will come for you, Raptor. The face you see in the mirror is the face that will destroy you," the Collector whispered, humming over his four-stone ring. The melody was a benediction, the words a curse.

"Did you not hear me, fool? I will hunt them all down, one by one, until the end of all time!"

"Leave them, Porros. They will never raise their hands against you. But we cannot let you go unhindered. You will live halfway between light and darkness, phantom and flesh. Between time and eternity."

Bright weapon still in hand, the Raptor screeled with rage and indignation, his dark hood falling back as he caught sight of himself in the fragment of the blood-smeared mirror. In horror, he saw his sandy hair and angular jaw disappearing into nothingness. Only his gray eyes remained under the hood.

"What have you done to me?" He flung down the glass and spun around the study, his bones afire, his dark red robes gathering and gathering speed. "I shall bring such a wind as you have never known, old man, and I will scour *your* image from this earth! I will scatter your belongings and I will bring your name to ruin after you," he screamed as he took to the air, his voice roaring from the heart of his whirlwind as it moved into the night sky.

The Collector lay slumped over his desk, blood pouring

from his neck, his pale hand clutching the chroniclave, still keeping perfect time despite the pandemonium around it. One thought repeated in his mind with each stroke of the pendulum: *No one knows the song! Mishra will surely leave the wall open if he does not use Claria's namesong!* There was no time, no time. The world was already going quiet before his eyes.

Outside the study door, Charga breathed in deeply, centered her strength, and focused on the bolt that lay between her and her master. At last, she could see it clearly in her mind. She gathered her will to break the wood, and began to split one fiber from the next, working from the inside out, as quickly as she could.

Inside, the Collector fought for consciousness as he sang Claria's namesong again, bringing the magic to it, and scratched a single glyph, the form of a tiny fingerprint, onto the bronze bottom of the chroniclave. He hoped it would be enough. Samor drifted into death thinking of his family, of the Holy Book, and how all things seemed to find their way home, even the beast, no matter how long the journey. The voice of the elf he had seen at the Chimes shadowed his last breath, reminding him, over and over, like the chroniclave's pendulum, that there *would* be time.

When Charga put the edge of her foot against the door this time, it broke cleanly and easily, but far too late. She found the smiling Collector still clutching his little musical clock, its pendulum beating steady time, the straining shutters banging a sharp counterpoint to the mounting wind squall.

Far to the west, the high red rocks shuddered, cracked, and then dissolved into powder as the Raptor lashed at them in his anger. An inch or two of the sharp red grit already covered the floor, the carpet's design now completely obscured. Reading the wind's direction and force, Charga shouted orders to the sleepy steward and sounded the alarm for her small company to assemble in the protected courtyard. She slammed closed the study door, racing to join them.

I will come back for you, my lord. I will not leave you to this tomb, unknown and unmarked. I heard everything that went on with this traitor. He is a dueco—*a double devil. I pray your forgiveness that I could not help you. Forever will I remember your teachings. Your daughter, your people, and especially the Raptor's own sons shall not grow up ignorant of them.*

She leapt the final stair railing and landed catlike in the courtyard.

"Go now!" she screamed over the howl of the wind and the squawking, frightened, parrots. Her lieutenants immediately urged Lesta and Claria, whose small mouth moved in cries of silent terror as the storm took her words away with it, in the direction Charga had pointed, toward the Neffian cliffs and their hidden caves.

Charga clenched her teeth against the stinging lash of the storm and her own grief, pulled her hood over her face, and fought her way back up the stairs to the study. Three feet of sand now covered the floor. The Collector's body lay all but obscured, his treasures scattered by the wind and covered over by the same sand that was burying him. Above the din and heave of the storm, Charga heard another sound: the unmistakable whine and split of timber and rock under the weight of tons of displaced desert. There was no time. She lunged through the sand and wrested the Collector's beloved chroniclave from one hand and the precious magical ring from the other as she straightened his limbs and arranged his purple robes over the body. She cleared the staircase again in a dazzling leap as the roof fell in, a huge piece of marble covering one corner of the study, entombing Samor between it and the wall in an instant.

Making warding signs and mumbling fearful prayers to Caelus Nin and the Seven Brass gods, the bewildered people of Sumifa fled before her, making for the cliffs, their chickens and goats squawking and bleating in front of them. Porros's two small sons clung to their nurse, and his wives herded together with the villagers like lost sheep, Sumifa's royalty mingling with its commoners for the first time ever. Charga could not see anything in front of her but the bright parrots sailing overhead like windborne pennants as the villagers dashed across the cold desert night to the shelter of the Neffian caves.

The shutters broke as the wind squall hit the house full force. It took the winds only hours to fill the study with sand, only a day to bury the house and wipe any trace of the city.

The Raptor rose high above the unnatural storm he had made, climbing the thermals and dropping into sheer dives until his rage had spent itself. He pulled himself over the dunes, trying to find landmarks, his robes fluttering in the wake of the storm, eternity yawning before him, the memory of the Collector's chroniclave ticking out a faceless, nameless, hopeless time.

There was nothing to see. Sumifa lay buried under a new desert, its unmarked face stretching for miles and miles.

The sun rose over the empty, shifting sands in quiet glory, its rosy fingers creeping through the Raptor's shadowy, outstretched hand as if he were not there. His other hand twitched and grasped at the shifting sand, the shimmering grains falling from dark, bloodstained talons.

PART
2

CHAPTER
1

Sumifa, present-day

"THE KING IS DEAD. HAIL THE KING OF
Sumifa! Long live the king of Sumifa!" The shouts of
ten thousand citizens of the new city filled the hot
afternoon and carried over the dunes to the old ruin.
Cheyne stopped his sketching to lift his head and sort
out the words. So old Thedeso had died. And his son
would take his place soon. Cheyne smiled under his
broad-rimmed hat and went on with his drawing,
deftly capturing the hard edges of the broken walls
with his charcoal, taking a measurement every now
and then with a stick to maintain his accuracy. Most
people thought diggers just hunted treasure. Mostly,
they were right. But like his foster father, Javin,
Cheyne was an archaeologist. He wanted more than
treasure; he wanted answers.

Cheyne took out his hand mirror and held it along the
inside of a broken edge of basalt block, checking for the
rock's stability, and for the scorpions that liked to breed
in those big cracks and would come rushing out by the
dozens, tails poised and pincers waving, when a man
put his foot unwittingly into their nest. Their sting

wasn't deadly—but it surely could hurt—and many a
deadly fall had been prompted by such sudden pain.
Satisfied that he was safe, Cheyne lodged his boot into
the crack and hoisted himself up onto the low wall for a
better view down the line of ancient blocks that had
housed the old city's olive press. He had finished the
sides; now he would draw the top of the old barrier.

The crowds in the new city had ceased their shouts.
From the top of the old press, Cheyne could see the
shining walls of the fortress town, whitewashed and
brilliant in the slanting sun. Tomorrow he would go
back there and find the tall elf again and get his
answers. He breathed on the little mirror to clean it,
wiped it on his sleeve, and reluctantly held it up for
inspection. No smudges. No streaks.

And, as always, no reflection.

Cheyne stared into the looking glass for a long
moment, trying to see himself, trying to see past the
blur that he always saw when he had to face a mirror,
but like always, nothing was clear. He put the spotless
mirror back into his scrip and made the measurements
for the top of the wall, thinking of the tall elf, his face
savagely scarred, whom he had seen in the city the last
time he had gone in with Muni for supplies.

*Tomorrow, I will find him, and he will tell me why
he haunted my childhood dreams . . . and what magic
it is that keeps my own image from me. He must know
who I really am. . . .*

"Lift! Lift! No, no, no, forward. Again. Again." The
shouts of the foreman rang through the still desert air,
directing the sweating men striving to shift a huge fallen
marble slab from an upright corner. There was a room
under the slab, the first on site with walls higher than a
couple of feet. In a moment more, they had succeeded in
sliding the chunk away from the corner, but then something besides the weight of the block halted the work.

"By the cracked face of Caelus Nin!" he swore. "Stop and stand clear. We cannot progress."

Muni, the foreman, waved the crew back and stood staring into the dark depth of the vault. The crew obeyed, one or two of them making signs of protection in the air as they stepped away from the opening. Muni glared at them and the gestures ceased.

"Javin, would you come over, please?" he called, his voice carefully void of excitement. A tall, brown-haired man of about forty-five, working at the other end of the twenty-foot-long block, shrouded in white robes, turned and made his way around the slab to see what Muni wanted.

"Look there," said Muni softly, his wide mouth curling in disgust and trepidation.

Javin peered into the opening, shading his eyes to adjust to its darkness. A dozen feet down below the broken wall slab lay, not the preserved remains of the long dead man they had expected to find, but the crumpled body of a modern day Sumifan, his black eyes frozen with fright at their last sight, a pool of congealed blood on the thin layer of sand beneath his head.

Javin's gray eyes went almost as wide, and deep furrows creased his brow. "By the seven stars! No one has removed the slab until today?" He looked at the foreman levelly.

"Yes, Javin. You may check Cheyne's drawing of the marble wall. He sketched this area late yesterday evening," Muni replied, his face inscrutable.

Javin shook his head. "That won't be needed."

Javin trusted Muni more than he did himself sometimes. They had worked together for years, traversing the huge continent of Almaaz in search of Javin's burning ambition: to find the fabled Collector. Back in Argive, Javin had become convinced that old Sumifa was the final resting place of the man who had been chief mage to the ancient artificer Mishra.

The climate of this region was deadly hot and the politics treacherous. The true nature of the dig had been kept secret, Javin giving out to the Fascini, Sumifa's royals and their courtiers, only that he wished to study the architecture of old Sumifa, the ancient buried city known and shunned for its mysterious abandonment long ago. The Fascini had not cared. They never had believed there was an old city. After all, no one had ever found it before. And archaeologists were just diggers, and diggers were just treasure hunters to them, whatever their reasons. As long as they gave the standard half of what they found to the city's coffers, and didn't stir up the locals against Fascini decrees, the court turned a blind eye.

Javin had brought with him only his foster son, Cheyne, who had traveled with Javin to every site he had dug in the last ten years, and Muni, who spoke every modern language in Almaaz, even some that didn't have words, and told the truth in all of them.

Javin nodded, and Muni brought his crew around him, asking for two volunteers to go down into the room to bring up the body. Finally, Rij and Hadi stepped forward, drawing their long, curved daggers from their hips. Disdaining the ropes, they leapt into the dim chamber.

"Pay these men double today. Give those two double that. Only make sure they stay quiet. Keep everyone else on the site down by the other side of the wall. Business as usual. And ask Zu to bring Cheyne up from the eastern perimeter. I told him to sketch the olive press walls today until we opened this room," muttered Javin.

Muni's crew had been handpicked and worked the most sensitive areas in the dig, but Javin knew that even they would have a hard time with this discovery. Sumifans were notoriously ancestor conscious, and a corpse, especially a fresh one, would send their officials into a frenzy of ablutions and liturgies and sudden new decrees forbidding further excavation on the site. If word got round to the city fathers that there had been a body, even the fragrance of his money wouldn't keep them from closing him down. Javin knew he was right on top of finding the old Collector's grave. And when he found the Collector, he would find the thing he really searched for.

For years, Javin's colleagues, all eminent scholars, had mocked his theories of where the old mage's grave really lay. Most of the experts believed that the stories of the secret societies and an Armageddon Clock and the fabulous wealth supposedly buried with the Collector or with the Clock were pure folktale, rehearsed and embroidered as local mythology by the primitive Sumifans. Others, who gave the Collector's story any credence at all, thought that the grave must be in the Chimes, a place largely associated with the Borderlands, a place more or less divided from the rest of Almaaz by a mysterious curtain of light held to be located beyond the desert and past the orc kingdom in an isolated mountain range. But the exact location of the Chimes was not recorded in either current memory or on an ancient map. Not that it mattered. Certainly, no one of any respectable academic standing thought the stories were worth acting upon.

Javin knew otherwise. He was the last living member of the Circle.

Recently, in a dark corner of the stacks of Argivia's oldest library, Javin had made a discovery that had sent him to Sumifa, against his greatest personal wishes. While cataloguing some old shards, he had found some scrolls packed inside a pottery jar made by the Sarrazan elves. The scrolls had mentioned details of Old Sumifa and the Collector in their stories, and the ley lines measured correctly for where Javin had begun to dig weeks ago. If Javin could but find the old mage's grave, then his writings, specifically the *Holy Book of the Confessors*, supposedly the original sacred text of his order, would surely be close by also.

There was a chance that Javin would then be able to accomplish what he had been trying to do all his life: find the Armageddon Clock and somehow disarm it. The secret of the Clock had died with Samor, and all through the hundreds of years since, the members of the Circle had passed down to their sons or daughters the mission of destroying it. But one by one, they had all been murdered, or disappeared with absolutely no trace.

The mages of the lost Circle, though their deaths had been as different as their personalities, all shared the same killers. They were the victims of the Ninnites, once their brethren in magic, now their sworn enemies, pledged to the service of a mysterious dark prince. The Ninnites, too, searched for the secrets of the fabled Clock, believing it to be the marker for inestimable wealth and power.

For the Circle, and for all of Almaaz, Javin believed, time was running out. When Javin was gone, there would be no one else to take up the search, no one, at least, who believed that the Beast of the Hours—supposedly a hideous, angry cockatrice, a creature even the Collector had not known how to fight—was what really awaited any who found and opened the Clock. The Ninnites had done a convincing job on the locals as well. Any Sumifan would scoff at the idea that anything but the treasure of the famous Collector was hidden with the Armageddon Clock.

And then there was the matter of Cheyne. Javin knew that if the dark prince, the Raptor, as the scrolls had called him, ever found the young man, Cheyne would be as dead as this corpse in the ruin.

He hunched down to inspect the body Muni's men had brought up. Plainly, the man had been murdered. Not a neat job: the corpse's throat had been cut, the jugular vein slashed with three parallel gashes, almost like claw marks. Almost like the favorite method of the Ninnites.

Javin bent to look at the back of the unfortunate man's head, brushing away a lock of dark hair from just behind his left ear. No mark of the double crescent. The man had not been part of the Ninnites, so this was not an example of the order's extreme discipline. But then why would the two-thousand-year-old renegade cult murder a modern-day Sumifan citizen? If he had been a common thief, Javin thought, there appeared to be nothing of value in the little room, and the man looked to have had no time to steal. Clutched in the corpse's stiff, whitened hand, Javin found only an ancient Sumifan family totem, like the hundreds they had already unearthed around the site: ganzite, inscribed with symbols from an Almaazan tongue older even than the ancient city. Hardly worth dying for.

Or killing for, he puzzled, laying it aside. Javin covered the body again, knowing little more now about the man than before.

Muni shook his head, anticipating Javin's unspoken thought. "He looks familiar, but I do not know him." The other crewmen repeated the same answer one by one as Javin questioned them.

The unknown man displayed the features of the majority of native Sumifans: dark curly hair, dark eyes, olive skin, and a strong, lean jaw. He appeared to have been about sixty, but if he had been a shepherd and spent much time in the weather, he could have been much younger. They called this place the anvil of the sun, and for good reason. One crewman suggested he might be part of the nearest nomadic tribe, but Javin dismissed that possibility immediately.

"He must have come from the city. Look at his clothes." Javin pointed to the man's flimsy shoes and thin shopkeeper's robes. "He wasn't ready to spend any time out here in those."

Muni squatted, crossing his hands in front of him like a big cat. "Javin, your son approaches."

Javin glanced up sharply to see Cheyne striding as quickly as he could manage through the deep sand, a look of alarm upon his face.

"Shall I greet him below?" asked Muni.

"No. Let him come on up. I want him to chart the room under the slab right away, while we are both here. He's more than twenty now, and he can take care of himself, but . . . "

"But you are still his father," said Muni, almost smiling, his dark eyes half closed against the hard desert light.

Javin nodded, a little undone. Muni had a way of disarming all pretense.

Cheyne cleared the last step, panting from the effort in the blazing noon heat. His face was dry despite the exertion—perspiration evaporated as quickly as it formed here. He gratefully accepted the water jug, threw it back native style across his shoulder, and took a long pull on it.

"Zu said you wanted me up here fast, Javin. What's going on? Did you find the Collector?" Cheyne gasped before he was quite through with the last swallow. He flashed a brilliant smile as the cooling water trickled down his neck, finding a quicker path along a leather thong at his throat.

Javin gestured to the dead man.

"Oh. I suppose not." Cheyne frowned, instantly comprehending the ramifications. "Not one of the crew," he breathed in relief. "But . . . who?"

"We don't know. Muni found him under this slab, in what looks like part of a house. As you can plainly see, he has been murdered. We have no idea who killed him or why. But we must keep this quiet, or we won't have a job by the afternoon bells. And watch out for yourself. The body can't be more than a few hours dead. Whoever did this is in sharp habit, from the looks of his method. The murderer could still be close," said Javin.

Cheyne lifted his broad-rimmed hat and ran his fingers through a thatch of dark blond hair, resettling the hat in exactly the same place. He stooped to examine the piece of marble that had been the dead man's crypt cover. "No scraping or pry marks around the slab—"

"We know." Javin slid his eyes over to the crew in warning.

Cheyne nodded and took out his bound tablet and a bit of charcoal. "Have you been down?" he asked Javin.

"No. But the Collector isn't there." The disappointment was written plainly on Javin's face. "I want you to go in and draw before anything else is disturbed. One of us needs to remain up here with the ropes," Javin replied.

He shaded his eyes with his hand and watched the last of the workers leave the site. "You know what to do, and I'll be right here. Muni will go in with you to hold the torch. Be careful. That body got in there somehow, and likely not by magic." *I hope,* he added silently.

"What about you up here alone?" Cheyne glanced around at the suddenly vacant site.

"I'll be fine. Just do your job and get back up here fast," said Javin.

Cheyne signaled for Javin to lower him and Muni with the plaited fiber ropes, which always looked too flimsy to take any weight, but had, for centuries, helped move the entire Sumifan civilization.

Inside the room, it was much cooler than on the sand, but the air was stale and thick and smelled of limerock. A fine layer of dust covered the several inches of sand on the floor, except for the wide stain of dark, fresh, dried blood. Cheyne carefully examined the sand around the stain, but found no disturbance. Muni stood exactly where he had first touched down, holding a lantern as Cheyne went over the room. Following the dim glow of the lamp, Cheyne sketched a window and a wide doorway, but they were packed with sand. The whole room, thought Cheyne, had likely been filled with it. A dark scar ran along the walls about head level, where the wooden frame of a roof had been. That structure had perhaps fallen into this story, a possibility that would explain the several roof tiles scattered on the floor. Dust became visible in the air as Muni moved the lantern around, swirling in thick currents and eddies with Cheyne's movements, but otherwise the place looked completely undisturbed.

Muni pointed to one corner of the room, where a three-foot-wide hole had been hacked in the wall, proba-

bly centuries ago. Looters had obviously excavated the
room long before them, taking everything of value, but
at least removing most of the sand as well. No footprints
marred its smooth surface. Cheyne resisted his first urge
to explore the hole and where it could possibly lead,
instead placing his measuring stick down by the wall and
then drawing the shape of it to scale. He touched the
stone, its coolness soothing his sunburned hand.

"Marble," he muttered. "Always eleven hagon
degrees cooler than the room temperature." The wall
was smooth and polished, hardly showing its great age
at all. One large crack, directly over the hole, ran from
ceiling to sand, but the other large slabs still stood
straight and square.

"Workmanship of the highest order," Cheyne said
softly. "It must have taken some doing to break
through that."

Not given to idle chatter, Muni only nodded. He held
the lantern out toward the broken wall until Cheyne
had drawn a texture sample and gotten a quick sketch
of the details of a collapsed set of marble shelves.

After a long look around the room, Cheyne decided
they could move on to the tunnel. As Muni knelt
beside it, something bright caught Cheyne's eye and he
held up his hand.

"Muni—look. Broken glass. Looks like it was a mirror."

Muni waved the lantern over the fragments again,
and Cheyne set down his stick, drew them, and then
picked up one of the longer pieces. Its silvering had
gone black long ago, but the front of the glass was uni-
form in thickness and had few scratches. Fine work,
again. Cheyne started to place the jagged glass in his
pack when Muni touched his arm.

"Let me have a look at the edge. I think I saw something else."

Cheyne turned the fragment over and, sure enough,
a dark brown substance filled some of the hairline
cracks in the glass. When he touched the edges, the
powder flaked away and fell to the ground.

"More blood?" Muni queried.

"If it is, it didn't come from our unfortunate fellow above. Look at the texture of the dust. The particles are far too fine to be only a day old," said Cheyne. He wrapped the glass in a clean cloth and put it in the pack.

"Let's see where this passage leads," he continued, bending into the dark hole.

"Your father . . ." Muni began, caution in his voice.

From the time Javin had taken Cheyne on his first dig, more than ten years ago, Muni had watched the odd, pensive child, a gifted artist even then, grow into one of the best young diggers he had known. Javin had insisted, partly because of the way he had found the boy—a subject Javin never discussed—and partly because they traveled to any number of less than safe places, that Cheyne learn the ten Argivan open-handed fighting forms and also to use a blade. Javin's care had made Cheyne deadly accurate with a dagger and better than most with a sword. Nonetheless, when things got dangerous, Muni tended to forget that Cheyne was grown up.

Cheyne let out a deep sigh, reminding him of that fact, and stirring several hundred years worth of dust into a small cloud, causing Muni to sneeze, which caused more dust, which caused more sneezing.

"My father is up there. We are down here. We have to do this," said Cheyne, laughing. "Are you afraid, Muni?" he teased.

Muni lowered his head and narrowed his leonine eyes at the young man, covertly moving his unoccupied hand to his sash, making sure of his dagger. "As you wish, Cheyne."

Cheyne bent again to the opening, this time dropping all the way to his knees as Muni passed him the lantern. Cheyne startled a bit as several hand-sized black scorpions instantly raised their claws and arched their tails.

"Vermin." Muni sniffed in distaste. "You are going in there?"

Cheyne gritted his teeth, held the lantern out as far

as he could, sending the scorpions skittering for deeper cover, and then drew it close again, motioning to Muni to back away.

"No. I'm not going in. There is no need. See for yourself."

Muni cocked a dark eyebrow at him, took the lantern, and looked into the crevice. Five feet into the wall, the opening was blocked with sand. A great knot of cobwebs crisscrossed the end of the short tunnel, their silken strands completely intact. The vermin had had the tunnel to themselves for centuries.

"Most adored Schreefa, jewel of the desert, luminous beacon of mercy, they have found Kalkuk the shop-keeper . . . ah, very, very dead, in a sealed vault out at the ruin. I thought you would wish to know." The dark-robed assassin bowed deeply to his employer.

"Well. That's too very, very bad." Riolla Hifrata mulled the words around in her mouth as if they tasted of poison.

Damn this jewel! she thought, rubbing the black pearl between her fingers. *Why can't I get it to work right anymore? Well, at least now I know where I sent the old boy. But maybe this is all right anyway . . . if those diggers are blamed for his death, perhaps the Fascini will shut them down. And the Raptor will then find better humor and stop charging me so much. Ever since they've been at the ruin, he's been ten times the beast he usually is.*

Riolla sighed and dismissed the assassin, who rose gratefully, having begun to feel the intricate, linked weave of the rug digging into his knee. As he backed out of the room, she trudged up the stairs to the top floor of her shop, thinking about her last attempt to work the pearl's magic

"Og, you old fool, however did you do it? How could you make the stones sing for you?" she muttered, reaching the landing.

She entered her bedchamber, drew the shades against the morning sun, and lay down on the gold-embroidered coverlet. Riolla's head had started pounding the moment she had tried to use the pearl to transport old Kalkuk's body the night before. It had been years since she had dared to attempt the stone, but alone and desperate, the Raptor's increasing demand for payments upon her, she had been forced to "collect" on Kalkuk. And Riolla knew, despite the fact that she was Mercanto Schreefa, that the Raptor would collect on her without a second thought if she were late with her protection payment.

It had been such a shame, really. Kalkuk was her best supplier; the man had come up with things none of the others could ever equal in value. She had never discovered his source, either. This time, though, poor old Kalkuk had missed his promised delivery—some kind of antique music box he had rambled on about, saying that it had been in his family for generations beyond counting, that it was so old that it might even have belonged to the Collector himself. Of course, of course; everyone in debt has such treasures. Riolla had smirked at him, marked his name on her list as delinquent, and gone on to other business. But when the Raptor had sent a summons for her to appear within three days, with double her usual payment, she had gone to Kalkuk's shop by herself, pressed him for the artifact, and he had threatened her with some old totem he had snatched from his shelf.

You shouldn't have done that, Kalkuk. I had to kill you then. She picked up a pumice stone and filed a snag on one of her long, sharp nails. *Word gets around if the Schreefa gets soft. Things just don't work right then.*

She sighed. Her head seemed to split with dark imaginings and the smell of dead seaweed filled her nostrils. She took a cup of tea to her lips, swallowing a tiny sip of the spiced brew. But it tasted of decay, just as had her breakfast, just as had her dinner the night before. Og had warned her about the pearl. Of all the stones in his ring, it was both the easiest to use and the most difficult to direct. The other times she had risked it had never been this bad.

Why hadn't the song done its job? She had sung it just as Og had taught her. She had meant to place the body in the middle of the Mercanto's sundial, before the scowling face of Nin, where it would have served as warning to the other businessmen and women who paid Riolla for her protection. Especially all those who had been just a little late. How had the body wound up out in the desert? Inside some old building? She hadn't even known there were old buildings out there. Imagine that, the ancient city of Sumifa was real.

Riolla paused, the stone in her hand growing strangely warm. She smiled a little. Then a little more. For if the ancient city were real, then why not the Clock itself? Maybe the treasure the silly Barcans were always looking for really did exist. This would bear further inquiry. When she could think more clearly.

So much for Kalkuk, she mused, trying the tea again, with no better results. *But I still don't have his payment, either.* And her own time was quickly running out.

A timid knock at her chamber door brought Riolla's head up too suddenly, the sound seeming to be pitched at the most irritating tone possible.

"Yes! Yes! Stop that. What is it?" she snapped, her own voice raking over her ears like claws.

"Schreefa, Prince Maceo sends greeting. He says to inform you that he has reconsidered your proposal."

"I still say there is no way anyone could have moved that block, and no way anyone could have used that tunnel, Javin," Cheyne repeated, slamming the water jug down on the camp table where he had spread his drawings of the room. A few stray droplets colored the bata-paper for a few seconds, then faded, drying quickly. "Go down there and see for yourself, if you like. It's just an old looter's hole, covered up by the sandstorms long ago."

Javin drummed his fingers over the drawings and shook his head. "I'm not saying you're wrong. I just don't like the alternative. The method looked too familiar. And by the way, you should stay close until this is over. They might know we are here after all."

"You mean the Broken Circle, the Ninnites?"

"Keep your voice down." Javin frowned.

"Javin, why is it every time we come up with something you can't explain, it has to be the result of some old grudge between a long dead bunch of sorcerers?" Cheyne met Javin's eyes and locked him in a long stare. "This time, I want to know."

"It is better you do not know yet. Besides, I couldn't tell you more if I wanted to. It's just not safe."

"Javin," Cheyne said, sighing, "if I were still ten years old, that would be the right answer. But I'm a grown man now. It's time for me to be on my own. Find a wife, find my own work. Find my *name*. I have to know what all this sorcery and lore you are always poring over and thinking about has to do with me. Who am I? What happened to the first ten years of my life? Why can't I see myself in a mirror like everyone else? Whatever you know about these things, Javin, I deserve to know, too. At last we are in Sumifa—and there is something about this place, this particular place, that feels so familiar to me. I have to be free to explore this place. Maybe here I will find someone who knows what this means—" he added softly, pulling an amulet from under his shirt, its odd marking, very like a tiny fingerprint, deeply and precisely etched into the end of the smooth, cylindrical stone.

Unwilling to answer, Javin started to rise and leave, his way of effectively ending every discussion about Cheyne's past. Then he sat back heavily on his low bamboo stool and looked at Cheyne for a long moment.

"We've been over this countless times before. Not yet. You have to trust me. Someday it will all be clear. But not yet. If my suspicions about this murder are correct, you are far safer not knowing. And as I said, don't go back to the city. Things are likely to be strained with the Sumifans until this murder is solved. I'll see you at the vault. We're going to go ahead and empty it. I know the Collector is close. He just has to be."

The ache in his voice went through Cheyne's heart like a dagger. Javin gathered the drawings and the water jug and headed out to the ruin again.

Cheyne gritted his teeth, using his frustration to rub all the harder at the totem he had found in the hand of the dead man when the workers had set about to carry the hapless Sumifan back into the city. Like all of the other family markers they had unearthed at the site, this one had a row of glyphs on it, and when Cheyne applied vigorous pressure, their outlines became clear and readable. If one read Old High Sumifan.

He dug his nail into the incised lines, clearing the deeper dirt away. The glyphs were really pictures, and Cheyne could make out a wavy line, which Muni had once said meant water, a stylized scorpion, probably a likeness of the ones he had seen in the vault, and a basket of some kind. Two others were too faint to decipher. He rubbed the ganzite block as clean as he could, fascinated by the way the colored light danced in its edges. He uncovered a basket and a boat. But there was still a stubborn smear near the bottom. He rubbed again, adding a little spit, and when the smudge still did not come up, he took a rough cloth to it. The mark seemed to be as permanent as the carved glyphs. Intrigued, Cheyne searched his bag of tools for a magnifier, found the fat lens, and held it over the totem.

Cheyne could hardly credit what he saw. Beneath a tough layer of dark soot there appeared to be a tiny fingerprint carved into the ganzite, its lines fluid and clear, an unmistakable match to the glyph upon his own mysterious amulet.

"Cheyne, I need you to come on out here and get the wall finished. We've got maybe another hour before it gets too hot to work," called Javin, from outside the tent. "Might as well do what we can. When word gets around about the incident, we want to have used our time well."

Cheyne found that his mouth was suddenly very dry, and it had nothing to do with the desert heat. "Coming, Javin," was all he could manage. His head swam with possibilities. He stuffed the totem into his pack, collected his gear and a water jug. He washed his face in the basin by the door, by long habit, avoiding the mirror that hung over it.

As the sun climbed to its searing zenith, Cheyne trudged to the north wall, finding, thankfully, a waning sliver of shade from the larger fallen stones to stand in as he drew. The time passed and he hardly thought of the stones he sketched, the shape of the totem's last glyph still burned upon his mind's eye.

By the last stroke of his ochre crayon, the shade had completely disappeared. Cheyne packed up and walked back to the cluster of tents, mulling over his next move. The amulet around his neck seemed heavier than ever before, and he felt it thump against his chest in time with every step.

The main tent was empty; Javin had not returned from the vault. But it wouldn't be long—not even Javin could stand to work in this heat. He thought to check the shed, hoping to take Javin's horse, but then remembered it had been commandeered to transport the dead man. Cheyne laid his drawings neatly on the table, refilled the water skin, pulled on clean robes, traded his hat for a native style kaffiyeh, and walked out onto the rough road toward Sumifa.

CHAPTER
2

MORE THAN SEVENTEEN CENTURIES OLD itself, the "new," shining city of Sumifa lay in a wide, flat valley between the eastern desert near the Fallajian territories and the western erg, which merged with the scrubland controlled by the fractious Wyrvil orc kingdoms in the west. The Nantas River, a slow-moving ribbon of silt-laden water, turned the valley green during the winter months, but even that dried up during the summers.

Since it was the month of Sul, the Nantas had reappeared, and Cheyne chose a path alongside it where he would be a little cooler from the constant breeze across the water. A herd of sheep bound for a drink passed him on the other side, the shepherds in their brilliant red-and-purple robes waving at him in succession as they prodded their thirsty sheep toward the water. Chameleons the colors of the blue-gray rocks sunned themselves in droves, bobbing their heads and racing instantly for cover when he strode by them. A lone skiff floated downstream, a red-haired Neffian slave at the tiller, another dragging a net full of shiners into the boat. Cicadas harped, their songs rising and falling in rhythm with the waves of hot wind coming in off the erg. Within the hour, nearly hypnotized by the heat and the low, flat countryside, Cheyne found himself at the majestic, golden Lion Gate bridge, the main entrance to Sumifa, capital city of Almaaz, oldest settlement in the west, the only part of the continent known to have escaped most of the flooding of the Great Thaw after the Wandering.

Architecturally, nothing much had changed in the years since Sumifa's population had moved from the basalt-and-limerock foundations that Cheyne and Javin were excavating to this huge, walled fortress town. Like the ruins at the dig, only on a far larger scale, the town was laid out in irregular concentric circles, each one with a gate of its own for better protection from attack. The gates were staggered inside the city, no two aligned, so that to walk into Sumifa was something like walking into a high, stout maze. In the records of the chaos that had followed the Artifice Wars, scribes wrote that these walls had preserved the city from siege by raiders and the fiery assaults of thirst-crazed military tribes wandering the dunes in search of their lost leaders. However, modern-day Sumifa made use of its fortifications in a way not evidenced at the old ruin. Between the poor and the merchant classes, and again between the merchants and the wealthy Fascini, stood the ten-foot-thick, twenty-foot-tall basalt walls, each a solid, grim reminder of the even more invincible, unseen divisions in the city.

The smell of roasting meats mixed with the strong odor of shirrir spice pulled at him, but Cheyne ignored his sudden, clawing hunger and passed over the sluggish Nantas and on through the outer part of town quickly and warily, keeping the totem firmly in his hand and his hand hidden in his robes.

Though the dig had opened a month before, this was Cheyne's first time in Sumifa alone. Always before, since Javin would not tear himself away from the site for a moment, Muni had accompanied Cheyne, and they had come for supplies or tools, or to bring a few small finds in to help appease the Fascini. They were in and out within a couple of hours, then back to work. But Cheyne took his time today. Things looked different somehow, a little more interesting. He remembered to keep to the middle of the wide, elevated road that twisted through the Barca, avoiding the pickpockets and the potholes, but kept a sharp eye out for the elf he was searching for.

As he came to the next gate, a half a mile into the city, one of the Fascini's royal purple sedan chairs, carried on four sides by ochre-painted Neffian slaves, suddenly veered, nearly pushing him off the highway.

"Hey!" Cheyne shouted as he fell roughly against a retaining wall, forgetting he had neither rank nor position in ancestor-worshiping Sumifa.

He fumbled the totem, but caught it just as a sharp reply came from inside the sedan and the slaves abruptly halted, all of them staring at him openly, their mouths agape. A pale, bejeweled hand snaked out of the purple embroidered curtain—a bit threadbare, Cheyne noticed from his new proximity—and twitched it aside. From the way the man sat so close to the side, Cheyne had the vague impression that there were two people in the chair.

"You dare to occupy the road when I have need of it? Doulos, ask this slave just why he is loose and who he belongs to. Demand of him his name."

The words could have been carved in ice, despite the searing heat. Cheyne grimaced at the irony. He had sought the answer to that very question all his life, and now it was the very reason he had defied Javin and come into town.

Still unable to see who had spoken to him, Cheyne dusted his hands off, picked up his pack, and walked closer to the chair. Before the nearest Neffian could repeat his master's question, or warn the young man with his eyes, Cheyne pushed back the curtain a little farther and received a sharp whack on the hand from the occupant's riding crop.

"Don't touch that, you renegade slave! I asked you a question. Who are you, and how dare you block the way of my runners? or place your unworthy hand upon my carriage! Do you not perceive who I am? Speak my words, Doulos," he ordered the Neffian, who began to repeat it all again, hysterics included.

Cheyne stood back, patiently listening and rubbing his smarting fingers, but thinking only about what he had seen of the people in the sedan. The woman was veiled, but the man was gaunt, black haired, green eyed, ashen skinned, and sported a thin mustache, twisted into a sneer. Though this was Cheyne's first actual contact with the Fascini, he had no trouble recognizing all the marks of Sumifa's leisure-loving, sickness-ridden upper crust.

But who was the woman? She wore no purple and no matron's veil. He knew that, on rare occasions, Fascini took wives from the richest families of the Mercanto, or from unprovable, if questionable, nobility in distant cities, but Javin had said that if you weren't born into the caste, you could never really belong, and the Fascini liked it that way. Fewer people, more wealth. Especially since the western caravans had stopped. Goods were ever more expensive and harder to come by. Of course, that also meant greater profit. For some.

The patient Neffian had finished and stood waiting for Cheyne to answer.

"I'm not a slave. I'm from the . . . east," Cheyne answered cautiously, remembering the problem out at the site. "I didn't see your chair in time. But your runners nearly ran me over."

"Oh, for Nin's sake, address the right-hand man, you fool. You can never talk directly to me. The east. The east. Where they have no culture, no appreciation for time-honored traditions. Where your persons of rank freely mingle with commoners, where slaves whose ancestors lived in actual caves deign to talk to royalty. Really, you foreign people should not be let

inside Sumifan gates until you know how to behave.
You have humiliated me. Do you know I could have
you flayed in the Four Most Awful Fashions for what
you just did? As it is, I am in far better humor than
usual. I will have you buried alive, instead," said the
Fascini, his voice rising with impatience.

While the Neffian took a deep breath and began to
repeat his master's words again, Cheyne shook his
head, perplexed as to which was his most grievous sin:
being in the way to be run over, or telling the Fascini
about it. He settled on the latter, but none too surely.
The Neffian shrugged his shoulders, a look of concern
replacing his careful blankness. Cheyne decided at that
point that the Fascini was serious about the burying
alive part. Cheyne was about to leap the guard rail and
try to disappear into the Barca when he heard his
reprieve.

"Maceo, he could not have known he spoke to the
royal heir of Sumifa. You have just been announced as
king this afternoon. He has done nothing to warrant
death." A small voice, raw with strain, pleaded with
the Fascini.

Maceo shot the curtain across its rod, leaving
Cheyne straining to hear the fervent conversation
within. The Neffian stared ahead again, unblinking
until he and the others simultaneously lifted the chair,
as if they had heard an order Cheyne could not. But
Maceo had the last word.

"Nameless idiot! Unknown fool! Today the woman
saves your worthless life. When I am installed as king,
if you dare to tread these streets, you shall pay for this
insult," the Fascini shouted as the chair swerved onto
the thoroughfare, a red ribbon falling from the
woman's side of the chair.

The next set of gates loomed just before him and
Cheyne slowly walked toward them, soon losing sight
of the sedan as the Neffians rounded a curve in the
highway, then turned off abruptly, heading, strangely,
Cheyne thought, toward the worst part of the Barca.

Despite the crowd that had gathered to witness his very public dressing down, all Cheyne could think of was the weeping woman.

Cheyne bent and picked up the red ribbon before a passing wagon ground it into the cobbles. It smelled of rich myrrh and bergamot, dark, strong scents both. He put it in his pack and passed through the gates, wondering what the face behind the veil looked like.

"I told you, I don't know, it could be Elclesian or Trufi ganzite. Or it could even come all the way from the Chimes, though *I've* never seen any of that fabled stone." The shopkeeper sneered, tired of guessing. "Looks like any other old totem except for that last mark and the odd cut. Where did you say this came from?" The slouching clockmaker set the totem on his cluttered counter and waited for Cheyne to answer.

"Thanks. Thanks very much for your trouble. It was an outside chance anyway; I know this sort of thing isn't really your business."

True enough. Cheyne had tried the clockmaker's shop just because it was there. It was the last place he had time for, and it had turned out to be by far the most distasteful.

Cheyne had wandered around the Mercanto for three hours, searching every antique stall and every art dealer's store he could find, and each time he had received a puzzled look or a shrug of the shoulders. As for the elf, his questions had provoked only laughter and the repeated response that no elves had been seen in Sumifa since before the Wandering. Worse, no one seemed to know anything about the last glyph on the totem, or even care, for that matter. Which made it very odd that the disheveled clockmaker continued to stare at Cheyne, his droopy face still lifted in expectation of an answer to his question as two greenbottle flies chased each other above his head.

Cheyne nodded his good-bye, returned the totem to his pack, and made for the door. The sun had moved over the westernmost part of the wall, marking it time for him to get back to the site. Javin would be mad enough already.

"Ah, perhaps I know of someone else who could help you with your dilemma," the clockmaker wheedled. Cheyne stopped at the door and turned around. "Her name is Riolla Hifrata. She is a worthy woman, well schooled in the antiquities. Here is her address."

The shopkeeper fumbled at the sleeve of his grease-spotted caftan and withdrew a small, dirty scrap of parchment with an even dirtier hand. His face unreadable, he slid the gilt-edged fragment toward Cheyne. One of his clocks began to click and bang in the back room, then every other one in the shop chimed in. Thanking the man, Cheyne grabbed the parchment and left the din, his ears ringing.

It seemed that the streets had emptied somewhat while Cheyne had been in the shop. Only one shabbily dressed vagrant hunched in the shade of a market stall, a nearly empty bottle in hand and humming to himself, completely unremarkable except for a truly enormous nose protruding from under the folds of his hood. Cheyne marvelled, keeping his amazement to a polite smile as he passed the man.

He read the card as he walked toward the Inner Ring Gate, wondering if he really had time to make this visit and then deciding that if Javin were mad already, Cheyne might as well make their confrontation worth his while. And after all, he hadn't run into any real trouble from the incident out at the site. In fact, aside from Prince Maceo, no one had given him more than a second glance.

The western wall cast a longer shadow than Cheyne would have liked, but the lure of the card was impossible to deny. Since his search for the elf had proved futile, this could be the one chance he had at finding out what the glyph meant. The Fascini might already be demanding that Javin close the dig, and if they had to leave, Cheyne knew he would never get back here again. He hurried through the vacant streets and quickly came to the address written on the small square of vellum.

"The Arcanum" read the painfully elaborate gold lettering on the sign. The little shop was built up against the Citadel's wall and as closely to the gate leading to the Inner Ring as it could be. Cheyne pulled the chime and waited impatiently for several long minutes while the peephole slid open, then several more until the door was unbarred to admit him. Apparently, the Arcanum served a rather exclusive clientele.

Inside the foyer, Cheyne was assaulted by the pungent odors of cinnamon, clove, and shirrir smoke, an illegal narcotic spice, probably smuggled in on one of the few remaining caravans, which traveled irregularly and eastward only. He stood in near darkness for a moment, his eyes adjusting, until he was able to see the woman who had admitted him.

"Hello. I have come to—" he began, but the woman held up a plump, razor-nailed hand to silence him.

"Yes, I know why you have come. Vinzo sent a runner the minute you left his shop. Please enter my counting room, where there is more light," the woman replied in a cultured accent, her voice an unpleasant rasp.

Cheyne felt a marked uneasiness, but allowed himself to be swept forward through a purple beaded curtain and into a well-lit room. Lining the white plaster walls of the room were stacks of books and scrolls, and on every flat surface rested some kind of clock or timepiece. No wonder the scruffy clockmaker had this connection. He had probably supplied most of these objects.

A steward spread a cloth on the red velvet chair Cheyne was offered while the woman settled herself directly opposite him, a small glass-topped table between them. On it, half a freshly cut blood orange glistened, and a small ruby-studded dagger dripping with the dark red juice lay very close to the woman's hand.

"My name is Riolla Hifrata. I have, as you see, a certain interest in antiquities. Perhaps I can help you. May I see the object?"

Cheyne hesitated, his gaze impolitely fixed on the creature before him. He had never seen anything like Riolla. She seemed to be a little older than he, but it was hard to tell—under the heavy, pale face paint, she could have hidden either youth or age. Her eyebrows arched up her forehead in thin, dark lines, and her bright pink smile seemed to be drawn permanently on full lips. Her eyes were vivid blue, the color of the high mountain lakes in Tarnrish, back home in Argivia. But the feature that continued to hold Cheyne's attention crowned Riolla's entire head. A bright, brassy sweep of curls rose to an impossible height and then cascaded halfway down her back, tendrils of it curling around her throat, framing her pendant: a single black pearl. Never had he seen such hair. Or such red hair. Though she affected the manners of the Fascini, Riolla looked as Neffian as the runners who bore Maceo's sedan.

"I said, may I see the object?" she repeated, a note of perplexing urgency in her voice.

"Oh. The object. Yes, well, I was wondering if you could help decipher the markings. I believe they must be Old High Sumifan, and it seems that no one reads that anymore. That's really all I need, you see." He fumbled, pulling the totem cautiously out from his pack.

"Of course, Muje . . ." She smiled, the corners of her mouth dimpling.

"It's Cheyne. Just Cheyne," he replied.

"Cheyne. Of course." She startled for a moment, then shifted her eyes distastefully away from him. He had no last name—an unforgivable sin in Sumifa. And he looked like a slave, with those blue eyes and that fair head of hair. "Just put it here." She patted the tabletop.

Cheyne hesitated, somewhat surprised. Cheyne wondered why Riolla had invoked the same rule of conduct as Maceo when clearly she was no Fascini, but he set the totem down on the table anyway. The steward picked it up, wiped it off, and handed it to her.

After a few moments of squinting at the glyphs, Riolla had written down six of the seven symbols and their meanings. She tapped the tabletop idly for a few minutes, giving the last glyph her complete concentration. The clocks in the room ticked and hummed in their particular rhythms. Riolla said nothing. Finally, Cheyne shifted uncomfortably in the delicate chair, its flimsy back giving forth a loud, grinding wrench. Riolla looked up at him and smiled mechanically, her answer composed.

Cheyne knew she was lying before she began to speak.

"This last one is the sign of the whirlpool. It is not seen often, for obvious reasons. The family looks to be of no importance either when this was inscribed or, certainly, later. There you have it."

She smiled even wider, waiting for his agreement. When he only looked away, she turned her attention to the totem again, pretending to admire its lines and the workmanship.

"Ah, where exactly did you find this piece, if I may ask?" she pressed gently, professional veneer thinly covering her intense interest.

"I picked it up out on the dunes," Cheyne said, reaching for the totem. Riolla feigned more appreciation and ignored his extended hand.

"Of course. You are a digger, no?" When he winced, her smile became tragic. "Cheyne, I like you. I am sorry I could not tell you that you had a valuable or important piece; I know how hard you people work for the little that you find. But I think I will make your coming to me worth your while. I do not ordinarily do this sort of thing, but I really want to help you on your way. I will buy this piece," she said generously. "I'll give you twenty kohli for it, and you'll never have a better offer, tell you why: it's really not worth even ten kohli—it's just that this particular totem comes from the time before the Wandering, and as you see, I collect things from that era." She waved her sharp nails around the room.

"Thank you, Riolla, but it's sort of special to me, too, even though it has no other value."

He swept up the totem from the table, his hand accidentally sending the delicate dagger sliding to the very edge of the little table, where it teetered on its hilt, blade pointing toward his host. Riolla followed the path of the knife and then slowly looked up at Cheyne, saying nothing. He stuffed the ganzite block into his pack and made ready to leave. Riolla's painted smile dropped an inch and her eyes hardened into glittering sapphires.

"Of course. That will be fifty kohli for the consultation, then. And leave my calling card here," she pronounced flatly.

After paying every antique dealer in the Mercanto, fifty-two kohli was all the money he had left. He reached into his pack and gave it to her, noting that Riolla's adoption of caste law didn't seem to affect the exchange of money, took the paper she had drawn the symbols' meanings upon, and left Riolla Hifrata sitting frozen in artful rage at her table, her calling card pushed under the sticky blade of the jewelled knife. Before he had found the front door, the steward had stripped the cloth from the velvet chair, folded it, and laid it neatly atop the trash heap in back of the shop.

Just as the Arcanum's door slammed behind him, he heard the last bells ring three times, a few minutes apart, signaling the closing of first the Citadel's doors, then the Mercanto's, and finally the outer gates of the Barca. That meant two walls to try to scale if he didn't make it in time.

He rushed down the narrow, winding streets, trying to

remember just how he had found the Arcanum to begin
with. The shadows confused and redirected his memory,
making certain shops appear where he had not seen
them before, and losing the prominence of other landmarks in their long crawl across the city. Cheyne began
to feel the edges of panic. He was a stranger with no
name and no standing, and now no money, caught in a
city where those were the only things that could pry you
out of trouble. And trouble, he had been told by Muni
time and again, always came out at dark in Sumifa.

Thoughts of Javin's distress at his absence rattled
through his mind as well—in all the times Javin had
taken him to help crew the digs, Cheyne had never so
directly ignored Javin's warnings. The trip hadn't even
been worth the expense of Madame Hifrata's information, much less Javin's trust. His concentration caught
up in this whirl of guilt and angst, he did not notice
the beggar he tripped over until it was too late.

It was a fortunate fall. Had Cheyne's head not
dropped as he rolled over the oddly familiar vagrant,
the well-aimed throwing disk that sailed over them
both would have taken it from his shoulders. The discus bounced hard off a basalt wall, brass blade ringing
sweetly as it spun into the sand.

"Stay low!" the beggar growled, listening intently to
the tone of the disk. "And follow me."

He drew his short dagger and rolled around the corner
of a bungalow, dragging Cheyne along with him. They
pressed themselves against the hot brick walls for a
moment, then when the footsteps passed by, the vagrant
motioned to Cheyne to follow him up a rope ladder.
Cheyne had little choice. He could already hear the soft
footfalls of the assassin heading back toward them, the
man no doubt having figured out their trickery.

Cheyne hauled himself up the rope to the flat roof of
the building, its surface baking his feet through his
boots with the lambent heat of the desert day. It
wouldn't take the assassin long to figure this out, either.
Cheyne was about to raise that point, but the beggar

had no intention of staying up there. He drew the young archaeologist to the edge of the bungalow facing the street where Cheyne had been attacked, and when the thug came trudging back the same way, let out a piercing wail and leapt off the roof onto the man below.

By the time Cheyne had found a safer way down a trellis, the vagrant had joined the killer in a knife fight, which was far more evenly matched than Cheyne would have thought possible. The vagrant had some acrobatic skills, and he was giving the assassin all he could handle, though neither had drawn blood yet. When he saw his chance, Cheyne waded in and threw a staggering roundhouse punch, dropping the assassin like a sack of salt.

Cheyne dusted himself off and took the ornate, curved dagger from the assassin's hand. It was the same one he had seen on Riolla's table, the juice of the orange still sticky on its blade.

"Oh, nicely timed," congratulated the vagrant. Cheyne turned to face his benefactor.

The beggar's hood had dropped in the scuffle, and Cheyne now saw why he looked so familiar. The beggar's nose was a veritable colossus, reminding Cheyne of the twenty-foot-tall head of Nin outside the crushed wall at the dig. The eastern face and the statue's gargantuan ears had long ago weathered away or broken off, leaving the head's stern western face an unbalanced joke for all time. As if he read Cheyne's mind, the vagrant quickly pulled up his ineffective hood, his sunburned nose still protruding noticeably from it.

"Wait—you were outside the clockmaker's shop . . ." Cheyne began.

"Yes. And now I am about to be there again, unless you give me a better place to be. . . ." The beggar crooked his finger toward the swinging sign on the raqa shop up the alley. "Nothing like a little rumble to work up a thirst. Would you care to buy me a drink?" Cheyne noticed that he swerved oddly, and moved to take his arm.

"Here, are you all right? Let me help you. But I can't buy you a drink. All I have left is two kohli," he apologized, searching for the coins.

Which were missing, of course. The beggar shook his head, his nose exaggerating the motion. "No, No. I'm perfectly all right," he wheezed heavily in Cheyne's face. The smell of soured raqa nearly succeeded where the assassin had failed. Cheyne realized he had discovered the apparent source of the beggar's remarkable bravery.

"Here. Please let me help you to some shade. I'll get water—" Cheyne said, fumbling.

"Water? No, I think not, my good man. What is called for now is vintage raqa, the sweet, crushed heart of the desert prickle, left at least a week in its delicious grief, and perhaps a loaf of solid bappir, probably the same age," the grinning beggar disagreed, his verbal abilities, like his bravado, seeming to rise to the occasion. "I'm fine, truly, young sirrah. A few bruises when I sober up. But then I'll *never* feel them now, will I? And thank you for the coins." Cheyne checked his pocket and frowned. "Now, now, a generous man will never go hungry. You can get out just the other side of that stall. Best be going now. Before that gentleman who wanted your head wakes up."

Cheyne knew he was right, but the bells had stopped ringing, and outer gates were closed by now anyway. He was stuck here overnight, and this poor soul seemed to be his only friend in the city, even if he had taken his last two kohli. He wasn't going to let him part company just yet. But when Cheyne turned to see where the man had pointed, the beggar immediately disappeared into the deepening shadows.

With no other choice left, Cheyne brushed himself off and headed for the curry stall where the vagrant had said was a way out of the city, hoping it wasn't a trick. The stallkeeper had raised a hand in a peculiar gesture when the beggar had pointed his way.

When he reached the tent, Cheyne eyed the roasting

morsels with keen regret. He must have looked ready
to drop with hunger, because the stallkeeper, clearing
his brazier for the day, left a haunch of lamb on it and
nodded to Cheyne as he seemed to melt into the wall.
The young man eagerly grabbed up the meat, not
minding the several grains of sand he found included.
The lamb was tough and dry, stringy and oversea-
soned, but Cheyne wolfed it down.

In another moment, he stood hovering in front of
the stall, licking his fingers, still wondering how to get
out of the Mercanto. Then he saw how the stallkeeper
had disappeared so thoroughly—behind the flimsy
tent, almost invisible in the deepening shadows, a large
crack parted the stonework. Cheyne looked around,
and finding no one to tell him he couldn't, took a deep
breath, scuttled through the narrow passage, through a
dark slaughterhouse, and out into the Barca. From the
well-worn path under the wall and the cloying smell of
old blood, both the butchery and the hidden entrance
had probably been there since antiquity.

Exhaling, Cheyne walked through the shabby streets
until he found the outer wall, and then studied it for
similar openings. Behind the hanging tent cloth and
lean-tos, he found dozens of such breaches, most of
them seemingly natural, that had been made in the
outer wall over the centuries.

*It looks so solid from the outside, but it's just layers
and layers of whitewash. I guess the Fascini wouldn't
repair anything they didn't have to look at,* Cheyne
mused.

Soon he was on the flat, dusty road back to the older
ruin, wondering just exactly what he would tell Javin.

CHAPTER

3

"DO I HAVE THIS STORY STRAIGHT? YOU DO
not have your payment because . . . you had your mark
in front of you, and you let him leave the shop? Then
he got away from your man in the streets? Riolla, I am
very disappointed in you. I thought I had taught you
better than to be so careless. And such an unimagina-
tive excuse at that." The hooded man spoke softly, but
his words pierced Riolla's heart. "And why would that
be? How many more like him have you let get away,
hmm? Did this particular young man distract you to
the point of blindness, or is your incompetence
because of your new 'love'?"

"I did my best, Raptor," Riolla countered, anxiety
making her words sound futile. She ignored the
Raptor's mention of her newest attempt to procure
the throne of Sumifa. "But Saelin, my best assassin,
says he is ensorcelled. It's as though he feels you
coming. Saelin reports that the digger dropped down
in the street at just the instant before the silent, spin-
ning blade would have struck him. Saelin the Butcher
has never come back without the head he was sent for
. . . perhaps there is magic here, or just very bad luck.
Some people are followed by such luck, you know—

they move through their lives with no care at all, never bowing to our beloved Caelus Nin, forswearing the ancestors, and nothing bad ever happens to them."

Riolla caught herself chattering nervously and stopped it. No true Fascini would ever do such a thing. The Raptor would not respect it. She moved to another tactic. One she knew the Raptor could not resist.

"Perhaps we might discuss future plans concerning this young man rather than past failures. I think he could be very valuable anyway. After all, he is a digger, and diggers are always after treasure. And I think this one has found something. He has been asking about a totem with a peculiar glyph on it, written in the old language," Riolla continued, mentally shoving her fear into a bag.

In the darkness of the hot room, which seemed especially hot today, Riolla waited for the Raptor to consider her tempting words. How she longed for an open window. . . .

The Raptor lived on the topmost floor of Sumifa's tallest building, smack in the middle of the Citadel, the central feature of Sumifa, a spectacular view at his command. But in all the many years Riolla had answered to this man, paid him for the protection he gave her several businesses, legitimate and otherwise, she had never known him to open a window, light a lamp, or leave the airless room during the daylight hours. She had never seen his face, and just now, as he paced back and forth in front of the dark stone walls, the only way she could pick out his location was by the rustle of his robes and the click of his heels on the black marble floor.

How glad I will be when I don't need you anymore, you cruel-hearted, self-absorbed, fear-mongering vulture. When I have married Prince Maceo, I will turn you out of this dark roost and clean this house. Saelin does not miss. If this digger has escaped my best assassin, then that young man may very well have the magic to lead me to the Clock, and its hoard, and then the entire Mercanto will look to me, and I will control what is paid and when. Maceo will be invested within the month, and I shall marry him upon the same day. And the Fascini will throw parties just to argue with each other about how and to which of them I am suddenly related, for I will be the queen of Sumifa. Maceo will, of course, come to an unexpected and tragic, though very sudden, death. And you, Raptor, when I have the treasure from the Clock, I will find a way to destroy even you. You will never make me feel common and unimportant again.

Riolla smiled to herself, ruby lips perking at the edges just a little, her eyes unfocused in the darkness. A slow trickle of sweat pooled in the hollow of her throat. Today, as always, she had removed the black pearl before her audience with the Raptor—it was the one thing she could not afford to pay him. She flicked open a flabellum made from the stiff white feathers of an extinct peacock and began to fan herself as the Raptor stopped pacing and finally spoke. His voice was hard and edged like Sumifan steel.

"Riolla, how many foreign diggers do your spies tell you work the site?"

"Three, Raptor. The leader, the linguist, and this young man." Riolla was puzzled by the question.

"And the young man . . . how old is he?"

"Well, I would guess him to be about his naming year, that is, if he had a name to take up," Riolla replied. Though she couldn't tell exactly why, things seemed to have taken a very bad turn here.

"And Saelin said he is ensorcelled? Magic? When, then? He must be the one. Of course I could not see him. How very, very clever of Javin . . . but he will pay for such boldness and such cleverness. His time, I believe, will shortly run out," the Raptor muttered to himself. Though Riolla understood none of his ramblings, she sat listening keenly anyway. Information was information.

"By the grace of Nin, Riolla, you have escaped death at the hands of your own assassin. If Saelin had taken this head for you, he would be taking yours for me."

Stunned, Riolla put down her fan and strained to hear what he said next. "But . . . I could do worse than to let this particular digger lead you to his hoard, bring it to daylight, and then inform him of my prior claim on it."

The Raptor started pacing again. "Yes. You will follow him. He will probably go west, across the desert. Perhaps a good long journey is just what you need. You haven't been getting out much lately."

Riolla began to fan herself again, squirming in her fair, delicate skin at the thought of crossing the desert and sleeping on the ground . . . at having to speak with commoners all day long. The Raptor said nothing for several moments. Riolla felt perspiration trickle down her back, but her fan kept its steady beat, counting out the seconds. At last she answered.

"As you wish."

The Raptor moved on to another question. "Riolla, what do you know about Kalkuk?"

"Kalkuk?" She coughed, completely off her guard. "I have not seen him for a while. . . ." If the Raptor knew she had killed the old shopkeeper, he would also want to know about how she had put him in the old crypt. The pearl . . .

"That is odd. He was found dead at the old city. Under very strange circumstances, from what my sources report. I wonder . . ." he breathed. Riolla did her best to control her fan, timing its languid sweeps to the same rhythm as before he asked his question. The Raptor said nothing.

"Perhaps the diggers did away with him themselves," she began. "Maybe he got in the way of their work, or tried to steal something they'd unearthed. That would make perfect sense. He was behind with his payment, which of course is why I myself am late," she improvised.

The Raptor laughed softly. "Or perhaps you have

found a way to make it seem so. If you are lying to me, Riolla . . ."

"Raptor, by the broken face of Caelus Nin and my most revered ancestors, I would be a fool to lie to you. I offer only a possible explanation for the untimely death of one of my best customers. I shall miss him sadly."

"You shall miss his regular payments sadly. And *your* revered ancestors are bought. But you will continue to pay Kalkuk's portion anyway, Riolla. Or I shall be forced to look further into his, as you say, untimely death."

Riolla knew when to be quiet. The Raptor paced the room for a while longer, then spoke again at last. "About this lucky young man. If he is who I think he is—if he is who I hope he is—I have waited a decade to find him again. I want him alive and unharmed. Follow him. As I said, he will go west. Discover his path before he takes it, so that you do not lose him again. Again I say to you, do not hurt him: do you understand? Your assassin was trained by Drufalden. He will have his pride to avenge. You must keep Saelin from that work. You are quite capable of your own work, I believe. If he is not left alive, how would the digger find the treasure for me, do you see?"

Long in the practice of reading this particular voice, Riolla noticed the Raptor's tone had softened, as though he felt he had told her a bit too much. She felt a little more confident. He was truly interested in the digger and his treasure. It made her want it even more.

"You have dealt with the peoples along the old route before," he continued. "Only do not forget that you are my agent abroad to all those whose boundaries you must pass. Take this with you. Give it to Drufalden for the surety of your army. I will collect it later myself."

An ancient coin with image of Caelus Nin on it, the eastern face on one side, the western on the other, chimed like a silver bell on the stones and rolled to Riolla's feet.

"I expect to see this again. I will send someone to rendezvous with you before you reach the Borderlands. Trouble me no more until you present me with the trove and the healthy person of this strange, elusive, young digger."

Riolla got up to leave the airless room, knowing she was dismissed, but not breathing much easier for it. Just before she cleared the threshold, the Raptor spoke again.

"Riolla."

"Yes, Raptor?"

"Pay your dues."

"Yes, I am angry. Cheyne, there is more at stake here than you know. If you were any younger, I would send you home. As it is, listen to the facts and act like the grown man you are. First of all, you told no one where you went today. Aside from the fact that we are now very shorthanded here, that put me into a bit of a stir until you returned safely. A body was found here! And we still don't know why, except that we could be right on top of the Collector's treasure. You go and disappear—what am I supposed to think? Aside from your little excursion, there is the matter of the rumbling in the ranks of the Fascini. The old king at least had a sort of tolerance for us. So long as we didn't bother him, he didn't care what we did with this forsaken sandhill. But Maceo is another matter. I expect King Thedeso won't be cold in the ground before his irritating son is carted out here to decree our immediate dismissal."

Cheyne started to say that he'd already met the heir to the crown, but had no chance. Javin continued almost without another breath.

"There could be a fight—I must refuse to leave. It's my last chance at the Collector. I need to know where you are at all times from now on." Javin dropped his head between his hands, elbows propped on his knees. "And I need to convince the Fascini to give us at least one more season. It would help if there were money enough to buy Maceo off, I suspect. But until we find the Collector's treasure, all I can do is promise him his share of it. Things will depend on my powers of persuasion. Judging from the way those powers worked on you today, the dig is all but finished," he added miserably.

"Javin, I had to go. Because of the grown man I am," Cheyne began, certain that Javin hadn't sent anyone to the city to look for him because he probably hadn't been missed until the guard had seen him light the lamp in his tent. Javin had had too much else to think about. "You just don't understand. It's not about the treasure for me. It's about who I am. That's a question you never had to ask. You knew your parents, you knew your country, you knew your work. I don't even know what my face looks like, or what my full name is. Everywhere on this continent we have gone, people have a surname. Even the Sumifans who live in the Barca have that. There are too many mysteries for me. I won't always work on your digs, Javin. I want my own life. My own name. How can I have a future unless I have a past? I need to know where I fit."

Cheyne was about to pull the amulet from under his shirt and show Javin the matching glyphs on the totem, but Javin whirled on him angrily, his patience worn away by the heat and the day's ugly discoveries.

"Cheyne! I gave you a direct order not to leave the site today. You disobeyed it. Why? Because you cannot see past your own small issues. If we—*when* we—find the Collector, I am sure that the answers to your questions will follow. But I need you to show some concern for something besides your own petty pains. Something far larger than your need for a name is at stake."

Cheyne's face began to burn with Javin's last words and he dropped the amulet back inside his shirt, a horrible new awareness dawning on him.

What did Javin care? For that matter, what had Javin ever cared? When he'd found Cheyne, Javin had been looking for the Collector, just as he was now. All

Javin had ever told him was that Cheyne had been the
only survivor of a vicious attack on a trading caravan.
Cheyne had turned the story over and over in his
mind, searching each detail Javin had supplied for his-
torical consistency, for truth. There were things that
just didn't seem right. For one, the orcs had done a
strange thing in killing off the drivers and the families
traveling with the traders. Usually, orc bandits, well
known for their laziness and lack of organization, just
took what they could carry in a lightning strike of a
raid and let the caravans go on, knowing they would
return via the same, the *only* path, laden with more
goods. It had taken some thousand years for the orcs
to understand that principle, and they practiced it with
consuming faith. Why, then, had they destroyed their
own livelihood for one haul of goods in that raid? It
didn't make sense. It never had.

Apart from his first name, Cheyne had never recovered any memory of events before that day. All his life,
the questions of why he had been part of the lost caravan or who his family was gnawed at him like rats,
growing bigger and more insistent with every new sum-
mer's end, the anniversary of the attack. Now it was his
twenty-first year in Argive, and also here in Sumifa—
that was the year a person took a name and left their
father's house—and still he had no more than the
amulet and Javin's shaky story to claim as his heritage.

For Cheyne, it seemed life had begun the moment
Javin had shaken him awake, pulling him from an
enchanted sleep, with only the strange amulet around
his neck as proof of the first ten years of his life. For
months afterward, he could not even talk. That's when
Muni had come. Muni was the best linguist there was,
and it had taken him nearly a year to get the boy to
speak coherently. All the while, Cheyne awoke every
night bathed in a salty drench of sweat, shaking and
terrified by indecipherable, recurring dreams—bizarre
images of color and light, of a tall, sear-faced elf, of a
man with no face.

Cheyne's dreams weren't the only ones in question. Before Javin could remount his dig, the Fascini heard about the hapless traders and permanently closed the caravan route, causing the elves to retreat into their magical forest, leaving no paths for outsiders through the curtain of light. As if that weren't enough, Javin had lost the support of future crew members—nobody wanted to go where the orcs were so vicious. Barely escaping them three times on the way back, Javin knew he could never make it across the hostile lands of the Wyrvils again alone, even if he could convince the elves to let him in. So because he had troubled to care for Cheyne, Javin had lost his chance to dig in the Borderlands for all time.

So why, when Javin faced the same loss again, would he *ever* care about Cheyne's desperate need to search out his identity? The perfect sense of it dawned on him with stunning clarity. Javin had too much at stake here to be distracted by anything—a man like Javin, who, before he had found Cheyne, had lost two wives in foreign plagues, who now fostered no friendships and sought no roots—to such a man, work was everything. Javin's heart was set on this dig. Come the Fascini or the whirlwinds, he would not be denied this last chance to find the Collector's grave.

"Look, Cheyne, I've had enough. I'm going to bed. Muni has found a man willing to stand guard at the vault. We've taken out most of the sand, but there's still a corner full of it. The Collector isn't down there, but I'm sure that it's his house. Maybe he's on the next level, but we have to empty this one first. Think you can help Muni for awhile tonight, while it's cooler? I don't know how long before the Fascini come. We need to move as quickly as we can," said Javin, his voice strained with fatigue.

"Sure, Javin," Cheyne answered hollowly.

As Cheyne made his way up the dunes, the three sisters, first evening stars in this part of the world,

appeared one by one in the deepening sky. Though the
sun had set an hour ago, heat lightning still flashed in
the west and the dunes still reflected the day's warmth
on his face and hands. Soon the warm air would turn
into a cold and constant breeze that would sweep over
the site relentlessly until dawn.

Cheyne mounted the topmost dune as the blue dusk
turned to complete darkness. He stood looking at the
fading horizon for a moment, the peaceful view soothing the pain of Javin's disinterest. Some of the old
palace's outer columns, invisible only a few weeks ago,
ringed the site like silent sentries. Their basalt heads
were chipped and cracked, or missing altogether. Still,
they looked regal to Cheyne as they cut even darker sil-
houettes against the flashing sky. Behind him, the broken shell of a round watchtower, probably the tallest
part of the ruin, rose in stark elegance.

He took out the totem from his tunic and held it to
the sky, watching the colors in its edges dance with the
lightning. He thought of the totem's glyphs and imag-
ined that it was his name, his true name, carved there,
sign of the beloved king of a great and mighty people,
holding a just court amid those tall columns, his ancestors' faces carved in the stones behind him and looking
on with approval.

He laughed aloud at the fantasy, sure that of all the
pasts that might be his, this was not one of them. His
voice echoed peculiarly in the columns just as the totem's
edge caught a strong flash of lightning and the rainbow
shot upward into the sky, the tight beam of colors softening to form the image of a woman's hand, her first two
fingers oddly crooked at the first joint. The vision was
gone almost before Cheyne saw it. Cheyne turned the
prism in every direction, trying to make the image appear
again, but the lightning moved off after a couple of minutes, and the sky was truly dark. He shook his head in
disbelief, thinking the desert played tricks upon his eyes,
that the lightning had deceived him. He put the totem
back in his pack and moved on toward the vault.

The high desert air tasted clean and pure, and the brilliant white stars nearly outshone the large moon and its small companion. Cheyne often marveled at the little moon—it had been an integral part of every ancient civilization he had studied. In Argive, each record of the moon's advent was the same, though. One night it hadn't been in the sky—the next night, it was, and it had been there ever since.

It just appeared there, no way of knowing how. Like me, he thought as he trudged up the dunes to the vault, where Muni leaned casually against the marble slab they had moved that morning. It lay in the same position, the plaited ropes in their original knots.

"I am glad you have returned safely from your adventure. My apologies, by the way, for the assassin, though you acquitted yourself admirably. I had my hands full with his three friends."

"You *followed* me?" Cheyne looked at him incredulously. Muni smiled broadly, his teeth showing very white in the darkness.

"No. I took a dead man home. On my way back, I saw your predicament." Muni held the ropes up and offered him one end, securing the other one around his own waist.

Cheyne did not move. Muni sighed.

"Cheyne. You come and go as you will. When our paths cross, it is my calling to assist if I may. A simple 'thank you' will suffice, my friend." Muni bowed deeply, as Almaazan man to man.

Cheyne was glad of the darkness. It covered his embarrassment. For the first time, Muni had just acknowledged him as an equal and he had nearly let his anger make him a fool. He returned the bow and took the rope. "You're not going down?"

"No. Kifran and I will stand guard up here. I will feed you buckets and empty the backfill. The only things likely to disturb you inside are the *living* vermin." He smiled.

Kifran, a large, bearded Sumifan, saluted Muni and

took his place by the tallest column. He was one of the men from the crew Muni ran, one of the few who did not believe in the old juma stories of an evil djinn which had once hovered over this place, bringing deadly sandstorms and making it uninhabitable, the very reason old Sumifa had moved to its present location. Muni's explanation to Cheyne had been more pragmatic: the community had simply outgrown its bounds, and the river had changed its course over the years, forcing them to rebuild across the Nantas to the west, where the town now rambled and sprawled, every so often adding another wall around the last when the population expanded. But the old legends had a hold on most of the Sumifan citizens—ask any Fascini's right-hand man, and the answer was the same. Old Sumifa had moved because it was destroyed by an evil force which still roamed the dunes.

"Muni?"

"Yes, my friend."

"By chance, did you see a tall elf in the city yesterday?"

"No, I did not." Muni laughed. "But if I had, or if I do, I will be certain that you are the very first person I tell."

Cheyne sighed and dropped down into the pit, the torch Muni had tossed in before him burning brightly on the newly swept marble floor. Several of Muni's despised vermin had scattered from the fire, and a couple of fancollar lizards, the scorpions' chief predators, skittered after them, their tiny claws clicking faintly on the marble floor. *Nature seemed to balance everything,* thought Cheyne, taking a bucket from Muni, scraping it full of sand, shaking it over the screen into another bucket, handing that one back up full, receiving another empty one.

The work continued rhythmically, uneventfully, for an hour, Cheyne's mind turning to his afternoon's adventure, wandering through the streets of Sumifa again, to Riolla's, to the fight with her assassin, to the odd helper he'd found and lost again so quickly.

What was it about this totem that made Riolla, the Mercanto Schreefa, want it badly enough to take his head? She had lied about the last glyph. Maybe she really did know what it said. Cheyne thought of the strange little man who had helped him. He wished he could have bought the beggar a hot meal or a bed for the night, *even though he stole my last two kohli,* Cheyne thought, smiling. At the very least, a loaf of bappir, that strange, sweet grain bread all Sumifans so favored. He vowed to himself that if he ever saw the big-nosed beggar again, he would find a way to thank him.

"Cheyne?" Muni called down. The empty bucket bobbed on its rope.

"Right here, Muni. Just thinking. Sorry."

There were only three or four feet of sand left to remove from the corner. Then he could sleep. With a mighty pull on the bucket, Cheyne tore into the job with renewed energies.

Just then, the torch burned into a knot, flaring brilliantly for an instant, illuminating the dark corner where Cheyne was working. He stopped in midscoop, something in the cascade catching the sudden light. Cheyne stepped back for the torch and brought it close over the fine sand. Just under the surface, the thick lip of a pottery jar decorated with intricate, bright goldleaf markings caught the torchlight again, its crescent shape unmistakable. Cheyne braced the torch upright in the sand, pulled out his hand sweep, and began to brush away the thin layer of grains. In minutes, he had freed from its gritty tomb several shards of a good-sized clay jar.

"Muni! I found something. Besides sand, I mean," Cheyne called up in an excited whisper.

But his old friend had stepped away from the portal for a moment—Cheyne could hear him speaking

sharply to Kifran above, but could not make out the
words. Agitation was not Muni's style. Troubled,
Cheyne turned back to the shards, grabbed up the
light, and shone it under the bright rim. More sand.
He quickly sketched the situation of the find, then
scooped his hand shallowly into the fragments, drawing out sand and letting the grains fall, their sharp
edges sparkling like gold dust in the soft light of the
torch. The sand inside the shards somehow looked
redder and sharper than what he had been scooping
away all night. And far more different from another
kind of Almaazan sand—grains blown around for centuries in the high, towering storms of the eastern erg,
settling to earth only when they became rounded, dull,
and unreflective. There were supposedly great deposits
of them hidden on the erg's surface. You could drown
in sand like that, no water for miles. Just sink into the
smoothness of it and keep sinking, until you were covered up. Like suffocating in silk.

But the crystals in his hand had been new when they
found their way into the jar—as if they'd just been cre-
ated, their edges sharp and faceted like little mirrors,
catching the light in glittering waves. He ran his hand
across the pleasantly rough grains, changing the pattern
of sheen from the light, tiny rainbows appearing in the
dark room for just an instant when the torch wavered.

Fascinated, Cheyne carefully dug more and more of
the fine sand from under the mouth of the jar. When
his hand struck the sharp edge of something, he leapt
backward, thinking he'd been stung by a scorpion.
Under the glare of the lantern, he saw a little nick on
his hand instead of a sting and, relieved, took up his
hand sweep to fish out a small, bronze-bound book the
moment before Muni's face appeared over the portal.

"Sorry, Cheyne, I thought I thought saw something
in the dunes—Cheyne?" Muni peered down into the
vault, a slow smile creasing his weathered brown face.
"You have found more besides vermin, I see," said
Muni, delight in his voice. "What do you make of it?"

"What? Oh, you mean the shards!" Cheyne chortled, quickly hiding the small book in his robes. He wanted a chance to look it over before handing it up. There was writing, and once a linguist got hold of a book, it could be months before he saw it again. "Yes, I have. I don't think the piece is Sumifan, though—the designs and clay are wrong, don't you think?"

"Hmm. We'll need to see it in daylight. Your father will be pleased. And that won't hurt right now," Muni said knowingly.

"Muni, I'm going to stop for a minute and record the patterns on these shards."

"Good idea. Only make haste—we have yet to empty the room. And something feels very wrong about the weather up here. I think I saw some sort of shadow moving toward the camp."

"That 'evil presence' the men are always talking about? Surely not you, too, Muni?" Cheyne laughed and pulled out his sketch pad, quickly roughing in the odd shapes stamped and carved onto the pottery fragments.

He was finished long before he called Muni to resume the evacuation of the sand—time enough to examine the little book and decide it was without a doubt what Javin had been searching for. *Now he'll understand why I have to find my past,* he reasoned. He tucked the book into his pack, saving it for Javin's eyes first. Muni, he knew, would understand. An hour later, they left Kifran to continue the watch alone.

"It appears I was wrong about the djinn. I have neither seen nor heard anything odd for some good while. But the feeling remains. So, indulge me, please, and sleep in the mess tent tonight. I will take yours. May the sun find you well, may your sleep be dreamless." Muni bowed his night blessing and removed himself silently to the workers' shelter, leaving Cheyne outside the dark main tent. Cheyne shrugged, knowing he would be there all night if he tried to talk Muni out of his precautions.

Across the floor, under the netting on a low cot,

Javin lay deep in sleep. Cheyne lit a small oil lamp and pulled out the book he'd found in the jar.

"Wake up, Javin." Despite his incredible excitement, Cheyne jostled his father's feet gently. "Look what I found." Cheyne produced the sketches first, saving the book for last and best, but Javin refused to move.

"Javin—" He finally held up the little bronze-bound book.

Javin snored soundly, stirring the netting about his face, the thin blankets tucked closely around the end of the cot to keep out unwelcome night visitors.

Disappointed yet again, Cheyne put the sketches on the table, sat down on the bench, and blew out the lantern. In the dark tent, his face toward the canvas, toward the east, he debated about leaving the little book for Javin to find in the morning.

He knew where the old pottery had come from. The signature stamps on it looked exactly like the ones on a matched set of grain pots Javin had said came from the Sarrazan forest. He had grown up with those two elven-made jars sitting at either end of Javin's big riverstone fireplace. And the elves' same signature glyph had decorated the tall elf's cloakpin. More importantly, all of them were originally word symbols in Old High Sumifan. Since he had first seen the elf in Sumifa, Cheyne had suspected the Sarrazan potters were the only ones who might still be able to read his indecipherable amulet and the totem's last carving. Now he was even more sure. But the elves lived in the Borderlands . . . past the western erg, past the Wyrvil territories, past the curtain of light. Beyond memory and time.

All right, Javin. I tried. I tried before, and I tried now to tell you about what I have found. But all you care about is your own little square of trouble. Well, that's fine with me. You have done your duty by your foundling—educated me, and sheltered me. Why should I expect any more than that? You took your chance in coming here to follow your dream. I must take mine now. You save your energy for the Collector. It's time for me to look for my own past. Cheyne's face grew hot with pride and determination. His mind was made up. He would quit the dig—Javin did the really important work anyway—and go to the Borderlands, no matter how far, no matter how dangerous.

And I will not look back, he promised himself. *I will never look back.*

He quietly lifted the keys to the supply hut from their hook above Javin's cot. It would have to be a short night. Tomorrow, before the three sisters winked out again and Muni would rise to relieve Kifran, before Javin would sense the light and lift his head, fastening single-mindedly on keeping his precious work going, Cheyne would be back in Sumifa, finding a guide for his own expedition.

Across the dunes, in the new city, a whirlwind churned the sand into a scouring spray as it moved through the Barca, tearing the stalls down and scattering crockery, blinding three men and a shirrir-drunken woman as they reveled on the rooftops. When the wind reached the Mercanto, it blew down the sign in front of Riolla's shop, then moved over the Citadel with a new strength, finally resting, hovering over the tall spire that was the Raptor's tower. Seconds later, the sand fell to the ground outside the spire, cascading down the basalt stonework like a waterfall.

CHAPTER
4

THE OLD BOOK HE'D FOUND IN THE JAR fascinated him. The parchment was in excellent condition, the dryness of the sand and the air in the crypt having preserved it beautifully. Its bronze cover was somewhat tarnished, and still bore the blackened, faint fingerprints of the last owner; the binding was pulled just the tiniest bit away from the spine. Oddly, for the book had obviously been well-cared for at one time, the last page of parchment was ragged and barely clung to the stitching. Flecks of something that looked very much like blood covered parts of that same page, almost as though something sudden and violent had happened over it. Cheyne thought of the bits of broken glass he and Muni had found in that same room and wondered if there were a connection.

He leaned against the Mercanto gates for a better angle in the soft dawn light, tried his magnifier again, but could not read the language. The last pages appeared to have been written with a steady hand, the style very tight and cramped, lines of Old High Sumifan carefully inserted between the other, unrecognizable lines. All but the final page, that is. The writing on that one was overlaid with more Old Sumifan

glyphs, and the new words confused their boundaries;
the bloodstains, for surely it was blood, blurred some
of it also. Without time and the knowledge of the lan-
guages, it was impossible to sort them out. Still,
Cheyne wondered why anyone would write over the
other words—and the closer he looked, the more he
realized that the glyphs were sort of *burned* onto the
page, rather than inked.

*If only I spoke Old High Sumifan. If only anyone
here did. Anyone that I could find again,* he groused,
thinking of the elusive elf.

The long journey west he'd set for himself seemed
more than he could accomplish in the clear morning
light and the rising desert heat. By the time he'd
slipped from the mess tent and slunk into the city
again, miraculously finding the same hole in the outer
wall he'd used the day before, he had also recalled that
he would need to somehow get past the western erg,
and after that, the Wyrvil orcs' stronghold. Even
sketchy memories of a quick run across the scrubland
and salt flats of that barren waste when Javin had first
brought him home were almost enough to check his
confidence.

Cheyne, at ten, had seen his first and only orc,
then—it was a dead one, but the thought of the creature's two-inch incisors, jutting brow, and green-tinged
skin still made him uneasy. Even in death, the thing
had seemed so feral and wild, more like a beast than a
sentient being.

But I have grown up since then, Cheyne reasoned.
Perhaps my memory is more terrible than true.

Cheyne gently closed the little book and placed it
securely inside his pack.

Business began early in Sumifa: the Mercanto's gates
swung open precisely as the gnomon's shadow struck
the fifth mark on the sundial. Cheyne strode through
and made his way to a stall he had noticed the day
before. Several ex-caravan guides had gathered there
already and stood waiting for other work, their hoods

low over their eyes and their sun-darkened hands avidly punctuating stories of recent adventures.

One fellow loudly extolled how his last fare had lost his shoe to a hungry drom, how the beast sickened and died on the spot from eating such a horrible meal, and how the man had limped home, leaning on the arm of his miserable guide the whole way. The next guide's fare had demanded to be taken to hunt the wild goats, a couple of miles off the regular route, where his feet were trampled and severed from his body in the goats' subsequent attack, and he had to be carried home on his miserable guide's back. The third guide's fare had asked to hunt in the cork forest, truly off the regular trail, had encountered a rutting canista and been stuck to a tree, driven through with the beast's horn, then devoured by the whole herd on the spot, before the very eyes of his guide and six esteemed persons of rank. So completely consumed by the beast was this last poor tourist that the miserable guide could find only his moneybag to carry home.

Amid the chorus of laughter the last story had provoked among the men at the stall, Cheyne stepped up and smiled, beginning to state his case. "Good morning, gentlemen, fine day. May the Twelve Blessings abound in your lives. Would any of you be interested in taking me over the western erg to the Borderlands?

The guides grew silent instantly and each wandered off to a different part of the street, the fellow whose story had won the day staring daggers at Cheyne's forehead. Cheyne shrugged and moved past them, up the winding cobblestone pavement toward the center of the Mercanto. After several hours and an equal number of encounters ending almost exactly like the first one, he came to a small raqa stall and sat down in the shade to rest. When the smiling attendant came with a small cup and a large bottle, he waved her away, taking a long pull on his water skin.

"No, no, no! You cannot sit there. You don't buy, you don't sit. No. Go away." The raqa server bellowed in his ear, her friendliness suddenly transformed into a toothless snarl.

Cheyne escaped the good-sized club she produced from under her counter by ducking through another stall, and then another, until he found himself turned completely around and, worse, out in the Barca again, still with no guide.

He wandered the dirty, narrow alleys of the south side for awhile, its ruby-lipped, green-lidded courtesans beckoning to him from shirrir-scented clouds and raqa-induced stupors. He smiled back at the girls, but they reminded him of the glittering lizards he had seen on the rocks by the river: pretty, but poisonous. He walked until he needed to refill his canteen, but the only place he could do so without paying was at the public well, famous among the workers at the dig for its unsavory contents. When he found the well, he hung his head under its covering, a huge flat rock supported by three smaller ones, a dolmen of sorts, for both shade and a look at what might be floating in there today.

"Oh, hello, there. We meet again," said a voice coming from somewhere behind what looked like an overlarge net bobber. Cheyne had seen that nose before.

"You? How did you get—?" Cheyne gestured at the dolmen.

"In the well? Fell. Must have. Say, could you lower the bucket down here and help me out? I'm nearly sober now, and I really don't want to experience this situation in that frame of mind," said the vagrant, the corners of a smile appearing on either side of the nose.

"Of course. Just wait there." Cheyne backed away from the edge of the well and then reappeared instantly. "Sorry. Where would you be going, after all?" he added, embarrassed.

The vagrant beamed up at him tolerantly. Cheyne turned away again, this time returning with a bucket and rope. Within moments, the beggar stood dripping in the street, waterlogged, but no worse for his baptism.

"Thanks very much, good sir. We have broken even, a life for a life. Although yours, it might seem, is worth far more to the Schreefa than mine," said the beggar, wringing out his robes.

"The least I could do," replied Cheyne, thinking he should find another place to get a drink of water.

After a moment of awkward silence, the beggar bowed gracefully, deeply, and introduced himself. "My name is Ogwater Rifkin."

"Cheyne."

Ogwater bowed again, ignoring Cheyne's lack of a surname. "Pleased. For the price of a bottle of raqa, Cheyne, I would be even more pleased. Drowning is hard and thirsty work."

Cheyne smiled bleakly. "Muje Rifkin—"

"Og." The beggar smiled hugely, revealing many perfect, very white teeth.

Cheyne began again. "Og, what money I have must go toward paying a guide and provisions. I'm sorry."

The beggar shrugged, his face falling. "No harm. A guide, you say . . . ?"

Cheyne nodded. Og's smile slowly returned.

"Muni? You'd better come out here. . . ."

Muni awoke thrashing again, his dreams full of the evil djinn, the voice in his ears unfamiliar. He sat up on the low cot, fumbling for a lamp before he swung his feet onto the floor, the precaution ingrained by years of habit. Before he could find the strikebox and the lamp, Kifran lifted the tent door, a torch in his hand. Muni instantly came awake when the light struck him and he focused on the guard's grim face.

"Muje Javin did not come this morning. I waited for him until first light, then came to find him. He lies ill in his bed, and he asks for you."

Kifran let the tent flap drop and waited for Muni to pull on his robes and boots. In another moment, they were both running toward Javin's tent, Muni reaching it first.

"My old friend . . . what happened?" Muni rasped, his voice heavy and the words coming hard. His old friend opened his gray eyes and tried to smile. Javin's face burned with fever, his flushed, sun-darkened skin drawn tautly over his angular features.

"How do you fight vermin? . . . They were here," he said softly, barely lifting his hand and pointing toward the corner of the tent. Muni followed the gesture to a single scorpion lying dead on the dirt floor.

"Scorpion? Javin, when? When?" Muni shook his friend back to consciousness.

"I don't know. All night, I could not move. I fought them in my dreams." He shuddered and fell silent.

Muni calmed himself, pushing down the thoughts of the irate Fascini, of the dig closing before they had found the Collector, of Javin dying here and now, and of his own helplessness to heal his old friend.

"No, no, Javin, you cannot die. We have too much to do, and you owe me a game of chess," he assured, trying to smile.

Then he turned to Kifran, who still held the torch at the door. "Where is Cheyne? Find him and go with him to fetch the doctor in the city."

Kifran bowed, lit a lamp for Muni with the torch, and disappeared.

That's not ordinary vermin, thought the linguist, who was something of an unwilling expert on the subject, as he moved to examine the creature. The dead scorpion, a large brown one, lay curled into a ring, its poisonous tail embedded in its own head.

Ah. The Ninnites. So they have found him again, Muni raged silently, understanding the symbol. The scorpion had been magically summoned, a creature from some other realm, not the kind that roamed the site, or hunched in the dark crevices of walls in the city. A creature out of its element. The Ninnites had tracked Javin from one end of Almaaz to the other, even to his home in Argive. No matter how often he moved along, no matter where he dug next, they always found him, but up until now, he had always seen them coming. Javin was a careful man, but this particular dig had been too much of a distraction.

Muni moved back across the tent to his friend, who was murmuring in his sleep. He brought an earthenware cup to the fevered man's mouth, forcing the tepid water past his swollen lips. Javin coughed a bit, and his eyes opened.

"I thank you. May your house be washed away in a flood of blessings." He grinned, choking again on the water.

"Be still, my friend." Muni poured some of the water onto a cloth and dabbed it to Javin's burning head. "Cheyne will soon bring the physician, and you will feel much better. Yes, you will live this time."

He found Javin's right hand, checked his pulse, relieved that it was strong. As he leaned over to place the archaeologist's hand back upon his chest, Muni also discovered the sting site: Javin's other hand lay by his side, the fingers swelled to three times their normal size, a small whitened whelp around a prick of dark blood on his ring finger. The wound appeared to be several hours old and looked horribly painful. Muni had seen a similar case before, when he had worked among the Fallaji mages—the poison would come and go, the wound would heal and fester, weakening the person until, eventually, it would sap their strength to the point that there was no more healing. Gangrene followed rapidly.

"You can recover, my friend. But listen to me, Javin: we will have to remove the finger, else the poison will spread. I'll bring more water for the fever. Just rest," he whispered.

"No, Muni, I will be all right. Already, I am feeling better. There is no need to take the finger. And I must tell you . . . what I saw in the dreams. . . . The man with no face. The Raptor. I could not move; I was powerless. He meant to kill me this time. I am the last one, you see. But it's all clear now; someone has told him about Cheyne. Where is Cheyne?" He sat up in the cot.

"Save your strength, my friend. The one after your son is Saelin. Yes, he is the chiefest of the Ninnite assassins, but he has failed once already; he will fail again. He is not so good as he thinks he is," Muni said, hushing him.

"No, you don't understand . . ." Javin protested.

"Muni—" Kifran opened the tent flap and held up his hand, a couple of pages from Cheyne's drawing tablet in it. "Javin's son is missing. All I could find were these."

CHAPTER
5

"HEY-HO, OG—BEEN BATHING AGAIN OUT OF season?" the swarthy barkeeper shouted as Og and Cheyne came into the raqa bar, its lewdly painted walls a record of anatomical wonder and its sawdust floors dangerous with giant, cracked zebramussel shells and fishbones.

It was too early yet for the midday crowd; only one other customer, a hooded man smoking an ancient pipe, sat in the corner, his hand rising as slowly as his smoke when Og nodded absently to him. They found a table near the door and sat down. Cheyne blew crumbs away from his side of the well-worn oilskin tablecover, the remains of last night's repast yet to be cleared from it. Og never noticed the puddle of sour raqa he dragged his sleeve through as he raised his hand for service.

"Pay no attention to the thrull behind the counter," said Og, annoyed.

When the man came out, Og signaled for two glasses and a bottle, but Cheyne shook his head, amending the request for water and two loaves of bappir instead. The barkeep gave him a smile and boxed Og on the ears as he went to fetch the much more expensive order.

"What did he mean, 'bathing again'?" said Cheyne,

smiling, his tone wary. "You weren't by chance waiting down there in the well on purpose for me, thinking you'd get that drink after all?"

Og looked mightily wounded. "By the three sisters and the Five Most Sacred Vows, I was not!" he declared, thumping the table. "I drown for no man."

"Then . . ."

"I'll tell you about it sometime. Later," said Og, the water carafe arriving. Apparently it was not often used—the vessel looked to be the cleanest thing in the shop. Cheyne poured for himself, but Og declined, frowning.

"Never touch the stuff. Not safe," he said, wringing his cloak out over the sawdust.

His throat now thoroughly parched, Cheyne ignored him and drank deeply, poured another glass, and drank all of it as well. He put one of the big round loaves of bread into his pack and tore into the other, offering half of it to Og, who took it eagerly, but did not eat. When Cheyne leaned forward on his low, cane stool, Og began his finest pitch.

"You seem a man of means and substance. Why is it you need to go across the western erg?" he quizzed.

"You *have* sobered up. How did you know that's the direction I'm going?" said Cheyne, amazed.

"You've been here in the city all morning, probably arrived before dawn. All the hunting guides go out before six bells, and it's past ten bells now. The only reason they wouldn't have taken you wherever you desired—for an extremely inflated price, I might add—is because they refuse to go where you ask for any price. And if they would not go there, it must be someplace very dangerous and far away. That would have to be in the direction of the western erg. The guides will not go into Wyrvil territory since the massacre," Og explained succinctly, sounding like one of Cheyne's better instructors at the Argivian institute.

The young man smiled, guessing where this was leading. "And how long have *you* been a guide, Og?"

"It's a new career for me, but I think I'll do exceptionally well at it." Og smiled back, his eyes crossing momentarily over his nose. "Got you home well enough last night, didn't I?"

Cheyne was sitting much too close for Og to actually focus on his face very well. Still, he could clearly see that from Cheyne's good-natured grin and his well-woven cloak that the young man would probably be good for a new pair of boots and maybe, if Og could work this right, a bottle or two of raqa after all. Though Og had no intention of leaving Sumifa, the young man was worth his time and had already provided better conversation than Og had had in months. Og began to feel just a bit of remorse over his dishonest intentions. But not enough to stop having them.

"And why is your success so certain?" said Cheyne, stuffing the last of the sweet bread into his mouth.

"Because I've been made redundant in my current occupation." Og rolled his eyes and then dropped his glance to the dirty tabletop. Cheyne smiled but did not laugh. He held Og's stare for a long time. "All right, because I have nothing else to lose," Og muttered, almost inaudibly. So much for evil intentions. Who could look at those piercing eyes and lie?

Cheyne sat in silence for a moment. Either Og was really good at panhandling, or he was telling some kind of hard truth. He decided to find out which. "And how do I know you can do what you say? You are a beggar, and I hardly know you," said Cheyne, as if he had his choice of guides.

"And you are a nameless stranger, who has yet to show another coin to me or even buy me a real drink. Well, do you want to go?" asked Og, knowing very certainly that he was Cheyne's only hope.

Cheyne poured another glass of water as he thought about it.

For an answer, he brought out the totem. "Ever seen anything like this? Not the ganzite, of course, but the last glyph on it."

Og shook his head, looking the object over as best

he could in the dimness of the shabby drinking house. The barkeep moved away from the doorway just then, and a ray of strong morning light caught the edge of the totem, sending forth a long bright ribbon of colors across the cracked plaster walls of the shop. The hooded man stirred slightly at his table as the rainbow washed over him and danced in the corner of the room. Og's eyes lit up as well.

"That's the second most beautiful thing I've ever seen," he gasped.

Cheyne bent forward, equally mesmerized, trying to see the woman's handprint the prism had shown him on the dunes, but it did not appear. "Yes. It is beautiful. What do you think?"

Cheyne could hardly believe he was asking the linguistic opinion of a beggar, but Og only shook his head again, as though he were completely accustomed to such queries.

"I think the symbols are from the old tongue. Most of the old totems use it. But the shape is odd, and I can't tell you what the last glyph says."

"No one can. Not here, anyway. That's why I need to go to the Sarrazan forest. The elves there still use these symbols to decorate their pottery work. They are the only hope I have of deciphering this totem," said Cheyne, his voice carefully lowered.

"Why is that so important? This is just an old totem. Except for its peculiar cut, there are thousands like it, more being made—and made up, I might add—every day. Half of the Fascini can't even read theirs. They just invent something they like, tell it to their equally ignorant friends, and it becomes the truth for all time. Why do you care what this really says? It's not *your* family totem, is it?" asked Og, a note of mock disdain coloring his voice. "This isn't some slog over the desert to find your name or anything, is it?"

Cheyne looked at him levelly. "I don't know. What if it were?"

"Well, I guess I'd need a map, then," said Og dryly. *I*

have gone soft, he thought, giving in to the remains of his moral code. *I cannot rob him. Yet, anyway.* The totem clearly showed a royal lineage—the boy could actually *be someone.* And he was a trained digger.

An idea formed in Og's raqa-deprived mind. This also might be the chance he'd waited for since Riolla had taken his ring and left him alone and almost powerless. If the lad were going to the Sarrazan forest, Og could wrangle a way to take them through all of the kingdoms where he stood a chance to steal back the ring's magical gemstones. Though it could be dangerous—Riolla had already sent her best henchman to kill the boy, and Saelin had a honed viciousness about him when he was satisfied; what must he have thought when the lad had gotten away from him? This totem must mean something pretty special to the Schreefa. Og pondered that for a moment.

The only thing that had ever driven Riolla to such lengths was her hunger for wealth. And the only treasure around Sumifa had to do with the Armageddon Clock fables . . . the old Collector and his vast, lost fortune. Now Og recalled how the ballads he had sung at the royal court about the mythical beast had fascinated Riolla long ago. While the young princess had fallen asleep during those songs, her companion Riolla had listened keenly, her eyes wide with wonder and belief. It figured. Only the Clock and the possibility of finding it would drive her to such desperation. Usually, the Mercanto's current Schreefa didn't dirty her manicured hands or her reputation with killing inside the city. Breaking hearts was more her style.

"Put that thing away," he snapped, suddenly finding the hooded man to be too much company. "The city has a thousand eyes and most of them are employed by Riolla. Or by the one who employs *her.*"

Cheyne replaced the totem's wrapping and put it back in his pack. "How do you know Riolla Hifrata?"

"Listen, we'd better get over to the mapmaker's place," said Og, rising from his stool.

Cheyne laid a coin on the table and quickly filled his canteen with the remainder of the carafe's water. Og was already down the street when he caught up to him.

"Og, how do you know Riolla?" Cheyne asked again.

"Everyone in the Mercanto knows Riolla, boy. She owns most of it, and what she doesn't, she extracts protection money from," said Og, dodging a water-laden donkey and weaving through a crowd of market-bound housewives. Cheyne had no idea where they were going.

"It's just up the way, a couple of streets over. I know we can find what you need there," assured Og.

"Og, wait. You and I haven't struck a deal yet. I don't know if I can afford you," said Cheyne, stopping amid the tight stream of dusty traffic.

Og went on for a good twenty yards before he turned around, pushed his way back, grabbed Cheyne's hand, slapped it, shook it, bowed three times and spat on the ground, almost missing the huge, well-shod foot of a passing blacksmith.

"May your pardon be begged." Og smiled up weakly to the insulted smith and yanked on Cheyne's sleeve, pulling him through the crowd to put the donkey and the market women between them and the smith.

"We now have a deal," pronounced Og, the hand behind his back busy with the "for as long as it suits me" sign common among traders of the Barca. "I will take you where you want to go. You will pay me half of the treasure."

"Half of the treasure? But all I'm looking for is the translation of this symbol. . . ."

"Don't try to fool a fool. You know what I'm talking about. The treasure from the Clock. And a bottle of raqa before. And a new pair of boots. Can't make that kind of a trip in these." He pointed to his sandals, their tops repaired with several different colors of cast-off rope.

"Well . . . "

"Deal! Now let's not waste any more time," Og pronounced, looking warily over his shoulder. The angry smith had skirted the obstacles and now bore down on them, intent on addressing Og's insult. "We have to be ready to go by tonight. Or do you want all of the people looking for you to find you first?"

Cheyne didn't get to answer. As the smith closed in, ham-sized fists waving, they rounded a corner, dove through another breach in the Mercanto wall, this one connecting to a fruit and vegetable stand to the Barca, and came out in a part of Sumifa Cheyne had never seen. In fact, it looked like a part of Sumifa that *daylight* had never seen.

Thousands of mangy yellow rats chittered and swarmed along the gutters, fighting for refuse dumped from the market Cheyne had just run through. Cheyne winced as Og hardly looked where he put his feet, seeming to dodge the rodents with practiced ease. Cheyne noted that the smell would have been overpowering had it not been for the blue cloud of shirrir hanging in the air. For another quarter of a mile, while Cheyne picked bits of onion skins and melon rind from his hair, Og navigated a trail through a maze of ancient garbage dumps, dice games, and shirrir parlors to bring them up to what had to be the worst-looking shop on the worst-looking side of the worst-looking back street in all of the city. Gaudy pastel paint peeled away from the walls of the stucco buildings and the high, irregular, windows had lost their glazing centuries ago. Piles of crates and other junk loomed over the alley doorway, as if garbage from all over the Barca had been deposited there for months.

In the midst of all this, Cheyne noticed a Fascini sedan, its purple fringe rippling as the Neffian slaves broke into a quick march. They pulled away from the front of the shop just as Og knocked softly in an intricate pattern on the heavy wooden back door.

Which opened somewhere in the middle of Og's percussion, a serving girl's small, irritated face appearing from behind it, much to his amazement and then to his distress.

"Where is Kalkuk?" said Og.

The young woman at the door winced, then motioned them quickly in with a bottle of linseed oil. "Dead. They just put him in the ground. You gonna be dead, too, if *she* finds you here."

"What's happened, Vashki? How Is Kalkuk dead? I just saw him the other day, and he was perfectly healthy, may he spend as little time as possible in the fourth purgatory," muttered Og, his voice as low as the girl's.

"He was found by the hired men working for that foreign digger out at Old Sumifa. They are trying to hush it up, but my man works out there, too, and said the boss sent them home early yesterday. Kirmah recognized Kalkuk. We all knew Kalkuk was behind with his payments to Riolla, but it was only by a few days and we thought he could come up with something. Diggers brought him in, and his kinswoman buried him this morning, early. Look, I gotta work and you gotta go. The lady's just back from an appointment and she is not happy. She's Kalkuk's niece; we worked together in here sometimes, but she's the boss now—"

"Vashki? Who are you talking to?"

Cheyne turned toward the sound of the voice. A fragrance filled the room instantly: bergamot and myrrh. The owner of the red ribbon, the woman with the prince.

"Uh-oh," said Vashki, resuming her work with practiced immediacy. "Now you get to be thrown out in style. Just like the fancy Fascini boyfriend in here before you. Young Prince Maceo himself!"

A slender woman glided into the room, the large package in her arms obscuring her face. All Cheyne could see behind the box was a tumble of black curls pinned up loosely with combs and red ribbons. She put the crate down on the counter. Cheyne's view improved. Stupendously.

Thinking about the dead man from the ruins, for surely this Kalkuk was the same man, Cheyne had said nothing up to now. He cleared his throat roughly in an attempt to introduce himself and show her the totem, thinking that she might recognize it and all the mysteries would be solved. But Og pulled at his cloak smartly, and the young man swallowed his words.

"We come in search of a map, my good lady. I have done business with your uncle for long years now. Vashki here tells me he has recently passed on. I hope it was none of the Five Fatal Fevers." Og bowed deeply, his nose all but touching the newly swept floor.

"Who are you? You both look familiar," said the woman, her eyes flashing darkly.

"My name is Ogwater Rifkin, professional guide, and this is my friend, who searches for passage across the erg to the far country. Your uncle sold the finest maps in all of Sumifa."

"You were part of my uncle's clientele?"

"Oh, yes, on many occasions. He and I did much good business together," said Og. Cheyne gave him a puzzled look, suddenly wondering if Og had had anything to do with the man's murder. "Well, at any rate, we did business," Og allowed.

Noting the lack of other customers, the woman glared at him for a moment, her eyes red and swollen, sighed deeply, and then motioned them around to the front of the counter. "Try not to touch anything, please." Her voice was tired and aloof.

"Oh, of course, of course. You have, ah, really shined things up here. I've never seen it look so . . . empty," said Og, searching for the stacks of brass sculpture filled with illegal Glavian shirrir, the stolen paintings waiting to be shipped on a midnight caravan, and the little piles of date pits that once littered the premises of his favorite black market. He marveled at what difference a day had made. The girl had worked fast.

"The shop, Muje Rifkin, is no longer what it once was. I am the cartographer who drew the maps—the correct ones—my uncle sold. I will ask you never to come again for the sort of business you no doubt conducted with my uncle. But today I will provide you a legitimate map for the legitimate fee in kohli."

Cheyne could no longer remain quiet. "Mujida, we are sorry for your loss, and thank you for serving us. My name is Cheyne," he said. "May I have the honor of knowing yours?"

Ogwater frowned his displeasure, thinking they would be there far too long now, and he really had reached his sobriety limit. His hands were beginning to shake and his mouth was dryer than the desert.

"My name is Claria. What is your final destination?" she replied, her voice a little less sharp, the first hints of a smile softening her angular face. Cheyne felt his cheeks go warm at the music in Claria's odd, lovely name. He almost forgot to answer her question.

"Uh . . . the Sarrazan forest, I believe," he finally sputtered out.

"The Borderlands?" she began, a strange look crossing her face. "Wait—I remember you now. Maceo almost ran you down in the street the other day. You're not from here. Don't you know—"

"He knows that's where he wants to go," Og hastily injected. Claria raised a dark brow, but said no more.

There was no way around it. He would have to see if she recognized the totem. Cheyne reached into his pack and brought out the ganzite block. Claria took it without his expected reaction, but was immediately intrigued with the carvings.

"Where . . . ?" Claria began.

"On site. Well, in a sort of crypt, actually." He thought better of telling her that he had found it in her dead uncle's hand. "I have to find out what the glyphs say. If you can read them, then we won't have to take the journey," replied Cheyne hopefully. Og slapped his forehead in disgust. Vashki giggled from the corner.

"On site? You are a digger? You must have been there when they found Kalkuk. Do you know what happened to my uncle? You must tell me. They would say only that he had been murdered, that Riolla had it done." Claria's eyes teared up again, and all Cheyne could do was shake his head.

"I am so sorry. I know less than you. Until now, none of us even knew his name. But I will tell my father. Perhaps he will want to speak with you," he offered.

Claria nodded, holding the totem to the light, forcing her mind back on the business at hand. Cheyne found that harder to do. Her eyes were so clear, so golden, as they wandered over the crystal.

"Why is it, if you are a digger, you cannot read the language on this totem? I thought that was supposed to be a digger's particular expertise," said Claria absently, picking up a glass to magnify the symbols.

"Because archaeologists are usually not epigraphers. And our linguist, the best there is, has no skill with this tongue, either."

Claria looked up. "Neither do I. I am sorry. I cannot read this writing. It is too old. But the last character— there is something very, ah, very strange about it, almost as though I have seen it somewhere before. . . ." Claria tapped the crystal, pondering. At length, she gave it back to Cheyne.

"No. But if you really must go to the Borderlands, I think I have something here that will do for you," she offered, ignoring both Og and Vashki, who seemed to be highly amused about something.

She looked out toward the street and, seeing no one, pulled a scroll from underneath the counter and unrolled it partway before spreading it full length on the tabletop. It was a fine rendition of Almaaz and the territories to its west, all the way to the Sarrazan forest and a little beyond.

"It's my best work. I took all the old maps I could find from caravan drivers who worked the routes before they were closed and drew this amalgam. This

is the only copy. The information is years old, but
nothing much ever changes in Almaaz. I hate to part
with it, but I need this sale to pay for my uncle's six-
teen days of requiem. Mourners are expensive."

"This must have taken months . . ." breathed Cheyne
as he traced a finger over the gilded compass rose.
Claria smiled and nodded, placed weights on each corner, then laid a piece of purple string across a possible
route for them around the western erg, down through
the grasslands and then over the mountains. "A long
and dangerous journey, Cheyne. What you seek must
be very important."

"More dangerous than you guess," mumbled Og,
tracing his own route. "We'll have to go through here
and there also." His dirty finger tapped first on the
Wyrvil territory and then another area where Claria
had skirted for a much longer, but far safer, way.

"How can you go directly through orc country, Muje
Rifkin? You have chosen the old caravan route—it is
illegal to travel that way now. You will surely never
return," she argued, wincing at the dark smudges he
had made on the clean parchment.

"We're in a hurry. I, uh, have old connections along
the route. I think we can pass unharmed for the most
part."

"For the most part?" Cheyne turned to Og, who
continued to stare at the map. "What do you mean?"

"Don't concern yourself. We'll take it. Please pay
her. We really must be going," Og decided, trying to
remember where the closest raqa stall was in this part
of town. Should be near the tanner's. They shared certain of the same curing processes.

Cheyne stared at the map for a long moment. The
route Og had chosen looked to be weeks, if not
months, shorter. Cheyne did not have the resources for
an extended journey. And perhaps, if he retraced the
old caravan route, something might look familiar
enough to jar his memory. "The route is illegal now,
you say?"

Claria considered for a moment. "It is closed for caravans. Anyone wishing to transport goods must clear passage with the Schreefa, because she gets a fee. People will not pay the fee now that the road is unsafe. Nobody wishes to brave such danger. The lost caravan was truly a frightful event. Some three hundred traders, at least half of them from Sumifa itself, were lost." She thought further for a moment. "I know of no order concerning citizens, though. But I would not bring it to the Schreefa's attention, even so." A look of pure hatred crossed Claria's face for a brief moment, but she found her composure and tallied their bill.

Og tapped his fingers in an irritating rhythm on the wooden countertop as Cheyne pretended to study the figures, all the while trying of think of something charming and gallant to say regarding the ribbon.

Toying absently with the tiny perfume bottle around her neck, thinking that she had asked too much for the map, Claria held her breath; perhaps Cheyne wouldn't buy it after all. Finally nodding, Cheyne fished around in his pack for the required sum, counted it out into Claria's hand, and rolled the parchment back into a tube. The business was done.

"You dropped this." He handed her the red ribbon. "I thought you might want it back," he said lamely. "And thank you for saving my life."

Claria smiled and took the ribbon from his hand, then tied it around the map. "Fair winds and waters, Cheyne." Cheyne's palm tingled where she had touched it and he felt his cheeks burning. He looked around for Og, but his guide had already breezed through the front door of the shop, leaving him to find his own miserable way once again.

"Ah . . . thank you. I hope we meet again soon. Perhaps I can call on you when I return." Cheyne bowed quickly to Claria, and then to Vashki, carefully placed the map roll into his pack, and raced after Og.

Claria watched him go, wondering if she would ever see him again. She pulled at the ring on her left hand, but it refused to come off. She smiled at the irony. Maceo had just bidden her farewell forever, but his engagement ring truly was stuck.

"Those manners didn't come from the Mercanto. Or even from the Citadel," teased Vashki as Claria found a crowbar and began to pry at the nails of the dusty crate.

"No . . . especially not the Citadel. But let us not pollute the air with words of Prince Maceo. He can have his well-connected, red-headed paramour and all of her money, money she robs from the pockets of the poor of this miserable city for 'protection' from the mysterious Circle. Who has even seen one of them? It is Riolla's own jackals she is protecting us from. And Maceo is a rank fool if he thinks for one moment she loves him, may she drown in her tears of happiness. She is just trying to improve her fortune. And he just needs her wealth to pay his physicians to cure him of all his imaginary diseases. But he won't need doctors pretty soon—she will kill him before ten days pass, and become queen of Sumifa. A blind man could see what she is up to. But surprise—both will get what they deserve! Ha, I am already over him!" fumed Claria, tears in her eyes as she rocked the crowbar back and forth violently on the crate's top.

"What do you suppose Uncle Kalkuk had saved in this old box?" she grumbled. "He sold everything he ever had at least five times over."

Vashki shrugged her shoulders. She had known Kalkuk since she was a little girl, and the only valuables he had were always still someone else's. Perhaps it was the treasure of the Clock—though nobody ever took him seriously, Kalkuk had always said it really belonged to his family. Vashki's heart began to pound as the old crate cover finally gave way and tore off, sticking to the crowbar. Claria tossed it down and reached into the container, raising a cloud of dust from inside it. Vashki fanned the air for a moment as

Claria brought out a tightly wound ball of waxed linen cloth and unwrapped it as she recovered her breath.

Then held it again.

When she turned back the last of the linen, an exquisite little clock, its bottom a carved wooden music box, its golden overlay a series of abstract lines of some sort, lay gleaming in the folds of the cloth. Claria tipped it over carefully in her hands, feeling the smoothness of the ancient wood.

"What is it?" Vashki was clearly disappointed.

"It's a chroniclave. A musical clock. I saw one once when I was a child. They don't make them anymore, no one can carve the gears," said Claria. The music works chimed and tinkled as she turned the chroniclave upside down, looking for the maker's mark and the winding key.

There was nothing but an Old Sumifan glyph, and that was fairly scribbled—no, burned—into the wood. Like a small fingerprint. The same as the one on— Claria's thoughts raced back to the totem the handsome young man had just walked out the door with. The handsome young man bound for the Borderlands. The one she would probably never see again.

"Well, that old pack rat," said Vashki, interrupting Claria's revelation. "Who would have thought Kalkuk had anything like this? Claria—it isn't the treasure, but you are rich! Look, its hands are made of gold! This has to be worth—"

"Hush, Vashki, I hear someone at the back door again. Maybe it's them," she said hopefully, "come back for something else." She wound the linen back on loosely and laid a half-finished parchment over the little clock.

"Perhaps," said Vashki, unconvinced. Og had been bound, after all, for a raqa stall. And the knock was not right. She set her bottle of polish on a bench, freed the crowbar from the crate, and started cautiously for the door, bar in hand.

She almost made it. The old door, full of dry rot,

burst inward as if a sand squall had hit it full force, and knocked Vashki to the floor, snapping her arm like a dry twig. She lay within a few feet of the alley—almost to safety. Two dark-robed men, one waving a burning torch, its acrid smoke swirling in the air, charged into the shop, armed with throwing disks, hooked daggers gleaming at their belts.

"Where is the foreign man? Where does he go?" barked the first, his kaffiyeh thrown across his face to muffle his voice. With her good arm, Vashki swung low with the crowbar, tripping the one with the torch. The rear of the shop suddenly blazed up as sparks from the fallen torch found Vashki's broken bottle of polish.

"The front! Now!" Vashki screamed, crowbar still in hand, as the second man bounded toward the counter. Claria snatched up the chroniclave and bolted through the front door, billows of black smoke and at least one assassin following her.

CHAPTER
6

"OG, SLOW DOWN," CHEYNE SAID PANTING,
catching him by the tattered sleeve. "Here's a bootery."

"I really want the drink first."

"But the bootery is right here. Let's go." Cheyne turned in to the open stall, its well-tanned wares hung from poles that surrounded the owner, who was almost finished cobbling a sole back onto an impatient customer's boot. Cheyne looked around while the man finished, collected his fee, and came to help them.

Every tap of the hammer caused Og's head to pound like the drums of Caelus Nin on the first night of Thanatas. By the time the bootmaker had stopped, Og could hardly see which pair of boots Cheyne handed him, let alone find his feet. He shook his head as if to refuse their style.

The bootmaker nodded as Cheyne found another pair, but when set beside Og's foot, they were plainly far too small. Smiling widely, the bootmaker found them in the right size, but Cheyne grimaced when he held them up. The flourishes that had looked appropriate on the smaller pair suddenly became hideous on the larger one.

"I'll give you these for twelve kohli. They were

ordered by a Fascini who would not believe me when I told him how tasteless the design would become in his extreme size. They have hung uselessly in my shop for two years."

"Not good big." Og frowned, but he tried them on anyway. "Of course, they fit." He grimaced.

"Ten kohli," said Cheyne.

"Deal," said the bootseller.

"He would have taken five," Og wheedled.

Cheyne handed the cobbler his money and they started for Og's drink. Og's furious pace slowed somewhat, his feet unaccustomed to such lavish confinement.

Four streets over, with the raqa shop in sight, another throwing disk sailed silently over Og's head, missing it by a good two feet.

"Riolla must really be angry at you!" cried Og, taking cover in a rug market as the crowd melted instantly from the streets.

"That wasn't meant for me." replied Cheyne, racing down the empty alley where the disk had come from. "Come on, Og."

Og looked mournfully at the raqa shop and dragged his well-shod feet slowly the other way.

When he found Cheyne, the young man had engaged three slowly circling, dark-robed men, their daggers drawn and ready to strike.

"Oh, no . . ." Og wailed. "This is going to take forever."

A strong hand grabbed him by the scruff of the neck. "Well, come on, then, let's help him!" Claria gasped, her face flushed with the effort from outrunning the thugs. "I'm first in line for him, anyway. This lot isn't going to take my chance at him now," she railed.

"What?" said Og, trying to stall his involvement with the daggers.

"My shop is cinders and my girl has a broken arm." She pointed to Vashki, peeking out from behind a trinket seller's tent. "All I've got in the world now is this."

Claria pulled the musical clock from beneath her robes. "And it's all because of you two. Him, mostly. Him with his sweet smile and pretty manners," she snapped. "Now get in there and keep him from getting killed. That privilege belongs to me."

Og wrung his hands in confusion and, he was sure, the latter, probably fatal, stages of raqa deprivation.

"Well, at least hold this!" Claria raged, handing him the clock. "And if you try to run off with that, I'll hunt you down like a snake. I'm going in."

From her place behind the purple tent, Vashki trained her black, pain-crazed eyes on Og. Og just nodded, rooted to the spot. Claria had accurately guessed his first thoughts upon seeing the bundle, but his feet had too many new blisters to run anyway. And he had run from Vashki before. Broken arm or not, she was fast.

Whooping a strange war cry, Claria threw off her cloak, drew the brass combs from her hair, and charged into the fray, catching one of the assassins above the eye with the combs' flashing teeth, instantly bringing him down.

Surprised at her courage and amazed at her quickness, Cheyne took his opening, stepped back, and threw a head-high kick with one foot, catching the first assassin's nose, then followed with the other foot, knocking the hooked dagger from the man's hand. The second assassin went down, yowling in pain as Cheyne's elbow rammed him under the ribs. The first one, his nose crushed and bloodied, sprang from behind, trying to rake his knife across Cheyne's exposed neck, just below the left ear. His face in tatters, the third assassin had risen and moved to Cheyne's right, preventing the young man's attempt to drop and roll, and pinning him by the right arm.

Claria found her breath and went for that one again; she'd heard the sound of breaking bones once already today. With a rake of her boot heel down the assassin's shin and a ferocious stamp of her foot on his instep, she broke his concentration before he could break Cheyne's arm, brought her comb across his ear, and the thug dropped to the ground, his foot giving way under him, his eyes blind with blood.

Cheyne broke free and fell away in a somersault while the knife meant for his throat caught the third man in the center of his chest. Claria whirled around, looking for the next opponent, but the others had faded into the shadows, leaving not so much as a footprint on the sandy cobblestones.

"Phantoms?" said Claria as Cheyne picked himself up from the gritty street.

"No," said Og. "They belong to Riolla. They can move like the wind. But they were real."

He made his painful way to the fallen man and turned over the body cautiously. Taking the jeweled dagger from the dead man's hand, he flicked away the dark hood with his new boot. Og stood over him, studying his face and the rose-colored tattoo of two crescents, their horns aligned but not touching, now visible just behind the undamaged ear.

Vashki came up, clutching her arm, to stand with the others.

"The clockmaker," said Cheyne. "The one who told me to go and see Riolla."

The assassin bowed deeply, the pain nearly unbearable for an instant as the blood rushed to the slashes on his face. He thought of ten particularly horrible ways to kill the digger and the girl before he brought his head up again.

"Thank you, Saelin. Well done. Await my further orders from the outer room. Help yourself to the tray."

Saelin left the beaded curtain clinking before Riolla finished her sentence, the strings of ruby glass swinging together in his wake.

"Saelin?"

Riolla looked up and shrugged, then untied the red

ribbon on the map to lay the parchment scroll out before her. It was an exquisite map, unquestionably worth even the cost of a dead assassin. The route Og had chosen was plainly marked where he had touched the clean parchment with his dirty fingers. Riolla shook her head in disdain. "He never takes the easy way . . ." she muttered. Then she paused over the map, noticing a certain familiarity about those particular locations.

"He's going to Rotapan's temple? The selkies' forest? Even to the Borderlands . . . by the broken face of Nin—he's not only going on the caravan route, he's after my ring-stones! That little wart! Who would have thought he had any gumption at all left in him, that broken down, raqa-wailing, dive-singing, flat-toned, honk-nosed vermin," she ranted, crumpling the map's corners.

"Saelin!" The assassin had just brought a shirrir-laced cake to his lips. "Take that garbage out of your mouth and get back in here! At the end of this, you can finish what you started in the alley. Get the horses. No, wait—have the men get my chair; it could be a long trip. We can't try to feed animals on this trail. We'll have to leave sooner than I hoped. They probably have a good start on us already," Riolla fumed, pinning her red mane up into a cooler style.

"We'll go as soon as I have spoken with the prince," she added, already formulating what she would tell Maceo.

Saelin shoved the entire cake into his mouth, put three more into his deep pockets, and thought how far more sweet would be his next kill.

"All right, Cheyne, or whoever you really are, let us have a few important words concerning the state of my business," said Claria as she snatched the bundle back from Og's trembling hands.

Cheyne dabbed at a cut on his lip with the sleeve of his tunic.

"Oh, here." She pulled a kerchief from her pocket and threw it at him. Too flimsy to reach him, it unfolded and fluttered to the ground delicately in front of Cheyne's feet. As he bent to pick it up, she continued her tirade.

"In one day I get that entire filthy mess cleaned up, throw out the vagrants and the lowlifes who used to trade with my uncle, hope to find a few new clients—"

"Like the one in the sedan who fled your establishment just before we got there?" countered Cheyne. "I think you'll remember that I've already run into him myself. Unpleasant business all around."

"You leave the prince out of this! He wasn't there for my work," she shouted, her cheeks reddening far beyond the exertion of the other fight.

"Oh?" said Cheyne softly, his smile crooked because of the swelling lip.

"You are impossible!" Claria snarled.

Og cleared his throat. "What exactly happened, Claria? Why were Riolla's thugs chasing you?"

She turned to him and began a long ramble about how they had burst in after he and Cheyne had left, looking for them, demanding to know their destination, then they torched the shop and chased her into the alley where they were now. Vashki had made it out the back door when Claria drew them after her. She had managed to take the clock, apparently her uncle's most prized possession, but the rest of the shop was currently going up in smoke, taking the entire street with it, right now, right over there. She ended by pointing a long finger to a large black cloud building above the Barca.

"I thought I smelled the smoke of a burning map shop," said Og. Cheyne marveled silently that he could distinguish that odor from all the others which continually assaulted them in the Barca. But then Og held his nose up to sniff the air again, and Cheyne remembered the beggar's outstanding advantage for such discernment.

"What, Claria, do you want me to do about all this?" asked Cheyne. "I don't know why Riolla wants to kill me, except that I refused to sell her the totem I found out at the site. But I have need of that myself. I thank you for helping me with the assassins, and I am truly sorry for what her henchmen did to your shop and your helper. I had no idea she was still after me, or even knew I was back in the city."

"Men! You think a little 'I'm so sorry' just fixes everything and you get to go on your fine proud way without cleaning up the mess you made. Well. I don't think so, not this time. I helped you—so you can help me. You're a digger. You're bound for the Borderlands. You can just jolly well take me with you on your journey, and we will divide the profits of your adventure as compensation for my damages. You'd think that with all this attention from Riolla that you have found the Clock."

Cheyne's eyes went wide with surprise. "What do you know about the Clock?"

"I know that the Schreefa of the Mercanto would never be so determined to catch you unless it had something to do with money. Since you are a digger, you must have found something valuable. Or know where it is. What else around here is valuable but the Clock?" She swept her hand upward, taking in the abundant squalor of the Barca, and narrowed her fiery golden eyes at him.

Cheyne said nothing, his face falling at the prospect of his quest becoming a full-fledged treasure hunt.

"You have found it, haven't you?" she said softly, all sarcasm gone from her voice.

"No. And I do not search for it," Cheyne answered firmly.

Og raised a hand in immediate protest. "Now, now, let us not speak so. We don't know that the Clock isn't within your grasp even now. But, Claria, I have already made an agreement with Cheyne for half of his profits. Why should we split the treasure of the Clock yet another way?"

Claria slid her bright gaze toward them and raised one side of her mouth in a sly smile.

"Because," she motioned to Cheyne's torn pack, the parchment roll missing from its pocket, "you may be a guide, Muje Rifkin, but I'm the only one who knows how to get there."

CHAPTER

7

SKETCHES IN HIS GOOD HAND, HIS OTHER
one painful and bandaged, Javin stumbled up the dunes
to the site where Cheyne and Muni had worked the night
before, hoping against his suspicions to find Cheyne at
work already, hoping the young man had just gone off
up here alone for awhile to sort his troubles out. But
when Javin mounted the last rise he saw he was alone.
He sat down on the corner of the weathered marble slab,
where Cheyne's familiar charcoal-smudged handprint
marked the pale stone suface. Javin placed his own hand
over it, wondering when time had made them equal. He
sat quietly, listening to the sigh of the hot wind and the
sounds of the brass sheep bells as the Sumifan shepherds
brought their flocks toward the riverbanks to graze. The
bells each had a particular voice; in the stunning quiet of
the windblown ruins, Javin had picked out three he knew
in only a moment or two.

*It must have been like this during the Collector's
time. When the Circle and peace had their finest hour.
When it almost stopped the war,* he thought, looking
over toward the new city, the river road clearly visible
from this height.

And clearly empty. Muni's crew should have been

making their way in from town. The Fascini would be on their way, then. Javin shook his head in frustration. If Cheyne had gone back into Sumifa, he could only wait for him.

Javin took out the sheaves of paper and idly shuffled through the drawings again, for the fifth or sixth time, searching for any clue that might lead to the Collector. But Cheyne had not put much detail into these quick drawings. He'd rendered the basic lines and measurements of the room under the slab. There was one sheet with few quick sketches of pottery shards that Javin had not noticed before. Probably from last night's work, he thought, scanning the dunes in the direction of the city again—no sign of the Fascini yet.

I might as well go down and see what he found. It will be the last chance I have.

He sighed, securing the plaited ropes to a large rock and lowering himself into the crypt. In another moment, he was out of the harness and over by the shards, matching them to the drawings.

Some Sarrazan work—older than I've ever seen, by the look of the clay. He noted the jar's grainy surface and its peculiar yellow color. After the cataclysm in the forest, the elves' clay was dark, almost red, and much smoother.

"This is before . . ." he muttered. The broken lugs of the jar looked very familiar, though. He ran his fingers over them, tracing the wavy lines and the intricate circles. Glyphs like the ones on the jars he had at home. Glyphs like the ones on the totem Cheyne had been polishing.

Ah, no, Cheyne! I should have known. I should have known. But I couldn't tell you any more. And now you have set forth toward the most dangerous part of all Almaaz with the cruelest assassin in Sumifa after you, he raged silently, quickly gathering the shards, wrapping them and placing them in his bag.

His mind racing, Javin began to climb back into the harness. There was no time to lose. As he raised himself up the rope, he paused, gathering strength—the descent into the crypt had been much easier on his hand and aching arm. As he hung there resting, panting, he twirled slowly back and forth, the new angle on the room intriguing him. From here, he could see light from behind a small crack about halfway up the wall.

He swung himself closer to the wall and caught hold of another crack to steady himself. With his bad hand, wincing, he removed his hand sweep from his belt and brushed away the dust and sand from the rift in the marble. There appeared to be something blocking light from the other side.

Something remotely the shape of a human hand, a couple of gold rings visible upon its fingers.

Excited, his heart pounding, Javin followed the line of the light and made out some kind of fabric, its purple dye still strong and dark. The juma records stated the Collector had been buried in his "robes of purpure royal." Javin could only hang there and stare.

By the Circle's sacred oath!

He pried as much of the wall away as he could, the marble coming out in small chunks, breaking along the main fracture line. After another moment or two, Javin had cleared an opening of about three inches at its widest point. He could see the body clearly. A stray shaft of sunlight overhung the desiccated mummy, illuminating the sunken face, the fragile, darkened skin. Thousands of years of the dry desert climate had protected the corpse so perfectly that Javin could see the man's final expression. Samor had died smiling, his face peaceful and serene, and the obvious haste of his interment had not changed it. Javin ached to get at his find, to discover the secrets of the body behind that wall.

I have found you. Samor, I have found you! He slapped the wall mightily with his good hand, frustration and joy breaking his heart. Laughing, Javin hung swaying like a pendulum upon the plaited ropes, tears streaming down his face.

But there was nothing for it. Even if the *Holy Book of the Confessors* was on the other side of that wall,

Cheyne was still in grave danger. Javin wiped his face upon his sleeve, drew himself up and out of the crypt, into the light and heat of the day.

I'll come back for you, Samor. I will not leave you here, unmarked and unknown.

With a salute, and the Circle's prayer of benediction upon his lips, Javin walked slowly to the mess tent, his head aching from the last of the fever, his heart from being torn in two.

He stuffed as much food as he could find and a skin of water into his pack, and was heading out of the tent as the first Fascini counsel chair turned onto the site.

"Your horse is missing and so is Kifran," said Muni, suddenly standing squarely in front of him.

"By the Seven, Muni, you can put a fright in a man!" said Javin. "My horse? Ah, I see. Kifran, you say. Muni, you will never see him again, but try to recover my horse, if you will. He will probably show up in some Fascini stable soon. But I must go now, horse or no. To the Borderlands."

"How can you think you can make such a journey with the poison not yet done with you? I beg you, let the surgeon take the finger, Javin. This is far from over," said Muni.

"I'm all right. The pain comes and goes; I'm moving fine again. The doctor has done all he can. I have no time to recover from an amputation. I need my hand now. I have to go after Cheyne."

"So he has found a direction for his quest. I am not surprised." Muni regarded Javin for a long time. "You are leaving the site to them?" He pointed to the purple-fringed sedans rounding the last curve before the broken face of Caelus Nin.

"I am leaving the site to you, my friend. I have no choice. He is my son." Javin dropped his head, took a deep breath, and then met his old friend's eyes.

"Muni, I found him. I found the Collector. He's in the wall, in the room under the slab. Don't let them close us down."

Muni smiled implacably and raised his hand in farewell. "We will be here when you both return."

"I need a horse. Has the doctor left?" said Javin.

"Yes, but you can still catch him." Muni smiled.

Javin ducked out the back of the tent and ran for the river, putting the ruins between him and the sedans, hoping he hadn't been seen.

"I hope I have not let you go to your death, my friend," Muni breathed to himself.

In a few minutes and a thousand apologies to the puzzled physician, Javin was on the back of the doctor's old horse, trotting toward Sumifa. When he cleared the Lion gate, he let the horse have its head. He pulled his kaffiyeh close, held his throbbing hand inside his robes, and hoped the doctor didn't live too close to the Citadel.

He had nothing to worry about. In what looked like the worst part the Barca, on perhaps the worst street, the ancient horse stopped and refused to move another inch. Javin climbed down, searching the storefronts and hovels for anything that looked like a surgery. He had no time for this, but he had promised the doctor he would return the animal and get a better one in Sumifa. In the third doorway on the street, a young woman stood waiting outside, one arm cradled in the other, her face ashen with pain. Javin brought the horse around up to the house. A blue crescent was painted crudely upon its door.

"Mujida, I am returning the doctor's horse. Is no one else at home?"

"He lives alone. I am waiting for him myself. My arm is broken. He set it last night, but it is aflame today. I need something for the pain. They have told me he was called out to the diggers. That is all that I know," she said wanly.

"How did this happen, Mujida? Is there no one else to help you?" said Javin, wondering why she didn't just take the pain-dulling shirrir, like everyone else in the Barca.

The girl smiled ruefully. "How can I request treatment at the hand of the Schreefa when she is the one who sent the one who broke it? The doctor will return soon. He will have something that will leave me able to look for work." She sounded a little stronger, her words full of anger.

"It is the fault of the diggers, I tell you. My man's work is uncertain, and now my work is gone, since the shop is burned. That young digger, the fair one, he has gone with my employer and a drunkard who pretends to guide them across the western erg on a treasure hunt. And all I have left is this." She held out a small bronze-bound book.

Javin could not believe his eyes. "Mujida," he said, his voice shaking, "where did you find such a book?"

"It dropped from the digger's pack in the fight. They were gone before I could give it back to him. But it is useless—the words are unreadable. The doctor likes antiquities, and it is clearly very old. I will use it to pay him. Should he ever return," she said miserably, eyeing the doctor's horse.

"Please—I would buy it from you, and you may give the doctor money for his efforts. There will be enough left over until you can find more work."

A moment later, for the price of two hundred kohli, Javin had the Collector's priceless *Holy Book of the Confessors* in his possession. "I have one more favor, please, Mujida," he said. "If you would tell me how the digger and his party travel?"

Vashki pointed west with her chin. "They are fools. They pass the caravan route. You will never see them again, and neither will I. But a thousand blessings upon you, Muje, for your generosity."

"It is I who have been blessed, Mujida." Javin bowed and left her with the horse for company, telling himself that the doctor would be there very soon.

He moved around the corner, sat down, and carefully opened the Book. A bright ray of light struck the pages and made the old words glow before his eyes, their hazy letters pale and red from age. But it was the Book. He closed his eyes and began the prayer that had once drawn the Circle together and made the Collector able to read the peculiar, veiled script. But there was no one to draw now, and no answering presence in his thoughts to await the words of the Book's spirit. He opened his eyes and read the first words that he saw: "Fear not." Javin breathed in the words with hunger, and they filled his heart to overflowing with joy of a sort he had never experienced. He sought to read on, but the script had reverted to its unreadable form. Javin closed the precious volume and placed it reverently inside his pack, buckling the straps with extra care. Time to find a horse.

From the shadows of the dark alleyway, through a crack in the old wall, a pair of pale eyes followed him to the livery.

The smell of night-blooming jasmine mingled with smoke from the fire, making it into a sort of incense, and wafted out over the desert on a vagrant breeze. The three sisters had all but disappeared in the pale dawn sky. Tired from their all-night walk, Cheyne trudged clumsily across a high dune, bringing a shower of sand down on Og, who had removed his new boots and walked in his old rope sandals. Miraculously, he had not passed out and died, as he had continually promised to do ever since the little party had left the city and its bountiful, untapped supply of raqa behind them many hours ago. But he was leaving a small trail of blood, dark drops in the dry sand, despite the bandages Claria had applied.

Cheyne shifted his pack, now considerably heavier for the food and other supplies they had scrounged before leaving Sumifa. To Cheyne's great chagrin, since there were now three of them to feed, there had not been money enough for even the worst of droms. They would have to go on foot.

"How far to that oasis, Og? It'll be full day very

soon. We need to find more water for tomorrow," said Cheyne.

"And a place to rest," said Claria. "We cannot let the face of the sun find us in the desert."

"It should be over those rocks there, the best I remember," obliged Og.

"The best you remember. . . ." Cheyne broke his stride for a moment, letting the little man catch up. Cheyne scanned the horizon. There were no rocks in sight. "Og, do you know where it is or not?"

"Of course I do. Keep walking. It's getting hot."

Cheyne was about to protest when Claria waved her hand excitedly and pointed to their left. "Look! I see the rocks. Come on." Sure enough, a low outcropping of sandstone glinted brightly in the first rays of the morning sun.

Finding new energy, they ran toward the bluff, leaving Og shambling behind, his feet ragged and bleeding from the long walk, the new boots, and a severe lack of raqa, he was sure.

The oasis had been recently used. Or abused, Cheyne thought. While there was plenty of fresh water, the previous travelers had left bits and pieces of their refuse scattered over the green carpet of cress at the edge of the spring, and the remains of a campfire scarred the center of the little clearing in the heart of a grove of date palms.

Claria gently placed her bundle in the mouth of a small shallow cave near the spring, took off her boots, tied up her long skirt, then walked into the cool clear water. She sank into the delicious spring, soft water-grass under her tired, sore feet, her skin drinking in the moisture, relieving the chaff and dryness of the desert air. Cheyne already had one boot off when Og finally managed to join them.

"Not yet. You wait while I go. One of us should stand watch," Og said, heading for the pool, where Claria had found a place deep enough to cover her shoulders. She lay back, her long curls fanning out over the water. Bright red-and-green parrots chattered in the trees overhead.

"Why?" said Cheyne, annoyed. There was no one in sight, no tracks, the birds haggled undisturbed over the abundant ripe dates.

Og pointed to something half-buried in the sand by the old fire. Cheyne put his boot back on, walked over to it, and took out his sweep to brush the sand away. Before the broom ever touched the object, he froze, his hand suspended in midair over a long-toothed, low-browed, hollow-eyed yellow skull.

"Orc," said Og. "Probably a rival tribe. The Wyrvils eat them. Or if they really respect them, or really hate them, or if they gave good sport in battle, they keep the heads. They build their temples with bones. This fellow must have been old or easy to kill. Skull was too soft to use in construction, so they left it. See that ridge just north of the rocks? The desert turns into scrub and the clouds coming off the inland sea drop their last rain there. That is the beginning of Wyrvil territory."

Cheyne drew his hand back slowly, an odd tingling making its way up his arm. He found a bit of broken bamboo and rolled the skull away into the bushes, then took the little man by the sleeve and led him back to the pool. Claria still lounged in the water, a couple of the parrots' feathers now tucked into her hair.

"How does a raqa-loving vagrant know about the weather and battle customs in Wyrvil territory, Ogwater?" asked Cheyne.

Og sat down on the grassy bank and put his miserable feet into the pool, sandals and all. "Ahhh . . ." He laid back and closed his eyes blissfully.

"Og." Cheyne persisted.

"Oh, all right," said the little man, his nose pointing skyward like a beacon. "I . . . was a songmage. A long time ago. Years and years. I was the best. Worked in the Citadel for the royal family. They treated me like one of their own." He cupped a handful of water from the pool and let it drain out onto the bank. "I could make it rain in the desert." He chuckled ruefully. "I could make it *snow* in the desert. Then I lost my ring, you know. The ring's stones helped me true the tones, find the right rhythms—make the magic work. Without it, the Fascini king had no use for me anymore. And, like one of his family, he banished me from the court.

"So I took whatever work I could get, and one day, I hired out to entertain a caravan of Mercantos before they were forbidden to cross here. We were hit by the Wyrvil on the way back from the mountains—and when I had nothing to give them, they took me prisoner. What could I do but sing, or lose my head? I sang. I was terrible; one of them, Yob, was impressed. Somehow, I had chosen his favorite drinking song as my debut and he thought it was a sign from the gods.

"They let me live. I stayed with his roving band for better than a year. When they finally ranged over to this oasis, I put them to sleep one night—for a couple of days—and escaped. Yob woke up and came after me, but the city guards drove him back. So he retreated, waited awhile, and then decided that I wasn't worth feeding all of the time anyway, and since he knew where I was, he could always arrange for his boys to sneak into the city at night and find me, drag me out here, or over to his regular camp, and make me sing for them whenever he wanted. Mostly weddings and funerals; same songs, you see." Og's voice trailed off into a quiet sob.

Claria had floated toward them and was listening intently.

"How did you lose your ring, Og?" she said softly.

Og sat up and brushed the tears out of his ears. "I gave it away. To Riolla."

Prince Maceo nearly choked as he tried to swallow a long draught of the fifth of his twelve regular medications.

Since that trouble with the juma some years back, his eyes had slowly begun to fail him. But he was certain there was a cure. For enough money, Maceo was also certain he could have it.

"When? I don't know when. I have only just proposed, Riolla. Is that not enough? Are we not engaged? I know you have no naming ring yet, but it is being specially prepared for you. You know there is the waiting period for your purification. Though I can barely wait to take you to wife, my darling, no Mercantan comes to the rank without undergoing a time of fasting, a time of self-denial, a time of change. A time, well, of accounting. And I want to be invested beforehand. My father's year of mourning has only just begun. I am king, yes, but officially, I cannot make policy until his year is passed. It is an evil beginning to take a throne before your predecessor is properly mourned."

"I do not have time for mourning, my dear," Riolla cooed, draping her veil over her face. "Grave things are afoot."

Maceo looked up from his medicines, finding something about her tone of voice disconcerting. Riolla smiled, meeting his glance with a look of total innocence.

"I have a short trip to take, Maceo. It's business. I want us to be married immediately after I return."

Maceo held his head back and dropped silvery fluid into both eyes, trying to relieve the pain. Nothing had worked for months now. He was all but broke from trying to pay the physicians, and the thought of that lustrous black pearl leaving his presence was almost more than he could stand.

No matter, he would soon be king. What did that mean? If Riolla left him for another, if he did not take this opportunity, all he could see was an image of himself penniless and blind in the Barca, and worst of all, the object of ridicule and disrespect. They would demand a new king, one with the necessary funds, someone who could bring back the grain. The Fascini

would pass him in their chairs as he stumbled around
the streets. They would mock his clothes and toss him
coins. Even Claria wouldn't marry him then.

He became just the tiniest bit depressed when he
thought of Claria. She had been so wonderful to him,
so genuine. What a pity she had absolutely no chance
of ever rising through the circles to become anyone he
could actually take to wife. She seemed to really love
him, had been so upset when he had to break it off. If
only she'd had a name! Didn't understand at all about
Riolla, and, well, the *necessity* of making the right
marriage, even if it wasn't the best one. Pity about the
ring, too. He should have asked for it before he told
her; Claria's fingers always swelled when she was
upset. But he'd get it back when he was king. Maybe
get her back, too.

Maceo brightened at that thought and put another
couple of drops into each eye. Someday he'd make her
see . . . it had been so awful telling her, and now all
this. He sniffed, wrestling his thoughts back to Riolla.

"Well . . . I suppose I could find a way to shorten
the mourning and the waiting period, since, of course,
I am king now, and your purity is renowned, my
pearl." He dabbed at his eyes, thinking quickly. "Why
don't I stay here and get things in order . . . and when
you return, we will be married."

"What a brilliant idea, my dear. I can hardly wait.
You will be true to me, won't you? I shall count the
hours while we are apart." Riolla ran her hand along
the edge of a gilded dagger, one of twelve that decorated her bedroom wall, arranged equally apart in a
circle around the two faces of Nin, their edges forming
rays like a noonday sun.

Maceo nodded vigorously, still unable to see.

"You *gave* your magical ring to Riolla, that—that
power-grubbing, backstabbing she devil? Riolla the

Schreefa, who killed my uncle for being three days late with his protection dues?" Claria slapped the water, showering Cheyne and sending a wave up into Og's lap. "Riolla, may she find her future blessed with too many of everything, who sent her assassins to burn my shop?" Cheyne smiled ruefully, thinking of his own encounters with the Schreefa and her thugs. "Are you out of your mind?" Claria's golden eyes flashed fire under her wet lashes.

Og stood up from his growing pile of date pits. "Yes. I am," he snorked. "Always have been, I guess, where Riolla was concerned." He found an aloe, broke off a leaf, rubbed its slick juice onto his blisters, and replaced his sandals.

Claria charged out of the water, wringing her skirts and shaking her dark mane of hair. She found a sunny rock halfway up the cliffside and sat down to rub fragrant oil into her skin as her clothes began to steam in the heat.

Cheyne watched her, appreciating how the light broke on the planes of her face, how the brilliant parrot feathers set off the color of her hair. How the air filled with that wondrous scent of bergamot and myrrh, and how she dabbed at her eyes again and again, turning her head away from them to do it. Then he looked at Og, completely puzzled. "I think you better tell her why, Og," he said quietly.

Og nodded. "Fair enough."

Claria whirled on him, waiting to hear his explanation, crouched and ready to spring her anger on him again when it wouldn't be good enough.

"Well . . . I told you I was a songmage. Well, Riolla once served in the Citadel—" He paused at Claria's sharp breath.

"Yes, Riolla was born a slave; she was not always the richest person in the Mercanto. Anyway, she grew up as a bought companion to a Fascini child, one of the king's daughters, actually, and the child thought so highly of her that she would pout and trouble her family if Riolla were left out of anything she did or wanted. So, when I was hired to tutor the princess in music and dance and acrobatics, Riolla was allowed to join in. When it became obvious to the old king that Riolla had the superior talents in these arts, he stopped the lessons.

"Some years passed. One day, when she had come of age, and the princess had become enraged that Riolla had taken her young man from under her very nose, Riolla ran away and found my house, invited herself in, and begged me to teach her more magic. I confess that I fell in love with her then and there. She was beautiful and young—all that dark red hair, those blue eyes. And she could sing. She seemed to be so interested in the songs, in how to find and channel the power, how to work the silences.

"I taught her everything I knew, and then drove myself to learn more so that I could teach her. Every day, I loved her more, risking even death if the king found out she was there. I wanted to marry her, to give her my name. It is an old and respected one, you know, whether I look like it or not.

"One morning, when I believed I had found the right words, the words that would make her love me back, I gave her the ring. It is custom to pledge a ring when you are about to give a name," he explained to Cheyne as Claria unconsciously twisted at the one on her own finger. "It was my most valuable possession, and I wanted her to know that her love was even more valuable to me, and that I would share everything I had with her. She took the ring, pretending to be honored, saying yes, she would marry me, that we would make magic together for all time. I was the happiest man under the sun. I went to fetch Bandro, who was the Mercanto Schreef at that time, to marry us."

"Well—what happened?" said Claria, frowning, refusing to be caught up in Og's romantic story.

Og looked up at her, his face bleak and pale behind his reddened nose. "When I returned, she was gone.

Everything she owned—and most of what I owned—had been packed and moved."

"So that's how Riolla got to be Schreefa!" Claria said, daggers in her words. "I knew she had to have had some kind of magic behind her. Maceo wouldn't fall in love with her otherwise."

"Oh, Maceo, yes. Well, she did use the magic, at first. She could spark a bit of a spell off the ring, but she never had the perfect pitch it required to really control the power in the four stones. Burned her house down once, changed some poor steward into a big white cockroach for bringing her the wrong drink. But in the end, she split up the ring-stones and scattered them. The first I heard about it on the street was that she had bought her freedom with one of the stones, then stole the gem back not three hours later. She gave the others out for political favor and privilege. Paid off the controllers of the caravan route."

Cheyne interrupted him. "This caravan route? Why would she need to do that?"

"Oh, well, the situation with the route is that the heads of the smaller factions of Almaaz let only Riolla's caravans go through unharmed for the price of the gems—otherwise, they would raid the caravans, and Riolla would end up with nothing soon—like the many other caravan owners she has driven out of business.

"See, this is, was, I mean, the shortest route to bring ch'mina into Sumifa. You can't grow it there, it's a mountain crop, and the main ingredient of bappir. Since the river dries up for six months every year, Sumifa lives off of it, actually. The longer route takes so much more time that the stuff spoils before it gets to the city. Riolla had cornered the market on it. She brought in tons and tons, converted it to a sort of meal that keeps indefinitely, and stockpiled it in those big round buildings between the Mercanto and the Citadel. Only her caravans were getting through, and so, Claria, that's how she got so rich.

"So now she doesn't actually direct all of the stones'

magic. Only I could do that, it turns out," he finished, still forlorn at the memory of better times. Cheyne looked away, and even Claria had momentarily faltered in her anger at Og.

"The stone on her necklace—is that part of the ring?" asked Cheyne.

"Yes. The black pearl of Nadrum. The one she used to buy her freedom. Its magic is easier to use than any other stone in the ring—not as exact a tone is called for. By itself, depending on a lot of things, but mainly the user, it can do anything from cure to kill. Very unstable, the pearl. But when it's used with the other stones, it provides bass and adds volume, amplifies the power I guess you could say, for my songspells. Even if all the other stones were put back together, Riolla could stand off their magic by sheer force of the pearl's dark, confusing noise. But it's very draining. You have bad dreams and pains for days after using it alone. Dreams of swamps and murky, foul places. Very unpleasant," said Og, wrinkling his nose.

Cheyne sat pondering Og's story for a while. One thing he knew: Riolla's caravan route had been closed for many years now. No matter how much ch'mina she had brought to the city, treated, and stored, she had to be getting to the end of it by now.

Still deep in thought, Cheyne removed his boots and tunic and entered the cooling spring. Despite herself, Claria could not help noticing how the water and sunlight played over his well-muscled body.

"Og?" Cheyne said, his eyes distant.

"Yes."

"Og, who else has the stones?"

Smiling, the little man considered for a moment. "The last I knew . . ." His face rounded into an endearing smile.

"What?" said Cheyne hotly, beginning to suspect the reason for Og's choice of routes. He pushed wet blond hair out of his eyes and swatted hard at a tenacious horsefly.

"Well, the selkies have one that Drufalden once owned, and the elves—yes, the elves—have the fire-bane, but they got it through one of their own, who turned out to be a traitor. Riolla had made some kind of deal with him for monopolizing the ch'mina, and he used the stone to kill the fields that were promised to other traders and such. Shalikre, I believe, was his name, dead now, anyway, but the elves use the fire-bane only to heal.

"And . . . the Wyrvil overking has one, the ajada." Og grinned sheepishly. "We could go there and you could see it for yourself. The overking, Rotapan—his name means 'One-lip' in orcish, but never, *never*, call him that—has had it made into a staff. Never leaves his temple; quite a place, really, everyone should go there at least once. He can do one or two things with the ajada, nothing really of much import, though. Nothing that would hurt us. Oh, and seems I've heard that it even protects him from snake venom."

Claria combed at her hair with her fingers, drying it quickly in the brilliant sun. "Would it turn the poison on an orcish spear?" she asked flatly, her face rigid and white with fear.

"I don't know," replied Og.

"Why do you ask, Claria?" said Cheyne, angrily ducking under the water again to avoid the horsefly.

The answer missed his head and twanged into the striated trunk of a date palm on the other side of the pool, sending the parrots into frenzied flight and their cluster of dates raining down upon Og's unprotected head.

"Oh. Well, you could have just said," Cheyne sputtered, surfacing.

CHAPTER
8

"THIS WASN'T PART OF THE DEAL, OG. YOU were to lead me to the Sarrazan forest, not straight into a war party of orcs. And you were supposed to be on watch. What happened?" Cheyne muttered under his breath as he worked at the ropes.

"I was upset. All that talk about Riolla. Every time I think of her, it seems to happen all over again. Besides, if we aren't dead right now, he's probably not feeling threatened enough to kill us. The leader is Yob, a Wyrvil underking. He has a camp not far from here. The two with the heads hanging from their belts are Rotapan's boys. See the notches in their ears? The orcs' ears, not the humans'. Rotapan bites them out himself when they enter his service. Yob is wearing his full battle gear; he's too dressed up for a routine hunting party. They're probably all going to the temple . . . quarterly payments or something. This could work very well for us, if I can remember a song or two. They can take us exactly where we need to go."

"You mean exactly where *you* need to go," groused Cheyne, his large fingers fumbling with the same knot for the fourth time. Og finally turned his face as directly toward Cheyne's as he could.

"Look, my friend, here's the situation. Rotapan has the ajada. I need those stones back, or you won't get to where you want to go either, plain as you please, and don't even think about turning back, because in case you don't remember, someone is hunting your head, too. Be calm. Save your energy. Tying us up is just routine for Yob. Impresses the big boys and gives him a chance to think, though that could take all day. Anyway, I'm terribly sorry, you know. About deceiving you, that is." Og ended, exhausted from his tirade. It was more than Claria could bear.

"Oh, once again, a man apologizes and he thinks everything is all right," she fumed. "'I'm so sorry, Claria, for getting you into this mess.' 'I'm so sorry, Claria, for not watching better, and for demanding we take the most dangerous trail possible.' 'I'm so sorry, Claria, but it could never be. We are too far apart in all the important ways.' Hey. That's my hand you've got now."

"Sorry—er, sorry," Cheyne muttered.

Then he sat up straighter, took a deep breath, and caught hold of the stubborn knot. "That's the last time I apologize for apologizing. Claria, I'm just trying to get us free. The inconvenience of having to touch me or having me touch you is temporary, I assure you. Now if you will just hold that end—good. Thank you." Cheyne unraveled the nest of knots with a quick jerk. "Now sit still."

"We can get loose and you want us to sit here anyway?" she grated.

"Please. No disrespect to your considerable fighting talents, but think about this: they are twelve and we are three, one lame. They have their spears and our daggers now, too. Let Og talk to them. Just cooperate for now. Besides, any one of them is twice as big as you are, Claria. Perhaps you didn't see the heads hanging from the biggest one's belt? Here they come. Og, you know them, you do the talking. And keep us alive, do you hear?"

"Of course," said Og, practicing his best diplomatic tone. "Take your cue when I give it; do something showy, if you can."

The orc Cheyne had guessed to be the leader sauntered over and towered over them, sniffing the air. "Og. You have been gone so long. My daughter cries every night for you. You are the only thing she does not forget. You did not say good-bye, even. You are missing her, too, perhaps? This is why you have come back to my desert?"

The orc's heavy teeth clacked together when he spoke, and two or three flies wafted in and out of his mouth, seeming very much at home there. Cheyne could not tell if he was smiling or not. Claria, the tension too much for her, broke into nervous giggles at the mention of a lovestruck daughter, shifting her head to squelch them and avoid the orc's odor, unmistakably the same as the slaughterhouse on a busy day in the Barca.

"Womba is well, I presume." Og smiled engagingly. "I have thought of her often. To tell the truth, Yob, we are just passing through, and we will pay you due honor by letting you escort us to the Borderlands."

Cheyne had to admit there was a certain power in the little man's voice; the orc did not squeeze their heads from their bodies instantly, as might have been expected in the face of such a demand. All the same, he was wondering if letting Og speak had been such a good idea.

Yob scratched his head, trying to figure out the convolutions of Og's reply, what benefit it held for him, and just who was in charge here. "You always make my head hurt, Og. I had forgotten this thing. Now you must sing for us."

The others in the group raised their spears and shouted a deafening cheer.

"Looks like they like that idea, Og," Claria teased.

"They like any idea. That's why Yob is the leader. He has ideas," said Og miserably.

"I will bargain with you, Yob. A song for our release and safe conduct. And maybe do you have a flask—"

"Og!" warned Cheyne.

"Maybe later. But I will do some magic for you right now."

Og curled his lip at Cheyne and began to hum softly, a low-pitched, almost tuneless sound that immediately got under Cheyne's skin and made it itch. Claria seemed to be squirming also. Then Og jumped free, flipped twice in the air from a standing position, held up his hands, and smiled hugely.

Yob jerked back as though stung, his yellow eyes wide with amazement. Before the others could react, he began to laugh in great rolling guffaws, shaking the teeth and bone necklaces that hung across his chest, making a weird sort of music himself.

"Good one, Og. Loved that one. Ha!" He wound down to a spitting chuckle. "Do some more."

Og whistled a little and began to pirouette and leap, his blistered feet completely forgotten, turning back-flips and somersaults, pretending to slip and fall, then catching himself awkwardly at the last moment. He found the skull Cheyne had flicked into the under-brush, found another one and a couple of shin bones very near it, and began to juggle them. The orcs dropped to the ground laughing and put down their spears.

"What's he doing now?" asked Claria, her shoulders aching from holding her arms behind her back.

"I don't know yet," replied Cheyne, laughing as heartily as the orcs. "But he has them spellbound. He's as good with them as you were in the fight back in the city. And I meant to say it earlier: thanks for the help. Where did you learn those old juma moves?

"What do you know about the juma?" Claria shot back at him.

"Well, just what I learned at the university," said Cheyne, trying to figure out what he had said wrong.

"Then you would have learned that there are no

more juma now," she said stonily. After a long silence, Cheyne tried a different subject.

"Tell me about Maceo."

"Maceo! Why do you want to know?" hissed Claria, suddenly angry again.

"Is he your lover? Check the ropes again," said Cheyne, leaning around her to follow Og's act.

"He was my fiancé, if you must know. But not anymore. Since he's about to be invested as king, he has accepted a proposal of marriage from Riolla. He told me just before you came into the shop, may her complexion glow divinely . . . from the drinking of poison. And I'm already over it, thank you very much."

Claria felt around her hands for the cast-off bindings. She turned her head sharply into Cheyne's nose when she did not find them. "Ow. You mean he really can do magic? Why do you care about Maceo, anyway?" she whispered, her face jammed uncomfortably into his stubbled cheek.

Cheyne smiled, enjoying her spicy perfume and the softness of her skin. "I care because I like to know who my enemies are. My friends, too. Listen."

When his audience was thoroughly mesmerized, Og launched into a song. Or it could have been a song at one time, Cheyne decided, disappointed. Og seemed to do well enough when he wasn't trying to make musical sense, but his voice, like any fine instrument left to the merciless desert wind and weather, or submerged in raqa, had deteriorated and become tuneless. With every verse, and the song had twenty-two, Og fell further and further from pitch. By the end, there was little difference between his voice and the croaking of the tree frogs in the pool behind them. Cheyne ground his teeth; Claria had placed her head between her knees in an attempt to cover her ears.

The orcs applauded rabidly; some were crying.

Og bowed deeply and touched his nose to the ground. "Now for the finale—" He glanced covertly at Cheyne, who nodded. "I will break the bonds of my friends before your very eyes. Truly a magical feat, since you tied them yourselves and know their incredible strength."

Og threw back his head and let loose a wild cry, the end of which was inaudible. Cheyne took the cue, grabbed Claria, and brought her to her feet in a grand, sweeping motion, twirling her around by the hand, her hair flying around them both in a glorious, dark swirl, rainbow ribbons dancing in the air. The orcs loved it. They whooped and thumped the ground, spit at one another, and applauded. Cheyne brought Claria back to earth, thinking it would be a good time for them to try to make a run for it. But Og couldn't let go of the note. As Og clutched at his throat, trying to stop the unheard song, Yob sprouted mushrooms on his shoulders, then two of his troops turned blue from asphyxiation.

And Womba appeared.

The warriors in Yob's tattered company gave a universal sigh of delight at her sudden arrival, but Cheyne's reaction was a great, unexpected compassion for Og, just when he had managed to begin to really despise him.

Disoriented, taken from her sleep, Womba shook herself, her little yellow eyes not believing what they saw. Her huge green face was covered in flaking mud, her coarse black hair fell in chopped, uneven lengths over her eyebrow. She yawned capaciously, revealing a complete set of red-stained teeth, her upper lip catching in a delicate sneer above a crooked canine. Pointed ears, pierced along the edges and hung with teeth and bits of carved bones, framed her face. She wore a tunic of gaudy ghoma skin, its leathery scales glinting orange and purple in the bright light of day.

"Womba!" Og rasped pitifully, finally able to let go of the song. Yob's daughter perked her ears at the sound of her name, coming fully awake. Instinctively, Cheyne and Claria scrambled to push Og under a nearby bush, but Womba had already seen him. She bellowed triumphantly, ran to his side, picked him up, and clutched him to her scaly chest in a death grip.

"Put him down!" Claria shouted.

Womba blinked feebly until she could find the source of the sound. Then she turned, Og still flailing in her arms, his suffocation advancing nicely, and stomped over to Claria.

"He is mine. You cannot have him. Mine," she snorted, jabbing a grime-encrusted fingernail at the girl and shifting Og under one enormous arm.

"Put him down, my dumpling," growled Yob, raking from his arms the wilting mushrooms, perfectly nonplused at her appearance. "I think I have traded them a path across the erg to hear the song about my finest battle. I had almost lost the words from my head about how brave I was. No one sings better than Og. Besides, you are killing him. I told you to be careful, they die so easily."

Dejected, Womba slacked her grip and Og fell unconscious at her scaly, corn-studded, feet. Cheyne stepped in and propped the little man up as he regained his senses.

"What happened?" Og said hoarsely.

"Oh, I think you'll figure it out. You all right now?" asked Cheyne, picking orange scales from the top of Og's nose and eyeing the restless orcs. They had found their spears again. The chance to leave was gone.

"I think we will take you to Rotapan, Og. He is smart enough to figure out your words. We leave now," said Yob, pushing his gnarled hand into his daughter's face. She had apparently already forgotten his words of a moment before. She looked at Og longingly through her father's splayed fingers and began to bray softly.

Cheyne turned resignedly to Og. "Looks like you'll get what you wanted, Og."

Og shrugged and held up his bony hands, feigning innocence, but not very well. "Just one minor detour in your journey. They can get us across the erg safely, too. Won't take long, might save some time in the end. What choice do we have anyway?"

Javin's mouth felt like cottonwool. He trudged across the erg in the darkness, the three sisters lighting his way, steering him ever westward. There had been no horse, no drom to be had in Sumifa. At least, no one would sell him one. From every livery he had tried, he received the same response: "We have nothing available today." Then silence, the attendants' eyes lowered and their voices fearful. It was as though they had expected him. The Ninnites had been there before him, of course.

Ahead of him, Riolla covered her eyes against the brilliant dawn on the western erg. It had been years—her childhood, really—since she had braved the full light of day; the Fascini never went out earlier than the late afternoon and not then without being completely covered. Sumifa's royalty were all very pale, and Riolla grimaced as she felt the sun penetrating the sedan's thin canopy.

She unrolled the map, checking for landmarks and direction, but until they passed the oasis, she had to hope that the Neffians knew where they were going. Riolla sniffed distastefully at Saelin, who drowsed in the other side of the chair, snoring softly, his long, curved knife loose in one hand and his sword resting in the other. She had had to let the assassin ride in the sedan when it became apparent that he could not keep up with the thin, wiry Neffians. She scanned the horizon, looking for Og and his friends, then checked behind, searching for any unwelcome followers.

She never saw Javin.

And Javin never saw the Neffian.

"Javin has left the ruin, presumably to find his son. He is wounded, but will not last long enough to do so. We have received a stroke of perfect luck from . . . from Caelus Nin himself, Raptor. The lad has fled his father and travels toward the Borderlands in the company of treasure hunters. He will search out the Clock and present himself to you without Javin's protection at the same time." The agitated voice fell silent.

"What you are telling me is that you have failed to kill the Circle's last mage," whispered the Raptor. "I like it not, Kifran. Such sloppiness is not what I have paid you so well for. I put Javin in his dream state—and I summoned the vermin. Was it too much for you to stay with him and make sure he was dead? Now he knows too much of me."

"Raptor, the water boy came to fill the jugs before I could make sure it was finished. I had to call for help, then; they would have killed me on the spot. The big foreman has a way with knives." Kifran scrambled for words, but found none of the right ones. The Raptor signaled to the tall, hooded guard at the door.

"Of course. So he does."

Kifran, thinking he was dismissed, bowed deeply, grateful to be leaving with his life.

"But so do others." Kifran never felt the guard's poniard as it entered his neck, pinning his tongue to the roof of his mouth.

"You know what to do, Naruq. I'll be watching," breathed the Raptor as the hooded guard reclaimed his poniard, wiped it on Kifran's cloak as the body slumped to the floor, and nodded.

The assassin replaced the blade in his silver cloakpin and strode out the door.

The sun broke over the dunes behind him as Javin drained the last of his water from his water skin. He looked up at the three sisters, almost faded from the eastern sky, and hoped his memory of the caravan route was accurate. It had been a decade, but he had once known this road well. His hand ached, the fire of the scorpion's sting now reaching up his arm in painful twinges, and his knuckles were swelled to rigidity. The wind had blown hard all night, but now, at least, it was at his back. The sun would be overhead soon; he would have to find the caves sooner. A mile or two more and there would be the refreshment of the spring, the cool of the date palms for the worst of the blazing day.

He collapsed fifty yards from the oasis. The Neffian caught up within seconds and hoisted him over his massive shoulders and moved into the shade of the palms with practiced stealth.

"Put me down here. Gently!" Riolla curled her bright pink lip in reprimand as the slaves let her chair down upon the thick carpet of watermoss near the little spring. She stepped into the green softness and smiled again.

"Saelin, wake up. We are here. The men have to rest. And I myself am so worn out from this rigorous journey that I must find a cool, dark place and lie down for the remainder of the day."

She picked her way over to the spring and waited for the Neffians to place her kneeling cloth on the ground. When she had finished her ablutions, Saelin had awakened and stood yawning and stretching by the chair.

"Most marvelous of maidens, you have led us to paradise," he said chortling, eyeing a cluster of dates high in one of the palms.

"Go on up, slave, and bring me those dates. I will await you." He motioned casually to the Neffian to retrieve the fruit. The Neffian bowed his head, but did not obey.

"He goes only where I send him, Saelin. Like you. Remember that. And I hate dates," said Riolla. The Neffians had begun to break out bappir and cheese, a skin of wine, and some oranges. Riolla did not invite

Saelin to join her. "You can stand guard at that rock."

"Of course, Schreefa," Saelin deferred, his smile magnificent while his left eyelid twitched with anger and his stomach growled fiercely.

He positioned himself at the edge of the oasis, looking toward the west, and settled in for the duration. But he was so hungry that he could not sleep. Instead, he began to pace the small shelf of flat rock above the spring, thinking about how he would dispatch the young digger who had so insolently escaped him the first time.

Two red-tailed parrots chattered overhead at the cluster of dates he had wanted. They busily devoured every date as Saelin eyed them contemptuously. He threw a stone at one of them, but the parrot was not of a mind to take the abuse and swooped over Saelin's head, flapping her wings and screeching in his ears, while her mate scattered him with droppings. He ducked her second pass, fell against the stone wall, and searched blindly for something else to hurl at the enraged bird. Saelin groped gingerly at a little recess in the rock behind him as the parrot continued her assault, but found nothing.

Nothing except Claria's chroniclave.

The parrots and his hunger forgotten, Saelin hunched close the stone wall and drew out the little bundle. He took his dagger to the neatly tied linen wrappings, and soon, before his astonished eyes, the little musical clock gleamed in the desert morning. Saelin grinned maliciously at the fine goldwork on the delicate hands, rewrapped the chroniclave, and stuffed it into one of the deep pockets in his robes.

Riolla would pay dearly for this little trinket. But he would have to sell at just the right time. . . . Saelin began to count his kohli as he finally drifted off to sleep in the cool shade of the rocks, the squawk of angry parrots following him into his dreams.

*   *   *

Riolla finished her repast with relish, the effects of using the black pearl having finally worn off, and wandered over to the caves. Riolla had traveled this route before, many years ago, on several caravans, but she had never taken time to explore the oasis' protective rock formations.

Not that exploration was her idea of fun. But today she was looking for a nice dark place, out of the heat, and the rock ledge above the spring offered the best chance of finding that.

"You there." She motioned to a slave, just sitting down for the first time in hours. "Go up there and look around. See if it's safe." She pointed to the caves.

The slave stood, somewhat stiffly, and, hiding his pain and fatigue behind a mask of careful blankness, climbed the rocks to the first dark opening. Riolla waited impatiently below, never noticing the well-trampled grass and the broken, yellowed orc skull just inches from her feet. The Neffian swung himself inside the narrow mouth of the cave and disappeared.

Expecting to be swallowed in total darkness, the slave instead found the cave to be brightly lit. From some other opening, some sink higher up the rock wall, a shaft of sunlight poured in, illuminating his path.

And some recent footprints.

Intrigued, he batted the torn, dusty spiderwebs out of the way and cautiously crept down the narrow, smooth-worn passage. The walls turned, and he inched around to the right, hardly breathing. He was met by a pair of gray eyes and a machete.

"Doulos!" the slave cried in alarm, then instantly lowered his voice. "You put the fear in me! Why are you here? Has you master dismissed you? Are you wanted? Does he hunt you?" The Neffian relaxed against the cool stone wall.

"Be hushed, Gahzi. Yes, I have run again. The master knows it not. Well, maybe by now. But he won't care. One less to feed, especially with the grain nearly gone. This is the last time, Gahzi. He promised to kill me if I left again." Doulos put down the knife he held. "But there is a reason beside looking for my brother Rafek this time. Look what I found." Doulos pointed to the corner, where a man lay sprawled in the darkness.

"Who?" said Gahzi, his pale eyes narrowing.

"One of the diggers. He is fevered. I followed him from the city and took his knife. Gahzi, he is from the Circle. He is the one. Like the juma stories say."

Gahzi shook his head in disbelief, then bent to check behind the man's ear, where the small tattoo of a blue circle showed plainly when Gahzi lifted a lock of Javin's sandy hair.

Gahzi stood dumbfounded for a long time, then finally said quietly, with great compassion, "You are imagining what we all so desperately want, my friend. The juma are all gone, Doulos. The dream is gone with them. How are you feeling these days? Does your head still give you those terrible pains? Do you still see the visions?"

Doulos sighed and held up his hands. "You see for yourself the mark and do not believe? I know what the others have always said of me, Gahzi. But here he is before you; this is no vision."

Gahzi opened his mouth to reply, but stopped when he heard Riolla calling from outside and below, demanding that he answer her.

"She calls. I think we are chasing someone, but I know not who. In our party, there is an assassin, very shoddy, and we four carriers. You know this place now belongs to the orcs? A large party has passed here very recently: beware. Stay hidden. I have never seen you. Doulos, go home; leave this poor man to his own fate. It may be that Maceo will not kill you. Surely he knows of your troubles, of your pain."

Doulos shook his head, smiled, and held up his hand in the farewell. "What has the prince ever cared for another's pain? Especially a slave's. Swear to me that you will not give us away to the Schreefa."

Gahzi nodded silently, returned the gesture, then ducked out the cave. "Honored Schreefa, the caves are dusty and full of vermin," he said, his voice a careful, vacant monotone.

Inside, Doulos smiled wider, promising to return the compliment someday. Riolla screwed up her face in disgust and went back to her chair, disappearing under the canopy.

When night fell, the Neffians awakened Saelin and took their positions under the chair, pushing westward, against the rising dunes and a stiff headwind.

When he was sure he heard them no more, Doulos went to the mouth of the cave and looked out upon the peace of the evening, the three sisters already riding high in the sky. It was time to go. Doulos crept over to Javin's side. Where the opening in the cave had been lit by day, stars shone down now, bringing almost as much illumination.

Something glittered beside Javin's good hand. Drawn by curiosity, Doulos reached for the shining object and discovered he had in his hand an old book. He opened it carefully, alert for the moment of Javin's waking. The old pages, pale in the starlight, stood up stiffly from the spine and wafted to and fro with his breath. They crinkled a bit under his fingers as he traced the lettering. He sighed in disappointment; the words were too blurry to read, in a language he could not fathom. Just then Javin shifted in his sleep, and Doulos quickly closed the old book and replaced it, never noticing that the last page, lighter almost than the air, lilted away in the darkness of the cave and settled invisibly in a dusty corner.

"Wake up, Muje." Doulos shook Javin's good shoulder gently, then waited for him to sit up and take the water he offered.

"Who are you? Where are we?" said Javin gruffly,

his voice dry and husky. His hand had grown cool, the pain nearly gone. Beside him lay the evidence that someone had lanced the sting again. He smiled at the man—from his light, short-cropped hair and dark skin, obviously a slave—and took another long drink. "Thank you. You have saved my life. What is your name?"

The Neffian smiled back. "I am called Doulos."

"Doulos, I am Javin. My other name is Argivian," he hedged. "You are a slave?"

Doulos lowered his eyes from habit. "Yes. Muje, I have run. Please do not send me back. If I go back, my master will kill me."

"I would not take you back, Doulos. Tell me—did you follow me from the city, or take up my trail even before?" Javin smiled.

"I watched you with the woman at the surgery. I came behind you from there," Doulos admitted.

"Why?" said Javin.

Doulos looked at him and laughed, great puzzlement in his voice.

"Because, Muje—you are the true king of Sumifa, and all of Almaaz."

CHAPTER
9

THE ORCISH WAR PARTY, ALONG WITH THEIR odd guests, moved across the erg slowly for the rest of the day, and for three more days, Yob and his men seemingly oblivious to the heat. When Cheyne demanded they stop to rest in the shadow of a huge rock, hewn, so said Og, into the likeness of Rotapan, they grumbled until Og sang Yob's song again. The humans slept and ate, Yob demanded the song yet again, with Og wearily obliging, but also causing some of the rock to peel away from Rotapan's majestic brow and come crashing down on one of them. Og made a new verse of it and the others applauded obliviously. By the time the song was over, they had forgotten who had been killed.

Soon after, they were moving again. Cheyne was beginning to develop some respect for the orc leader, despite himself. Yob halted the group on several occasions, sniffing the air, pointing to a stretch of sand, and then promptly directing them around it.

"What's he doing?" Cheyne asked Og after the second time of having to add two or three miles to their path.

"Sandmire. Dry quicksand. He can tell somehow.

Smells it, I think. For some reason, the Neffians know how, too," replied Og. "The sandmire seems all right at first, because there is a thin crust of regular sand on top of it. But one step into it, and you are lost. Legend has it there are people, full caravans, still falling to the bottom of sandmires."

Cheyne nodded, remembering Javin's words about the sandstorms, and tried to fix the territory in his memory, but found it impossible without landmarks.

That afternoon passed, like the others before, in heat and dulling sameness, until the sun lowered before them and Cheyne noted, almost surprised, that the erg had changed into scrubland. Serrano, Claria had called it. A few low, gray-leafed trees, their trunks twisted and wind-battered, bordered long, flat stretches of patchy sawgrass and thistle. The grass had turned a dormant yellow and whistled dryly as they passed, but the thistle bloomed gloriously, thousands of spiky purple heads stiff and proud against the constant wind.

To Cheyne, this country looked even more hostile than the desert; where there was long clean space on the erg, the serrano was littered with sandspurs and briars, thorns and razor-edged cacti. It smelled of sagebrush and juniper and the peculiar sharpness of candlestaff, those upside-down-looking giant trees that managed to live in the most severe of climates, their barren branches reaching skyward like long straight roots, a single bunch of red, waxy leaves at each terminal. Their interiors were hollow, and travelers had used them for centuries as emergency shelter and shade. You could smell a candlestaff grove before you ever saw it—like burning pitch mingled with attar of roses, their fragrance filled the breeze. Sure enough, a mile or so later, a great forest of them sprouted up from the rocky floor like gnarled, blackened hands, their fingers burning at the ends.

High above the pungent trees, several packs of horned canistas hunted the ridges. Their eyes glowed

red even in the day, and their eerie, laughing wails
rode the wind over the dry valley. Twice they came
upon the canistas' recent kills—the carcasses looked to
have been lions, but it was hard to tell, with nothing
left but bones and flies. Yob's second-in-command had
wasted no time in gathering the trophies. The heat
seemed to be more oppressive, too, but that could
have been because they'd had so little rest, thought
Cheyne.

"Who do you think they were?" whispered Claria as
they trudged along in the orc war party. Og had recovered somewhat, both from his blisters and from
Womba's heartfelt advances, especially since Yob had
tied her hands behind her back.

"What? Who?" he said, his mind still on the bones.

"Them. The heads on his belt. Who were they?" She
shuddered, pointing to the big orc walking in front of
Og.

"You don't recognize them?" asked Cheyne.

"Should I?"

"They were two of the 'phantoms' we fought in the
alley. Look behind their ears. See the tattoos? Same as
the one that didn't get away."

Claria squinted hard, trying to catch a glimpse of the
double crescent marks they had seen on the other
assassin. When the big orc missed his footing going up
a dry gully, he paused to right himself, and she saw
them clearly. "Oh. Do you think they were still following us?"

"Probably. My guess is that Yob saw us coming a
long time before we saw him. If he had wanted our
heads, he could have taken them as well. The spear
was just a calling card. Og here is some kind of
favorite—with this tribe, anyway."

Claria walked on in silence, her hood pulled low
over her eyes against the strong wind, thinking of her
chroniclave, still wrapped in its linen covering, hidden
in the little cave back at the oasis. She hated leaving it,
but had not wanted to risk the orcs' rough hands on it.

It would keep well enough in its dry, dark hiding place until she could return for it. She walked on with her head down, careful of her own footing, avoiding the prickles and shifting sand.

In a few more miles, Cheyne smelled salt in the air and looked up to see a gull circling overhead. "Looks like we're not far from the South Sea."

Claria shook her head. I don't think so. Yob is taking us steadily west. A long, long time ago, this whole area was underwater. When the land emerged again, the flood left a small inland ocean at the edge of Wyrvil territory. It's called the Silver Sea."

"I remember passing over it once. There was a long bridge."

"You have been on this path before?" said Claria, startled.

"Not precisely, and it was long ago. Coming the other way. We were in a hurry, and it's been a long time, so most of it doesn't look at all familiar." He paused, thinking. "I was with the lost caravan."

"You? I thought no one had survived that attack. The Fascini proclaimed the route closed and told everyone the travelers had all been killed. Lots of strange rumors about that in Sumifa right after the Great Purge."

"The Great Purge?"

"Happened when the last Fascini king thought the juma were getting too powerful. The old king was Maceo's father. He's dead now, but when he thought the juma were about to seize the city, he had them all murdered. Imagine, that old man afraid of a bunch of women living above the oasis in those caves."

"I thought the juma were a fighting order. Maybe he had some reason to fear them," said Cheyne, recalling some of Claria's moves in the altercation in the alley.

"They were—a thousand years ago. And they still could have been; their mastery and knowledge of martial arts have never been equaled. But there were never enough of them to revolt outright—they believed their

main purpose in modern times was to prepare the way
for the true king of Sumifa. The old king was afraid
because of their words. They would draw great crowds
to their camps, then talk to them about the old days,
when the Neffians—can you imagine?—the slaves were
in power. They would talk about how there would be
one of them who would come back, from some faraway
place, who bore some kind of special mark, and he
would free them and restore the country to prosperity.
Of course, it would get really awful right before he
came: the djinn would be most active, there would be
famine, and so forth.

"Well, there were always enough hungry people in
the Barca, and enough slaves, to make serious trouble
for the Fascini. Enough of them believed what the
juma were saying: that it was time for the change to
manifest and the new king was on his way. So, in a fit
of fury, the old king sent his raiders and henchmen
and the mercenaries Riolla provided and wiped out the
juma, thinking that all the rumors and rumblings
would stop," she explained.

Cheyne laughed. "*Did* they stop?"

"Well, no. The seeds of revolt were already well
planted. But without the juma, there was no one to
organize the coup. Perhaps you noticed the strain
between the Fascini and the Barcans." She laughed,
then abruptly changed the subject. "But you were talking about the lost caravan. . . ."

"Well, I don't remember very much. In fact, I remember nothing before the attack," Cheyne said miserably.

"Should you remember?"

"Yes, I should. If only I could." He walked in silence
for several steps, then continued. "Everyone but me did
die, and the orcs supposedly took the bodies. Javin
found me hiding and took me back with him. That's my
first memory of the whole ordeal. When the Fascini
finally came after their goods, they didn't even find
bones. Speaking of which—look up."

He pulled gently on her cloak. The orcs had halted

and Yob was giving instructions for two of them to hail the sentries in his name.

At Cheyne's warning, Claria dropped her hood back and stopped. Two or three feet in front of them, the flat scrub they had been walking through abruptly dropped away. Some hundred feet below stood a strangely constructed walled settlement. A long, sparkling ribbon of water, the Silver Sea stretched out behind the fortress's central feature: a huge, gleaming white temple. Even from this distance and height, Claria could see that it was undeniably built of bones.

"The Wyrvil temple. My uncle told me about it. He used to travel a lot in his younger days, hunting for artifacts. He got this far once—used to boast that he was the only human ever to see the outside of Rotapan's temple and live to tell the story," she breathed.

"Then you'll improve on his tale. Looks like we're going inside," said Cheyne.

Yob waved at the guards standing at the temple's gate and motioned Og to lead the way down the steep, nearly invisible trail cut into the cliff.

Riolla put down her spyglass in amazement. She clicked her long, red nails nervously on the telescope's casing, trying to decide her next move. Og did have a lot of gumption, she had to admit. Either that, or the orc was bringing them as gifts to help with Rotapan's current renovation. She'd heard he'd started the twenty-fifth story on that hideous, top-heavy stack of bones. Who would have thought there were that many skeletons in all of Almaaz? Except, perhaps, in the closets of the Raptor, she thought, wincing.

Javin stared at Doulos until he remembered to blink. "What did you say, my friend?" He fumbled in his pack for a candle and a firestone, struck a spark with the stone and brought flame to the candle, seeing plainly for the first time the Neffian's painted face.

Doulos nodded vigorously and reaffirmed his words. "I followed you because you are the rightful, true king of Sumifa. I understand that you travel in disguise, for they would kill you otherwise. Look around."

He took the candle and raised it to the walls in the cave, where Javin could faintly make out a series of pictographs etched into the stone, colored in vivid rainbow hues and spanning the entire length. Javin had seen a few of the characters before—on the juma scrolls at the university.

"See, here are the prophecies of the first juma, inlaid with ground pigments of precious stones so that we would not forget."

Doulos began to read the glyphs, his voice swelling with the import of the words. "There will come one from far away, out of the Circle, bearing the precious Book, and he will be the New King of Sumifa. His eyes will be like the dawn sky, he will have fire in his hands. He will destroy the djinn and bring freedom to all of Almaaz. . . ."

Javin waited for him to finish. "You can read? Is it not illegal for Neffians to read?"

"Muje, all of us can read this language. It is our very own. We helped invent it, hundreds of years ago."

"Where do your people come from, Doulos? Why are you the slaves of the Fascini?" said Javin.

"We come from right here, Muje. We are those who are of mixed blood—part Fascini and part common Sumifan. I will tell you the story.

"A long time back, before the desert swallowed the old city, there was an evil prince, a worshiper of Caelus Nin, who turned into the wind and wrought great destruction. He was a sorcerer, and as he fought one of the Circle, another sorcerer, he killed the man and then caused the desert to cover his own city. It was said that nothing could harm him but one of his own. So he tried in this way to destroy his family so that none of them would ever break his power. He killed the first of his own sons when the boy was but a child.

"The boy's nurse found the child out in the desert, where it looked like he had fallen prey to thirst and then to the vultures. But the old nurse knew it was the sorcerer, for she had seen him once, stalking the children, and he had a claw like a hawk's. So to save the other child, she cried aloud to all the city that the younger son, too, had been slain, had fallen into a sandmire. It was the time of the Wandering, before we learned how to read the face of the desert, and many things of that kind happened. But she hid the younger son in these very caves—they were first known as the caves of Neffia, after the name of the little spring below us.

"While the boy grew up, the juma taught him many things: about the magical order of the Circle, some of whom yet lived, about the old city, about his father. Then he did not believe anymore in Nin and hated the god of his evil father. He chose, instead, to worship as the juma did, after the sayings and beliefs of the Circle, because they had believed in peace and tried to save the land from great destruction at the hands of the warring brothers long ago.

"He was a born fighter, but he went forth from here disguised as a meek herdsman, married a Sumifan slave woman, and his family lived in peace, enjoying the freedom of the land outside the city walls for a great many years, herding sheep and living in tents. They sought out the surviving members of the Circle and protected them as best they could, for the djinn had sworn to find and kill all of them.

"They became the Neffians, a large nation, but a peaceful one. Enough time passed that the evil prince, who had lost his human form, was satisfied that none of his line was left to bring him down. All of Sumifa believed it, too. The people had no one left to follow, and no hope.

"Then came the time of the erg raiders, after the great war. Sumifa needed leadership and fortification badly. So the evil sorcerer put another in the place of his sons, one that would do his every bidding, and declared that he was the ruler of Sumifa. This ruler then began to build the great walls and became fearful when the shepherds would not pay their tribute money to Nin to finish them, for the evil prince demanded much kohli from the new king, or he would kill him and replace him. So the new king went out to the desert with his armies and captured the shepherds after much horrible fighting, took all they had, and made them his slaves. He made us cut the blocks, lay the courses, and finish the walls that became our prison with our own money and our own sweat and blood. That king was the forefather of all the Fascini now. I suppose we are enslaved now because we lost our war then.

"My father was born into slavery, and his before him, and the others before him, back a thousand years. Sometimes our masters have been good to us, mostly they have not. When we have run away, we have used this place to hide, and when the juma yet lived, they helped us as best they could, hiding us for a night or two until a caravan would come and take the runaways with it toward the mountains.

"I have been here once before, when I was very young. My brother and I, his name was Rafek, had run. The old king was our master, but he sent armed men for us. Rafek had gone with a caravan two days before, but they had no room for me. I went back rather than make trouble for the juma. Look, there is my mark as a child. And Rafek's." He pointed to two small handprints near the floor.

"And there are the names of all of us who have passed this way. The names of your people, Muje." He swept his hand toward the ceiling of the small alcove.

Javin expected to see the names in the Neffian language carved into the ceiling; instead, he could barely make out some odd shapes. But when Doulos moved the flame under them, he saw hundreds and hundreds of handprints outlined in red ochre and charcoal, as though the hands had been hastily placed against the rock—no time to carve a name—and the colored earth blown onto them, causing an exact print to remain when the hand was removed, like a wordless signature. The handprints looked like the wings of a thousand birds in flight, one upon the other. They spanned the ceiling of the cave, the long, bunioned fingers of old men and women next to the small prints of children and the entwined hands of lovers.

Javin had dug the fabulous ruins of the known world, had seen with his own eyes in the light of precise measurement the gemstone mosaics of Karjzia, and the gold-embossed, hand-painted funerary portraits in the vaults of Tralinga, and they had not moved him. But here is this dark cave, lit only by a small candle, the hurried marks of the hope of runaway slaves overwhelmed him.

"What happened to all of them, Doulos? Did they find freedom?"

Doulos shook his head. "Some, like Rafek, made it out with caravans, when the traders passed through here to take on water. We have never heard again from them, but I know they lived. They must have. Our people—your people, Muje—are strong warriors still, well able to survive if they got the chance. Perhaps some settled somewhere outside of Almaaz. When they are strong and many, they will come for us.

"But most who ran away were brought back to the city. Their graves lie in the desert, outside the city walls, unmarked. These are now the shape of their names and the way they are still known to us."

Doulos gave him back the candle. Javin sat in silence for a while, mulling another question that had presented itself.

"Doulos, you mentioned the djinn. Will you show me the glyph for that word?" Javin had heard Muni talking to the crew about this term.

"Yes, the djinn—you know, the evil wind." Doulos pointed to a drawing of a pair of circles, one of them broken. "Here it is called the 'dueco,' the double spirit. Not just the divided thing, but that which causes division. It is an old word, a hated word. In the juma writing, it always stands for the evil prince."

Javin listened as Doulos read on, and when the slave had finished, he spoke, his voice quiet and gentle. "Doulos, you have followed me here because of these stories? You have risked your life by leaving your master for the marks on these walls?"

Doulos lifted his head and looked Javin straight in the eye. "Yes, my king. And I will go with you wherever you journey. I will be your protector and your servant. I have believed I would see this day since I was a child."

"Doulos, please understand this. I . . . I can't be the king. I'm only a digger, and I'm looking for my son, who has left our camp to travel to the Borderlands. He is in terrible danger. He is pursued by one who would take his life. That's where I journey: into danger and uncertainty. Away from Sumifa, to the farthest reaches of Almaaz, not to the throne of the Citadel. I am one man alone. I could not free anyone from the Fascini. I can only hope to find my son before he is killed."

"Muje, I have spoken. My word stands. Upon my name."

Doulos closed his mouth and held up the palm of his right hand in the candlelight, then took a bit of ochre from the cave floor in his left hand and placed his right upon an empty space on the far wall. He blew gently upon the powdery ochre and removed his palm, leaving a sharp outline of every finger on the smooth cave wall. He beckoned to Javin.

"I would ask that you leave your mark to stand with theirs in faith for their freedom, Muje. And to witness my oath."

Javin could hardly refuse the man who had saved his life. He rose and placed his good hand next to the print Doulos had made and let the Neffian mark the image upon the warm cave wall. He stepped back and looked at his own finished print. Javin smiled to himself. The shape of the hand he saw was a perfect copy of Cheyne's.

CHAPTER
10

YOB STOPPED THE PARTY OUTSIDE THE GATES of the bone temple, saluted Rotapan's guards, shook his spear at them, reminding them again of his name, and waited for them to swing the heavy doors open. Cheyne mentally sketched the enormous building, thinking that someday, if he lived through this, he would put down it on paper for Javin.

They moved into a dry, dusty yard, where a few stone-and-shell dwellings had been irregularly scattered and several ragged squadrons of orcs drilled with hooks and chains. One or two bodies lay along the sidelines, casualties of the day's practice. Yob dismissed his group and came back to Og, who still stood cowering in Womba's awesome shadow. Cheyne and Claria kept their distance; every time Claria came closer, Womba bared her huge teeth and roared her deafening jealousy.

"We will see Rotapan now," said Yob, yawning. "Womba, go to the western sentry and wait for me. Tell the arms master I will see her when I have delivered my report."

Yob's daughter moaned and let large tears form in her eyes. Yob glowered at her, shaking his spear, and she left, obviously pouting, now and then hissing at Claria, until she disappeared behind the temple.

Relieved to be rid of his would-be paramour, Og fell in beside Cheyne and Claria as they mounted the threescore marble steps that led to the temple's main entrance. Oddly, the stairs seemed to vibrate beneath their feet with a kind of keening, a doleful wail coming from deep under the temple. Og placed his hand over his heart for a moment until the tones died away. Claria shivered, unable to make sense of the sound. Cheyne took her arm, and they continued up the stairs.

"This will be tricky. Rotapan can be, uh, difficult," Og said. "He's not very impressive upon first glance, but he's a deadly fighter, more ferocious for his lack of size. Nobody can beat him with an edge. That's how he got to be overking, actually. Just don't panic when we get to the top; I'll take care of it. And, well, watch where you put your feet," Og assured them.

Cheyne nodded, noting that the bone temple was really a secondary structure, built on ruins perhaps as ancient as the ones he had just deserted in Old Sumifa. Cemented into broken walls and between tall, scallop-shell-capped marble columns, the rib bones of huge sea creatures served as the building's major supports. Some kind of long tusks framed many of the windows. The temple's friezes and archways were decorated with the skulls of all kinds of beings Cheyne could identify, and many more he had never seen before, each reverently housed in separate niches formed of long bones. Despite Og's admonition, at the last step Claria shrieked, pointing to something in the darkness of the main doorway. Yob turned around, laughing nervously.

"That is Sister Krota. Rotapan keeps her out here because she is so mean. Rotapan says if she likes you, she will not try to strike. But I don't think she likes anyone. Every time I come to make the tribute, she bites me. Takes me days to get well."

Yob sighed and motioned them toward the biggest

rattlesnake Cheyne had ever seen, a foot-wide specimen coiled tightly on an uprooted sapling that had been wedged into the bottom of a huge, broken, overturned ceramic pot. Krota suddenly flicked her tongue at them, shook her rattles menacingly, and drew her head back, preparing to strike. Yob prepared himself, teeth clenched and yellow eyes squinched shut. But Og jumped in front of Claria and whistled a low note, gradually raising the pitch as she and Cheyne and Yob flattened themselves to the hideous wall and made their cautious way around the snake. Og let go of the note and hopped to the other side of the temple doorway. The rattler stretched back on her perch, fangs bared and frozen in the striking pose, one lidless eye fixed coldly on Og.

"She'll stay that way until I revoke it," assured Og. "I think."

Claria, recovering her composure as they moved into an anteroom of sorts, looked over her shoulder at the rattlesnake, then pulled on Og's sleeve. "Why does he call her 'sister'?"

Og smiled. "Because she is Rotapan's sibling. One day they were having an argument, and quite by accident, *he* claims, he bewitched her with the ajada. Then he couldn't undo the magic, but I don't think he tried very hard, either. Now he keeps her out here because he can't control her like the others. She tries to kill everyone who passes. Can't blame her," he replied. Yob stopped walking and laughed nervously.

"Others?" said Cheyne, his eyebrows raised. Og shrugged as Yob cut in.

"He's over there. I will go before you and make my report."

In the dim light of the temple's rotunda, Cheyne waited for his eyes to adjust, the sound of gentle friction all around him. When he could see again, he instantly preferred the blindness. From every corner, every niche, and statue, snakes of all colors, patterns, and lengths clung and draped, hissed and coiled, dropped and slithered. And every one of them bore the marks of being poisonous.

"By the seven stars and the three sisters!" Claria's fingers flashed through all of the warding signs she knew. "I've had enough. No treasure is worth this. I'm going back to get my inheritance. I'm cutting my losses, and that will be that last I see of you two and your friends here," she muttered.

"Why do you wish to part company before we have met, woman? I think I must take that personally. That sort of attitude will irritate the Lord Chelydrus," a cracking voice from somewhere in the midst of the snakes boomed under the rotunda, the chamber's acoustics magnifying the tones and scattering the sound all over the building. Something in that voice made Cheyne's skin crawl even worse than the snakes did. Yob snapped his feet together at the heels and bowed deeply.

"Yob reports to Rotapan with quarterly tribute," he shouted. "Six dozen warriors slain from Glom's tribe. Fourteen from Puffer's. Five droms, eight hundred kohli, and two heads, taken in combat from Riolla's spies. Three lost. But their bones were recovered," he finished, after a pause to count everything up on his fingers and toes.

Silence answered him. Cheyne shifted his weight to the boot Claria wasn't standing on. She seemed completely disinclined to move; the several inches around Cheyne's feet looked to be the only place the snakes shied away from.

"Og, you say? Og is back? Well, of course he is— you would be moaning in pain from Krota's greeting otherwise. Oh, do bring him over here. Send the heads to the masons. Tell them to place them facing west, so that Riolla's other spies may easily notice them. That was a good piece of work, Yob, though somewhat late in coming. You must tell me, after the feast and the great sacrifice, how you managed it. The Schreefa thinks she does not need Rotapan anymore. From her

safe city, she sends her spies to kill me. She does not
honor my Lord Chelydrus. We will see if she can't find
it within her power to reopen the caravan route now. I
do so despise that woman. And you have something
else, I see," he crooned.

Yob released his breath at last, his report seemingly
acceptable.

"Yes, Overking. I was confused and decided to let
you decide what to do with these humans and Og."

Gently nudging a couple of twenty-foot-long yarn-
snakes out of the pathway, he ushered his charges to
the throne, somewhat more visible after Yob brushed
handfuls of baby bushmasters from Rotapan's feet.
Cheyne looked on with interest. Rotapan's throne
must have been part of the original furnishings of the
building; some of the same seashell decorations had
been worked into its design. Its carved red marble
gleamed with a high polish.

Somewhere during the short walk to the throne,
Claria's fear of the deadly reptiles turned to curiosity.
None of the snakes seemed the least bit dangerous,
their movements languid and lazy. She knew some to
be natural enemies—why did they tolerate each other,
and how was it that Yob could handle them? Just as
she was about to ask, Rotapan raised himself from the
throne and stood before them, smiling.

Though she recognized traces of a resemblance,
Claria decided instantly that the statue in the desert
had been sculpted by an artist whose flattery bordered on deceit. But at least now she knew how he
had gotten his name. Rotapan stood only four feet
tall to begin with, and looked older than the rock in
which he'd been immortalized. Blue eyes, set far too
closely together, peered out from a slightly overhung
brow, and gray fuzz covered his chin. Wisps of pale
hair crowned his head rather than the lush waves the
desert artisan had provided. His upper lip lay completely hidden under a huge silver mustache, leaving
the lower one to protrude prominently over his weak

chin. His features, like his speech, were decidedly human, though his skin tone and the clawed hands and feet gave away his half-orc heritage.

Uh-oh, she thought. *That probably means he's much smarter, and much more dangerous.*

Rotapan dismissed Yob with a wave of his staff and stood watching as the orc gingerly made his way to the door, the sea of writhing reptiles closing quickly over his wake. The overking then rested his cold gaze upon Claria.

"I am Rotapan, Rex Serpens to the ten tribes. You will answer me, woman. Why do you offend me by declining an audience? You may address me as 'Overking,'" he said, his right hand wandering up and down his staff.

Claria had forgotten his first question. She stood transfixed by the scepter's glowing red stone, cleverly set as a third eye in a gold viper's head, its fangs bared, at the very top of the staff. Cheyne prodded her gently and she found her voice.

"I meant no disrespect, Overking. Snakes make me very nervous. I don't like them," she replied, flustered.

Rotapan grinned slyly, showing the two tiny, sharp fanglike teeth left him. "Neither do I, woman. But what is your name, and who is your tall companion? Something about you smells familiar, like a rat we saw lurking around the outside of the temple once. Speaking of rats, have you any notion of the esteemed person who travels with you?" he ended sarcastically, and motioned to Og, who had remained remarkably quiet since they had come through the door, his focus entirely upon the red stone in the staff.

With the mention of his name, Og bowed to Rotapan.

"Forgive the woman, Overking. She knows nothing," Og said, pitching his voice in a pleasant, warm range. Claria shot him a deadly look, but let him continue. "Her name is Claria, and her companion is Cheyne, a digger." Cheyne's dazed face matched Claria's.

"Archaeologist," Cheyne interjected.

Og went on. "We seek only passage to the Borderlands. We hope to return with treasure, and with such would gladly pay your fee for safegoing."

With the word *treasure*, Rotapan's nose crinkled up like a dried fig, and he cackled loudly.

"You come into my temple with two stinking humans who don't have so much as a second name between them and expect me to believe you are hot on the trail to treasure? You cannot be serious." He began to cough with laughter, finally doubling over in some sort of spasm and almost dropping the staff.

One of the puffadders lying near Cheyne's ankle made a sudden movement toward Claria, its mouth wide with aggression. Rotapan hastily tightened his grip on the rod and brought it down sharply on the marble step. The adder dropped harmlessly to the ground, leaving Claria gritting her teeth to keep from shrieking.

"But perhaps you *think* you are serious, I see," the overking continued. "Hmm . . . You have told me lies before, Og. Your head is already promised to me. Should I collect your bones now, or wait for you to make me richer? It's also time for another sacrifice."

He eyed Cheyne suspiciously. "You are a digger? You hunt for lost things, lost hoards? What time has buried, from the glorious days of antiquity?"

Cheyne nodded.

"You smell strange, digger. I wonder if you are not sent here to dig up my kingdom. Perhaps you are sent by Riolla? Remain where you are. I must consult my cabinet."

He stepped gingerly through the coils of a boras and over a ghost cobra, its white scales reflecting the glow of the red gemstone in the ornament, and banged the staff on a large wooden cupboard.

"All right, Og, what's this about a sacrifice and when is he going to let us go? We have to get out of here," whispered Cheyne, adjusting the cord on his amulet. "That's your ajada, isn't it?"

Og nodded. "Yes. He hasn't really got the hang of it, though. The ajada trues my music. The way he's working it, that power looks to have somehow drawn nearly every snake in this part of the world to him. Interesting. And the sacrifice—apparently for Chelydrus—the monstrous water snake he says lives in the cauldron—is something he does every now and then, when things aren't going all that well. Like now, I guess—the closed caravan route means he never sees most of what the northern tribes take off the longer road to Fallaji. There's talk that one of the underkings is getting pretty powerful up there. Oh, and don't worry; nobody else has ever seen Chelydrus—it's a figment of Rotapan's imagination."

"How comforting. Og, *what* precisely does he sacrifice?" asked Claria, tight-lipped and pale.

"Um, well, I'm sure we'll figure something out before we have to talk about that. Keep your eye on me. We may have to run for it, if this gets personal," said Og, silently working out a scheme to retrieve the ajada.

"Silence!" shouted Rotapan. From the drapes of his robe, the half-orc slowly took a long bone carved into the shape of a key and unlocked the cabinet doors, swinging them wide.

This time, Claria was beyond shock. When three shelves full of shrunken heads began to bat their eyes and yawn, she just dug her nails deeply into Cheyne's hand. He wondered how snake bites could possibly be more painful.

"His enemies," whispered Og. "He uses my stone to animate them and make them tell him the future. Again, the stone governs truth, so they can't prophesy lies. They still hate him, though. He can't do anything about their venomous words."

"Why the two empty spots?" murmured Cheyne.

"One is for the riverking, Wiggulf. Didn't you hear him when we came in? He sings all the time in the water dungeon under this temple. Rotapan would have killed him by now, except that he enjoys torturing him with captivity and he's more than a little afraid of selkies, even though orcs have been known to eat them. . . ."

"Orcs eat anything, even other orcs. Why is Rotapan afraid?" said Claria.

"Well . . . some time ago, Drufalden—"

"Drufalden? You mentioned her before," said Cheyne.

"She's queen of the cold country, has a fortress of ice up on the biggest mountain in the range, along the Borderlands," answered Claria. "The last of the Three Sisters, they call her. A long time ago, when everything was locked in ice, her ancestors' kingdom covered most of Almaaz. They've never gotten over the Thaw."

"As I was saying, Drufalden had another of my stones. The caravan route passes through her lands, so Riolla had to pay her off, also. But the ice queen got a little careless with her water sapphire. Lost it as she was bathing in a stream that feeds into the selkies' river. The stone washed right down into a fish's mouth, quick as you please, and in a day or two, it was on Wiggulf's table, decorating his lunch. Of course, he knew what it was—that harpy had been using the stone to freeze the waters upstream from him for years. Little by little, she was advancing toward his kingdom, pushing his clans together and starving them out, trying to take control of his waterways, forcing his fishing farther and farther toward Rotapan and the Silver Sea."

"And his poison," added Cheyne.

"Yes. And drying up the sea at the same time, just to irritate Rotapan. So Wiggulf, or rather his family, has held the stone for awhile—as both a balance against his life with the orcs and as a threat to Drufalden."

"How so, Og?"

"The best I can figure, the waterstone works with sound that can make solids of liquids and liquids of solids. No doubt Riolla taught each of her minions just enough to make them dangerous with the stones, and their lack of natural ability makes things even more uncertain, but if Drufalden could freeze Wiggulf out, he could possibly bring down her mountain of ice just with the same stone. And Rotapan is afraid that all that melted ice will make the Silver Sea suddenly rise and swallow his kingdom. Orcs don't swim, remember? If Rotapan were to survive that, and still have his stone, he could do some harm to Drufalden, too. It's been a delicate balance. I don't know how he survives, but Wiggulf keeps singing his strange song down there in the dungeon, year after year, waiting for help."

Cheyne nodded as he recalled the eerie wail they had heard as they climbed the stairs. "The other space in the cabinet?"

"Is for me. Gambling debt. I went for double or nothing on the staff and lost. Game was rigged, of course; you should never trust an orc, much less a half-orc," Og ended, motioning their attention to the cabinet, where the heads had begun to chatter.

"Hallooo! Well, it's about time, now. Puffer, are you still up there? Shake the straw from your ears and wake up," said one of the heads on the lowest shelf.

"Of course he's still up there. Where else would he be? You say that every time the doors open, Glom," snapped another one, its eyes sewn shut with long, black stitches.

"You know it's the rule of order to recognize the speaker for the house. Mind your tongue, Rasper," replied the first head, managing to sound as wounded as possible.

"Order! O-O-Order!" sputtered the head on the top shelf. "Now, this session of the war cabinet will begin." He called roll, and when all the heads had answered, he announced, "We are all present and accounted for, Overking. How may we serve you today?"

"I have need of determining whether these humans are sent to imperil me. You may commence to prophesy," intoned Rotapan, facing the cabinet, closing his eyes and banging the staff down three times. The red stone cast a pestilential glow on the shriveled heads.

Puffer opened his puckered mouth and began, the relish in his voice all but garbling his words. "Not since you took me in your greatest battle, Overking, have I been so honored to tell you that, though they are not sent by Riolla, indeed, these three are come to work you the gravest of harm—"

"I wanted to tell him about the gravest of harm part! Overking, upon my sworn oath to destroy you, I say they will bring down your kingdom, and there will be nothing left of it but white dust," Rasper broke in. The other heads began to cheer wildly.

"Order! O-O-Order! The Right Honorable Rasper will refrain from interrupting. The speaker recognizes Clutch," bellowed Puffer.

Clutch snorted and giggled, savoring his response. "By the spear you put through my eye, the tall one is the nemesis of Chelydrus himself, the one you fear above all, and he will break your staff and let the short one take your magic!"

"Ooo-me next, Puffer," said a shrill female voice, somewhere from the left side of the cabinet.

"Proceed, Sawsa," said Puffer.

"Ooo-by the fang of the adder you sent to bite me, the girl will laugh at you."

"And why is that, you simpering whinny?" Rotapan raged at the head, shaking his staff in her face.

"Because they have all escaped!" Sawsa gleefully shrieked, and the other heads began to trill and gibber with abandon, Puffer calling for order every second or two, only adding to the uproar.

Whirling to face Cheyne, Claria, and Og, Rotapan opened his eyes. True to the prophecy, they were nowhere to be seen, having slipped away as easily as the snakes slithered into the cracks of the temple walls. He banged his staff and slammed the heavy wooden door shut on the council's hilarity, catching Glom's left ear in the hinge. A hideous muffled wail arose from the cabinet. Rotapan rapped the staff sharply on the door and the wail ceased, but the exertion brought on one of his coughing fits, and he hacked and spit for a full minute before he could even summon speech.

"Yob!" he boomed, the rotunda's chamber echoing his anger out in great waves to the steps outside.

Yob, his eye warily on the entranced Krota, snapped to attention and raced back into the temple. "Yes, Overking?" he answered tentatively.

"Where are they? They have escaped! Were you asleep at your post again? They must have run right past you! I knew it—they smelled like trouble from the beginning! I will hunt them down and feed them to these writhing reptiles and make of their blood the supreme offering to my Lord Chelydrus. You brought them here—if you wish to live, you bring them back—dead!" he screeched, pounding his staff on the head of an unfortunate mamba. "Your daughter, who, by the way, I had seized as surety against your tribute report, just in case you came up short yet again, will now serve as my hostage until such a time as you come back with their bones."

Yob gulped and bowed, then dug in his claws as he leapt over the coils of vipers and back out of the temple after Og, Cheyne, and Claria. Rotapan was hard on his heels, shaking the staff and ranting about a laughing woman. Yob stopped short at the steps, an odd roar, seemingly from under his feet, shaking the building ever so slightly. Yob looked down, but forgot the noise immediately when he saw, in the soft sand at the bottom of the staircase, human footprints leading toward the inland sea, the only part of the temple's grounds that fronted no wall. For generations, the sea itself—and its raging whirlpool, the cauldron—had served to protect Rotapan's western front. He looked toward the wind-whipped water, meeting the prospect of the chase with utter chagrin.

He seemed to remember that orcs cannot swim. That was just before he remembered Sister Krota.

Who had come out of her trance.

Yob saw only a tiny flick of her tail, heard the barest whisper of a warning, and then another strange, echoing roar from the water dungeon as Krota sailed at him like a javelin. Trying to duck her strike, he fell against the nearest column, dislodging a delicate elven skull from its place deep in the wall. Rotapan, coming right behind him, broke into another coughing fit from the exertion of the short chase, his grip on the staff failing as he doubled over again. The staff clanged down the marble steps, and Krota recoiled herself. Yob snatched Rotapan away just as the snake struck again with the force of a war hammer, bashing her head into the bone wall and leaving herself limp, stupefied, and powerless just long enough for them to roll the rest of the way down the stairs.

"You goblin-hearted fool!" cried Rotapan, oblivious to the fact that Yob had saved his life. "Where is my staff?"

Yob looked up the stairs, thinking that he had seen it as he tumbled down. But the staircase was empty.

For about three more seconds.

A low rumble began to shake the ground beneath them. Then something fell from the topmost stair of the temple. It was the elven skull. It landed near Rotapan's foot and bounced several inches up in the air. Yob picked it up, reverently brushing the sand from the slanted eye sockets.

"Sorry, Overking. I'll put it back." He began to climb back up to replace the skull when the rumble grew much louder and a strange, hollow music descended upon them as the top seven stories of Rotapan's temple began to drift slowly down in a cacophonous heap.

Their eyes upon the collapsing temple, they did not see Og reach from under Krota's pot and snatch up the staff and vault over them to safety as hundreds of bones rained in a sharp, hollow melody down behind him.

From her vantage point on a cliff high above the temple, Riolla patted at her brow and adjusted her hood.

Hmm . . . They left the temple . . . how extraordinary. Short audience. Old Rotapan must be furious; they are running hard. And is Maceo's cast-off love in some distress? Poor thing. They should be coming right back up here, where I will have a lovely chat with the digger and then grind Og into powder.

Riolla waited for a moment, thinking on the riches that would soon be hers. It would be a simple matter for her to coerce this young digger into leading her to the Clock, once Saelin had the girl in his clutches. But something wasn't right—Og's little group was running toward the Silver Sea. And—he had the staff! Then the top of the temple began to collapse and Riolla understood. She dabbed her upper lip, cackling loudly when she saw Rotapan hike his robes up and run after them.

"Oh, how delightful! The journey continues. I had no idea this trip would be so much fun, Saelin."

Saelin only snorted from his cushion. "Perhaps, my ecstatic empress, they stand a wonderful chance of being impaled by some of those bones, or drowned. I should like to see that as a matter of professional interest, though, admittedly, I will be very disappointed if I cannot be the one to use the girl's own weapons on her, then take the digger's head."

Riolla stopped laughing as Saelin's words conjured the vision of Cheyne dead of the bonefall, or of her chance of finding the Clock and its hoard drowning in that whirlpool.

"Onward, and double-quick! Follow the little wart with the staff," she cried in alarm.

Saelin looked at her in horror. "Honored Schreefa, I meant I should like to see it from up here!"

Riolla waved his words away and plunked herself into the seat next to him, sending Gahzi and the other weary runners hurrying down the far side of the cliff, toward the shoreline as the sedan followed behind.

Seconds behind her, Javin and Doulos crept over the bluff Riolla had just deserted.

CHAPTER

11

"RUN FOR THE SEA! NO NOT HERE, TOWARD the other side of the old bridge, you two! We have to try farther down—the cauldron!" wheezed Og.

Cheyne reached back, took Og by the cloak, and slung the smaller man over his shoulder. "Og, they are right behind us. Better an uncertain swim than a certain death. You *can* swim, can't you?" huffed Cheyne.

"No. Absolutely not. You should know that from the well in Sumifa."

"I still think you were faking that you slipped in."

"Truly, I was not," said Og. "Yob won't want to follow us into the water. He can't swim, either. But there's the whirlpool—and the monster."

"You said Chelydrus was imaginary!" barked Cheyne.

"I said no one had ever *seen* him," countered Og.

"Will you two set your minds and mouths to figuring out a way to survive Yob's spears first?" called Claria from in front. Somehow, even on the run, she had removed her boots, shoved them into her pack, and tied up her skirts.

"What were you doing in the well, Og?" Two nearly accurate spears chunked down to Cheyne's right and left.

"I was practicing, actually. Trying to get my voice back. Riolla had actually cast her glance my way the day I met you. I had hopes of, well . . . I fell in, but found that singing over the water seemed to help bring the magic. After all, I was still afloat when it summoned you, wasn't I?" He laughed.

Three more lances sprang up in front of them, causing Cheyne to veer, nearly dropping Og.

"Hey, will you be a bit more careful, there?" complained the little man.

Cheyne smiled despite himself. But then he got an idea, and none too soon: his boots hit the surf as a rain of spears fell at the shoreline.

"Can you find the same magic to float us over this water?" Cheyne asked while he swam out, still supporting Og. Claria raced ahead, doing a remarkably quick breaststroke.

"I really need more than this one stone to lift all of us. . . ."

"There's a bit of a sandbar here," shouted Claria, her mouth just above the waves. "I can feel bottom, but the tide is rising, and there's an undertow. Hurry, Og. Sooner or later, it looks like everything goes down that vortex."

Cheyne caught up, dumped Og in a shallower place, where the water came up to just under his nose, and removed his own footwear.

"Og, can you do anything with what you have now? Ow!" Cheyne winced as he stepped onto something hard and sharp. He reached down and brought up a large, broken conch shell, poured out the sand and water it held, then began to examine its markings, his injury forgotten in the new curiosity. Claria ducked her head under a wave to hide her smile.

Og held his hand over his eyes, bobbed up and down on the sandbar, and peered around them. On all sides, the sea rose and fell in a liquid rhythm, deepening from pale green to dark blue only yards out from the sandbar. The cauldron's spray filled the air, making rainbows in the sunlight. The only thing Og saw was a bit of flotsam tumbling strangely in the tide out a few yards to the left. But it seemed to be moving on its own power.

Og clapped his hands in glee. "Yes! I've got it," he bubbled, losing his footing to the rising tide. "Though the results may be variable. . . ."

Cheyne moved over and held him up in the water.

"Give me that shell and lift me as high as you can," Og sputtered. Cheyne lifted him to his shoulders.

"Hurry, Og. The tide is moving quickly, and the orcs on the shore show no sign of giving up. Unless you can work your magic, we're done for," said Claria. She took the oncoming waves with ease, but clearly did not enjoy the ride. The water looked clear enough, but tasted foul and metallic and smelled of decay.

Og turned his head and pounded on it just above his ear, removing the water inside. The shell at his lips, the staff in the other hand, he began to hum a middle-range note, not far from the sound of the waves crashing on the shoreline, punctuated by a series of honking whistles. A red light appeared around his head, its surges seeming to make the music visible. While there was a strange, compelling rhythm to the performance, Cheyne felt relieved that Og hadn't attempted another song. The notes were astoundingly powerful and astoundingly loud.

Og kept it up for a couple of minutes, and then pointed all around. "See? There—there, and over there. They're coming."

Cheyne looked toward shore and thought Og meant the orcs, who had tired of waiting and were now, at Yob's sharp prodding, stepping delicately into the water, holding their spears above their heads. Then Claria called his attention back to the open sea.

"Look! What's that?" she marveled as a string of stepping stones seemed to gather and stretch toward the far shore, its line oddly the same height and unnaturally straight, the red light hovering above it.

Og just grinned under his nose and made a flourish above his head with the staff.

"After you, my lady," he offered.

"They're alive!" said Cheyne in amazement, as a sea turtle the size of a sedan chair swam up and presented its mottled green, weed-fringed back to them.

Claria climbed up onto it, carefully avoiding the sharp edges of the colonies of coral and gooseneck barnacles that clung along the edges of the slick plates of the turtle's flat shell. Og quickly followed, and the two of them pulled Cheyne up just as the first wave washed over his head. They stepped shakily from shell to shell, the turtles placidly treading water nose to tail, and made good progress toward the far shore.

Then Cheyne looked back. Og's amplified spell had called enough turtles to stretch from shore to shore, but something was wrong: they were not swimming off before the orcs could also use them.

The results, had indeed, been variable. Not only were Yob and his warriors bounding along after them, Rotapan himself, furiously unbalanced, charged over the turtles' backs, shoving any of Yob's javlineers in his way to their watery deaths.

"You'll not escape me this time, Ogwater! Your friends will be my lord's dinner, and you will finally come home to my cabinet where you belong. And give me back my staff!" he wheezed. His thin hair lay plastered to his skull and his glorious mustache drooped heavily.

When he reached the part of the tortoise bridge closest to the whirlpool, he stopped abruptly and bowed to the roiling cauldron, making a long series of elaborate gestures in the air. Yob's troops far in front of him, the shore far to the rear, Rotapan suddenly realized where he was—out in the middle of the sea— and froze to the shell he stood on. But there was another reason besides the very good one of not being able to swim. Coming along behind him, four tired, frightened-looking Neffians bore a sedan chair, its pale silks fluttering in the sea breeze.

Rotapan wasted no time. "Great spirit of the mighty circular tides, mover of the waters, serpent of the Silver Sea, rise up and save your humble servant! I beseech you to engulf this threat to your worshiper!"

But the only thing that rose from the cauldron's steamy mouth was a hiss and a geyser of water, which rained down upon Rotapan, knocking him from the shell into the swirling waters.

Riolla opened the canopy on her chair as the Neffians picked their careful way over the turtles' backs, waving and grinning wickedly at Rotapan as he bobbed and struggled to stay afloat.

The half-orc was not the only one to look back. "Og, Claria—move along. We have company," said Cheyne. He could see Rotapan's mouth moving, shouting over the waves, shaking his empty hands first at Riolla and then at them. "Faster, Og!" he shouted.

Over the turtles' shells they ran, until the water changed from dark blue back to green, and then to paler green. When Cheyne could see the beach clearly, he caught Og by the hood and jumped from the last shell, Claria already swimming hard before them, obscured by the foaming breakers.

Rotapan had disappeared. Riolla sighed and tossed a feather at the last spot she had seen him floating, then moved past without another thought. But the chair was leaning heavily; she looked to the left and saw a Neffian struggling to keep his footing, the weight of the sedan finally becoming impossible for the exhausted slaves.

"Saelin—it appears the chair is too heavy. Catch up on the other side," she said as she pushed the assassin from his seat into the dark water. Riolla immediately slid to the center of the chair to maintain the Neffians' balance. "Carry on." She motioned, wrinkling her nose at the heavy, cloying odor of the sea.

Saelin gurgled under the frothy waves, the weight of his heavy robes and weapons taking him down immediately. He grasped at Gahzi's ankle in desperation,

but only managed to pull the screaming Neffian into
the sea with him. While Gahzi sank like a coin in a
fountain, the other Neffians struggled to right the
chair.

Og, still riding Cheyne's shoulders, Cheyne, and
Claria fought a strong shoreline current as they tried
time and again to reach the beach. Yob and three of
his javlineers were catching up fast.

But Cheyne discovered there was a new problem,
the results being variable, of course. Wave after wave
of the Silver Sea now bristled with the vipers that
Rotapan had ensorcelled with his staff.

The ajada had drawn them into the brine, some
immediately drowning, most managing to swim along
nicely, their heads straining at the waves, following the
staff with rapt devotion. Several raced far ahead of
Riolla's chair, toward the orcs, swifter in the water
than on land. Within seconds the snakes would be
upon them.

"Og!" Cheyne shouted. "Do something!"

The songmage had lifted his hands, preparing to dis-
enchant the turtles, when he saw Rotapan surface and
climb back onto the shells closest to the whirlpool.
Rotapan swore and sputtered, the waves crashing over
him as he clung to the turtle's slippery back with his
hooked claws.

Riolla yawned and frowned as she noticed the half-
orc's reappearance. *How unfortunate,* she thought.

Og stopped the spell and began to laugh uncontrol-
lably at the site of the flapping half-orc, his silver mustache drooping like a walrus's, his bony, green arms
flailing as he went down again and resurfaced.

"Og, hurry!" shouted Cheyne, not finding the delay
at all funny.

A brown viper cruised within inches of Claria's
heels, straining to wrap itself around her ankle.

"You old buzzard! Who will take whose head now?"
Og taunted the drowning overking. Og shook the staff
at him every time he surfaced for further torment.

The brown viper lunged and twisted its rough, saw-toothed underbelly around Claria's ankle once, opened its mouth, and struck blindly at her foot, missing only because she jerked her foot underwater at the snake's cold, sharp touch.

"Og!" The songmage jumped at the power in Cheyne's voice, ceasing his laughter.

And dropping the staff. He had finally noticed Riolla.

Cheyne had no time to deal with it. He dove for the brown viper, snatching its wide, flat head from Claria's kicking limb, and pushing its bared fangs under the waves, squeezed with all his strength. The snake coiled and twisted around his arms, then caught hold of his neck, the choking pressure and pain from its grip caus-ing Cheyne to surface again and again as he wrestled with the viper.

Og watched in despair as the current quickly carried the scepter over the churning waves and into the mouth of the cauldron. The other snakes, still in its magical thrall, confused and churning the water, began biting one another and racing over the waves toward Rotapan, who had again caught a slippery turtle and was clinging to it for all he was worth.

The cauldron toyed with the staff, the light of its red ajada stone unquenched by the whitecapped waves. It danced merrily on the edges of the vortex, and then bobbed underwater for a time, only to reappear moments later in the same place.

Rotapan grabbing wildly for it from his handhold. Chastened, distraught, Og remembered his purpose, waiting until he was sure Riolla would not be drowned, hoping that Rotapan would be, and hummed into the conch shell. Without the staff . . .

But the red light fragmented and dissolved, and the confused turtles instantly broke formation and swam off.

Last in the chase, Riolla found her chair sinking and taking on water quickly, the three Neffians having abandoned their posts in the onslaught of angry, waterborne vipers. At last she disappeared into the dark waves. Caught totally by surprise, Yob dove with his turtle, who stayed under almost longer than the orc could bear, but then surfaced again close to the far shore. Yob broke the water with a huge gasp, never so glad to see land in his life, and promptly passed out, tiny waves lapping at his chin as he washed in to shore.

Farther back, Rotapan found himself trying to swim amid a roil of serpents, many of which had tired and began wrapping themselves onto whatever solid thing they could find in the sea. Struggling to break from the whirlpool's currents, the overking slung two kraits and a copperhead from his arms, screaming in circles of terror. He would have surely been swallowed by the cauldron had not Riolla floated past, her sedan chair bedecked with hissing reptiles and moving under the power of a turtle who was trapped underneath. As he lunged for a handhold, she batted at the half-orc's clutching fingers with her fan, a sneer of mild distaste on her overpainted lips. Og watched her blissfully, his heart now pounding from more than the hard run across the turtles.

Finally on shore, the brown viper dead, Cheyne motioned to the forest. "Og, come and now," he panted. "Claria says we have two choices: the old caravan road that leads toward Drufalden's mountain, or straight through that thick wood."

Claria stood silently watching him gingerly dab at his neck as she wrung out her robes. The dead snake lay in loose coils a few feet away, but her ankle was raw and still twitched from its touch. Claria shivered, thinking how close it had come to biting her.

"Here, let me do that. Please," she said, reaching up and taking his hand away from his neck.

While Og hurried up the beach, Claria quickly cleaned Cheyne's abrasions as he scanned the thick, swaying pine trees that marched westward just a hundred yards from the shore. Enough cover, he thought, if they could get in quickly. He checked his pack for his boots and then for the totem, finding it sticky with salt, but secure. But the little bronze-bound book was gone. There was no time to look for it now.

"Og!" he rasped impatiently.

"I know. I'm coming. But isn't she lovely? Just like a queen." Og sighed. Claria shot him a killing glance at the mention of the word "queen," but said nothing.

"Hey, what is that?" Cheyne pointed to something caught in the shallows, rocking back and forth in the waves like a piece of driftwood.

"It's the staff! I thought it gone forever," cried Og, throwing his boots off as he charged into the water to retrieve the ajada.

"Not so fast—that's mine!" shouted a voice from the breakers.

Rotapan, covered in a cloak of seaweed, a water-shy coral snake wrapped around his head like a crown, bobbed under the shallow water. When he broke the waves again, Og, Claria, and Cheyne had disappeared once more, right before his very eyes, leaving only one of Og's castoff boots, and the sound of Claria's laughter rising on the wind through the tall pines.

"Well, what a lovely job you have done with the power I gave you, Rotapan. 'Rex Serpens,' was it? I have seen that stone do a lot more than draw reptiles." Riolla chortled as she shed her bobbing chair, sopping pink silks and all, and stepped out onto dry land.

Before the water became too shallow, instinct had called the trapped turtle back out to sea, but Riolla's lambskin boots had never so much as touched water during the entire ordeal. One or two little diehard asps leapt from the wreckage of the sinking chair and wriggled toward the drier sand, their horned heads disappearing beneath the low dunes in seconds.

Rotapan envied them their concealment. He sat on the white beach, exhausted and powerless to fend off Riolla's digs. He had also forgotten the coral snake around his head until it sensed a lack of movement, unwound lazily, and fell about his narrow shoulders in bright loops. Remembering that he had no immunity to its bite now, Rotapan sat terribly still, puckering his face in disgust and trying not to breath until the snake had completely departed its perch. He cast an irritated eye upward, where Riolla stood fanning herself in the humid heat and listening to the cicadas choiring in the pines.

"What do you want of me?" He sighed, beginning to smell like dead seaweed. Riolla breathed through her mouth.

"Oh, first I think you might want to repay me for the heads your war party took from my assassins. I wasn't nearly finished with them yet, you know. And they are so expensive. Drufalden seems to want more and more for less and less these days," she replied.

"How? The staff and its stone are gone—back in the hands of the songmage. What can I do now? And what of my Lord Chelydrus? The ajada helped me to talk with him. The magic is departed, and so my cabinet will not be able to advise me; the heads of my enemies are surely good only as gargoyles now. And venom—venom will be very hard to come by without the staff. . . . How will I ever know when Chelydrus demands an offering?" Rotapan moaned.

"Yes. I know. I am quite sure he will be very displeased with you now. But I would let you have the red stone again if you help with a certain task I have in mind," she lied. "And you do owe me."

Rotapan's shoulders straightened. "Perhaps I can be of further service after all." He smiled, his little blue eyes distant and strange.

"I need a small force of fighting men, Rotapan. Swift of mind, fleet of foot, and tough. So no orcs, understand? I need soldiers I can count on, who will obey me.

We'll take the path that veers toward Drufalden's mountain. She will supply us with more Ninnite loyals."

"Well, yes, she certainly has enough of them. But there are the slaves. The slaves are a different matter. What if they see me?"

"It's been ten years, but it's true they probably haven't forgotten you. But they're *slaves*, you spineless vermin. You are the Rex Serpens! So remember: loyal Ninnites only. My best men have come from Drufalden's training grounds, the two most recent of which are spending eternity as gargoyles on your temple. Well, until the top half fell. That reminds me— Saelin? Where are you?" she called loudly.

She shook white sand from the toe of her dainty boot, dabbed at her hair, searching for something to secure a fallen curl with. She finally settled on Rotapan's now useless bone key, which still hung dripping from the sash at his tunic. He gave it over reluctantly.

"For the glory of Lord Chelydrus, I can do this," he said, staring at the ruin of his temple. He couldn't be sure from this distance, but it looked like it had stopped falling. Perhaps the old parts were still standing—the prophecy hadn't yet come true. He could rebuild. . . . "Where do you want them and when?" he snarled.

"Have them assembled at the Borderlands. As soon as they can get there. You will tell them to wait for my orders when I arrive."

"The *Borderlands*?" Rotapan twitched his mustache with a grimace of unbelief. "You can't get there from here. The elves— How am I supposed to—" He fell silent when he saw her expression. "Right. The Borderlands."

"We must hurry. We'll take the old caravan road toward Drufalden; I suppose you can go with us until we reach her mountain. This business must be concluded forthwith. I have a wedding to attend. Where *is* Saelin . . . ?" she muttered.

CHAPTER

12

FAR DOWN THE BEACH, NEAR THE MOUTH OF a small river, Yob came to consciousness, stinging bluewinged flies buzzing at his ample ears. He raised his waterlogged head, blew his nose, the resulting honk scattering several curious shorebirds, and sat up. He looked seaward, remembering he had come with a company, and tried to discern if any of his warriors might have made it to shore. But the waves and the beach were empty but for debris and washed-up clothing; he was alone.

Well, not quite.

When he turned to look in the other direction, standing in the shallow water where the inland sea and the little river met was a large furry creature, sunlight glinting off something shiny at its ear, holding a clam in one paw and a rock in the other.

Yob made a startled sound deep in his throat. The creature did not twitch a whisker. After a moment of regarding the orc, it lay back in the water, bashed the long, thin clam on the rock, oddly discarding the meat but saving the shell.

Yob suddenly became overpoweringly hungry. It had been a hard day.

Drooling, he lunged into the brackish waves after the creature. The otter playfully slipped through Yob's claws, tossed its stone aside, and bellied up to the shore. Yob made another swipe at it, but this time he found himself with an eyeful of sand and armful of rock hard muscle. The razor-sharp clamshell pricked at his throat.

"Be nice." A woman's deep, sultry voice breathed into his ear. "Let me go, or the sharks will be gathering for an early dinner when the riptide takes your body out to sea, and you'll never see that daughter of yours again." Yob relaxed his grip on the woman's arm. She slithered behind him. "Thank you. Now don't turn around until I tell you."

Yob was in no condition to argue. Half-drowned and suddenly very lonesome, he did as he was told. The hunger had subsided, too. He gingerly touched the little cut on his neck. Hardly more than an orcish lovebite, but the pain was growing intolerable. He wondered if the shell had been poisoned. There was a rustle of fabric at his back. He craned his head as far as he could without causing more pain, but could see nothing of the woman.

"All right. I'm dressed now. Turn around slowly. What's your story?" the sultry voice demanded.

Yob scooted around in the sand to face a small woman clad in iridescent brown ghoma skin, razor-clam shell still in hand. She blinked slowly at him, her eyes silver and huge, her face and body dark as night. Her hair lay in slick curls down her neck and danced at her broad forehead. Yob couldn't quite place what was so very strange about her until he noticed her ears: tiny, flat against her head, and pointed like a mouse's. Or like an otter's. At the lobe of the left one, affixed to a golden earring, there dangled a glittering gem the colors of fresh, deep water.

"I am Yob," he said. "I don't remember my story. Who are you?"

"Can you not guess? I thought you greenskins were

always good for a game." She smiled, the blue-and-purple gem flashing.

Yob shook his head, making himself dizzy; he hadn't guessed right all day. The woman chuckled and gave him a mock curtsy. "I am Frijan, daughter of Wiggulf the Riverking. And you are my prisoner, orc. Get yourself up and march. We have a long way to go on land, since I know your kind cannot swim."

Yob stood up. As he towered over the woman, he remembered how big he was and began to laugh. "Your prisoner? I am Yob! A Wyrvil overking. You are a little selkie. It is funny that you say this thing."

"The cut on your neck will kill you inside three days if you do not come with me. My father is the only one who can reverse the effects of the poison. Still funny, orc?"

Yob's yellow eyes widened with amazement and he clutched his neck, the pain growing more intense as he thought about it. After a moment or so, Frijan pointed the way, and they began to walk into the pine forest, following the river.

"I need some fresh water to rinse my clothes and this salt off my skin," muttered Claria as she led Cheyne and Og ever deeper into the wood. "It's been a long time since I've heard anyone behind us. The old maps showed a river running through this forest, and I can even smell it. Could we please stop and wash?"

"Not yet. I want to make a couple of more miles before we camp," said Cheyne, looking over his shoulder.

The trees crowded over their trail, and the ground was dry, loose sand, littered with seasons and seasons of pine needles and stickaburrs. Hard country in which to track. Still, he felt the presence of followers.

"Og, step it up. Stop dreaming of Riolla. She would have drowned you back there without thinking twice. Come on. You're supposed to be my guide, not the other way around."

"I know. I know." The little man sighed, one ugly boot in hand. His waterlogged sandals still squished a little. "I just wish it were otherwise. I just wish she loved me like I love her."

Cheyne gently pushed the songmage in front of him and hung back for a moment, listening. Not far away, to the right, he knew he had heard someone moving among the trees—someone who seemed to know their way. From Claria's estimation, that's where the river lay. The trees seemed less dense there as well, affording him a protected view. He stood silently listening to the whisper of the cooling wind in the fragrant pines.

And then he saw them. Yob, his shoulders stooped and his hand at his neck, lumbered along not fifty feet away; behind him a dark-skinned woman walked as if she owned the forest and everything in it. It was Yob who made all of the noise. The woman moved as though her feet never touched the ground, as though she swam through the air. They seemed to be walking with purpose and speed. And Yob seemed very unhappy about all of it.

Cheyne slowly let go of the bough he held in front of his face. In a few steps, he was back with Claria and Og and had bade them to stop.

"Ogwater, it's your old friend, Yob. And he looks to be injured, though he's on his feet well enough. A dark woman walks behind him, and I think she has a definite destination," he whispered as the trio crouched low under the pines.

"She'll have a definite purpose, too. She must be a selkie," replied Og, his face furrowing.

"A selkie?" said Claria.

"Yes. Riverfolk, you know. Change from humans, or nearly human form, to otters and such, depending on their clan. Live in the forest here, further upstream, but they know everything that happens in the water. She must have found Yob at the delta. Selkies really love three things in life: games, baubles, and fishing in the tidal pools. They used to frequent these parts, before

Rotapan poisoned the Silver Sea." Og smiled. "But I've never been this far west. That's just a guess, from what the orcs say and the old ballads I know about them."

Cheyne idly drew his foot across the speckled white sand. "Why would she want an orc, Og?"

"Oh, I would think she's taking him home with her. Remember, Rotapan has had their king in his water dungeon for years now. Something of a trade-off, I would guess. . . ."

"Rotapan doesn't strike me as caring much about anyone except himself. Why would he ransom Yob?" asked Cheyne.

"He wouldn't. But Yob would ransom Womba," Og said slowly. I was hiding under Krota's broken pot—I heard Rotapan say to Yob was that he was holding Womba prisoner until Yob brought all of us back to the temple. Well, actually, just our heads."

"How would the selkies know that?"

"If Womba is in the water dungeon, they know from Wiggulf himself. He sings constantly. Nothing happens in the water without the selkies hearing of it within the hour."

"Let's follow them. If nothing else, we'll find our way through the wood safely," Cheyne said, thinking of the canistas he had seen earlier; a bedraggled group of exhausted travelers would be just the sort of prey the beasts liked best.

Warily, he led the way. Claria took the middle position, keeping a sharp eye on Og ever since she had seen him mooning over Riolla. The songmage clutched the serpent-headed staff tightly, the red ajada covered with a shred of Og's overshirt. Every so often, when Claria cast a glance at Cheyne, Og would look behind him, tuning his ears to any sound that might mean they were being followed. Especially any sound like Riolla's voice.

An hour more into the pine forest, the trees began to thin into deciduous, understory saplings, which provided almost no cover. Cheyne dropped the party back

several hundred yards, trying to keep quiet in the
rustling, drier leaves that lay scattered under the dog-
woods and maples. Claria moved well in the noisy rub-
ble, but Ogwater sounded like Yob. Finally, at the
river's edge, in the relative shelter of a huge, storm-
fallen willow, Cheyne bade them stop.

"Looks like we can wash now, Claria. We'll need to
take to the water if we want to continue to follow
them. How far upstream are we, anyway?"

Claria had already waded into the clear, cold water.
A low mist hung inches above the river, almost like ice
crystals suspended in the air.

"Brrr! The water is like ice! It shouldn't be this cold
this time of year. The leaves haven't even fallen," she
complained, quickly splashing down and wading out
again. "I recall that there is some kind of enlargement
in the river around here soon. I drew it about four
miles into the forest-sort of an island in the middle of
the stream. That's all the traders' maps showed. We
should be very close to that," she replied.

"That would be the rock of the main lodge.
Wiggulf's personal quarters are supposed to be as big
as a banquet hall," said Og. "I know a song—" He
began to hum, but Cheyne hushed him with a glare.

"Come on. Back in the river."

"Not me. We won't last ten minutes in that water,"
said Claria, still shivering. "Besides, how are we going
to follow them into the main lodge? It'll be surrounded by selkies, won't it?"

"I'll take you."

They all turned at once toward the husky voice. The
female selkie stood smiling before them; at her side,
Yob shook violently, his face as pale as a dead leaf.

"Let's go. This greenskin is fading fast on me. He's
too heavy to carry and they never float, and I need to
keep him alive for awhile. He'd probably like that, too.
I finally had to come back for you because you were so
slow. He hasn't got long before he falls down. But now
you can carry him when he needs it." She waved a

graceful hand at Yob, then motioned to a nearly invisible path in front of them.

Cheyne looked cautiously over his shoulder, the sensation of being followed rising up his back again. He fully expected to see Riolla and Rotapan bearing down on them. What he saw instead made him only a little happier. Two dozen burly, bearded men, skin the same color as the woman's, long coral knives in their hands, appeared and encircled them. Water droplets gleamed in their dark curly hair and clung to their beards. Bits of colored shells and sea urchin spines dangled from their ears and necks and at the belts of their ghomaskin breechcloths.

"You didn't think the riverking's daughter travels alone, did you?" Frijan beamed.

Yob remembered something, then, stirring out of his stupor.

"Daughter . . . Womba . . ." he cried softly. "The temple fell down, and you are left there, my little flower."

She wished he would stop that infernal singing. Womba shook the iron bars of the water dungeon and let loose with a mighty roar, causing the grizzled old selkie to cease his mournful song for a moment.

"Oh, good one. A few more of those and we'll be out," he chittered appreciatively. "Pray tell, orcess— why do they have you in here?"

Womba hung onto the rusty iron gate, the strong tide lapping up to her neck, and fitfully scratched at a bit of gray seaweed caught on one of her chin whiskers. The saltwater was ruining her dress, and if it rose much higher, she would surely drown. When she didn't answer, the old selkie flipped his tail playfully and resumed his song. Womba sighed and contemplated how much energy it would take to catch and eat the old furbag. But then she would be alone down here, and that, despite the dolorous singing, would be much, much worse. It had taken eight armed guards and a net to get her in here. She must have been really tired, she told herself. Such weakness was inexcusable. Og would not want her now.... A large tear formed in her right eye and dropped into the rising sea.

"Oh, please, don't make it worse. The water will drown you soon enough without help." The old selkie chuckled as he swam over. He floated on his back and looked up at her, compassion and pity radiating from his huge brown, shining eyes. The bright sunlight on the water outside the dungeon sparkled through the arched gate and played against the ceiling, its soft overhead rays making his gray whiskers gleam silver.

"For whom do you cry, orcess?" he squeaked, his voice small and strange in Womba's ears.

"What?" she sputtered.

"Is it a young warrior? Your mother? A long lost friend?" The old selkie paddled around her slowly, keeping just out of swatting range, his words echoing off the wet, salt-encrusted walls of the dungeon.

"I have shamed him with my weakness; I let myself be taken prisoner. He was destined to be my husband, and now he's with *her*." She began to sob.

"Who? Who?"

"The finest songmaker in all of Almaaz: Ogwater Rifkin. Oh, did you mean the ugly woman? I don't know her name. I could care less. And she smells." She gurgled, the rising waves making her speak in gasps. She roared again with frustration.

An answering rumble overhead made them both look up just in time to see a large crack form in the vaulted ceiling and widen before their astonished eyes. The old selkie clapped his paws together and danced and twirled and dived in his excitement.

When he surfaced again, the crack had spread to the gate, and Womba was cowering against it, all but drowning. "What's happening? The temple is going to fall on me! My hair . . . my wedding dress! This is my wedding dress!" she cried between gulps.

"No, no, no, we'll be fine. It finally worked! My song has weakened the structure over the years and your lovely roar has triggered the collapse. See? You are not so weak after all. . . . Ha! I've beaten your prison, Rotapan, you old poisoner! And I have beaten you!" he shouted to the ceiling. Then he whirled to Womba, who was plastered to the iron gate like a big green barnacle. "Look, you push on the bars. That's a big, fine girl; you can do it. Think of your loved one."

In the first stages of panic, Womba could have moved mountains. Her little yellow eyes glazed over and her lips curled into a snarl as she nudged the gate with her shoulder. The bars sprang loose instantly.

And sank instantly.

"No, no, let go, orcess! Let go of the gate!" shouted the selkie, diving after her. But Womba had a death-grip on the gate, her shriek rising from her mouth in huge, pearly bubbles. The selkie rolled his eyes and dove after her, trying to distinguish her face from the morass of seaweed and barnacles growing on the lower part of the gate. In clear water, it would have been a difficult job; in the silty tidewash, it was impossible.

Wiggulf went up for air, wondering why he even cared that Womba was drowning. After all, her kind had put him in this wet pit where he had languished for years, living off the fish the tide brought in, and the crabs and mollusks that favored that dark, protected walls of the dungeon. He'd never been dry enough to change back into a man. But they had put her in there, too. Somehow that was enough.

He dove again, finding Womba's huge hand, claws still locked around the bars of the gate, and opened his mouth to bare two savagely sharp incisors. He clamped down on her scaly fingers with all his might. It worked. She let go of the bars and grabbed viciously for him, chasing him up from the sea floor to the surface, rage and pain in her salt-blinded eyes. Wiggulf barely escaped her proven grasp.

"Enough, orcess! Leave off! I mean you no harm. You are safe—look, see?" He pointed toward the open sea. "We must swim now, out of the gate. Just hold your breath." He panted as Womba clacked her teeth at him and fought to stay above the waves.

"But I cannot swim, you rodent!" she whuffed, spewing him with water.

Wiggulf had not thought of that. But there was no time to work it out; the temple had begun to collapse, a few small bleached, hollow bones plinking here and there into the sea like the beginnings of a hard cloudburst. Soon, he knew, they would be unable to get far enough away before the top-heavy structure crumbled, sending huge chunks of marble, heavy monaurochs skulls, and enormous whale bones crashing over their heads into the bay.

He swam out past Womba, nipping her as he went, and waited as she followed, her anger providing enough propulsion to get her out of the dungeon. Wiggulf circled her again and again, teasing and poking at her, until he had maneuvered her several yards out from the dungeon, toward something he had spotted floating in the water: one of Rotapan's favorite decorations, a massive gargoyle made from a bunch of large, round skulls lashed together, which bobbed in the waves like a coconut raft. Wiggulf swam under it and towed it to Womba, who grabbed onto it with all the strength she had. When he was sure it would remain afloat, Wiggulf tugged at the lashings, slowly bringing the strange raft along.

The sea was high—the whirlpool controlled the current—so he steered Womba far to the right, close to the ruin of the causeway, just as most of the temple broke apart and fell. It was a sight Wiggulf had awaited for years. He turned on his back to watch and grinned so widely that his whiskers tickled his ears. "Ha! You old poisoner . . . builder of bone lodges! You have done this to yourself. Good-bye, Rotapan."

Womba looked back also. The bones crashed into the sea behind them, what remained of the temple disappearing amid a puff of white dust. A lone boot, its workmanship exquisite, its decoration exquisitely tasteless, floated up beside Womba.

"Og . . ." she cried, reaching for the boot, hugging it to her chest. "Og . . . oh, and Papa, too . . ." she moaned, about to lose her grip on the raft.

Wiggulf sighed. It was hard work, saving an enemy.

"Hold on, orcess, over there is part of the old bridge. We can rest there until the tide goes out again. I will swim to my people and bring you help. You will be safe here: the water never rises above these rocks, and the piling is hollow—our fishers once used this place as shelter in storms."

Wiggulf pulled himself up a cairn of crab-infested rocks, once part of the destroyed bridge's pilings. Womba clawed up the rocks after him, hugging the boot, and fell into an exhausted sleep as soon as her feet were out of the water. The blue fiddlers and the spiky red crabs, their black-tipped claws clacking at their new find, swarmed over Womba momentarily, but Wiggulf batted them off, taking one or two to taste. For years, he had eaten crabs. And since the crabs ate the remains of everything else in the sea, they had held the most poison in their flesh. Wiggulf spat the bitter meat out in disgust. He could wait until he got home; it wasn't that much farther to decent food.

He dipped back into the water to clear his paws of the foul smell, hopped back upon the dry piling, and began to preen his fur, awaiting the transformation. It had been years since he had taken the shape of a man. He wondered what it would feel like to be dry. Seconds later, he knew.

CHAPTER
13

"WHAT DID YOU SAY?" SNAPPED FRIJAN. "About the temple?"

"He's right. Collapsed just as Og left. Most of it anyway. The last I saw, the first seven or eight stories still stood, if somewhat shakily," said Cheyne. "You are thinking about your father?" he asked the selkie.

"Yes. Did you see him?" she asked.

"No. But we did hear him just before the temple fell. Perhaps he escaped."

"Perhaps he did. Perhaps he is right here behind you," said a voice from over Cheyne's shoulder. Frijan turned, her face incredulous.

"Father? No . . . how can this be? My sire is no bent graybeard."

"And my daughter no tall, strong woman. You forget, child, how long I have been imprisoned by the poisoner. I forgot, too. It was, to say the least, a shock to find myself with bent back and bowed legs. The poison has done me grave harm, it seems. Fortunately, I met the delta guards, and they helped me to cover most of the damage up with this rag."

He leaned hard on his newly cut walking stick and pointed to his ill-fitting tunic. Claria eyed it closely, noting that the design looked remarkably like the decoration on Riolla's slaves' garments. Cheyne and Claria introduced themselves, and when it was Og's turn, a strange smile crossed Wiggulf's lips. He held out a short, webbed fingered hand to each of them.

"Greetings to you all, and welcome to my kingdom. I am Wiggulf, the riverking, and I apologize for my inability to meet you properly. I have just escaped, with the help of an orcess, of all people, from the Wyrvil water dungeon. The poisoner is dead!" He laughed, bowing painfully to Cheyne, Claria, and Og. Wiggulf straightened abruptly when the others did not share his laughter.

"No, Riverking, he is not," said Cheyne.

"What? But I saw as we escaped—the bone temple has fallen into the sea. Rotapan never leaves, except to pour out his poisons upon the waters of the cauldron. But you say he lives?" Wiggulf took a few steps toward them with the aid of his walking stick.

"He and the Sumifan Schreefa follow us, Riverking," said Og. "Rotapan, um, seems to believe this stone is his." He held up the staff, its serpent's head still covered with the rag. Even so, Wiggulf drew back instinctively at the sight of the poisoner's rod.

"Where did you get that?" he asked roughly.

"We retrieved it from the waters as we ran from Rotapan," said Cheyne quickly. "The stone in the serpent's eye truly belongs to Og, and was stolen from him many years ago."

"Then our stone was also yours to begin with . . . for the four were all from the hand of the same workman, cut to fit one to the other. Just like the old stories, which say our kingdoms used to be joined." Wiggulf considered the thought, a frown crossing his wizened face. "We must hurry to the lodge."

The others made to follow him but, Frijan hung back, still uncertain. Wiggulf could bear it no longer. "Please come to me, Frijan. I have missed you . . ." he said quietly, holding out his thin arms to his daughter.

As Frijan embraced her father, Cheyne turned and
looked behind him into the forest, remembering his
last words to Javin, an unbearable feeling of sadness
overwhelming him. He jerked his head back suddenly.
No. I will not look back, he thought, setting his jaw.

Claria studied his bitter expression closely, but said
nothing, her thoughts interrupted as Og drew closer, a
look of terror on his face.

"Did you hear him? He said Womba escaped with
him. That means she's on her way here. We have to
leave as soon as we can and go on toward the mountains," he whispered to them both.

"Why? There are enemies still on our trail, we're all
tired, we need more suitable clothing, I need a chance
to think, and before we try for the Sarrazan forest, we
have to get some provisions," said Cheyne. "Unless, of
course, you can sing all those things out of the air for
us right now, Og." He winked. "But maybe that's not a
good idea—we might see Womba even sooner. . . ."

Og did appreciate Cheyne's attempt at humor.

But Wiggulf and Frijan heard Claria laugh and
moved to join them.

"What about this one? Did he attack you?" said
Wiggulf, pointing to Yob, who had been lying all this
time almost hidden upon the forest floor. The color
had completely drained from the big orc's face, and he
was still trembling violently.

"No, Father. I found him half-drowned by the sea.
He was to help with your ransom. I cut him with a
razorclam to make him cooperate. He'll die soon, I
think. We can leave him here; it's far enough away
from the lodge. The corbies will take him inside a day
or two," Frijan replied.

Wiggulf met his daughter's eyes, a look of surprise
and disappointment clouding his face. "My child, the
terrible burden of my absence has made you hard. No,
Frijan, we cannot let him die. There is no need. He
deserves life as much as any of us."

The old selkie bent over the orc and examined the

cut. "Ah, time is short. The wound is already sour.
Once the cut of the razorclam was not even serious,
but now, since Rotapan's been dumping his poison
potions as sacrifices to that imaginary water worm in
the sea, the smallest nick is deadly. Well, best get on
with it. Give me the stone, girl."

Frijan's silver eyes went wide with disbelief. "You
would use the stone on one such as this? One of the
enemy, who held you captive in that pit? Father, how
could you? At your best, your strongest, using the
stone for the life song always made you ill. It will kill
you in this weakened condition."

"So you never were going to make Yob well? You
were just using him until you got what you wanted?"
said Og.

"You *know* this orc?" she said incredulously.

"Well, he has done me several favors, I suppose you
could say. It's kind of a complicated relationship," said
Og.

"Stay out of this, little man. To me he is but an orc,
so I am his enemy. Don't make me yours, too," she
snapped.

Og threw up his hands and withdrew behind
Cheyne.

"Well, somebody either help him or kill him," said
Claria. "I can't bear seeing him suffer."

Wiggulf beckoned to his daughter again. "I said give
me the stone. I am still your father, and your king.
Obey, Frijan."

Out of old habit, Frijan submitted, tearing the water
sapphire from her ear and handing it to him. "I cannot
watch this! You come back, after all these years, after
all my waiting and hoping, and now you will go, this
time forever, inside the same tide. For the sake of a
filthy greenskin!"

She bounded away into the forest, leaving Wiggulf
holding the dark stone to his heart, his eyes following
her sadly.

"I love you, Frijan," he whispered, knowing she did

not hear him. "And you have kept my kingdom well. But I am still king, and this creature has not come to my kingdom of his own accord. His blood is on our hands. And it is true, his kind would not help us in the same situation. I have spent the last ten years in my enemy's prison; now that I am free, I will share none of his ways. The life song must be sung."

He closed his gentle eyes and began to hum. The water sapphire twinkled and glittered in response, its colors changing slowly from deepest purple to pale blue and back again. Wiggulf's strength seemed to wax and wane along with the colors.

"Is there nothing we can do to help him?" said Claria softly.

"Not that I know of. The stones are Og's. I know nothing of their powers," Cheyne said helplessly. Og began to pace and mutter behind them.

"Wiggulf will die that way. Too much random power. It'll stop his heart. He can't make the tone true enough, can't direct it outside himself without—" Og stopped, noticing suddenly that Cheyne was staring at him.

"Without what, Og?"

Og creased his forehead with a grimace and held up the cloth-covered staff. "Without the ajada. But I haven't sung the life song in a long, long time. If I tried it, using both stones, and I missed the notes, it could kill me, too, and Yob would still die. And Wiggulf could never manage both stones. That's a very powerful song," he said miserably. "Far more powerful than the one I sang for Yob and his company at the oasis. You do remember what happened there when I couldn't release a note."

Cheyne nodded and turned back around to see Wiggulf shake violently as he lost his breath. Yob lay stretched on the forest floor, his face blanched and slack, his eyes closed and still. But Wiggulf raised his silvery head and continued the song, spending himself without thought.

Or effect. Finally Og could bear it no longer. He parted the way between Cheyne and Claria, and laid his hand upon the old selkie's head. Wiggulf opened his eyes and saw that Yob was no better.

"Let me try, Wiggulf. I have the sister stone. Perhaps it will help, perhaps not. Results may be variable, of course." Og chuckled lamely, uncovering the staff. Instantly the ajada began to gleam redly in the bronze serpent's head.

Wiggulf drew back again from the fanged effigy.

"No, I cannot. He lies upon my land; he is my responsibility. And put away the poisoner's wand, I beg you," panted Wiggulf, his face as pale as the orc's.

"Like your stone, the ajada itself is not evil, Wiggulf. The user determines the use of its power. Command me to your service," said Og. "As king, you can do that. Please, there is no time. And your daughter should have her father back. Let me try—I think . . . "

He took a deep breath and looked at Cheyne, knowing his speech had yet to convince the selkie. Cheyne nodded slowly, his eyes never leaving Og's.

". . . I *know* I can do it," Og finished strongly.

"Please, Father. Let him," a voice said quietly. Frijan stepped back out of the forest, returning to his side.

"Yob's stopped breathing," said Claria, watching the orc's chest.

"I will let you try on one condition," wheezed Wiggulf. "I vowed that the poisoner's staff would never rule in my lands. Break the staff and take the stone from that serpent's head. Then you may make your attempt."

"Agreed," said Og instantly.

Cheyne snatched the rod and banged the red stone loose on a large river rock, then broke the staff under his heel in one swift motion. Claria dove for the ajada, and desperately, Wiggulf put his hand upon Og's head, spoke a word none of them could understand, and changed places with the songmage.

Og smiled weakly, took the ajada from Claria, holding

it in one hand and the water sapphire in the other, and began to sing the same song Wiggulf had attempted. The water sapphire seemed to catch fire in Og's hand, its dark blue depths lighting to an intense brilliance with the notes of the life song. The magical light blossomed over Og's head again, the ajada's red mingling with the sapphire's shades of blue and purple.

Cheyne could hardly believe his eyes, much less his ears. Og's voice had become resonant and clear, full of life. Tears formed in Claria's eyes and spilled unbidden down her face. Frijan broke into joyous laughter as Wiggulf's back and legs straightened, and the pall of Rotapan's accumulated poisons lifted from his face. As Og finished, the stones' light receded. The skin on Claria's ankle was smooth, Cheyne's neck no longer hurt, and the selkie king stood on his own, marveling that his twisted body was restored and whole.

And Yob woke up.

"Where . . . am I? What is this place? Womba?" he rasped weakly, raising himself on his callused elbows.

"You are in the territories of Wiggulf, king of the selkies," said Cheyne. "And Ogwater has brought you back from your final journey, Yob."

"Your daughter is safe also, orc. We escaped together, she breaking down the dungeon gate. We managed the swim to the middle of the Silver Sea. I left her waiting in the shelter of the old bridge ruins for the help I promised. It will take a while for my people to rig a raft for her, but she will be along shortly," said Wiggulf.

Yob smiled hugely and threw himself onto the songmage in a crushing hug. His strength, apparently, had been completely restored. "I will never forget this. My house owes yours the life-debt, Og," said Yob.

Then a shadow of confusion passed over the orc's face and his skin prickled visibly. He put the songmage down. "I was cold and tired. Then I saw the land beneath the hills. I saw the old ones, waiting there. I saw a great city, full of bright things, strange machines, and also many bones. Where was this place I went to? I did not see any of you there. Then I heard a terrible sound, like your singing, only very bad. The sound reached into my chest, hurting like a dagger, and pulled me from the darkness, and then I am here." He looked puzzled. "What are you doing with Rotapan's staff, Og?"

"Um, this won't hurt a bit. Just stand still, Yob," said Og, as he took up the bronze end of the broken staff and swung it mightily at the orc's head.

The impact would have killed a man, but Yob's eyes suddenly cleared, and he grinned again.

"Feeling better now? You just had a bit of the death shock hanging about. You'll forget all about it in a little while." Og tossed down the staff.

"About what?" said Yob. "I'm hungry. Let us hunt."

"No, no. We will feast in my lodge. You will honor my homecoming with your appetites." Wiggulf laughed. "Frijan, let us bring our guests to a bountiful table. Tell the guards to fish for a feast. The hall will be merry tonight."

"But Father—we have so little. How—?" Frijan began.

"The table of a generous person will never be bare, daughter. We will have plenty." Wiggulf hushed her. "If nothing else, my girl, there seems to be an abundance of crabs!"

Saelin woke up with a fiddler crab on his face. And a few hundred more dancing on his chest.

He lay sprawled upon one of the old bridge pilings, the one closest to the beach. Saelin sat up abruptly, and when the crabs scurried to find their holes, the one on his face dove for the nearest long, thin nostril. Saelin slapped hard at the crab, then recoiled in pain as he smacked his sunburned face, still tender with the cuts from Claria's combs. The assassin bellowed and snorted until the hapless crab was evicted, then sat back down to think about all of the ways he could kill Riolla and get away with it. The sun was going down, and the waves on the Silver Sea had quieted to gentle swells.

"By Nin's empty glass, I must have been here all day," Saelin muttered aloud, taking another swipe at the curious crabs, who had ventured forth sideways from their holes once it seemed safe again. They instantly pulled back into their small dark tunnels, brandishing their blue-and-red claws behind them. But Saelin could still see their little gleaming blue eyes, held high on stalks above their heads. "Stay there, or I'll have you all for dinner!" he threatened.

Instantly, his stomach reminded him that he had not eaten since yesterday. Time to try for the other shore, before he was stuck here all night with the sea fog cold and wet upon him. His outer robes were long gone, shucked against the deadly pull of the cauldron. If he stayed here, he knew he would freeze to death. He looked at the beach and the water between. There was nothing for it.

Saelin removed his short tunic, wound it into a tight ball, and slung it around one shoulder and onto his bare back in hopes of reducing the drag of the water as he swam. He gritted his teeth, smoothed his dark mustache, and dove into the cold sea, thinking about the little music box he had found and left in the sedan chair, wondering if it had survived Riolla's crossing.

Visions of how much kohli it would bring again filled his head: how he would spend it raqa bars, recounting for his guild members how he had never yet lost a single head he'd been sent for. The memory of Cheyne's incredible escape from their first encounter burned in his mind with each stroke toward the shore. And that woman's combs! His freshly opened cuts stung with the salty water. They would probably scar his handsome face. . . . He would bring those combs back as a trophy—perhaps he would even kill the digger with them after he had dispatched the girl.

By the time he reached the shoreline, he had convinced himself that he could find the little clock and had changed his mind about Riolla. But not about Cheyne.

Far down the beach, Javin pulled himself from the swirling surf, clutching in his good hand a waxed linen-bound bundle, red ribbon still tied around it, that he had pulled from the wreckage of Riolla's sedan chair.

"What is that, Muje?" said Doulos, coughing up more of the salty seawater.

"It looks like a little clock—very old. It seems to be dry, despite its recent treatment. Sort of like us. Thank you for your help in the water—I would never have made it without you. Where did you learn to swim so well, Doulos?"

Javin sat back on his haunches and gave the chroniclave a small shake. When he was satisfied that it had remained watertight, he tried to get it to work. "Oh. It needs a key," he said, turning it over.

"I learned to swim in the Sumifan River, Muje. During the wet months, when I was not the old king's carrier, I worked my birds on the river. When we were children, before he left, my brother Rafek and I had twelve cormorants, and they fished for us. The prince sold the fish for much kohli."

Doulos's eyes followed the flight of a waterbird to the far side of the Silver Sea. "I miss my birds, but my friend will care for them now," said Doulos, spotting and retrieving one of the drowned orcs' spears, which had washed up a few feet away. "Muje, lost things always find their way home. If there is a key to your clock, we can find it." Doulos smiled. Javin smiled back, humoring him.

"It's a remarkable piece. Probably . . ." Javin wiped at the smudge on the bottom of the clock. It did not come off. Doulos waited patiently for him to finish. "Probably someone loved it," the archaeologist improvised. The smudge looked like a glyph. In fact, it looked like the same glyph that was on Cheyne's amulet.

"Muje, look . . . your hand." Doulos frowned.

Javin put the chroniclave down. The scorpion sting had flared again badly, despite the cold seawater and the drawing action of the salt. The wound was turning black and would have to be lanced again before they could go on. Javin took out his knife, shoved it hard into the sand several times, then struck his firestone against a rock. He held the knife over the firestone, and slowly put its heated point to the swollen sore.

When Javin came to, Doulos was pouring water over his face with a shell. "Don't worry, Muje. It has been only a little while. But the assassin passed not fifty feet away from us, moving toward the mountain. He must be trying to catch up with his party. You should rest a while. They are taking an easy road; the Schreefa is now on her own feet." He chuckled. "She's taking the old caravan route, I think, so your son must still be going that way. It is probably overgrown, but far more passable than the forest."

"I know that route, Doulos. Come on. We're losing the light. I'll be all right. We have to get to Cheyne."

CHAPTER

14

AS THE ODD GROUP WALKED UPRIVER toward the selkies' lodge, Og dropped back a bit and fell in beside Wiggulf.

"Um, sire, I was wondering if you could tell me just a bit more accurately when you think the, ah, orcess you left on the bridge piling will be arriving at your lodge to be reunited with her father . . ." he whispered nervously, thinking Yob could probably still hear him. Wiggulf turned and smiled, his large front teeth white against the shadows of the darkening forest.

"Oh yes, of course. Well, I would suppose her to be coming soon, unless the guards meet trouble. I take it you do not return her affections."

"I have been promised to another for many years," Og said delicately, as Yob's left ear twitched a bit in his direction. "I could never break that vow."

"I see," said Wiggulf, his bright eyes twinkling.

"Soon, you say? When might you be reckoning as soon, sire?" Og waited for more information, but the old selkie held his peace, an odd smile upon his lips. The songmage gave up and caught back up with Cheyne and Claria.

"She's coming. What are we going to do? You know

what kind of trouble Womba can be. If she sees me, she'll never let me go. You have to protect me," he pleaded. Cheyne shook his head.

"Og, you have just sung us over the sea, turned a rash of vipers away, and brought Yob back to life. What can we do to protect you? You are holding half of your power again, in case you hadn't noticed," said Cheyne wearily.

It occurred to Og only then that Wiggulf had not asked for the water sapphire to be returned. Even more strangely, Og noted that he had not thought once about stealing the gem for himself. He opened his hand and looked at the stone.

"Oh. So I do," he said quietly.

They walked the next mile in companionable silence, watching the woods for unwanted company, though Wiggulf had agreed with Cheyne that it was unlikely Rotapan would follow them until he could find reinforcements, now that Og had the staff. But Riolla was very resourceful. And Wiggulf was quick to recount that she had long ago allied herself with Drufalden, the queen of the cold country, and the selkies' other main enemy.

They stopped on a rise about a mile from the lodge. The sentry, a man with skin the color of copper and a head of short, blond hair, saluted Frijan readily, but had to be told his king was also present.

"Forgive me, sire, and be welcomed." Somewhat shaken by Wiggulf's changed appearance, it was all the young guard could do to sheath his coral knife and lower his bow. "It has been many tides since you were home. There has been much activity here this day. We have watched as a party of three travelers passed on the old caravan road, and then two more came in stealth behind them. The first group appeared to be going toward the queen's mountain, the last seemed to be following them. All wore their hoods low and walked on foot. We could not give them names, though one, strangely, resembled the Wyrvil king himself."

"Thank you, Dunsan. We are bound for the lodge. Send ahead to them," said Wiggulf. "Watch well, my friend. You are the very image of your father, you know."

"Safe waters, sire," said Dunsan heartily, his eyes already back upon the road.

Wiggulf led them on without comment, his thoughts his own counsel in the early gloaming. The forest seemed to grow more dense the closer they came to the lodge, and a light mist swirled among the trees. The nightbirds flew from branch to branch, awaiting the small prey that scurried before the rustle of many tired and noisy feet.

"What do you think Riolla is up to?" Claria whispered to Cheyne.

"Would you credit my words if I told you that I truly do not know? I'm sure it has something to do with the totem, but I know no more."

Claria pulled out her combs and rearranged her hair. "What about your family? Are you alone?" she offered.

"What about them? Javin is all I have. He's just a foster father. Not the real thing. And right now, he has enough to concern him with worrying about me ever finding anything else about who I am."

Claria said in amazement, "You don't know who your family is? You don't have a name? But you are foreign—surely you have a name from your home country."

"Did I introduce myself with one? No, I have no name. No home country, either. That's why I'm going to the Sarrazan forest. The elves—"

"That's your final destination? Cheyne, there are no maps of the Borderlands. That place is so strange that time itself seems to bend around it. The elves come out of the forest only to trade their wares. What makes you think you will find them when they don't want to be found?"

"I have seen one in Sumifa. They are the only ones who might know."

"That's absurd. There haven't been elves in Sumifa since—"

"I know, since before the Wandering." Cheyne sighed, recalling receiving the same reply during his futile search for the tall elf in the city. "But I did see one, and if he isn't in Sumifa any longer, at least I know he came from the Sarrazan forest. As I said, the elvish potters are the ones who will know."

"Know what?"

"About the last glyph on the totem I found at the dig. They still know the language. They use it on their wares as decoration."

"The totem . . . that's your quest, isn't it? You think the totem is your real family's." The picture of her chroniclave and its matching glyph flashed in her mind for the first time since she had opened Kalkuk's crate. "What has this got to do with the Armageddon Clock? I thought that's what we were after."

"That's probably what Riolla is after. That's what Og is after, I suppose it's what even *you* are after. I told you back in Sumifa that I was no treasure hunter."

Claria backed off. "So you did. Fair enough. I never thought you really meant it, though. I've never known a man who would swim oceans and wrestle vipers and tramp across deserts for anything that he couldn't spend. You are a very unusual man, Cheyne . . . forgive me."

"It's all right. Sorry you won't get what you came for."

"I have no name, either," she went on, ignoring his last comment. "I was about to have one—Maceo would have given me his. I would have been queen for the rest of my days. He told me so, and I believed it would have been true. People would have respected me, would have had me to tea and named their children after me. I wouldn't have had to lift a hand— Neffians everywhere. But now that won't happen."

"If that was your only choice, I wouldn't be too sorry if I were you."

"How would you know what it's like to live in Sumifa without a name? How would you know what that feels like? People won't look at you, won't meet your eyes. They talk about you as though you weren't in the room, if they let you in the room to begin with."

"I just meant that you seem like someone who needs more out of life than to be waited on."

"Oh . . . like what?"

"Like a regular challenge, something that would make your talents shine, keep your mind sharp. You handle those combs like an assassin handles blades. You don't run from a fight—in fact, I'd bet you go looking for them sometimes, don't you? A woman like that doesn't sit still and be waited on very well."

Claria turned her head from him, letting the darkness hide how flattered she really was. Something about this cool-headed outlander confused her, made her think of herself differently than the way she had planned her life. Trouble was, she rather liked it. Though she had crossed the desert, been attacked by hostiles, and swam against time and tide to save her life, she had never had a better time in all her city-living days. Cheyne wasn't hard to look at, either. And he was right. Thoughts of herself as the queen of the citadel were somehow less appealing out here. She considered all that she might have had with Maceo, against what she had now—the only thing she truly owned, the chroniclave. It didn't seem so uneven anymore. As she turned the possibilities of what the matching glyph on the chroniclave's base might mean, one thing was becoming very clear. She would have to tell Cheyne about it, whether it meant giving up her inheritance or not.

"I have something to tell you . . ." she began weakly, but he did not hear her.

"Look, that must be the floating city." He pointed through the trees at what looked like a marooned forest, piles of timber and branches stuck on a bit of rock in the sluggish stream. All along the water's edges, bits of debris tilted and bunched, frozen in an icy, haphazard hedge.

Wiggulf stopped to take in the sight of his home. Then he began to cry. "What has happened to it?"

"The ice queen has frozen the mother waters, Father. Barely a trickle of the mighty stream that once flowed under our feet in the lodge remains liquid. Our people are starving for fish and have taken to hunting the forest, instead—I tried to tell you how little food we have. But you are home now. All that will change," said Frijan.

"It looks to me like the river is still pretty high," said Og.

Wiggulf shook his head slowly. "Not a tenth of it remains passable. None of the rock used to show. Where the stream passes under the lodge, there—that is the way all of it once was." He halted them at the icy shoreline and waited for the guard to appear.

Cheyne found himself fighting to focus on the misty island in the middle of the river, but after awhile, if he persisted in looking at just the same place, it took more definite form. He could make out what looked like a log jam, huge trees cut down and hauled into place to form a sort of floating barrier. A very effective one, he thought. If people tried to walk out on that, falling would be inevitable, and if the cold water didn't kill them, the disturbed logs banging together could easily crush swimmers before they ever got to the lodge. Then from the mist itself, Cheyne thought, six more selkies appeared before them and saluted Frijan.

"Your king is home. Clear the way for him and his guests," she commanded, and they immediately dove under the icy logjam, disappearing in the dark waters. In a few moments, the timbers parted, and several huge otters bobbed and swam in the wake.

"Go, orc. They will see that you don't drown. Just lie back and relax," said Wiggulf.

Yob obeyed, having little strength to do otherwise. The otters caught him from underneath and ferried him somewhat roughly to the lodge, but his head never sank below the waterline.

"Can't you do some magic here, Og? I don't want to dip into that water again." Claria stood frowning at the river's edge.

"I'm a little worn out, if you please. And I haven't had a drink since before we left Sumifa," said Og, his eyes bleary and tired behind his huge, sun-blistered nose.

"Are there no rafts?" asked Cheyne.

"We keep nothing around that would provide access to our lodge by our enemies. Unfortunately, it discomfits our friends as well. It will be a quick crossing, though the water will be unnaturally cold," said Frijan to the others. "Concentrate on your breathing and know that we will be there to bear you up should you falter."

Claria set her jaw and went next, under her own power, then Og with Cheyne's help. Wiggulf and Frijan brought up the rear, visible only as sleek, dark streaks under the low fog.

As the cold, black water swirled around his head, Cheyne felt rinsed of the layers of salt from the seawater, his skin soothed by the river's gentle current. But for Og clinging to his back, he could almost have fallen asleep, sinking down into frigid peace, forgetting why he had ever wanted to be anywhere else. At length, Claria brushed against him, and he reached numbly for the rock that appeared in front of him.

"Cheyne, are you all right?" She crawled up after him onto the river-worn boulder.

"I think so. Yes." He shook his head, clearing it, his thoughts coming sharper and faster again. A few seconds passed before Wiggulf and Frijan appeared from behind them.

"You did well. Despite our best efforts, the water is still fouled with deathsleep from Drufalden's cold heart. Let's get inside where the fires are. You're all shaking," said Frijan, climbing over the smooth rocks to a wooden platform.

Og slung off his pack and dripped steadily, regarding the selkie's blue-and-purple earring, which he still clutched tightly in his hand.

"I might be able to help you," the songmage managed to stutter, despite his chattering teeth. "But I'll need to ask to keep your stone," he added quietly, his eyes upon Wiggulf.

"My daughter knows the state of our affairs with Drufalden far better than I at this time, Ogwater. I must defer to her judgment."

Frijan shrugged, pointing to the doorway. "When Drufalden's heart thaws, the river will be warm and the fish will return. Until then, we suffer her icy curse. And we need the stone. I can never give it up."

"No, I mean, I could really help you. With the river," said the songmage, reluctantly handing the sapphire to Frijan under Cheyne's hard glance.

Frijan peered at him intently, then turned to examine Wiggulf's solemn face. "All right, we will counsel together."

Cheyne and Claria helped Yob up the slippery, ice-encrusted stairs, and soon they were all resting, higher and drier, in the great hall of the lodge around a crackling driftwood fire.

"Move faster, Rotapan. I have never been this cold in my entire life," complained Riolla through her chattering teeth. "How does Drufalden bear this?"

She pulled her thin silk robe around her shoulders more tightly and gave the half-orc a bit of a kick. He turned on her with sharp little fangs bared, but then remembered that Saelin, who had wordlessly joined them moments earlier, was once again at his heels, and hurried his steps a bit more. It was hard going. Drufalden's mountain was really an old burned-out volcano, and the sides were covered in alternate patches of thick ice and barren lava runs, which were encrusted by layers of hardened ash and natural glass

fragments. Here are there, steam vents offered relief
from the frigid air and the bleak landscape, their pockets of lush greenery scattered like so many oases over
upon the mountain.

"Look ahead—I see a rising mist, honored Schreefa.
Perhaps there is warm spring there." Saelin pointed to
a low-hanging white cloud just ahead of them. "In any
case, we are losing the light. Perhaps camping would
be preferable to this current misery?"

"Yes, I believe there might be a warm spring over
there. There used to be one on the caravan road, I
recall. Perhaps I can be warmed, after all." She gave
Rotapan another boot toward the rising steam, much
to Saelin's relief. "We camp for the night. Rotapan,
you will climb the mountain, make the arrangements
for the army, and return to us here."

"What? Am I not just as weary as you? You would
send me up there alone?" whimpered Rotapan.

Giving him a grimace and no more, Riolla entered
the small but dense jungle that had grown up around
the warm spring. Huge arrow-shaped leaves dripped
condensation off their pointed tips and the warm
spring filled the thick air with a soothing gurgle.

"Your archenemy has no more power than you right
now. I have it on the best authority that she'll see you.
Saelin will go with you as your bodyguard. Stop whin-
ing, Rotapan," she admonished, giving the crestfallen
Saelin a signal to find some food. "Drufalden's spies
have surely told her we are here. Their eyes are everywhere. Do you forget whom I represent? I'm sure if
you explain that the Raptor himself has interest in this,
she will listen. Here, take this."

She handed him the coin the Raptor had given her.
Rotapan looked at the gold piece with keen interest,
then dropped it into his deep pocket. She picked a
spotted orchid bloom from a low-hanging limb and put
it in her hair as Saelin summoned his last bit of
patience, bent a short tree, and cut down its hand of
ripe miniature bananas for her.

Rotapan curled his mouth into a silent, bitter sneer as he turned toward the trail up to the summit, up to the ice-ridden castle, Saelin close behind him, Riolla's whispered instructions fresh in his ears. High above, at the mist-shrouded summit of the old volcano, Rotapan thought he saw a dark whirlwind stirring the snow into a blizzard.

"Do not harm the young man. Do not touch him, do not let him be touched by any of your Rimscalla guards," said the Raptor.

Drufalden's pale, almost colorless, eyes followed the shadowy figure as it paced back and forth in her darkened chambers. She studied the sway of the crimson cloak as it brushed over the polished floors, never quite touching them. The click of the Raptor's heels echoed through the carved ice hallways and played against the stone archways like music over water.

Here, inside the mountain, she had always been safe, never really believing this man, if he were man, existed. But here was the Raptor, just as Riolla had said so long ago. Just as her mother had spoken of in her raving madness, before dying in the coldest dungeon in Almaaz. Drufalden wondered how he had moved past her guards; his cloak showed no evidence of travel, or of the snow that locked her land. And just as Riolla had said, he had demanded near darkness and that every reflective surface in the room be covered. And Drufalden could not, no matter how hard she tried, see his face. The hood concealed every feature, and his voice seemed to come from the air around her ears instead of from under that dark red hood.

It had been a long time since a man with any power had stood in her presence. It was . . . enticing. How refreshing and invigorating it was to have a new mystery, a new territory to . . . explore. Drufalden smiled alluringly into the shadows.

"Cooperate with my agent, let the digger pass unharmed to the Chimes, and you will have your trinket back, and the Wyrvil kingdom along with it. And by the way . . . your tribute to Nin is long overdue, Drufalden. We can begin with that coin the Wyrvil will give you. I hope your spies have already delivered the rest to Riolla's shop."

"So you will heal our waters, but your price is our stone?" said Frijan, her eyes upon Og.

After a hearty meal of fish and zebramussels, Frijan and Wiggulf sat with Og over cups made of conch shells, drinking mead in the low firelight of the lodge's great hall. Og stretched lazily, but his eyes were sharp and attentive behind his bulbous, peeling nose.

"Yes. I think I can bring the warmth back to them. Melt the ice upstream," said Og.

"The stone is our only defense against two enemies, Muje Rifkin," she countered.

"If I melt the ice that keeps your waters locked, Drufalden's kingdom falls to ruin. It's only the cold that keeps her magical forces alive. They are made of ice and thought alone. And Rotapan has only an imaginary god to contend with. He is of no real threat without this ajada. It seems to me that this is your only hope of recovery. Until her spell is broken, your waters will continue to freeze, the ice continue to creep toward your lodge. Moving again and again will force you closer to the poisoner's waters. If you give me your stone, I can take care of that problem, too."

"Perhaps. But what guarantee do we have that you will break Drufalden's icespell? We have tried and tried ourselves, ever since we found the stone. Nothing works for long. How do we know you would not melt the waters for a day or two, be on your way, and then they would freeze again? And how do we know that Rotapan will not find a way to take back the ajada from you? He stalks you now, and has the Sumifan Schreefa to help him. We cannot protect you beyond our own borders," said Frijan. The water sapphire glittered at her ear.

"No," she continued. "I will tell you right now that I cannot consent. It is better to have power that we have not learned to use than none at all."

She left Og at the table and moved toward the center of the hall, where a huge log crackled and sparked in the heart of a natural fireplace, a hollow rock formation that rose from the riverbed through the rafters. More than a hundred selkies sat rapt at a game in progress as Frijan found a place next to her father. Yob had showed them a Wyrvil game with daggers, and the competition had become serious.

Wiggulf had to stop his ears with his fingers when Yob's dagger sank into the cross-cut tree round's center yet again. In the fifth and last round of their game, the big orc had struck home every throw, besting even the selkies' finest marksman. With years of Javin's demanded practice behind him, Cheyne was the only one who could still throw as well, and if he made his target now, he would win the match. Wiggulf looked around his beloved hall with chagrin. If Cheyne missed, Yob would very possibly tear up the whole lodge in celebration.

"I will bet you that gold ring the orc wins. The man is good, but this is an orcish game," whispered Frijan to Claria.

Claria quirked her mouth at the selkie, her feelings stung beyond reason at the challenge. She twisted Maceo's ring on her finger, wondering if it was still stuck, but it floated easily over her knuckle. Strangely, Claria realized she didn't care if she lost the ring. She cared only that Cheyne won.

"All right. My ring if he loses. But your coral knife if he wins," said Claria, her hand awaiting Frijan's on the bet.

"May I have part of this wager?" said Og, suddenly at Frijan's elbow.

"What would you have to bet, songmage?" asked the selkie.

"My other stone. For your stone. Since you won't part with it any other way, let me give you a chance for both of them."

Claria met Og's blank face with horror, but he kicked her sharply under the trestle table before she could make a sound. From deep in his sleeve, he brought forth the ajada, hummed a little low song over it, and put it on the table in front of Frijan. The selkie's eyes widened with amazement as her sworn enemy's source of power glittered within her reach. The human had only to miss, and he was long overdue. She looked up at Og, unable to resist such a possibility.

"You're on," she said amid the noise and shuffle of other wagers and the dull clink of shell cups. Og smiled genuinely while Claria snatched up his brimming cup and downed its contents in one toss.

The dank, smoky room became very quiet as Cheyne, completely unaware of what rode on his skill, loosened his shoulders and stepped back to throw. He glanced at Claria, who smiled at him a bit drunkenly, and drew back his arm. Yob's little yellow eyes followed his every motion, his face tight and drawn, his sharp claws drumming lightly on the tabletop, where he nursed a bucketful of mead. With no further thought, Cheyne brought the dagger to its mark in a quick, hard throw. It sank deeply into the center of the tree round with a satisfying *thunk*.

Wiggulf strode over to check the degree of accuracy, pulled out the dagger, and proclaimed, "He has crossed the orc's cut! It is a perfect throw!"

The selkies cheered, Frijan handed over her coral knife to Claria, and Og raised a new cup in salute, wishing fondly it was full of raqa instead of Wiggulf's cloying mead.

Cheyne took a mock bow, chuckled at his victory, and went to shake Yob's hand. But Yob only looked at Cheyne with stunned silence. He set the mead bucket down quietly, and Wiggulf held up his hand for silence. The chatter stopped immediately. Yob took a deep breath and raised his hand to Cheyne.

"No one has ever bested me, human. You own my service now. I offer you my life."

"What?" Cheyne blinked as a strong whiff of woodsmoke washed over his face, and when it cleared, Yob still had one hand in the air, but the other held his own dagger at his heart. "I await your choice, human. My life or my death."

Cheyne looked for Og in the crowd, and the songmage stepped out dramatically, bowed to Yob, and began to explain.

"Such a thing is customary among the Wyrvil. If a Wyrvil takes on an opponent in this game, he or she must win or their life is forfeit. Yob is a Wyrvil underking. This very game was the way he won his kingdom," said Og. Yob nodded, his eyes trained on Cheyne.

Cheyne stared back in disbelief. "You have played for your life?"

The songmage pretended not to notice the look Claria threw him as he pocketed Frijan's earring.

"You did not know? This game is always for life. Had you lost, you would be my subject now, or you would have to take your own life. But say what you would have of me. Service or death," said Yob, unflinching.

"Yob, I am unwilling that you should die for such foolishness—"

"It is no foolish!" roared the orc.

"All right. All right. Then . . . service. Live, my . . . friend," said Cheyne, still baffled.

Yob's knees buckled under him as he returned his bulk to the bench. He sheathed the dagger and raised his drink.

"To service," he said, and the selkies nervously joined the toast.

"His entire kingdom is yours now. That's all the land outside Sumifa from the oasis to the scrubland," whispered Og excitedly to Cheyne.

Cheyne pulled the songmage back into the shadows, picked him up bodily, and dangled him by his collar out the only window in the lodge. "What do you mean, letting me throw with him? I could have lost my life to that big greenskin! And you would have lost your fee! Does this make any sense at all, Ogwater? Hmmm?"

Og hung onto Cheyne's arms for all he was worth. The mist had cleared and the ice in the river was clearly visible under the bright starlight. "I knew you would win!" he choked out. "There was no need to make you nervous. We need the water sapphire!"

"So that's it? You had a *side* bet? Ogwater!"

"It was the only way I could get Frijan to give it up. Selkies can't resist a game, you know, especially if you put something shiny in front of them. And as I just, ah, said, we need the water sapphire." Og looked down at the dark, cold water. He could already feel his feet tingling. "Someone has to heal these waters! We must have this stone."

"*You* must have this stone! *I* must get on to the forest as quickly as possible and stop letting you drag me into your old, unsettled intrigues."

"Uh-oh," said Ogwater, his attention diverted to the shoreline, where a mist-shrouded figure dropped a loose log into the river.

"What now?" asked Cheyne, tiring of his threat, and hauled Og back in through the window.

"We have company," moaned Og. He turned to Wiggulf, eyes blazing with desperation. "I'm sorry, Riverking. I have to go now!"

The songmage clutched the ajada and the water sapphire together in his hands and began to sing for all he was worth. Before Cheyne could reach him, he had disappeared in a swirl of light the color of fire.

CHAPTER
15

OG'S BOOT FIRMLY IN HAND, WOMBA BOARD-
ed the log she had freed from the icy riverbank, and
charged into the freezing river, disdaining the help of
the delta guard, oblivious to the water's icy touch.
Within seconds, she had spanned the current and
climbed dripping onto the dock. She shook herself
from head to foot, entered through the lodge door, and
made a dash for Og.

Who, of course, had disappeared completely. Yob
held his arms out for his damp daughter, but she
hardly saw him.

"Where? Where is he?" She began to sniff the air.

Claria slid slowly behind Cheyne, but it was too late,
Womba's keen nose had already discerned the faintest
smell of bergamot and myrrh.

"You! You have taken my Ogwater! You have
bewitched him. I will make war clubs of your leg
bones and earrings of your ugly white teeth!" she
shouted so loudly that three of the selkies scattered to
the other side of the lodge.

"As you can plainly see," said Claria indignantly,
"Ogwater is not with me." She lifted her hand to her
hair with a juma flourish.

Womba bared her teeth. It occurred to Yob and
Cheyne at the same time what was about to happen next.
Cheyne stepped between them and gently, firmly, took
Claria's hand—and the comb in it—into his own just as
Yob threw his massive arms around his daughter.

"I am so glad to see you safe and well and beautiful,
as always, my little flower," rumbled Yob, tightening
his arms around her like iron bands.

"Muje Rifkin is indeed gone, orcess. We are not hiding him," Cheyne repeated.

Caught in Yob's powerful embrace, Womba curled a
nostril back and sniffed the air, unsatisfied with that
possibility.

"Then where has he gone?" said Wiggulf.

Frijan stared miserably out of the portal into the
dark, cold night. The river swirled under her, and the
three sisters winked in and out of the cloudspun sky.

"I cannot answer you, Father. But I have done a terrible, unforgivable thing. I have lost the waterstone to
the songmage."

She continued to face the riverbank, her tears dropping into the dark currents below. Wiggulf came up
beside her and put his short arm around her.

"Yes, yes, you did, but this time I think the best has
come of it, daughter. And do you not know that if I
can learn to respect and understand people who have
been my enemies, there is nothing I would not forgive
in you? Look."

He nodded to the water below. The glassy shelf,
ever present around the shoreline, had completely
melted, and the ice-locked brush had already been
swept away. The river seemed wider, faster. Frijan
heard the grind and shudder of an ice floe breaking up
far to the east.

"You see? He has healed our waters. The stone was
always his, Frijan. It has been our privilege to keep it
safe these years until he came for it. It has been so
from the beginning. The stone found its way back to
him, daughter, just as I found my way back here,

where I belong. If it had not happened this way, it would have been another. Have peace, daughter, you were only trying to do a good thing for your kingdom. And next time, you will know better than to game with Ogwater."

Cheyne cleared his throat from behind Wiggulf's back. "Riverking, it has been a long day and a long night. We will need to rise early and be on our way to the forest."

"Oh, of course, of course, Cheyne, but how will you ever find your way?" Wiggulf chuckled.

"Well, it's just beyond your borders, is it not?"

"In a manner of speaking. The elves are fairly particular about who comes to their homeland. Only they know the passages through the curtain of light; if you try to enter without escort, you will never find your way out of the woods. We have seen many travelers, sometimes years after they entered the elves' territories alone and unbidden, come stumbling out, so confused they did not know their own names anymore. What is it you seek there, boy?" Wiggulf cocked a dark silver eye up at Cheyne and waited for him to answer.

"I doubt I would find myself wandering and forgetful of my name, sire. I won't even know what it is until I find the elves." Cheyne smiled ruefully. He took out the totem to show Wiggulf the mysterious glyph. "I need for them to translate this."

"I see," said Wiggulf. "Well, then we will help provide for your journey. And I will take you as far as the curtain of light myself. I want to see the land again, anyway. We will leave tomorrow."

He motioned to a couple of young, moonfaced boys playing at pickup sticks, and they sped off in different directions to gather food and clothing for Cheyne and Claria.

"Looks like it's just us now." Cheyne turned to Claria and smiled crookedly, like the day when he had split his lip in the fight in Sumifa. A little scar from that fight, very new, still puckered a bit.

She smiled back, covertly twisting the ring on her finger on and off, courting its loss through the wooden slats in the lodge floor. The river moved below, dark and quiet and deep.

Cheyne bowed to Wiggulf and made his way to one of five pallets, already laid out by the boys. Yob immediately lay down inches from him, so close that the orc's breath cut through the air between them like a poisoned knife.

By the window Womba gazed over the thawing river and up at the moons as she constantly sniffed the air. When she finally caught the scent she was hoping for, no one saw her slide out the door and lower herself onto the loose log and pushed off over the mist-covered water.

Long after the fires of the great hall had been banked, and the tired group had given themselves to their fragrant, overstuffed pillows, Cheyne lay awake, staring into the dark, bark-covered rafters and thinking. Gentle waves rocked against the lodge's sunken pilings, and he could see the moons and the three sisters dancing on the dark water through a crack in the flooring. Yob snored to one side and Claria lay curled a few feet away on the other, her black hair spilling over the pallet and onto the polished wooden floor.

The parrot feathers from the oasis were long gone, but one red ribbon wove itself through a small braid at her temple, and one of the brass combs was still tucked safely behind her ear, inches from her fingers. Her blanket had fallen from her arms and she shivered at the touch of a sudden draft from under the lodge. The fragrance of bergamot and myrrh wafted lightly over him, and before he knew it, Cheyne was reaching over to cover her bare shoulder with his own blanket. Her hand lay between them, and he smiled as he studied her long thin fingers, the first two, so like the hand in his vision, crooked at the first joint. They were a little pale from the cold floor, and he almost put his hand over hers to warm them.

Just then the fire flickered and Maceo's ring gleamed brightly on her third finger, a constant reminder to Cheyne that Claria's heart still belonged to another. One who had betrayed her, no less. He shut his eyes against the thought of it. Claria shifted in her sleep and burrowed back under her covers, and he inched back to his own bed, his mind and heart completely at odds. He didn't know exactly when he had started to love the girl.

Only that he would somehow have to stop.

He rolled over on his pallet and tried to think about anything else. In the morning, Wiggulf would lead them through the winding paths of his watery kingdom to the curtain of light at the edge of the elves' sanctuary. At least then he would discover his name. And wasn't that why he'd come all this way?

Claria opened her eyes at his sharp motion, but did not move. For an hour or more, she had pretended to sleep, unable to calm her mind. Since the long walk in the forest to the lodge, all she could think about was the strange exhilaration and brightness she felt. It seemed the farther she went from Sumifa, the more free she was. Every sense seemed sharpened out here, and her skin had grown dark with the sun. Gone were the headaches she constantly fought in the city, the malaise of the dusty streets and dry days. The journey thus far had been the most arduous thing she had ever experienced, but she was thriving.

What if Maceo could see me now? What would he think? she wondered. Claria realized that she wasn't even mad at him anymore and didn't care that he preferred the Schreefa. Her time with Maceo seemed like a distant memory after the last few days. The heavy gold band felt like a shackle on her finger. She just wanted to return the ring and be done with him. He, after all, was certainly done with her.

Beside her lay Cheyne, a man with no name and no ring to give her. He was by far the bravest man she had ever known. But that same bravery made him too driven to notice her, too polite to look her way. Claria knew she would always have his compassion, but she could never hope for his love. She let tears well up in her eyes and fall, but made not the slightest sound. When this was all over, at least she would have a good story for Vashki.

But that was probably all. As soon as Cheyne reached the Sarrazan forest, he would have no need of her anymore. There would be no treasure to divide. And Riolla would probably never let her back into the city, once that man-eating canista was on Sumifa's throne, may Maceo live long enough to appreciate his bride for her true value.

Claria shut her eyes and tried to fall asleep. Tomorrow would be another long day. Another day closer to Cheyne's destination.

Javin's hand had begun to burn again three miles ago, but he had said nothing to Doulos. The slave would have begged him to stop and take care of it, and they would have lost sight of Riolla and her odd companions. The trail blazed through the mountain scrubland was clear enough: two sets of human prints and the twisted claw marks of the half-orc. Rotapan, Doulos had called him—supposedly king of the ferocious Wyrvils.

The night had begun with a clear sky, but the higher they climbed toward the mountain, the less of it they could see. Finally, Javin could bear the pain no longer, and he motioned Doulos off the trail.

"Let's camp here for the night. We can't see the trail anyway. But that means they can't, either. So here is as good as anywhere. There are some big rocks over there that will make for good cover," he whispered. "Why don't you look for some tinder for a fire?" Doulos nodded and made for the rocks.

When the slave was far enough ahead, Javin peeled back the old bandage and held his hand close, trying to see the wound. But it was futile: the night was too dark and the mist too heavy. He hurried to catch up with Doulos before he lost him in the fog.

In a few minutes, Javin's firestone had sparked a low flame for a fire within the sheltering ring of boulders, and they were hunched over its flickering light.

"I hope they don't see this light, Doulos. Granted, we could probably take them, but the idea is to let them lead us to Cheyne. Your friend Ghazi was of much help with that information," said Javin softly. "I'm sorry he didn't . . . "

"He knew his life was worth very little to the Schreefa. But I am sorry, too. She never let him learn to swim, you know. Her slaves never worked the river," said Doulos. "I have lost many friends, Muje. But each time becomes no easier for the previous experience."

They sat in silence for a time, watching the fire. At length, Javin took out his knife and began to pass it through the flames.

Doulos looked up at him, puzzled. "Again, Muje? It has been only a few hours."

Javin nodded. Every time Javin lanced it, the sting had closed over and appeared to be healing, but then the dark poison rose up inside and the fever came upon him, the fiery pain shooting up through his hand and arm all over again, just as it had that night back at the ruin. If he could get to Cheyne and then to the Borderlands, if he could just find the forest . . .

"Doulos, do you know anything about the Sarrazan healing legends?" said Javin, cleaning the knife in the sand.

"Not much, Muje. Only that the juma said no poison could stay there. They dance, the elves. They whirl and beat their magical rhythms on the forest floor with their feet, and the evil is drawn from wounds, and the poisons lose their power. That's what I know, Muje. Why?"

"If that's where I were going, would you go, too? I have heard the stories, too."

Javin passed his knife back and forth over the fire again, put a fold of his tunic in his teeth, then applied the tip of the knife to the wound. He bit down hard on the cloth hard as the hot knife seared his skin, opening the tough scar and relieving the poison's awful pressure. The stench was hideous. He relaxed, breathing hard, his face flushed and red with exertion. It was worse every time. The skin thickened more and the poison welled up from deeper and deeper. Back at the ruin, Muni had wanted the doctor to take the finger. Javin had since thought better of his friend's harsh wisdom and brutal compassion; a quick chop then would have saved him this savagery at his own hand time and again. He felt along his arm and up his sleeve, where the swelling strained and pulled at his darkening skin. Muni had been right. Now the bite threatened his entire arm.

Doulos sat thinking about Javin's question, his blue eyes catching the firelight. "Yes, Muje. I have sworn it. It is true that there are many stories about how the forest moves, how time changes or stops in there. How men have been lost in a wavering curtain of light as they rode in plain view. You would not go without good reason. The juma stories also say the elves' medicine is hard to bear."

"The cure cannot be worse than this," said Javin.

"Muje, the juma said the poison comes out only when the elves dance and call down the holy lightning. Strikes you in the heart. Hurts much worse."

"But it heals."

"It heals. Or it kills."

Javin slouched against the cold rock, letting the chill take the heat from his face. Doulos banked the fire for the night and stood up to take the first watch.

"I will wake you when the moons pass the sisters," the slave said.

Javin nodded, rebandaged his arm, and found his blanket. Doulos climbed the rangy oak above them, settling back on a large bough and wrapping his robes about himself against the cold night.

Doulos never knew when he drifted off, but when he awoke, the moons were not only past the sisters, but nearly down. High over Drufalden's mountain, one bright light flared briefly through the fog, then died like a falling star.

Then there were six stars. Then twenty. The wind changed, and the unmistakable odor of canistas assaulted Doulos's nose, their foul, musty scent choking him. The slave whirled around, his spear ready. But there were too many targets. The canistas blinked redly at him through the white mist, then dropped their huge jaws open, and he could see their long, bright teeth. One of them began to chuckle, a low, almost human laugh. *Like Riolla's laugh,* Doulos thought, *like the Schreefa about to eat you alive.*

The laughter spread, growing louder and louder until the Neffian was surrounded with the hideous sound, his ears ringing with pain, his eyes suddenly unable to find the leaping, cavorting canistas as they prowled the foggy campsite, circling closer and closer to Javin.

Doulos knew if he made a sound, they would all spring upon the wounded man as one and tear his king to pieces before Doulos could reach him. If he didn't shout a warning, they would only move in steadily, playing their game, ripping and teasing Javin to death, and then turn upon Doulos himself. It seemed hopeless.

Doulos looked skyward, mouthed a silent prayer, and raised his spear. If he was going to die, he would take some company with him. He backed up one step, bracing himself, and felt the massive oak at his back like another fighter. Doulos put his foot into the next branch down and lowered himself to the ground, ever so slowly, holding his breath, listening beyond the hideous laughter for sounds that Javin was conscious.

One more limb down, and he would be able to throw the spear. . . .

In the darkest hours of the night, Cheyne finally found sleep, but no peace. The bad dreams of his youth came back, this time with an intensity and sharpness he had not experienced since the months directly after Javin had brought him home for the first time. Over and over again, he saw the figure with the clawed hand drop down onto him, ready to devour him, and the shape of the totem's glyph flashed in front of his eyes like a bright beacon.

Then the dream shifted to a terrifying new image. He saw Javin, his hand awash in flames, the fire about to consume his body, fighting dark shapes in the moonlight. The three sisters tilted overhead, and a hundred gleaming red eyes burned in the darkness, circling and closing on Javin.

Cheyne awoke, his lungs strained with unvoiced agony. He sat up and peered around the lodge, slowly remembering where he was. Claria lay still and lovely in the darkness, moonlight glowing on her skin as it shone down through the lodge's skylight. But Cheyne thought he was still dreaming when, out of the shadows of the smoky lodge, stepped a tall elf, his face divided by a long scar, a silver chain for his belt and a brooch carved with the glyphs of the Sarrazan potters upon his breast.

"You!" Cheyne shouted. "Who are you? Have you been following us, too?"

"Who's there?" said Wiggulf sleepily from the far side of the hall.

The tall elf held up his hand, long thin fingers pale in the low firelight. "Forgive me, Riverking, for the intrusion. But I have urgent business with your guests and have just come from the Treefather with a message for the Argivan."

"Naruq? Is that you? You are always welcome here. But why do you come under the cloak of secrecy?" said Wiggulf, ambling over, dragging his covers, his round face troubled.

"There is one who seeks this man's life." Naruq pointed to Cheyne. "And his killer has been watching me for a very long time. I have risked enough by coming here, by showing myself in Sumifa before. I could make no direct contact."

Cheyne threw off his blanket and stood up, hand on his dagger. "So you *were* in Sumifa. I know Riolla's henchman is spoiling for my head. That's no secret."

"It's not the assassin Saelin you need consider. Although that fight outside Riolla's shop was a little too close for my liking. You handled yourself well, though. And you make friends fast, it seems."

"Who is the Treefather?" said Cheyne.

Wiggulf pulled at his bushy beard. "He's the Sarrazan elder. The Ancient. He never leaves the forest. No one knows how old he really is, but there are rumors that he was around at the time of the Wandering. If anyone would know what your totem says, he would."

"And he does. He has been expecting you since the lost caravan. He will answer all your questions. Time is of little consequence to the Treefather, but not to you. The curtain will part for us only for another hour."

If the elf had pierced him through the heart with his own knife, Cheyne could not have been more surprised. It was the answer to his every prayer. He had come so far on sheer hope. And to find the answer to his greatest need, he had only to go now, this minute, with Naruq.

And leave Javin to his death. The dream had followed him into consciousness. With every passing second, Cheyne's conviction of Javin's predicament grew even more certain.

"Naruq, I can't go with you."

Claria looked at him through sleepy, unbelieving,

eyes. "Cheyne, why not? This is what you have come all this way for," she said groggily.

"Because Javin's in danger somewhere behind us." He crawled out from under the thick covers and found his boots. By now, the whole lodge had awakened and Frijan had lit a candle with an ember from the fire.

"What is it? Intruders?" she whispered, looking out the window toward the riverbank.

"My father . . ." Cheyne began.

"I will go with you," said Claria, rising and folding her bedding.

"No. Please. I don't—"

"Need help? Really?" she interrupted fiercely.

"I don't want to worry about you, too. Please. Please," he begged her, holding her hands in his, Maceo's ring a cold reminder of their different paths. "It may already be too late."

"Then I will go," another voice added. "My nose can find them in the dark."

Cheyne turned and saw Yob looming over him in the eerie light of the low fire. His big jaw was set and he had found a spear.

CHAPTER

16

"JAVIN!" THE SHOUT ECHOED THROUGH THE
rocks from Doulos's left.

"Cheyne?" came the weak answer. "Is that really
you?"

A hail of stones rained down on the snarling, laughing canistas, and they broke off the attack and scattered through the low brush in all directions.

"We are here, Muje! By the tree," cried Doulos.

Just then, the canistas, no longer confused, herded
back together and bounded through the brush and
charging Cheyne and Yob. Half the pack separated
and circled warily around the orc while three others
took turns rushing Cheyne. The beasts were quicker
than anything Cheyne had ever fought, and seemed to
enjoy dancing in and out of his dagger's range, snapping at his heels as he whirled around and around,
keeping them away. The others, wide grins on their
slavering jaws, paced around Yob and began to narrow their circles.

They were within seconds of closing in when Doulos
began to yell an ancient Neffian war cry at the top of
his lungs from the tree. The shrill sound bounced
around the flinty rocks and echoed off the mountain-

side, causing the canistas to hesitate just long enough for the big orc to drive through their circle and reach Cheyne. As they met, Cheyne pressed himself to Yob's back, and when the canistas rejoined the attack, two of them had their throats slit before they knew it. They fell slowly, never seeming to notice they were dying, their jaws continuing to snap and snarl. The others hopped over the bodies of their packmates with no concern. Frustrated, Doulos could not aim his spear for their constant motion.

"Over to the fire, Yob," cried Cheyne. The orc grunted his understanding and they began to move slowly, a step at a time, toward the dying fire. "Good. Get ready."

Cheyne took his opening when one of the beasts jostled another and fell into the firepit. The fire caught at its fur instantly, but the beast died before it felt the burning as Doulos finally got his opportunity to stab it. Cheyne leapt away from Yob, retrieved the spear with a quick jerk, and rolled the dead canista off the embers.

He took the stick on which Doulos had roasted a rabbit and stirred the embers into new life as Yob moved around behind the fire, keeping the rocks at his back. The canistas drew back, growling low. Cheyne cautiously worked the fire until it caught on the greasy stick, then he advanced on the canistas, swinging the flaming stick in the midst of them.

He tossed Yob the spear, then ran from behind the firebed, crushing the pack together, causing them to turn and bite one another in their fear and frenzy. There were still too many. At least they still couldn't get to Javin. The biggest of them broke from the fur fight and loped off a short distance to gather speed, then ran back at Cheyne. Cheyne stood his ground as the beast charged, and opened him from breastbone to belly with his dagger as the canista leapt onto him. Their leader dead, the others scattered, wailing and crying and snickering into the night.

"Good fighting, master. We don't have long," said

Yob. "They'll come back again. Canistas are a worthy enemy. They never give up."

"Neither do I, Yob. We'll play until we win," said Cheyne, wiping the dark, sticky blood from his dagger and hands. "Come on."

They found Javin with Doulos crouched protectively over him, quietly weeping. Javin appeared to have lost a lot of blood from several bites. Javin was calling for his son. Cheyne bent over him, straining to hear what his foster father was saying.

"Cheyne . . . I thought I would never see you again. Are you safe?"

"Yes, very safe. And so are you, now, Javin."

"I found him . . . the Collector."

Cheyne smiled, his ears alert for the canistas. "I'm glad, Javin."

"There is something you must know." Javin's breathing had suddenly become shallow and far too fast.

"What's wrong with him? He's not hurt that badly." Cheyne clutched at Doulos as he ground out the words. Doulos pointed to Javin's exposed arm, where the poison had advanced up to his shoulder.

"He says it was the Raptor. He followed you because you are in terrible danger," said Doulos, his face bleak in the starlight. Cheyne let the slave go and bent closer to hear, hoping Javin had the strength to say what he intended.

"The caravan. You were right, Cheyne, I never told you . . . all. But if I had, the way I hid you from him would never have worked. I was on my way to the forest with that caravan to dig for the Collector. When the Raptor came, you were bringing water to the animals. One of the droms had loosened its hobbles, and you had gone far afield to find it. By the time you returned, the Raptor's agent, an elf with a scar across his cheek, had killed everyone but me. But he didn't know about you. That day, when you came back from the wood, I took you and hid you from him.

"Your amulet . . . for centuries, we have passed it

down one to another, in the Circle. It was the Collector's, and some of his magic has remained upon it. I am no good with magic, but I used the amulet to take away the picture in your mind of your identity. That's why you cannot see yourself. If you do not know who you are, then he cannot know who you are.

"Cheyne, the Circle ends with me . . . I am the last. The Raptor, he has hunted us down over the centuries, finding us no matter how well we hid. Many times, I have been within his grasp, and he let me go. This time he tried to kill me. It could only be because of you, and the Clock . . . "

"Because of the treasure?" Cheyne repeated incredulously.

"Yes, but it is you he wants . . . has always wanted. You are the one, you see . . . "

Cheyne looked up at Doulos, who shook his head in bewilderment. Doulos hushed Javin for a moment, listening. Cheyne raised his dagger, thinking the canistas had returned. They waited in silence for awhile, but heard nothing else. Doulos slipped around the boulders for a look, but found only Yob, his spear firmly in hand. From the high branches of the big oak, Naruq leapt and landed without a sound, already counting his fortune.

Cheyne was still holding Javin's head when he began to talk again. "The Clock is really a weapon, made by the Collector long ago, when the brothers fought. The book—"

"Javin, you have the book? The little bronze-bound one? I . . . I found it in the crypt and took it with me. I'm sorry, Javin, I was angry with you. I should have left it for you. I thought it lost forever!"

"It's all right. The book must explain how the Clock works; it has to. The juma writings say . . . it's where the Collector left his clues. You cannot let the beast get out. The Raptor still believes the crystal wall shields a treasure. He will stop at nothing to get it— and you. He is a madman, no man at all anymore . . .

part phantom, his hand a claw." Javin collapsed without another word.

Cheyne huddled over his father for a long while, until Doulos pulled him away and covered Javin with his outer robe.

"What do you know about this?" Cheyne asked Doulos.

The Neffian shrugged his shoulders, took the book from Javin's pack and gave it to Cheyne, who shook his head sadly.

"Only the Treefather can read this. And I've missed my only chance to get through the curtain of light."

With Saelin following at a safe distance and the wind taking his words the other way, Rotapan trudged up the dark, windy mountainside, cursing Riolla loudly and with great exuberance. It made him feel better. More importantly, it made him warm.

Icicles had formed on his long ears by the time he had cleared the tree line. His ill-shod feet were cut and bleeding from the unavoidable patches of obsidian and broken lava, and the only thing that kept him moving upward was the thought of those talking heads and their miserable prophecy. As long as there was a chance to rebuild his tower, to regain his staff, he lurched onward. In his mind, he had already redecorated the topmost pinnacle of the new temple with Riolla's head. The great Lord Chelydrus would enjoy his offering of her adder-poisoned blood.

The higher he climbed, the more an ice cloud obscured his vision. Soon, only the steady strain of moving upward and the dark patches of the barren, wind-scoured rock beneath his feet guided him. He began to imagine smells and noises in the cold fog. A whiff of wet fur and a low growl behind him. The padding of heavy feet in the snow off the trail. The pant and whine of wolves.

And Saelin nowhere around. He should never have trusted Riolla's assassin to watch his back. Fighting for breath, Rotapan quickened his step, looking for possible weapons on the trailside and sending small rocks plinking down the path behind him. He broke stride to pick up a large piece of obsidian, but his hands were so stiff with cold that he fumbled it. When he turned to retrieve the dark glass, he found himself standing within three feet of the biggest white wolf he had ever seen. Rotapan froze in his tracks, cold weapon in hand.

"It will be sweet, that day when the Lord Chelydrus appears to me before my people. Then they will believe," he said aloud, trying to chase his fears with the sound of his own words.

"Believe what?"

The voice behind him was strangely accented. He turned his head to see a gray-eyed Neffian in furs and a silver slave collar and his other companion, the white wolf's mate.

"Don't move. Do you need help? Are you lost?" said the Neffian.

Rotapan turned his head slowly to face forward again. The wolf stood silently gazing at the half-orc for several seconds, then his lips rippled, his nose lifted in a snarl, and he began to growl almost imperceptibly. Rotapan knew if he made the slightest move, the bigger wolf would be upon him. He felt himself close to passing out from fear and lack of air.

Worse still, the other wolf had moved soundlessly closer to his back. He could feel its hot, rank breath upon his neck. Probably the female, thought Rotapan. She might be a little smaller. The male pulled back into a half-crouch, tightening to spring.

Rotapan swallowed hard, took a deep breath, then shrieked a wordless prayer to Chelydrus at the top of his lungs as he tried to run past the female. She whipped her claws into his back as he went down, but Rotapan somehow found her neck and managed to

bring the rock across it, opening her throat with a
frantic swipe of the glass. She yelped once before
dropping. Instantly, the big male sprang over her body
with a magnificent leap, but Rotapan ducked and
caught him in the belly with the same edge that had
killed his mate.

Rotapan looked around for the Neffian, but there
was no sign of him. He cautiously kicked at the dead
wolves, all the while straining to see into the deep mist
where more of them might be waiting. But all he heard
was a hungry pup's distant whimper.

Let him go, thought Rotapan. *He'll starve on his
own, and I can be on my way.*

As he turned to go, Rotapan noticed some sort of
metal band around the female wolf's neck. "Like that
Neffian's collar ... the slaves will come for me now,"
he muttered. "But let them do their worst. Mighty
Chelydrus has protected me. And you I did not need,
worthless Saelin!" He searched his pocket making certain Riolla's Ninnite coin still rested there, and walked
on.

He worked another hour scaling the steep path, slick
with snow and black ice, and finally came upon a more
level road that led into the castle's keep. Before him,
white with five or six inches of fresh snow, stood
Drufalden's crystal gates. If the slaves were going to
ambush him, this would be the most likely place.
Saelin had said there was some kind of secret entrance
just outside the gate, which the slaves used when they
slipped out to hunt.

The thieves' colony supposedly lay just beyond this
point, with Drufalden's castle further up the mountain and within the old volcano's protective shell. If
Rotapan could manage to get past these gates, he
could slip in and deliver his order, asking for a legion
of his own to take back to his temple. After all, he had
the coin. How would Drufalden know until he was
gone that Riolla's orders were any different?

Rotapan slowed his pace and kept to the shadows of

the rock wall, where the mist seemed to linger. But before he had taken another three steps, white-shrouded guards stepped out from the gates and advanced stiffly toward him, swords drawn.

"Stop where you stand!" shouted the one on the left.

Rotapan plastered himself to the rock wall. His knees knocked together and his breath came in gasps. Unbidden, stories of travelers lost on this peak, checking their maps and freezing open-eyed and standing, came racing to his mind. The coin, in his hand for the last few feet, was losing its heat even faster, and felt as though it were stuck to his palm like a searing brand.

The guards shuffled through the heavy snow and stopped a few feet away from him. "We hear you. Show yourself, slave. We have warned you about leaving the colony without our escort," said one of them, his eyes strangely vacant, his breath making no mist in the frigid air.

Rotapan could not move. But from the other side of the path came a faint sound. The Neffian crouched behind a snowbank, holding a whimpering wolf pup inside his furs. Rotapan breathed a slow sigh of relief when he realized he was not the guards' objective. At the sound of the pup's cry, they moved in on the Neffian, affording Rotapan a strange revelation. The guards' skin was as white as their stiff robes, and when he looked directly upon their faces, he could almost see the outline of everything behind them. They looked as though they were made of the same ice that covered the entire top of the mountain. They carried swords made of brilliant crystal and their words hung in the air like the sound of steel on steel.

As they came forward, the Neffian released the pup and silently bade him to stay, then broke from his cover and shot past them as they clashed their swords over his head. The slave ran in through the gates, then took to the even steeper path toward the main entrance of the slave colony, the guards following stiffly, but with amazing speed. Rotapan shrugged and slipped through the silvery gates into the vacant courtyard.

The mist had thinned and the light from the moons and the three sisters sparkled over hundreds of intricate ice sculptures, making the courtyard seem alive with strange animals, flowers, and trees. The half-orc stood transfixed, forgetting the cold, forgetting the guards and the coin in his hand, forgetting his mission and Riolla.

For there in the midst of the cavorting ice sculptures, occupying a massive block of ice, complete with carved waves and the surge of the cauldron, reared the shining, glossy shape of a sea dragon.

"Chelydrus!" breathed Rotapan.

"Amazing, isn't it, Wyrvil? These were carved when her people ruled most of the continent, before the great Thaw. Some say all of them really roamed the world at that time." Saelin's voice came drifting past Rotapan's ear.

"Bow your knee to the god of the waters!" Rotapan snapped, irritated that anyone else would be sharing his audience with Chelydrus. "And just where were you when I was dragged and bloodied and mauled by those wolves?"

Saelin gestured mockingly at the ice sculpture. "Right behind you. Conserving my strength. You didn't seem to need any help. Let's go. The Rimscalla guards won't be long with that slave. I'd rather not have to wait on them."

Before Rotapan could move, Saelin threw a blindfold over his head and jerked the knot tight, setting his dagger's edge at the half-orc's scrawny throat.

"Nobody sees the way in, Wyrvil."

And you won't see the way out, either, he chortled to himself, pointing Rotapan in the direction of Drufalden's castle.

CHAPTER

17

RIOLLA HELD THE SPYGLASS TO HER EYE
and tried to find Rotapan and Saelin through the
mountain mists. For some time, she had been able to
follow them up the craggy sides of Drufalden's
stronghold, but now she had lost them.

"I don't like this one bit."

She collapsed the glass into its casing and ate
another banana. It was getting a bit lonely in the warm
spring's bower. Riolla shifted her deep blue eyes over
the tropical foliage, checking for movement or intruders. It had not been the best of ideas to stay there
alone, but she could not risk putting herself on
Drufalden's home soil without more protection.

The steady dripping of the condensed steam from
the plants had begun to annoy her. Her hair drooped
and her clothes were soaked through. She so hated wet
places; full of noxious mold and mildew. She stirred
the little fire at her feet, trying to get dry, but the heat
was making her sleepy. The steamy spring gurgled
invitingly a few feet from the fire. If she were already
wet, she might as well enjoy it and stay awake at the
same time. Riolla looked around one more time and
then began to undress.

Across the spring, Og grabbed the trunk of a banana tree to keep from breaking his neck as he tumbled gracelessly out of nothingness and into what appeared to be paradise. His song had taken him away from Womba, but he had no idea where it had dropped him. As he had held the stones in his hand and sung an unmaking spell, the last thing he remembered thinking about was . . . Riolla.

And to his astonishment and incredible delight, there she was, lounging in the midst of the warm spring with an orchid in her hair. Og blinked, thinking he dreamed. An orchid. Just like the one he had conjured for her the day he had proposed. Og's heart broke all over again as he looked through the thick tropical undergrowth. His nose poked into another hand of bananas for camouflage.

Riolla took her time in the misty waters, her head floating just above the bubbling surface. But when she rose to leave the spring, Og noticed for the first time that she was very, very naked. Enraptured, he shut his eyes, trying to orient himself, then looked up to try to find the three sisters. The swirling mist obscured the sky for the most part, but Og could make out the familiar constellation now and then when the firmament cleared for a brief moment. Everything looked pretty much the same as it did at the selkies' lodge, except that he knew he had moved a little west. This had to be the warm spring at the base of Drufalden's mountain.

Placing the two gemstones in his bag, Og began to plan quickly. Womba would surely be coming after him now that she knew he wasn't at the lodge, and he could return to the selkies' river any time before daybreak, when Cheyne had said they were leaving for the forest. But first, he wanted to get just a little closer. Just to be with her again. Just one last look, while she didn't know he was looking, while they were alone together.

He shoved his nose back into the bananas just as

Riolla slipped back into her robes, an appealing pink flush upon her white skin. Og's sudden motion made the tree sway enough to attract her glance, and while she stopped to listen for a moment, he steadied the tree, not risking even a breath. But it was too late. Riolla, having seen the tree's hand of ripe bananas, smiled greedily and moved through the wild growth with glee, her eyes fastened on the heavy, golden bunch.

Og could do nothing but await the inevitable. Riolla yanked at the biggest banana on the stalk, and Og came tumbling out of his hiding place, holding his battered nose.

Riolla only barely contained her shriek. She did not at all contain her wrath. "You! Where did you come from? Have you been watching me, you ugly little raqa-fogged peeper? Saelin!" she called, wanting Og to believe he was moments from losing his head.

He picked himself up from the slick, vine-covered ground and drew himself to his full height, faced Riolla, and looked deeply into her furious eyes. He had waited years to be able to speak to her and he knew exactly what he was going to say.

"I . . . I love you, Riolla," he croaked, his voice cracking miserably.

She wrinkled her nose in distaste and gingerly grabbed him by the collar, marching him through the lush ferns and club mosses over to the fire, where she tied him to a thick-trunked rubber tree with vines, stirred the fire up angrily, and sat down to decide just how she could hold the old stickaburr for ransom.

"Saelin, I'm waiting!" Riolla's sharp voice cut through the mist several yards away from the warm spring's thick cover.

When no one appeared or answered her, she strained her ears again, keeping a dagger in Og's ribs to assure his silence as well. Several more minutes

passed without another sound from the mountainside.
Og waited peacefully, never offering any attempt at
escape. After all, he was exactly where he had dreamed
of being since Riolla had left him. The gag was tasting
a little nasty, though, and his nose hurt horribly. Og
finally turned his face away from Riolla long enough to
rub his head against the rough tree bark to scratch a
mosquito bite.

And came eye to eye with Womba.

He couldn't even scream.

"Ngah! Ngah!" he managed, but Riolla, still unsure
of their solitude, shoved the dagger back into his ribs
and craned her head the other way.

Womba looked at him all doe-eyed and dewy, and
was about to tweak his bindings loose and carry him off
when another visitor appeared out of the mist and took
a seat at the fire. Womba's nose, confused by a sudden
abundance of strange smells, had missed the intruder.

"By the empty jar of Nin, Naruq! Why are you here?
Can you never announce yourself like anyone else? I
might have killed you before you could have been recognized," Riolla sputtered.

The tall elf smiled sardonically. "I doubt that very
much, Schreefa. Very much indeed. As you were told,
I am your guide through the curtain of light. You have
taken a prisoner, I see. Although I think this one was
not so difficult. Hello, Ogwater, is it?"

"Ngah. *Nagahhh!*" Og cried.

Ignoring the elf, Womba nonetheless withdrew,
fearing she had frightened Ogwater. A swirl of steam
brought a new, particularly strong scent, her little yellow eyes hardening with what the smell suggested.

"Ngah, Ngah!" repeated Og, but Riolla had forgotten him.

"Not much of a conversationalist, is he?" said
Naruq. Riolla studied the elf for a moment. "I haven't
seen you since the route was closed. What have you
been up to?"

"Nothing I care to discuss. But I have a bit of information you might like to hear. For a price, of course," said the elf.

"How much?"

"I think half of what you let the digger find under the Clock will do."

Riolla looked at him levelly. But he knew he had guessed the truth.

"Surprised that I knew you planned to take it all for yourself?" he continued. "I could have told the Raptor back in Sumifa, but then I would have had to do your job, too. And this way, we both get what we want. You can have Sumifa, but I want Sarraza and what lies below it."

"What do you know about the Clock?" growled Riolla. Og perked up his own ears, but pretended to drowse from fatigue.

"Enough. But you don't."

"What do you mean? she hissed.

"Well, there is the matter of how it works."

"What do you mean? Stop toying with me, Naruq."

"The digger has what he needs now to find and open the Clock. It's in that book his father has carried with him all over Almaaz. You did not know you were being followed? Yes, I thought that might bring a pique to your complexion. But the digger and his book are not a problem, even if he gets the Treefather to read it for him."

"Why not?"

"We now have something he wants."

Naruq stood and parted the foliage behind him to reveal Claria, her golden eyes molten with anger, her hands and feet tied, and a gag in her mouth.

Already agitated by Claria's perfume, Womba could contain herself no longer. When she saw the girl, she roared and leapt from her hiding place, ripping the small tree that Og was tied to from the ground by its roots. Og bounced free from it just before she swung it. Naruq, caught totally by surprise, barely managed to dodge the blow himself. Riolla rolled her eyes, the orcess's appearance just one more inconvenience. Claria could only roll under another sturdy bush and hope for the best.

Womba missed her again and again, each swat of the tree breaking it farther down its shaft until the orcess held only a stick of kindling in her scaly hands. Naruq had drawn his dagger, but could not get his aim until she turned her face toward him and he brought the knife across her cheek with a vicious slash. Her eyes full of blood, Womba bellowed again, grabbed Og, who had not yet worked free from his ropes, and ran into the night.

"That was brilliant. Now he can go and tell the digger what we plan to do," said Riolla.

Naruq chuckled, wiping his dagger on Claria's robes. "Oh, but don't you see, Schreefa? The orcess will take him as far from the others as she can. By the way, you did check his pockets, didn't you?"

"Of course not. Why should I; he didn't even have Rotapan's staff. You expected me to actually touch him? It was all I could do to tie him up, the little cockroach. He would never hurt me anyway."

"He had two of the stones."

Riolla's face went ashen. Naruq looked down his long angular nose at her with disdain. "The digger is headed for the Treefather. He's the only one who can read the book. I'll have to take him into the forest, so I'll hear what the old graybeard has to say and be back as quickly as I can. Your job is to take care of her while I'm gone. Don't hurt her or let her get away, Riolla. You need what only I can provide, or you'll never get to the Clock . . . think on that, and be grateful I have decided to give it to you."

Riolla sneered at his back as he melted into the forest. Then she turned to Claria and smiled, her mouth a little pink rosebud of false pity.

"We meet for the first time, my dear. I had hoped you would see me at the wedding. Maceo was quite taken with you at one time, I know. But of course, all that is over now. And your little insignificant life will be over soon, too. I'll just take his ring back to him for you."

Riolla reached for the ring on Claria's finger, and to her great surprise, the girl did not try to draw back her bound hands. Instead, she wiggled her finger, now swollen again, right under the Schreefa's nose. Riolla cocked an eyebrow at Claria and tried to remove the ring.

Which, of course, would not come off. Claria laughed behind her gag. Riolla was not amused.

"Ah . . . well, then. There are other ways, my dear," she cooed.

Rotapan finished reciting Riolla's request and fell silent.

"All right, Wyrvil. Hand over the coin," said Drufalden, tapping the arm of her throne with a long silver nail.

Rotapan blinked and rolled his eyes, adjusting them to the blazing brightness of Drufalden's chambers. Saelin had removed the half-orc's blindfold only after they had been escorted through the maze of ice and stone that formed Drufalden's personal corridor.

Rotapan fished into his pocket and reluctantly brought forth the Ninnite coin. Drufalden examined it carefully, at last satisfied that it matched the Raptor's description.

"You just saved your miserable life, Wyrvil. I've been waiting for years at the chance to have you standing before me. Tell Riolla her escort will be waiting. I'll send five hundred of my finest assassins to wait at the curtain. She can meet them there.

"Get him out of my sight before I forget myself, Saelin." Drufalden waved her hand at the assassin.

Saelin smiled, bowed, and dropped the blindfold neatly back over Rotapan's head. As they moved through the frozen corridor, the air seemed strangely warmer and smelled different. Rotapan felt water beneath his feet. Then he heard a peculiar sound.

Like the thawing of a river. Like the cracking of ice.

Saelin heard it, too. There was half a mile of corridor left to go. The assassin ran for his life, splashing down the long maze, leaving the half-orc to stumble blindly into the melting walls, the roof of the corridor already dissolving at a rate far faster than a natural thaw.

Rotapan tore off the blindfold and raced after the assassin, Saelin's footprints a fresh trail in the sugary ice.

Exhorting Chelydrus's mercy the entire distance, Rotapan coughed and wheezed through the slippery corridor, the roof raining icy water down his neck, but holding up in spite of the sudden thaw. The half-orc slid the last several feet out into the courtyard, barely avoiding a drenching puddle of slush, picked himself up, and looked around for Saelin. The assassin had vanished.

Leaving Rotapan with nowhere to go. Except home. He wrapped his thin cloak about himself disgustedly, set himself in alignment with the sisters, and proceeded through the melting courtyard and down the mountain.

Behind him, Drufalden's crystalline kingdom seeped into dirty rivulets that became muddy streams, which then emptied into the rivers below. By the next day, ice that had stood in walls a hundred feet high would flood the land below the mountain and end up pouring into the Silver Sea. Rotapan paused as he passed by the remains of the magnificent sculpture of Chelydrus, now a featureless lump amid a growing puddle.

"Mighty Chelydrus, you alone survive, your face perfect and your form without blemish. Nothing can touch your glory. I will rebuild your temple, my lord. Only see me safe home, and I will raise it again. I will hold the staff again. I am Rotapan, Rex Serpens to the ten tribes!" he shouted aloud, and moved down the mountainside as though he still were.

Behind him, the slave the guards had taken, his face beaten raw and one of his eyes already swollen shut, slipped out of the corridor and waved his hand in a sharp downward motion. The wolf pup came bounding out of his hiding place in the rocks and leapt playfully into his arms. The Neffian knelt painfully and let the wolf sniff his wounds, but hushed him when he began to whimper, then led him into a dark crevice under an overhang at the edge of Drufalden's courtyard.

"Rafek! Where you been? What happened to you?" the voices seemed to come from all around the Neffian as he moved from the secret entrance of the colony to the main cavern.

"There's no time to explain. The guards have melted! Yes! Even as they beat me—I was out hunting with the wolves and couldn't get back to the doorway before the guards sensed me—but the guards just turned to water before my eyes. I thought I was dead and dreaming. Now I see that the whole place is going—something has changed out there."

A hundred old Neffians, all past work, but still bearing the silver collar with Drufalden's mark, looked at Rafek like he was mad.

"You can't mean that, man, look at you—it's probably from the beating. But where are Jepli and Carsh?" said one of the older men, whose name was Salmak.

"The Wyrvil king killed them both. Only Q'Tarin survives." The wolf pup licked his hand at the sound of his name.

"The . . . Wyrvil king? You saw the Wyrvil king up on this mountain? Rotapan, who traded us all into slavery again when we had run from Sumifa?" Salmak began to shake his head and roll his eyes. A few of the others politely covered their toothless smiles.

"I did. I thought he was a lost traveler at first and I tried to help him. For that kindness, he killed my wolves. From the guards' loose talk, I know that another, an assassin, took the Wyrvil in to see Drufalden herself. I didn't see the assassin when I came out of the corridor, but the half-orc is on his way back down the mountain now. Apparently alone," added Rafek. "I tell you, things have happened. The New King is at hand, just like the juma said. My brother Doulos was right—we are about to be free! Where are the house servants? The men in the mines? The smiths? Ask them if this kingdom is not melting. Or look outside for yourself if you don't believe me!"

The old man smoothed back his thick mane of white hair and pulled on his silver collar, then motioned one of the others to take a cautious look out the secret entrance.

"All right, Rafek, calm down. If Silufe brings back water, we will act on this," the elder said, giving Silufe an empty cup to take with him. In a few moments, Rafek's eye was bandaged and the other man had returned with a smile and a cup of water.

"The guards are gone. But the assassins have manned the courtyard," said Silufe. Rafek settled, glad that they finally believed his news.

Salmak smiled in his white beard. "I never thought I'd live to see it. But perhaps we have a chance now. They are just men and women. We could not fight magic. But we can fight flesh and blood and bone. We will have to plan carefully. There are still many more of the assassins than there are of us, but we will have our chance." He pulled again on the silver collar. "She is not invincible anymore."

Rafek hugged the wolf pup and stood up to leave. "Take care of Q'Tarin. I'm going after that Wyrvil snake."

"Rafek—the Ninnites will take you down in a heartbeat. The courtyard is crawling with them," said Silufe.

"I have to go. It may be the only chance we have at him while he's alone and unprotected. And he killed my wolves, Silufe. You know I cannot let that go." Rafek threw on a heavy cloak and crept back out to the secret entrance.

He had to wait only a few minutes before the assassins gathered in the center of the yard to light their rations of shirrir. When their backs were turned from the wind, Rafek moved shadowlike out of the rocks and down the trail.

And Q'Tarin, who had bitten every hand that had tried to restrain him, trotted silently behind.

CHAPTER
18

RIOLLA BROUGHT FORTH HER LITTLE JEW-
eled dagger and flashed it before Claria's golden,
unflinching eyes.

"You think we will need this to remove the ring?"
asked the Schreefa.

Claria shook her head, her gag still in place.

"Good. Now you take it off."

Claria held up her bound hands.

"Nice try," said the Schreefa, bringing the dagger
closer.

"Riolla!" Saelin came crashing into the dense undergrowth like a falling boulder. "Gather yourself. There
is no time. We must move to higher ground immediately," he puffed.

"Ah . . . well done, my esteemed empress. Is this a
special treat for your honored servant?" He brought
his hand to his face, tracing the raw, red scratch lines
of Claria's comb.

"What are you talking about, Saelin? Why do we
have to leave here now? And where is Rotapan?"
Riolla replaced her dagger.

"When the melt began, there was no time to dis-
pense with him as you had planned. But I am sure he

is dead. I left the Wyrvil in the palace's corridor. Do
not fear—he'll never find his way out, and the Wyrvil
tribes will continue to remain hostile to the ice queen.
He was blindfolded and the walls were melting. I am
sure the corridor has fallen in on him. He delivered
your message and Drufalden has summoned your
sabers. They will await you at the Curtain."

Saelin kept looking up toward the mountain.
"Schreefa, there is a wall of mud ready to come down
on us. We must move now."

Riolla kicked at Claria to get her on her feet. "The
old coot must have used the selkies' stone," she muttered. "Never mind. We need to move fast anyway, but
I wish your dagger had found Rotapan's heart instead
of leaving him to chance. No matter, he is out of the
way, and I don't have to pay him. Perhaps, Saelin, you
would do well in his old position."

The assassin bowed and smiled under his dark mustache. It was enough to make him forget all about the
lost chroniclave.

Ogwater bounced along atop Womba's massive shoulders like a bag of melons. The orcess had not slowed
her pace since she had thrashed her way out of the
jungle and into the forest that surrounded the selkies'
river. Og had no idea where she was taking him, but
wherever it was, he thought it was too far.

Until he saw Dunsan. The sentry ran toward them,
his face hot with exertion.

"Where have you been? We have been searching for
you at Wiggulf's most urgent order. Do you not know
that the mountain falls also? This place will likely
remain dry, but you could be trapped here until the
river recedes."

At the sound of Dunsan's voice, the battle frenzy
departed from her, and Womba looked at him as
though she did not comprehend his words. But

Dunsan's appearance had stopped her long enough for
Og to squirm loose from her grip and drop gracelessly
to the ground.

"I have to find Cheyne. Does he yet lodge with
Wiggulf?" the songmage asked.

"He left to go to his father. They are up the path a
bit. I can lead you," said Dunsan, slicing through the
ropes still binding Og's hands.

Og strode quickly after him, with Womba right on
his heels. Dunsan wove through the forest until they
came upon Cheyne's party. Yob and a Neffian were
with him: they were transporting a wounded man
between them, moving along the path Cheyne and Og
had taken to the selkies' lodge earlier.

"Cheyne! Yob! Help!" he cried.

Cheyne halted the group, and Yob took off after his
daughter. Moments later, he came walking back with
Womba, unconscious and draped over his shoulders,
with Og rubbing his bruised hands, but making his
own way beside them.

Cheyne had no smile for Og. "Where have you
been? We needed your help." Og followed his stony
stare as it fell upon the wounded man.

"Well . . ." For once, Og was speechless. He bent to
look at the man, but when he touched Javin's cold
hand, he drew back. "He's dead. Who was he?"

Doulos bowed and answered. "He is the young
Muje's father, the true king of Sumifa. And he lives
yet. But if we cannot get help for him, he will die very
soon."

Og pulled at his scrip and emptied the stones into
his hand, making ready to sing the life song. But after
the first few notes into the melody, the light generated
by the two stones faded and died away, leaving Og
croaking the words out of tune and so tired he could
hardly move.

"What is the poison? I cannot unsing this," he marveled.

"It's the Ninnites' dark magic, Og."

"Then we have to get him to the Treefather. The firebane is the only stone that can counter this. The elves know how to bring the magic to that one even better than I did," said Og. "Come on. There is no time to lose."

Cheyne began to lift Javin into a more comfortable carrying position.

"Wait . . . maybe there is something I can do anyway. And I have news, Cheyne. Our friend Naruq has none of your good in mind. He works for the same one as Riolla, and he works for himself, too. He had planned to lead you into a trap. Riolla will have five hundred Ninnites waiting for you after you find the Clock for her. And . . ." He swallowed hard, not wanting to tell the next part.

"And what, Og?" Cheyne said quietly.

"And Riolla has Claria."

Rotapan halted in the depths of the forest to sniff the air, fearing the sounds behind him. For several miles he had heard the rumble of the shifting mountainside above, the rush of the rising river, and worse, far worse, the snap and rustle of dry twigs beneath the feet of a careless follower. He pointed his nose in the air, closed his eyes, and concentrated on the smells the wind brought. *Neffian? And another wolf?*

Rotapan was puzzled. *And very close, now. . . .*

So close that when he opened his eyes, he saw them standing before him, the Neffian's face bruised and grim, a good-sized club in his hand. Rotapan braced himself against the tree trunk at his back and fumbled for the dark obsidian blade he had used on the wolves up the trail.

"You lost it a couple of miles down the mountain, Wyrvil. But you're on different ground here. No rocks. It'll do you no good to run any further. You and I have a trade to make," said Rafek. At his feet, the half-grown wolf pup sat poised to leap, his teeth bared and a low growl rising from his throat.

"A trade? What kind of a trade?" croaked Rotapan, his hands groping at the tree trunk.

The Neffian moved closer, a step at a time. "Your life for all the lives of my people that you sold to Drufalden, after they had paid you in labor on that monstrous temple to let them pass freely through your kingdom. And your life for the lives of my wolves. Hardly seems a fair trade, does it? You owe far more than you can pay. But this will be a start!"

The Neffian lunged at Rotapan, bringing the club crashing into the tree trunk at the precise place where Rotapan's forehead had been a split second earlier. Rafek leveled his club again while the wolf pup leapt upon the fleeing half-orc; his weight, if not his skill, brought Rotapan down instantly.

Pressed under the pup's big paws, Rotapan struggled madly in the soft, sandy pine forest floor, groping at the cast-off cones and needles under the tall, swaying trees, but finding no weapon. When Rafek whistled the pup off him, Rotapan crouched cowering on the ground, mumbling to himself, his eyes glassy. Rafek moved in to finish it.

Rotapan shut his eyes and screamed, crawling backward across the prickly ground like a cornered spider. Rafek raised the club.

It would have been over instantly had Rotapan not touched a piece of wood. He snatched the thick pole from behind and blocked Rafek's angry blow, then dodged the next two as he came to his feet. The wolf pup wove in and out, trying for the half-orc's throat, but Rotapan swung the makeshift weapon around himself madly, keeping the pup at bay. Rafek charged at Rotapan again and again, their staves clashing loudly over the river's rising voice, until Rotapan noticed that the staff he held was actually half of his broken scepter, the brass serpent's head still adorning one end.

He yowled in rage and swung the heavy ornament at Rafek's head with all his might, his sudden attack catching the Neffian on his blind side as the slave raised his club again. Rafek stood for a moment, the club poised over his shoulder, a look of amazement on his bloodied face. Then he dropped over backward, the weight of the club taking him off balance. He was dead before he hit the ground.

The wolf pup leapt viciously at Rotapan, but the half-orc hooked his broken staff over a low-hanging limb and swung himself up the tree, making his way high into the tall pine. Q'Tarin tried to climb after him, falling back time after time, barking, finally settling into a low keen for Rafek. But in the dense forest, with the rush of the river nearby, his requiem went unheard.

Up the tree, Rotapan sat hunkered over, nursing his scratches and bruises, his hands wandering over the broken staff's ornament, the serpent's third eye now just a dark pit above its long, bared fangs.

The girl had laughed. The staff was broken and the ajada gone. But his tower, faintly visible in the dawning day, still partially stood. Mighty Chelydrus would have his sacrifice of poison yet.

"Riolla has Claria? What do you mean?" Cheyne looked at the bedraggled songmage incredulously.

"Well, um, Naruq came into Riolla's camp with her, that's all I know. Needless to say, I was very surprised to see her. You, too," Og added.

Cheyne grimaced. "So she'll be wanting to trade Claria's life for the treasure under the Clock, is that it?"

"That would be what Naruq hinted at. He said you had some kind of book. . . ."

"What we have is a sick man who won't live the rest of the night without help," said Cheyne. "Let's go! Dunsan, will you tell Wiggulf what has happened?"

"I will. He will be distressed about Naruq. They were very old friends. Come with me, orcess. You need some help with that cut."

She had awakened, but the loss of blood was telling on Womba. Though it meant leaving Og, she did not protest when Dunsan turned her toward the lodge and fell in behind her. Cheyne gave Doulos the signal to raise Javin, but Og raised his.

"Wait. As I said, I can do that at least. I still have the stones. Join hands."

Og took a breath and summoned his strength, bent over the two gemstones and began to sing, concentrating hard on the Sarrazan forest.

A place he had never been.

Naruq felt the surge of the curtain when Og took his party through. The elf stopped in his tracks and began to run back toward Riolla's camp. A quick check told him they had moved on and why: three feet of mud now covered the camp and clogged the spring. Naruq took to the trees, running the arboreal highways with greater speed and ease than the uneven ground of the forest road could provide. He caught up with Riolla just as she came to the edge of the curtain.

"Stop!" Naruq jumped down lightly in front of Saelin, who had his dagger drawn and ready. "Put that away, assassin. You were about to lose yourselves." The elf glowered.

"Where?" said Riolla, looking all around. "I don't see anything but trees, and the road goes straight through the forest."

"Watch," said Naruq, as he walked a few yards down the overgrown road. Riolla's jaw dropped as the elf shimmered into nothingness, then stepped back toward her, appearing to be solid again.

"The curtain parts over there. Come on."

Naruq motioned them off the road. A quarter mile

later, they stepped through the invisible curtain, the air around them charged with unseen power. Where there had been only forest and sky before, Mount Sarrazan loomed over them, the sunrise glinting off a sparkling crystal mirror high upon its rocky slopes. Claria breathed in the pure air and felt her strength return. Riolla and Saelin exchanged looks of triumph.

"Yes. That's Mount Sarrazan. Beautiful isn't it? Wait here until I return. And remember, Saelin. We need the girl." Naruq vanished before Saelin had risen from his mock bow.

Og set them down in a bramble, but he knew they had passed through the curtain. So did the elves.

From every tree above them, the silver-haired Sarrazans dropped down, some carrying bows, others armed with blow pipes and darts fletched with tiny, brilliant feathers. All of them wore shades of green and brown, blending perfectly with the summer-clad forest. In fact, Cheyne had a hard time finding them if they stood still for any length of time. He raised his hand in greeting, while Doulos and Og shook off their dizziness. Javin remained unconscious.

His bow drawn, one of the elves stepped forward, looked at Cheyne carefully, then smiled. "The Treefather is expecting you. But where is Naruq? He was supposed to bring you in at one of the portals." The elf's voice seemed to carry toward them on the breeze.

"Naruq is a traitor to you. I'll be happy to tell you about that after we get this man to your healer," said Cheyne, climbing out of the thorn bushes.

The elf bent, holding his hand over Javin, but not touching him. He frowned his concern, motioned to the others, and they came forward quickly to lift Javin lightly between them.

"It's not far. Just follow. And only believe. He clings to life yet."

Cheyne did not notice anything special about the next two or three miles. Then suddenly the trees parted before them, leaving a clear view of a gleaming wooden causeway leading up to a massive living fortress.

Cheyne caught his breath at the sight. A wide ring of trees taller than Rotapan's temple rose against the backdrop of the dawn sky. The trees all bore peculiar markings, softly limned in the clear, red light. Curious animals twirled upon themselves and grasped their tails with hooked mouths. Ribbons of intricate scroll-work wrapped around the trunks in thirty-foot-high bands, and several of the trees appeared to have words carved into them.

Words in the language of Old High Sumifan.

CHAPTER

19

THE DIGGER HAD TOLD THE ELVES ABOUT
him now, so it was only a little more difficult moving
in and out of the fortress. But long in the service of the
Raptor and his Ninnites, Naruq was an expert at such
things and rather enjoyed the challenge, when he
thought about it. He settled himself into his hiding
place in the meditative cell nearest the door just as
Cheyne and his party entered the Treefather's chambers through a series of connected portals, their lacy
roofs covered in wild rose and berrybramble. Yob
waited outside, positioning himself, as usual, by the
doorway.

"Place him here before the stone," said a warm
voice, compassion seeming to carry in every word.

Cheyne looked up and around as he helped Doulos
position Javin on a long table, the central feature in the
large, airy room. Behind the table, a small glass container held a white gemstone suspended in water.

"That's the firebane. They keep it in the water so the
power accumulates around it. When it was set in the
center of the ring, the other stones did that," said Og
quietly.

Cheyne nodded and looked around. Rising to the

vaulted ceiling, columns carved from whiter wood
than Cheyne had seen outside braced forty or fifty
intricate, curving ribs that met high overhead in an
elaborate filial of stylized leaves and acorns. Pale light
filtered down from a few high windows, and as his
eyes adjusted, Cheyne realized that the columns were
carved to look like tall, thin trees themselves. Cheyne
could find no break in their grain, no beginning or end
to them, and with a shock, he realized that he was
standing in the hollowed interior of the biggest tree in
the fortress.

In calm efficiency, the Treefather rose from his
prayers and stood to greet them, going immediately to
Javin. "Hello to all of you, and be welcome here in the
sanctuary of our forest home. I am Luquin."

He smiled as he worked over Javin, checking his
pulse and his pupils, his breathing, the several new
gashes the canistas had given him, and finally the site
of the scorpion's sting. After they had passed through
the curtain, Javin had begun to stir in his fever, to
thrash and jerk and mutter. He seemed worse than
ever now, but Cheyne held his tongue, watching the
Treefather carefully.

Luquin was taller than most of the elves they had
seen in and around the fortress. His face shone with an
inner light, and his gray eyes crinkled at the edges only
a little when he smiled, which seemed to be often.
Luquin, seen anywhere other than his home, would
cause almost anyone to stop and stare, to wonder about
his every feature, to become mesmerized by his movements and the sound of his voice. Here, Cheyne
thought, he seemed to be just another part of the tran-
scendent beauty, the towering majesty of the forest and
the fortress. Here, it was his hands that pulled Cheyne's
eyes to them as though they had a power of their own.
They were not the hands of a person who spent his
time in soft work. Luquin's hands were rugged and
knotted, their many white scars testament to far more
than a life of contemplation.

As the Treefather touched the swollen area around the sting, Javin began to stiffen and contort in bone-breaking spasms, and Doulos cried out. Luquin did not seem distressed and did not stop, but called for two of his assistants to hold Javin on the table. Cheyne and Og drew Doulos away, soothing both him and themselves with low words of assurance.

At length, Luquin looked up at them and told them the truth.

"It is very bad. His spirit has already left his body. It wanders, but we will dance." He smiled. "Prepare the stone," he said to his assistants, who bowed and removed themselves from the room.

Still hiding in the cell near the Treefather's chambers, Naruq frowned his impatience behind the door, waited for them all to leave, then slipped out of the narrow doorway and faded into the green depths of the fortress hedges.

Moments later, the silent call had gone forth, and in the center of the fortress common the elves had gathered from their work, many still with clay upon their clothing, some with wooden tools in their hands, and others with farm implements strapped across their backs. They stood together in a loose circle, the Treefather in the center, with Javin, still unconscious, stretched across the same finely carved table. In his gnarled hands, the Treefather held the firebane, now dry and glowing in white brilliance, its inner flames flashing rainbows.

"He'll chant for awhile in the old language, then the lightning will come. Best move back," warned Og, but neither Cheyne nor Doulos stepped away.

"All right, then," Og pronounced, and held his own ground, too. Yob, a little disturbed at the sight of so many elves, waited a few paces behind them.

The Treefather held the firebane high and began his

prayer. His voice magnified with every syllable, until it became so loud that Cheyne could not distinguish the words any longer and thought he heard only the roar of many waters, or the sound of thunder. When it became almost unbearable, the wind bore down on them, the elves linked hands and began to stamp their feet in a quick, complicated rhythm, and the firebane flashed its light into the sky above Javin's contorting body.

Cheyne had to shield his eyes and he could feel the crackle of the power on his skin. The Treefather quickly stepped back just as the bolt of lightning struck Javin's chest, lifting him off the table and into the air several inches, then dropping him hard back onto the wooden surface. Immediately, the light disappeared, the noise ceased, and the Treefather collapsed as the two attendants moved to catch him. The elves continued their dance until he rose, holding the firebane, then stopped in unison with a quick double stamp.

Cheyne let go of the breath he had been holding.

"The work is finished," announced Luquin shakily, and the elves broke the circle, quietly departing the common, leaving Cheyne, Og, and Doulos with Javin, who lay still now on the carved table, his face deadly pale, but the scorpion's sting completely gone.

"Is he . . . ?" Cheyne began. The Treefather held up one hand.

"He lives," said Luquin, then he bowed and left them alone with Javin.

All that day, Cheyne waited for Javin to wake up. Cheyne spent the time looking at the little bronze-bound book, thinking, and running his fingers across the glyphs on the totem's smooth face. When the elves brought Javin inside the Treefather's chambers at the middle hour, Cheyne sent Yob and Og to eat, but Doulos would not leave. When the Treefather entered for his afternoon prayers, Cheyne and the slave jumped to their feet, a hundred questions on their lips.

"He lives, and I believe he is healed. But I cannot tell you when he will awaken. It could be anytime. Or it could be much longer. But here, we pay little attention to time . . ." said Luquin, smiling.

"But I need to know that he's all right. And I need to know what he wanted to tell me in the forest." Cheyne put the book down, picked up the totem, and turned it over and over in his hands.

"Muje?" said Doulos. "Remember that you have many other things to ask."

"What does that matter if Javin doesn't wake up? I . . . I got him into this mess by leaving before he could find the Collector. He told me to wait. I should have."

"But Muje, he came because he wanted to. And you came back for him, leaving what you thought was your only chance to see the Treefather, just as he left his work to look for you. If you do not ask about the Clock, all that he cared about will be as dust."

There was time, not many days ago, that Cheyne would have answered that all Javin cared about was dust anyway. Old dry, dead things that had nothing to do with the living people around him. But not now. Cheyne knew Doulos was right, but it didn't ease the pain of guilt in his chest.

The Treefather looked long into Cheyne's troubled eyes, then gently took the book from him.

"I know what you seek, Cheyne. And I will tell you what I can."

He turned through the fragile pages of the little book, shaking his head at first, then stopping at the last several leaves. Finally he took the totem and held it to the light. Luquin's brow creased as he studied the last glyph. Cheyne waited patiently, but his eyes were on Javin.

"The last glyph is a woman's name. The marker—that fingerprint is feminine—but I cannot read the letters. It's inscribed with magic." he finished.

"A *woman's* name," breathed Cheyne, hardly believing his ears. "Then that means the totem . . . "

"Is a woman's totem, yes," said Luquin gently, his eyes full of compassion. "But it's much more than that, Cheyne."

"What? What do you mean?"

"It's the key to the Armageddon Clock."

"The—"

The Treefather nodded. "Your book says so, at least. Cheyne, do you know why Javin sought the Collector?"

"Only so that he could find the Clock. It was his . . . great quest."

"Yes. Because the Collector was the one who invented the Clock. Let me read something to you."

He began slowly, pronouncing the words first in the old language, then repeating in the modern tongue. "The Clock shall have a key. It shall be the totem of my daughter Claria, to whom I bequeath all my knowledge, and all my possessions, and to all of her line successively shall it be so—"

"Did you say *Claria*?" asked Cheyne before Luquin could translate. Og mirrored his startled response.

The Treefather raised his eyes and nodded. "Yes. It's an uncommon name, even in the Collector's time. May I go on?" Cheyne nodded, a peculiar smile lifting his lips.

"The key shall fit the twelfth spire, the tallest, I believe, from the edge of the middlemost part of the valley the elves call the Chimes. When it is inserted into the cleft in this spire, and the spire is made to be whole once again, the slightest breeze will cause the other spires, in their peculiar properties, to sing until they shatter, and the void they leave shall summon the godscream from the erg, and the ensuing power of its voice shall break the crystal door."

And give up its treasure to me, thought Naruq, eavesdropping again from his hiding place. This was going to be far easier than he thought.

"Want to make a trade, digger?" Naruq stepped out

into the shadows of the chamber, still hidden but for
the light that sparkled from his silver cloakpin.

"Ah, Naruq. We have been looking for you," said
the Treefather, unperturbed. "It seems you have found
employment outside the colony."

"And your skills are yet sharp, ancient one. But not
as sharp as mine. What about it, digger? The girl for
the totem?"

"I don't think so, Naruq."

"Too bad, since that beast Riolla employs seems
hardly able to keep his hands off her. Appears he has
some kind of professional score to settle with her. And
with you." Naruq chuckled. "Care to think again?"

Cheyne looked helplessly at the Treefather, who
only nodded and smiled.

"You must do what you must," said Luquin, his long
finger gently tapping the book. *There is more,* said his
eyes.

"Then I will set the terms," said Cheyne. "You will
meet us at the Chimes before dark, alone. When I see
the girl is well and unharmed, I will give you the key."

Naruq cocked a silver brow at him and laughed.
"We will be there." He stepped backward, seeming to
melt into the shadows.

"Are you sunstruck, man?" shouted Og.

"No, I am trying to buy some time to think of a way
to bring Claria to safety without giving him the key to
the Clock, Og," replied Cheyne.

The Treefather eyed Cheyne curiously. "There is
more here that you should know. Naruq is very bright
and a talented woodsman, but he has never learned to
consider the entire forest before he chooses his trail.
Here is the rest of what the Collector wrote. 'The beast
is pure evil, a thing of terrible beauty and the bringer
of terrible fear. I have looked upon it and lived, and
that is a horrible blessing. I have put it to sleep with a
common spell, amplified by my brothers in the Circle.
It is all we could do . . .'"

For a long time, the Treefather read to Cheyne and

Doulos the account of the battle the Collector had fought, of his pain and loss, his agonized decision to give Mishra the doomsday weapon he sought, and how he had arranged the keys so that it would destroy the beast the first time Mishra tried to summon the creature.

"But the last page is missing, Cheyne. Here is where it was torn away." Luquin showed them all what Cheyne had already seen.

"The writing stops in the middle of a sentence about the Collector's killer—'The Circle is betrayed, the Raptor has come for me in his evil wind, but he can be destroyed, yet only by the one who—' This part looks like he burned it into the script over other words, as though he were in distress and had no time."

The color had drained from Cheyne's face and he hardly felt the Treefather's gentle hand on his shoulder.

"Cheyne? There is more," said Luquin.

"Go on."

"The same name on the totem is inscribed inside the back cover."

I know. And it's on the amulet that Javin said he used to protect me from someone he called the Raptor. But he was fevered and babbling. I still don't understand what the glyph means to me." He pulled the amulet from beneath his tunic.

At the sight of the amulet, Doulos broke into a huge grin.

"That's the key!" he shouted.

"No, the book said the totem is the key," said Cheyne.

Doulos could not be dissuaded. "I mean the key to the *little* clock, the chroniclave, as your father called it."

He ran excitedly to the cabinet where Javin's pack had been stored, retrieved the clock, and brought it to Cheyne.

"See? The very same mark. I told him if there was a key, we could find it. Try it, please, Muje."

Cheyne examined the chroniclave, turned it upside down, and found yet another inscription of the same glyph. "Where did you find this, Doulos? It's Claria's. She had to leave it in a cave at the oasis when Yob surprised us," he said, taking the amulet from beneath his tunic.

"The king found it as we left the sea," Doulos said, shrugging his shoulders.

Without taking the amulet off, Cheyne inserted its end into the slot, gave it a cautious turn, and removed it. The chroniclave sprang to life with song, a lilting melody that played over and over, filling the room with a sweetness that thousands of years had not dimmed.

"That's the most beautiful song I ever heard," said Og reverently. There is magic in it, I can tell."

His glance fell upon the totem in the Treefather's lap, and he remembered the day Cheyne had first shown him the artifact. "May I see the totem?"

Luquin gave it to him. Og held it up and turned it as the music played, catching the sunbeams from the high windows in the hollow tree. Suddenly the room filled with a burst of brilliant light, a rainbow seeming to bring fire from the totem's edge and sending a tight ribbon of color into the depths of the dim chamber— the outline of a woman's hand sparkling into the darkness. Cheyne found himself mesmerized at the image of the hand, its first two fingers slightly crooked, until the vision disappeared with the last notes of the song.

And then he remembered Claria's hand on the polished wooden floor of Wiggulf's lodge in the dying firelight, how her first two fingers had exactly the same little crook in them, just at the first joints.

He looked at Og, who nodded in silent agreement. "The totem belongs to Claria, too. The glyph writes her name, just as it wrote the Collector's daughter's name."

Cheyne wound the chroniclave again and Og tried the name, as the Treefather had pronounced it, against the song. The syllables and accents fit perfectly.

It took a few minutes for everyone else to find their

voices. In the meantime, Cheyne gave the clock's pendulum a little push, and the clock's hands jumped to life, as though they had been waiting for his touch.

"What does this mean?" he breathed. "All of these things must have belonged to the Collector. He says in the book that there was a namesong that would destroy the crystal door forever. This must be that song. Og, do you think you can sing this? We may have the way to save Claria without letting loose the Beast of the Hours!"

"Well, results—" Og began. Entertainment was one thing. Even healing, he knew he could do. But this was . . . this was the Armageddon Clock.

"No," said Cheyne. "This will have to be certain. No variation. No 'almost right,' Og. This will have to be perfect. Can you do it?"

Og tried the little tune in his best voice. It cracked. He tried it again. It cracked again.

"I need the stones, I think." He looked longingly at the firebane. "All of them."

CHAPTER
20

"HURRY UP, YOU LITTLE NAMELESS COM-moner," Riolla prodded, her voice vexed at having to climb down into the bramble-ridden Chimes. "We have to be there on time."

"It would be so much easier, my queen, if you just let me divide her up among us, so that the burden of her portage would be lighter and quicker," Saelin added wickedly. Claria shot him a deadly look above her gag, but moved a little faster anyway.

Naruq led the group from far ahead, scouting for possible traps. At his signal, they stopped amid the towering spires and waited. He advanced alone to a rise above the valley and stepped out of sight behind an old hickory tree. Above the valley, the wind had picked up considerably. Drufalden's five hundred sabers, scattered plainly in sight around the mountainside, waited for Riolla's command.

They did not have long to wait. Cheyne, guided by one of the Treefather's attendants, came into view almost immediately, Ogwater at his side. Bound by his oath, Doulos had stayed with Javin. The attendant waved farewell, and Naruq stepped out from the tree's cover. The assassins began to advance to their positions.

"I see you are a man of your word, digger. Look for yourself. See if she is not there in the valley."

From his place on the hillside, Cheyne could see straight down to where Saelin stood impatiently over Claria, who was bound to a ganzite spire.

"Let her go. When she's up here, you'll get the totem," said Cheyne, his eyes stony and hard as he watched the assassins ring the valley. "Are you so afraid of a digger and a songmage that you need an army?"

"Saelin!" called Naruq, turning to leave.

"Wait. All right. Here. Now let her go." Cheyne held out the totem.

Naruq took it, smiled, and called down into the valley again, his words echoing off the spires like the sound of flat stones thrown in a shallow pool. "Saelin! Let her go."

Cheyne watched anxiously, but no one moved from the spire. When he looked back to Naruq, the elf had disappeared. But the sabers had not.

"Well, you didn't expect him to really do it, did you?" said Og.

"No. Of course not. He'll open the Clock. With this wind, it could be anytime. Are you ready?"

Og blanched, straightened his back, and nodded.

His mouth was so dry he couldn't even say yes.

Riolla snapped her spyglass shut and stood by the spire Naruq had indicated. Claria, still gagged and bound, had been lashed to the crystal with tough cords of bark rope Naruq had taken from the fortress. Saelin stood by, leering at the girl, waiting for the moment Riolla gave her over to him.

When the elf appeared beside him, the assassin startled and nearly lost his footing on the rock-littered valley floor as he fought the reflections all around him. Claria had enough courage left to laugh. At least until

Naruq blew the debris out of an opening in the spire just over Claria's head, polished the four sides of the slot with his cloak, and inserted the totem. The spire reclaimed its missing piece with a sound click.

He turned to Riolla and smiled, his silver eyes dancing. "I'll be going now," he said, and disappeared into the mirrored maze before the words registered on her ears.

"You can't leave us here!" Riolla cried, her voice echoing all around, following the reflection of her worried face from spire to spire. She grabbed Saelin's arm and popped open her spyglass. "You watch ahead. I'll direct our path up the mountain."

They began to stumble out of the valley as fast as they could, leaving Claria amid the resounding swell of the wind.

Above the valley, behind the crystal door, the Beast of the Hours awoke to the sound of a distant ringing, like the call of Ninnite prayer bells on the wind.

Up on the hillside, at first there was no sound at all. Then the force seemed to gather under their feet and the rocks hummed low and steady, shaking so gently that only by looking at the pebbles rolling around on the surface could they tell there was any motion at all.

"It's begun," said Cheyne. "They've put the totem in the correct spire. The first key is in place. And they've left Claria tied to the spire. Og, I don't know how long I have, but I've got to go down there, army or not. Claria will never survive what the Collector said will come next."

"Cheyne, the wind has already picked up. The storm gathers over the erg now. Look!" Og pointed to the darkening sky, the few clouds over their heads beginning to swirl into a spiral pattern. Toward the north, a low, pale cloud loomed.

"That's the sandstorm. The godscream. When it hits,

we'd better have taken cover. That wind carries enough sand to grind down this entire valley," shouted Og. "You can't go down there—"

Claria's shriek rose from the valley floor, sounding like a thousand women. Cheyne grimaced and called over his shoulder, the wind taking his words to Og's ears instantly.

"Sing it shut again, Og. You're our only chance."

And then Og stood alone on the outcropping over the valley, his eyes on the crystal door above. He swallowed hard, his hands shaking and his knees about to buckle. All he could think of was how badly he needed a hard slug of raqa. Or even just a taste.

The wind bore down on him, and he braced himself against a big hickory tree, clutching the three gemstones in one hand and waiting for Cheyne to emerge from the valley with Claria. Little by little, the rising din from the spires' vibration filled his ears until he could not hear anything else. One by one, he saw the spires begin to shatter, their music passing from the range of his hearing into pure destruction. Holding fast to the tree, he didn't see how anyone could survive the onslaught in the valley.

Anyone except Womba.

Og could not believe his eyes. There she was, making her way across the tormented valley, pushing spire after broken spire away from her, with only one arm protecting her eyes. Two of the assassins lay crumpled in her wake. Og took a deep breath and steeled himself. There was no time for him to get away and no place to go. He turned away, gathered his concentration, and thought of the song.

Above, the crystal wall shook and trembled with every new assault from the powerful desert-borne winds. Og held his voice, hoping for a moment of respite from the wind, a moment when he could hear himself sing the song, truing the notes as he went.

In the Chimes, Cheyne wrapped his face in his kaffiyeh, put his head down, and pulled himself from spire to spire blindly, some shattering over his head, unable to see any sign of Claria. With his thoughts on Claria alone, he had forgotten the assassins, but they had not forgotten him. Two of the closest had placed themselves between him and Claria, their sabers sheathed, but their intentions plain. They would not let him pass. He had simply charged through them, run into the thick of the ganzite crystals and disappeared into a thousand reflected images of himself. None of which he could see, he thought ruefully. Several of the assassins had followed him in. Three of them lay dead from falling crystal, and two more still wandered blindly in the fury as Cheyne pressed on toward Claria.

Og looked through his thin kaffiyeh toward the crystal door and knew he could wait no longer. He began to put voice to the memory of the little tune as the windstorm finished its work in the Chimes.

All Cheyne could see was dark, swirling sand. But when the lightning struck the Chimes, it charged the spire in front of Cheyne with brilliant power, arcing from peak to crystalline peak in jagged, haphazard paths, giving him an instant of light to steer by. He saw Claria huddled next to the only spire still standing, beside it, a pool of molten glass sizzled around a shortened spire, the ganzite slowly dripping down itself to the dry valley floor in glowing, burning red lumps. The churning wind tore at Claria's robes and the airborne sand had all but flayed the skin from her hands. But he had seen her, and she had seen him. Coughing, Cheyne collapsed against another spire, oblivious to its danger, and thought he would die there, amid the smell of molten ganzite and sulfur, and the pandemonium of the godscream.

Then the worst sound of all reached his ears: absolute silence. The wind ceased as quickly as it had begun, and for a moment, Cheyne thought he had gone deaf. But then he heard the spilling of sand from his robes as he shifted, and the tinkle of the crystal chimes as the lightning's last charge scattered to exhaustion.

And Claria's raw shouts, so near that when his ears seized upon the sound, he was at her side in a heartbeat. His hands stiff with sand-covered blood, he fumbled at Riolla's ropes like a man with no touch at all, but at last he cut through the thick cords, brought Claria to her feet, and began to run with her to the edge of the valley, to the deep, sheltering caves.

"I'm here, Claria, hold on. We'll be out of here in just a minute, I swear to you, I will not fail you," he muttered through painful, cracked lips. Cheyne knew they had only seconds before the crystal door gave way and the Beast of the Hours, so long entombed, so long at bay, would spring back into its unconquered realm with the fury of three thousand unanswered years.

Above the Chimes, Og stood helplessly watching the storm progress. The song had not worked. No matter what he did, the ring-stones would not respond. And he knew why. He needed Riolla's pearl to ground them. With the increased energy the three of them could now produce, Og could not govern and direct their magic without the pearl of Nadrum.

I have failed again. Riolla was right all along. I am just an—

"—old fool. Having trouble here?" A shrill laugh cut through the wind and Og turned to meet it. The Schreefa and her assassin stood behind him.

"Riolla! Oh, Riolla, what have you done?" he cried.

She set her jaw in contempt. "I'll bet those are the very same words you said when I left you," she shouted. "You haven't changed one bit, you raqa-spoiled howler. But I have. You are looking at the next queen of Sumifa. Get used to addressing me as Your Majesty. As soon as that door opens, I will be sole owner of all that has lain untouched and unclaimed for centuries!"

"What do you mean? Don't you know?" Og stared at her miserably. "Riolla, if I cannot unsing what you have put into motion, the Beast of the Hours will come crashing through that wall and destroy everything in its path. There will be no kingdom for you to rule! Riolla, you have unleashed a cockatrice! There is *no* treasure!" Og screamed at her.

"Oh, take your act back to the orcs, Og. Any moment, I will be the richest woman in the world," she crowed.

Og could not remove his eyes from her for the time it took for his heart to beat three times. "I love you, Riolla. I always have. Give me back the pearl."

"Oh, please. You—" She stopped in midsentence, staring behind and above Og's shoulder, a smile forming on her face.

He turned to look as the first crack spread across the smooth surface of the crystal door. "Give me the pearl, Riolla, it's our only hope!"

Then he turned and began the song again, tears welling in his eyes. Riolla touched her disheveled curls with a graceful gesture, spun on her left foot to make a regal exit, and nearly fell into a bottomless abyss that opened up directly in front of her. Saelin was nowhere to be seen. All around them, the earth began to break apart, thundering into pieces and falling away in massive chunks from the mountainside. She realized that she and Og were trapped on a pinnacle of rock, and she fell to the ground as it began to shake violently under their feet, his song unable to reach the needed volume to stop the godscream. Still, Og stood bravely singing Claria's name over and over as the mountainside crumbled around him, bits of rock and huge pieces of sod bursting from its sides.

Through the sandstorm, through the wind-whipped forest, and now caught in the shifting, rock-strewn gorge, Womba struggled to climb up toward the light, clinging to the sheer walls of a newly opened ravine for all she was worth. Convinced that Og would never make it down from the rocks without her help, she set her massive jaw and dug into the earth in fierce determination to rescue him. Inch by painful inch, never sure which handhold would give from the slightest pressure, she pulled her considerable weight upward, panting and grunting, tears of pain streaming down her face. Her bone necklaces snagged on exposed rocks, dirt and debris showered onto her head and shoulders, and her wonderful ghomaskin dress hung in shreds. Still, she made her way ever upward toward Og.

The wrenching of the strata filled her ears with its roar until, ten feet before she would clear the edge of the ravine, light broke through, carrying with it the sound of Claria's name echoing all around her, in a hundred voices, all of them Og's. Womba burst into fresh tears, felt herself falling back into the pit, her strength broken by the sound of her rival's name. But Og was still trapped. Womba beat down her rage and tears, promised herself the pleasure of carving the Sumifan woman's bones into ten thousand beads, and kept climbing.

With a bellow of triumph, she scrambled over the top of the pinnacle just at the exact moment the final crack shot across the gleaming face of the crystal door. Og didn't have time to move. He only saw Womba stand up and throw herself in front of him as a brilliant burst of light flashed when the full voice of the god-scream hit the crazed crystal, shattering it completely. As the beast opened his faceted ruby eyes, Womba caught the full force of his furious stare.

"Don't look at his eyes!" Og shrieked.

But Womba stood for a brief moment, a look of rapturous love on her face, and then dropped to the ground, her features seemingly carved in basalt, her body turned to stone. Stepping slowly out of the Collector's ancient prison, the beast lifted his iridescent wings, raised his head, and began to hiss and screech. The sound raked across Og's heart; it was a sound he knew he would never forget.

"By the cracked face of Caelus Nin!" shouted Riolla. "What is that?"

His eyes on Womba, Og quickly whipped his cloak over their heads and turned his back to the emerging beast.

"Don't look at his eyes! Whatever you do, don't look at his eyes!" he shouted in her ears. "Now do you believe me? Give me the pearl before I can't do anything about this."

Riolla whimpered, thinking of the lost treasure, her unpaid dues and the Raptor's wrath, of the horror that they could hear awakening behind them. She angrily ripped the pearl from her neck and handed it to Og, who clasped it firmly together with the other stones, the firebane positioned in the middle of the group. He began to sing, summoning the magic as he had done when his voice was perfect, when his heart was filled with love instead of pain.

And the magic came.

Above their heads, the rainbow light rose and wove itself into ribbons of gold, purple, blue, green, and bloodred, their streaming banners widening and widening until they blanketed the doorway, covering it in light, while the beast tore and clawed at them to no avail. The cockatrice raged and flapped its wings, but the more it struggled, the more the light entwined it, until at last it lay hissing and subdued behind the broken crystal. Og continued to sing, the beast fading with every note.

Below, sheltered in the first cave they had found, Cheyne and Claria looked at one another in amazement. The wind had stopped. The only sound they heard was Og singing Claria's name, over and over, his voice pure and true.

CHAPTER
21

SEVERAL MILES AWAY, BEYOND THE CURTAIN of light and the Sarrazan forest, atop his dangerously fragile perch in the pine tree, Rotapan turned his back to the gale and marked the passing of the godscream overhead, its noise blurring with that of the surging river. When the windstorm moved off toward the Borderlands, the waters became quiet, and he could not see his temple for some sort of rippling, shining curtain that seemed to hang before it in the sky. Rotapan stared at the barrier for a moment, not comprehending. His world had changed too much in the last few days. He wanted to go home, lick his wounds, and seek the counsel of Chelydrus.

And it seemed he could. The wind had cowed the wolf pup beside his dead master below. But in the length of time it took Rotapan to make that decision, the world changed again.

The strange curtain suddenly dropped, revealing his shining, broken temple for a split second before the waters from Drufalden's melting glacial kingdom, which had flooded the Silver Sea, came thundering down again, rushing instantly to the other side of the dry seabed and over the gleaming bone pile, covering the temple to the last standing spire.

When the tidal surge receded, no trace remained that there had ever been a temple on the shores of the Silver Sea. Rotapan, his eyes tearless and dry, slid slowly down the rough tree trunk, walked out of the forest toward the high, deadly waters, and let the thrashing riptide take him. Before he fell into the airless tunnel of the cauldron, he thought he saw the scaled face of Chelydrus, laughing.

Riolla clung to Og long after the silence told them they were safe. The beast was gone, Og knew, back to wherever it had been summoned from, and would never trouble them again. But all around them, the world lay broken and altered. He disengaged Riolla's stiff hands from his cloak and turned to see if Cheyne and Claria had made it out of the valley.

Beside him lay Womba, still clutching Og's lost boot in her clawed fingers. He gently removed it from her grip, held the stray boot for a long time, then took the mate from his pack and put them both on to find that they finally fit comfortably.

"You really did think you loved me, didn't you?" he said to Womba's stony face. Somehow she didn't look as ugly anymore.

"Yes. I did," said a raw, brassy voice behind him.

Og startled, his heart racing. But he knew Riolla was gone before he ever turned around. He suddenly felt very foolish, and very tired.

"Og?" called Cheyne from below. "Ogwater, are you safe?" His voice seemed small and far away.

"Yes. I am. It's over." Og answered, moving toward the sound.

"Stay where you are. We can make it up," said Cheyne.

Several long minutes later, Cheyne lifted Claria up the last few feet and then followed her. "Well done, Og. Well done. Your—your voice is back, isn't it?"

"Yes, it has been fully restored."

"I'll buy you that drink now, if you like." Cheyne smiled.

"No." The songmage shook his head sadly. "I just want to go home."

Then Cheyne saw Womba. "The cockatrice?"

Og nodded. "I don't know how to tell Yob. She shielded me from the beast. I would have met its gaze before I could stop myself."

"I'll tell him. You did your best. She died in battle, and he'll be proud."

"What about you?" said Og. "Where will you go? You still don't have a name."

"No. I don't. But Claria does."

"What?" Claria said weakly.

"Yes. The totem was yours. Came from your family. And that means you are the Collector's heir. You could . . ." He bit the words off hard and fast, or he wouldn't be able to say them. "You could marry Maceo now."

She wiped the tears from her eyes, the fine sand ground into her skin from the winds making the motion even more painful. "Yes. I guess I could." Maceo's ring seemed to burn on her finger.

"Well, then. Og was right. It's over." Cheyne swallowed the fire in his throat, and felt it surge through his body like the godscream.

"Where will you go now, Muje?" said Doulos, the dim light of the Treefather's chamber obscuring his features. "You know that I must stay with him."

Cheyne had expected no less. Doulos would never

give up his hope that Javin really was the true king of Sumifa, the hope of the ancient juma writings and of every slave since the Wandering. But it was a comfort to Cheyne to know someone was that loyal to his foster father. And a thorn in his side, as well. Cheyne thought of his last promise to himself when he had left Javin sleeping, the poison of the Ninnites already working in his body. *I said I would never look back. Now it's all I can do.*

He smiled and nodded to Doulos. "I know. I'm glad you are with him." Cheyne looked over to Javin's sleeping form, laid upon a soft pallet of green boughs in the center of the chamber. "He's here because of me. The least I can do is find out about the Holy Book. There has to be a way to read the rest of it, and even if the last page is lost, maybe I can find some of those answers, too. This Raptor—it's him I have business with. And I still don't know who I am. But maybe that doesn't matter as much anymore."

"Of course it matters," said Claria quietly. "How can you say that? Who you are was important enough to Javin to risk everything for. You have to keep searching, Cheyne. But this Raptor—whoever or whatever he is—if he killed the Collector, if he is that old, he has great magic. How will you fight such an enemy? How will you fight a whirlwind?"

"I don't know. But I have to try. Claria, the Collector's story also said he had hidden away great wealth, the glory of the old kingdom. The Raptor has never stopped looking for that. And he won't. But it's *your* inheritance," Cheyne reminded her.

Claria dropped her eyes, hoping the light hid her unshed tears. This journey had begun with her hope of a name and a dowry. Cheyne had given her back the chance for the first, and he was offering her the chance for the second now.

Why does it feel so awful to get what you wanted? she thought. She looked at her newly healed hands, Maceo's ring still upon her finger.

"I suppose so. But you have made some enemies. Yob will be of no help—he has gone back to bury Womba, and Wiggulf has more than he can handle with the floods. Dunsan reports that Naruq is nowhere to be found, and Riolla is garrisoned at the curtain of light with her borrowed army. Will you try to go back to Sumifa?"

Cheyne smiled bitterly. "I don't know. Just remind Og to tell Muni he'll see me soon enough."

Og, strangely quiet since their close brush with the beast, rolled the four gemstones over and over in his hand, then spoke up softly.

"I'll tell him," he promised. "But I'll tell you this, too. You cannot go back to Sumifa, Cheyne. Maceo wants you dead. And on the way back from the Chimes, I thought I saw Saelin. That one will never forget that you have escaped his expertise many times now. He will require your head to answer his shame. And then there is Rotapan. . . . Why don't you let me go with you? I promised I would guide you."

"And I promised you half of what we found. Which turned out to be a great deal of danger and trouble. Besides, you were a terrible guide, Og." Cheyne laughed. "And Claria needs your magic to get home. It's a long trip."

He took her hand in his and kissed the two fingers with their little crooked first joints. "Fair winds and waters, Claria."

Claria could not trust her voice to answer him. A few seconds of awkward silence passed, then Og began to sing over the stones, his brow wrinkled in concentration. The magic came to the stones, white light pouring over the songmage and the girl as they faded into the brightness. In a heartbeat, they were gone, the scarlet flash of Claria's hair ribbon lingering for a brief moment afterward in the myrrh-and-bergamot-scented air.

High above the shattered Chimes, a dark whirlwind

scattered the broken ganzite crystals and stirred up stinging clouds of sand as it passed slowly overhead, searching.

(To be continued)

TERI McLaren, under the name Teri Williams, has coauthored two previous novels, *Before the Mask* and *The Dark Queen*, and the short stories, "Mark of the Flame, Mark of the Word," published in *The Cataclysm*, and "The Final Touch," published in *The Dragons of Krynn*.

She teaches literature, medieval culture, and writing at the University of Louisville, in Louisville, Kentucky.